continued . . .

WAKING NIGHTMARE

DEADLY SINS

THE MINDHUNTERS

KYLIE BRANT

BERKLEY SENSATION, NEW YORK

THE BERKLEY PUBLISHING GROUP
Published by the Penguin Group
Penguin Group (USA) Inc.
375 Hudson Street, New York, New York 10014, USA
Penguin Group (Canada), 90 Eglinton Avenue East, Suite 700, Toronto, Ontario M4P 2Y3, Canada
(a division of Pearson Penguin Canada Inc.)
Penguin Books Ltd., 80 Strand, London WC2R 0RL, England
Penguin Group Ireland, 25 St. Stephen's Green, Dublin 2, Ireland (a division of Penguin Books Ltd.)
Penguin Group (Australia), 250 Camberwell Road, Camberwell, Victoria 3124, Australia
(a division of Pearson Australia Group Pty. Ltd.)
Penguin Books India Pvt. Ltd., 11 Community Centre, Panchsheel Park, New Delhi—110 017, India
Penguin Group (NZ), 67 Apollo Drive, Rosedale, Auckland 0632, New Zealand
(a division of Pearson New Zealand Ltd.)
Penguin Books (South Africa) (Pty.) Ltd., 24 Sturdee Avenue, Rosebank, Johannesburg 2196,
South Africa

Penguin Books Ltd., Registered Offices: 80 Strand, London WC2R 0RL, England

This is a work of fiction. Names, characters, places, and incidents either are the product of the author's imagination or are used fictitiously, and any resemblance to actual persons, living or dead, business establishments, events, or locales is entirely coincidental. The publisher does not have any control over and does not assume any responsibility for author or third-party websites or their content.

DEADLY SINS

A Berkley Sensation Book / published by arrangement with the author

PRINTING HISTORY
Berkley Sensation mass-market edition / August 2011

ISBN: 978-0-425-24270-4

BERKLEY® SENSATION
Berkley Sensation Books are published by The Berkley Publishing Group,
a division of Penguin Group (USA) Inc.,
375 Hudson Street, New York, New York 10014.
BERKLEY® SENSATION and the "B" design are trademarks of Penguin Group (USA) Inc.

PRINTED IN THE UNITED STATES OF AMERICA

10 9 8 7 6 5 4 3 2 1

For my newest granddaughter, Harper Sophia,
with love and anticipation—looking forward
to tea parties, dress up, and shopping trips!

Acknowledgments

A great deal of research goes into my books and I always reach out to experts for help. A big thank-you is owed to Kathleen Hartnett for your fascinating details regarding the duties of Supreme Court clerks. A specialist in the Office of Public Affairs of the FBI Washington Field Office offered insight into FBI's Evidence Response Team and answered questions on some procedural details—you know who you are! The generous assistance I received from both of you left me seriously questioning where I was during Career Day at school.

Joe Collins is my go-to guy for weapons questions, and he came through again when it came to researching my sniper's weapon and how he'd set up his shoot. As always, thanks for the input! Mark Lohrum, Purdue University Cyber Forensics graduate student, provided the cell phone spyware expertise, which scared me away from ever opening links on my phone.

Washington, DC, and the surrounding area is one of the loveliest in the country. Although I've made several visits, I needed frequent assistance regarding neighborhoods, routes, distances, etc. I'm grateful to Jeff Welter, longtime resident of the area, for filling in the gaps in my geographical knowledge and proving at long last that he's more than merely a pretty face ☺.

As usual, any inaccuracies that occur in the story are solely the responsibility of the author.

Chapter 1

Despite what it said in the Old Testament, death was rarely the result of divine intervention. Often nature could be blamed. More frequently another person was the cause. On that drizzly gray evening in early November, nature had an alibi.

If Supreme Court Justice Byron Reinbeck had known what fate had in store for him that day, he'd have spent less time writing the scathing dissenting opinion on *Clayborne vs. Leland*. Which in turn would have had him leaving his chambers at a decent hour. That would have negated the need to stop at his favorite sidewalk vendor for flowers to take to Mary Jo, his wife of twenty-five years. She was having a dinner party that evening, and he was running unforgivably late.

But not being blessed with psychic powers, he pulled over at the sidewalk in question. Danny Shelton was there, rain or shine, until the snow started flying. And he never folded up shop until he'd sold his entire inventory.

"Mr. Reinbeck, good to see you." A smile put another

crease in Danny's grizzled, well-worn face. A three-sided awning protected him and his wares. A small propane heater was tucked in the corner of it. "When you called, I put 'em back special. I got just the thing." He sprang up from his battered lawn chair with a surprising spryness.

Byron turned up the collar of his overcoat, belatedly remembered the umbrella in the backseat. Hunching his shoulders a bit, he pretended to contemplate the bouquet of yellow roses thrust out for his approval. He suspected Danny stocked them daily, on the off chance that Byron would stop.

Yellow roses were Mary Jo's favorite.

He reached for his wallet. "You're a lifesaver, Danny."

The other man's cackle sounded over the crinkle of the wrapping paper he was fixing around the bundle. "You gots to be in big trouble for these flowers not to do the trick."

A quick glance at his watch told Byron that he was only a handful of minutes away from "big trouble." He withdrew a couple bills, intending to leave without waiting for change.

He didn't have a chance to turn around before the sharp *crack* of the rifle sounded behind him. But he saw the splash of crimson on the front of Danny's stained brown hoodie. A second later pain and shock paralyzed Byron's system before he pitched forward, his lifeless body crushing the fragrant long-stemmed beauties against the makeshift plywood table.

———

Adam Raiker rapped softly at the door of the library. Although there were three occupants in the room, only one voice bade him to enter.

Because it was the one that counted, he eased the door open, his gaze going immediately to Mary Jo Waverly-Reinbeck. "Everyone's gone."

Even grief stricken as she was, there was no mistaking the command of the woman. The red sheathe she wore accentuated her pale blond hair and ice blue eyes. She was brilliant and witty, and had been known to dismantle a seasoned defense attorney with a few well-chosen lines. But it was her devotion to one of Adam's closest friends that had endeared her to him.

Tears still running freely down her face, she held out a hand to him. "Thank you, Adam." He went to her, aware of the impatience emanating from the other two in the room. He took her hand in his, and at her urging sank into the seat beside her.

FBI Deputy Director Garrett Schulte leaned back in his chair and offered Adam a polite smile. But there was no pretense of civility from the other man. Curtis Morgan served in the Department of Homeland Security in some capacity, Adam recalled. Given his presence here, it was a position of some import. Regardless, it was Byron Reinbeck's widow who held his attention.

"Gentlemen." She took a moment to wipe at her face with a tissue. "I'm sure you both know Adam Raiker, by reputation if not personally. Adam is a dear family friend." When her voice broke, she paused to compose it. "I'd like a few moments with him now. We can resume our discussion in fifteen minutes. If you'd excuse us?"

Schulte and Morgan exchanged a startled glance, but the deputy director recovered first. "Of course." When he rose, the other man followed suit. "Is there anything we can get for you?"

"I'd like a copy of the investigative report updated daily and delivered to me." Even under the circumstances it was difficult for Adam to suppress a smile at the men's uniform reactions to Jo's crisply worded request. "Perhaps you can discuss the details involved for making that happen."

Without another word, the men moved to the open door. Went through it. And when it shut behind them, Adam knew the woman had successfully distracted the two from his presence here. They were going to be kept busy employing a duck-and-dodge strategy that would allow the investigation to continue in confidence while still placating the widow of one of the most powerful men in the country. Their focus on her connection to Byron Reinbeck also meant they'd underestimate the fact that Jo Waverly-Reinbeck was a brilliant assistant U.S. attorney in her own right.

If the situation were different, he might feel a bit sorry for them.

"Thank you"—she squeezed his hand and sent him a watery smile—"for making the necessary calls. For getting the people out of here . . . God. I just couldn't deal with that."

"What about the kids?" he asked quietly. The couple had two sons, both blond like Jo, both in their teens. So far they were being shielded from the news of their father's death.

"They're with my parents. They'll keep the boys away from the TV until I can go and tell them in person." Her chin quavered once before she firmed it. "We discussed this. Byron and me. Given our professions, I always thought I'd be the likelier target. God knows I've had plenty of threats. Remember the Calentro drug-cartel trial last year? Somehow the U.S. Marshals Service managed to keep me safe through that, but Byron hasn't had a serious threat in years. And still . . ."

Because there were no words, Adam released her hand to slip an arm around her shoulders. The passing minutes were filled with her soft weeping, which caused a growing desolation inside him. Helplessness. There was nothing he hated worse.

Moments later, she drew away, mopped her face. And he recognized the determined expression she wore. "You've told us often enough over the last couple months, but are you truly okay? Completely recovered?"

The non sequitur had him blinking. "The bullets caught me in the one area of the chest that wasn't already scarred. I'm still a bit miffed about that, but otherwise, I'm fine."

Her gaze was intent. "Who will have jurisdiction on this? The bureau?"

"DC police will have been first to the scene. Marshals will have sent backup. Then you have the FBI and Homeland Security, just for starters. It'll depend on what's discovered at the crime scene. At the location of—"

"Of the shooter," she continued for him. Her tears had stemmed, as if she'd successfully willed them away. "With Byron a sitting justice, we're likely to have every alphabet agency coming out of the woodwork trying to get a piece of this." Her smile was fierce. "I've read the justice reports. Regardless of 9/11, the agencies still haven't learned to share intelligence. I don't want Bryon getting lost in a bureaucratic pissing match."

He couldn't refute her logic. Although he'd left the FBI years ago, Adam had been an agent long enough to recognize the potential pitfalls of the upcoming investigation. "What are you proposing?"

"They won't keep me in the loop of the investigation." She waved away any response he might have made. "I know they can't. That's not my forte anyway." Her pause then was laden with expectancy. "But it is yours. And that of your agency."

With certain regret he answered, "As good as we are at Raiker Forensics, there's zero chance that the feds would invite us to consult on a case of this magnitude. They'd see it as a duplication of services for one. And my relationship to Byron would be considered a conflict of interest." Although given the man's far-reaching career thus far, he was likely personally acquainted with several top officials in both the FBI and DHS.

"Perhaps under ordinary circumstances." A small sound was heard in the hallway. Jo lowered her voice as she reached out to grip his hand. "I have a few hours to trade on the expressions of sympathy that will be coming my way. Having the sitting U.S. attorney general as a former boss is about to come in handy. And I fully expect the White House to call soon. President Jolson is responsible for Byron's seat on the Supreme Court. I think he'll grant his widow this one favor."

Shock flickered. "Jo, if you accomplish that, I'd be working with the task force put together for this case. And given its sensitivity, I couldn't—"

"Report directly to me? I know." She leaned forward, her

expression urgent. "But I trust you. Byron trusted you. And if you're on this case, I won't worry because I know you'll cut through all the bureaucratic bullshit to get the answers." Her voice grew thick with tears again, although there were none in her eyes. They gleamed with purpose. "I want my husband's killer. And if things get messy, I want the real facts, not the sanitized version or whatever the feds deem publicly palatable." Her grasp on his hand tightened. "Before I beg my former employer and the president for a favor, Adam, I'm requesting one from you."

I've never asked you for anything, Adam. I'm asking now.

There was no reason for Jo's words to have memory ambushing him. To evoke the image of another time years earlier, of another woman with similar entreaty in her eyes. In her voice. Turning away from that woman had been the right thing to do. He still believed it.

And still lived with the searing regret that lingered.

He looked down at their clasped fingers. Her pale smooth skin contrasted sharply with the furrowed scars crisscrossing the back of his hand. Some decisions, made for the best of reasons, left haunting remorse in their wake. This one didn't even require a second thought.

"I'll do everything I can."

"The prudent thing to do—for all concerned—is to bow out gracefully." FBI Assistant Director Cleve Hedgelin looked at a point beyond Adam's shoulder as he parroted the suggestion, which had no doubt stemmed from a loftier position in the agency's hierarchy. But it was equally likely that Cleve shared the sentiment. He might have been Adam's partner eight years ago, but he'd stayed on at the bureau. Had risen in the ranks of the Criminal Investigative Division. An agent didn't do that without learning to toe the political line.

And after the spectacular ending of the last case they'd worked together, Cleve likely harbored his own reasons for keeping his distance from Adam. "There's nothing that you can add to the case, and your involvement is a needless distraction."

The office was outfitted more grandly than the cubicle Adam had been assigned when he'd worked in the Hoover Building. He settled more comfortably into the plush armchair and sent the man a bland smile. "Stop wasting time. Attorney General Gibbons has already approved my full inclusion on this investigation. The president himself assured Jo Reinbeck that her wishes in this matter would be heeded. The agency's objections to my presence are expected and duly noted. Let's move on, shall we?"

An unwilling smile pulled at the corners of Hedgelin's mouth. "Same ol' Adam. You never were much for small talk."

"Is that what that was?" When his thigh began to cramp, he shifted position to stretch his leg out. "And here I thought it was the usual bureaucratic BS. The bureau's been painted into a corner with Gibbons and Jolson weighing in but still thought it was worth a shot to appeal to my more tender sensibilities."

"You never had many."

"And I haven't developed any in the time since I left. Tell your superiors you gave it the college try and I'm not budging. So." His hands clenched and unclenched on the knob of his cane, an outward sign of his flagging patience. "Catch me up."

Cleve smoothed a hand over his short hair. It was more gray than brown now, but his pale brown eyes were covered by the same style gold wire-framed glasses he'd favored eight years ago. His build was still slim, but the intervening years had left their stamp on the man's face. Adam didn't want to consider what showed on his own.

"We've got more agencies than we can handle jockeying for position in this investigation."

"I imagine that kind of juggling comes with the job."

The assistant director grimaced. "You have no idea. But in this case it means doling out pieces of the case to teams comprised of agents and members from DHS, USMS, the DCPD. . . and now you."

"Nice to know I'm not crowding the field." Adam wasn't without sympathy for the man's position. But the emotion didn't run deeply enough to have him bowing out and making it easier for Hedgelin or the FBI. He'd made a promise to Jo. She'd done her part. She'd gotten him placed on the investigation. He had no allusions; it would have been her connections—and Byron's—that had landed him here. Despite his past in the agency—or perhaps because of it—his presence would make them uneasy. His last case for the FBI had ended dramatically—and almost killed him. Although he didn't care about such things, to some it had made him a hero. But because he'd chosen to cut his ties with his former job, the bureau might regard him much differently.

That part didn't matter. The investigation did.

"You'll be partnered with two of our seasoned agents. I believe you know both from your time here. And Lieutenant Frank Griega will be your liaison from the DCPD." Hedgelin dropped into his high-backed leather desk chair and shot Adam a small smile. "Given that our best guys in the Behavioral Analysis Unit were actually instructed by you, we'd be interested in any profile of the offender you put together."

Adam inclined his head. Since he hadn't made a point to keep up with many from the bureau once he'd left it, he had no idea who was still left in the BAU. But Cleve was right. Profiling had been a specialty of his while he'd been an agent. Now it was his employees at Raiker Forensics who received his tutelage. "Of course . . ." His pause was meaningful. "But it'd help to get some background on the case first."

The agent leaned forward and stabbed at a button on his desk phone with the stump that remained of his right index finger. Adam wasn't the only one who bore old injuries from the last case they'd worked. He rarely considered his own. When it came to human nature, it was only the scars on the inside that were worth noting.

Moments later the door to the office opened, and a man and woman entered. With a glance Adam determined that Cleve was right. He did know the agents. His gut clenched tightly once before he shoved the response aside by sheer force of will. He'd had recent dealings with Special Agent Tom Shepherd, as well as knowing him slightly when they'd both been with the bureau.

But his reaction had nothing to do with Shepherd.

"You recall special agents Shepherd and Marlowe?"

"Of course." Adam gave them a curt nod.

Shepherd's broad smile complemented his aging-Hollywood-golden-boy looks. "You're looking a sight better than you did a few months ago in the Philly Critical Care Unit. I heard that the doctors took to calling you the miracle man."

Her voice and face devoid of expression, Jaid Marlowe raised a brow at him. "Just a word of advice, you aren't actually bulletproof. Next time you have an assassin after you, try Kevlar."

"Now that I've discovered bullets don't bounce off me, I may have to." His tone was as mild as hers. No one would suspect that only a few short months ago Jaid had sat at his bedside clutching his hand, silent and pale, her wide brown eyes drenched in tears. In a medicated fog at the time, he might have thought she was an image produced by his subconscious. She'd taken up permanent residence there eight years ago, like a determined ghost refusing to be banished.

Cleve stood, taking three oversized brown folders from a pile on his desk and leaned forward to pass them out. Flipping his open, Adam saw it contained copies of the case file. Regardless of the minutes wasted trying to convince him to bow out, a file had already been prepared for him.

The thought vanished when he focused on the pictures contained in the first manila folder inside. There was a clutch in his chest when he recognized his friend crumpled on top of the stained, broken plywood, bright yellow roses crushed beneath him. The depth of emotion blindsided him.

He took a moment to acknowledge the feeling before tucking it away. Subjectivity crippled an investigator. Turning those feelings into purpose was the only way to help Byron Reinbeck.

"Any word from ballistics?"

Hedgelin nodded. "The kill weapon was a .308 Remington Model 700. Full metal jackets. Which explains Shelton being killed with the same bullet. Passed through the justice and into him."

Adam riffled through the pictures, plucking out a few to arrange on his lap atop the open folder, side by side. After studying them for a moment, he looked up. "The shooter was in the parking garage across the street?" At Hedgelin's nod his gaze lowered again. "Second level, most likely. Easiest thing to do would be to back a van into a slot facing the street. Open the rear doors, take the shot, and then drive away."

"Second level, southeast corner," Cleve affirmed. "Check out the scene photos." There was a note in the man's voice that alerted Adam. He shuffled through the pictures in the next folder. There was little to see in the images. No sandbags that might have been used to support a rifle. No shell casings. The shooter had coolly taken the time to pick up before fleeing the scene. There was nothing except . . . he squinted his one good eye at a photo of what looked like an ordinary five-by-eight white index card encased in a plastic Ziploc bag. On it was scrawled one word in what looked to be red marker.

Wrath.

As if reading his thoughts, Jaid said, "*Wrath*? The shooter was angry at the victim?"

Flipping through the rest of the photos in that file, Adam stopped at one that showed the card before it'd been disturbed. "Oh, he wanted this to be found, didn't he?" Adam murmured. He'd first thought the bag protecting the card was an evidence bag used by the crime scene technicians, but now he realized the shooter had left it that way. Encased in plastic, with a fist-sized piece of broken concrete holding it in place on the pebbled flat roof of the building. "Wrath. One of the seven deadly sins." Feeling the others' eyes on him he looked up. "Not that I'm all that well-versed in the tenets of Catholicism, but I had some exposure in my youth."

"A passing exposure, obviously." Jaid's wry remark had the corner of Adam's mouth quirking.

"It didn't take, no. Much to the Franciscans' despair."

"As it happens, I am Catholic, so I had the same thought." Hedgelin took a large manila envelope off his desk and opened it to shake out a single photo. Bracing himself with one fist planted on the desk, he leaned forward, holding the image up for them to see.

"That's not Reinbeck," Shepherd noted, shifting to better view what was obviously a crime scene photo.

"This victim's name was Oliver Patterson." The assistant director paused, but when no one commented, he went on. "He had a global investment and securities firm. Patterson Capital."

"One of the too-big-to-fail companies that plundered unfettered until the financial collapse a few years ago." The victim's name and his company triggered Adam's memory. Both had been on the receiving end of some unbelievably bad press after the upheaval, which worsened when the obscene bonuses paid to top executives came to light. Adam assumed Patterson had ridden out the rocky times with help from the government-issued bailout funds. He recalled that the news stories surrounding the man's death had been lacking in details. "When was he killed, last week?"

"Nine days ago in the parking garage of his building on I Street Northwest. Stabbed. You can't tell in this picture, but there was an identical card left at the scene." Cleve's expression turned grim. "It was impaled on the knife left in his heart."

Intrigue spiking, Adam guessed, "Avarice."

The assistant director nodded. "Close enough. The word *greed* was written on the card, in red marker, much like the one found at the site of Reinbeck's shooter. Another biggie according to church dogma. The DCPD is compiling copies of the complete report on that ongoing investigation. Griega will get it to us when it's ready."

"You think these two are serial killings?"

Hedgelin raised his hand as if to halt Jaid's line of thought. "Let's not get ahead of ourselves. DCPD tells me that the detail about the card got leaked three days ago. Wasn't picked up by all the media outlets, but it was out there. No way to tell if we've got a copycat or if the same person killed both men. The manner of deaths was completely different. We're a ways from tying the two homicides together at this point."

"But the religious connotations of the notes gives us a link worth following up on."

The assistant director didn't reply to Shepherd's observation. Instead, he took off his glasses to polish them with his handkerchief, a habit Adam recalled from their time partnered together. "We're in the midst of having all the evidence gathered from the Patterson homicide transferred to Quantico, where it will be given top priority. If there's a link to be found, we'll soon know about it. We still have a large group of DCPD officers canvassing the area surrounding last night's shooting."

Despite his cautionary note regarding a serial killer being responsible, it was obvious the bureau was looking closely into a connection between the cases. They had to. "What about the threats the justice received? Depending on how many clients took a bath in the financial collapse, Patterson probably had more than his share of enemies, too."

Adam's comment elicited a nod from Hedgelin. "Since it's the USMS Judicial Security Division's duty to anticipate and deter threats to the judiciary"—his voice was heavy with irony—"they have a thorough file on any targeting Reinbeck. It'll take some time to compare them to those received by Patterson. You won't be involved in that end of things. Right now you're headed over to the Supreme Court building to help with the interviews there. It's the JSD's turf, so play nice. With over three hundred permanent staff members alone, it's going to be a daunting task. You'll be part of the contingent focusing on the staff that worked most closely with the justices. There are close to forty clerks, four fellows, administrative assistants, and God knows who else in there with direct access to the judiciary. Your first focus will be on Reinbeck's clerks and his administrative assistant."

His attention shifted to Shepherd. "Take Raiker to security and pick up a temporary ID badge for him." His smile was thin as he included Adam in his glance. "They'll need to take a picture for it. Shouldn't take longer than fifteen minutes or so."

Barely restraining a grimace, Adam rose. Photos were a necessary evil at times, but one he avoided at all costs whenever he could. It clearly wasn't going to be possible this time around. And the realization already had him feeling surly.

When the agents rose, Hedgelin looked at Jaid. "Agent Marlowe, if you'd stay for a minute?"

The order couched in the request had Adam's instincts rising, but he didn't look at her as he and Shepherd headed to the door. He'd been given a reprieve.

He had the next ten or fifteen minutes to figure out the best way to handle working with the woman who represented the biggest regret of his life.

Since she wasn't invited to sit again, Jaid remained standing, her eyes fixed on the assistant director. The pseudo-civility that had permeated his voice for the earlier briefing had vanished. The gaze he regarded her with was hard. "I had an opportunity to speak to Shepherd earlier. I'm going to tell you the same thing I told him. I want Raiker supervised at all times. He doesn't conduct interviews alone. He doesn't follow up on any leads without one of you accompanying him. The bureau may have had its arm twisted into including him on this case, but damned if we're going to sit still and allow him to turn this thing into another chapter for his sensationalized memoirs."

There was absolutely no reason for his tone, his words, to have her hackles rising. Feigning puzzlement, she asked, "He's writing his memoirs?"

Hedgelin sent her a sharp look, but she knew her expression was blank. She didn't wear her emotions on her face anymore. Adam Raiker had begun that lesson, all those years ago. Life had completed it.

"I'm certain you know what I mean. You're to keep him firmly contained within the investigative parameters you're given. In addition to the report you or Shepherd file online nightly, I want details on Raiker's behavior. His thoughts about the case. Who he talks to. Anything he says of interest."

In short, she was to spy on him. Just the thought filled her with distaste. She'd run her share of surveillance ops in her career, but informing on another member of her team was especially abhorrent. More so since she suspected his most grievous crime was his mere presence in this investigation. The petty politics involved in the agency was her least favorite aspect of the job.

But she knew how to play the game. Or at least how to appear to. "Understood."

He stared hard at her, long enough to have to her flesh prickling. "I'm told you knew him when he was with the agency."

"I took a class he taught for the BAU." The words were delivered in a bland voice. And didn't reflect the sudden weakness in her knees. "Worked a couple cases with him after that."

Hedgelin gave a nod, as if satisfied. "It's to our advantage that you and Shepherd are on a friendly footing with him. That should keep him off guard. Just be sure you don't let that friendship interfere with your duties regarding him."

"It was a long time ago."

He picked up a folder from his desk and opened it, clearly dismissing her. "Join them in security."

Without another word Jaid turned for the door. She'd

seen Adam twice in the last eight years. Each of those times he'd been in CCU, clinging to life. It had taken a wealth of strength to accept this assignment, realizing it would place her at his side for days, possibly weeks, on end. She'd convinced herself that she could handle it. Could handle *him*.

But it had never occurred to her that she might be called on to betray him.

Chapter 2

"Have you developed a sudden disability we should be aware of?"

From her position in the back of the black Suburban, Jaid was alerted by the dangerous note in Adam's ruined voice. It had always had a low timber. But one of the many scars resulting from his last case for the bureau was a knife wound across his throat. The injury had caused irreparable damage to his vocal cords.

Looking out the window, she noted that Agent Shepherd had pulled into one of the few handicapped parking spots on Maryland Avenue. Then she took in the identifying placard he'd hung from the rearview mirror and braced herself for the explosion. She was no expert on Raiker. Experience had taught her that. But she knew he'd despise being treated like a cripple.

Looking a little sheepish, Shepherd turned off the ignition. "The lot's full, and the nearest parking garage is Union Station. I don't want to waste valuable time cruising the streets looking for a spot when we could be conducting interviews. Unless you'd rather put business off for an hour or so while we do?"

The seconds that ticked by then were like waiting for a detonation. Then, his jaw tight, Adam opened his door and exited the vehicle. That he'd put the case before his own emotions didn't surprise her. The job had always come first with him.

Before heading toward the building, Shepherd raised the back hatch of the vehicle. The three of them took off their weapons and holsters, and locked them in the gun safe inside. Then they made their way to the nearby side entrance of the gleaming white-marble structure.

Although Jaid passed the building countless times during the week, she'd only ever visited it once, and that was on an elementary school class trip. Those details were fuzzy.

She squinted across the plaza toward the domed Capitol. Despite the earliness of the hour, there were a few people scattered about, strolling by in small groups or snapping pictures. Most wore jackets, as she did. Because of the DC humidity, November could still bring mild temperatures. It'd been in the sixties all week. But mornings and evenings were cool. Neither Adam nor Shepherd, however, wore anything over their dark suits.

The building had been taped off and closed to the public, so the people entering were likely law enforcement or employees. Regardless, security at the side entrance was tight. She waited her turn to have her ID scrutinized and to step through the metal detector. A thirtysomething Supreme Court Police officer holding a clipboard detached himself from the group standing just inside the vestibule and approached after they'd cleared through. Shepherd flashed his shield and introduced them. "Shepherd, FBI." Indicating each of them in turn, he continued, "Raiker and Marlowe. We're conducting the interviews of Reinbeck's clerks and office help."

The man bent his head over the clipboard and ran his pen down the list of names on it. A moment later he looked up. "Your interviewees will be shown to the justices' dining room on the second floor. I'll take you up."

"Second," Jaid muttered to Adam as they fell in step behind the young officer and Shepherd as they were led to an elevator. "The justices' chambers and the clerks' offices are on the main floor. Wonder who's in charge of searching Reinbeck's?"

"You were busy on the trip over," he observed.

"Googled the building. Haven't been here since I was a kid. You?"

"It's been decades," he admitted, without adding details. Which was par for the course. She'd always had to pry to elicit the slightest hint of personal information from him. Which had just made every nugget gleaned seem more valuable.

A part of her squirmed inwardly at the naïveté of the woman she'd been. Green and overeager, both in the job and in their relationship. She never would have survived as an agent or as a female if she hadn't finally heeded his advice to guard her emotions. Harness her control. There was no better model of both than Adam Raiker.

But Jaid had never been particularly grateful to the man for the lesson.

She watched him now from the corner of her eye as they stood waiting for the elevator doors to open. He'd despise sympathy, so she allowed herself to feel none at his altered appearance. His hair was still dark, his remaining eye a vivid laser blue. The black eye patch covering the other gave him the look of a modern-day pirate. John LeCroix had been responsible for its loss eight years ago, as well as the scars that marked Adam. The nerve damage that had resulted from the wounds to his leg had him relying on a cane for support, and she knew him well enough to realize how much he must hate that.

But his shoulders were still wide, his back still straight. And as the elevator doors opened and the lone woman inside exited, the look she sent Adam was pure female appreciation. Because the years had only polished the aura of command shimmering off the man. Had only enhanced his devastating attractiveness.

She wedged herself into the corner of the elevator and gave silent thanks that she had long since grown immune to both qualities.

When they'd been shown to the large dining room with its gleaming paneling, the officer said, "All four of Justice Reinbeck's clerks have arrived. Do you want to interview them in a certain order, or should I just show one in?"

The three looked at each other, and Shepherd shrugged. "Any order will do."

Jaid sat between the two men and placed her briefcase on the long polished table. Popped it open.

"Okay if we rotate taking the lead in the interviews?"

She looked at Tom Shepherd, a little surprised at the diffidence in his voice. Jaid didn't know the man well, but his self-confidence used to border on cocky. Originally coming out of cyber crimes, his rise in the agency had earned him the nickname Midas. Every case he touched came out golden. Until his team had failed to resolve a kidnapping of a multimillionaire's daughter. It was Adam who'd eventually cracked the child-swapping ring a couple years later, when one of his agency's cases intersected. He'd been credited for the safe return of that girl and dozens of other children. From what she'd heard, Hedgelin had banished Shepherd to the field office in North Dakota, likely because of the resulting embarrassment to the division. She wasn't sure how he'd landed back in DC, but apparently his tenure in the frozen north had taught him a little humility. "Fine with me."

Adam only nodded.

A few minutes later there was a knock at the door. "Lawrence Dempsey," the officer announced.

A tall, exceedingly thin man with a headful of straw-colored hair entered. "This is horrendous. Absolutely horrendous." His blue eyes, below brows so light they were nearly invisible, were troubled. "Justice Reinbeck was a brilliant jurist. A scholar. He was doing great things for our country. That something like this could happen is a staggering commentary on second amendment rights run amuck in our nation today."

"Please sit down, Mr. Dempsey." When the man took a chair across the table from them, Shepherd made introductions and began leading the man through his educational background and employment history. They already had that information in a dossier on each of the people they would interview today, but the man visibly relaxed during the recounting of the familiar. It wasn't until Shepherd got to the questions regarding his work relationship with Reinbeck that he showed any signs of discomfort.

"What was Justice Reinbeck like to work with?" Shepherd asked.

"Awe-inspiring," was Dempsey's prompt answer. "His mind . . ." He shook his head, as though words failed him. "He needed only a couple paragraphs of a memo to get the grasp of a petition. He could summarize the most complicated brief in just a few incisive, articulate sentences."

"I knew Byron for a long time," Adam put in. His black-on-black pin-striped suit was almost a twin to the one Dempsey was wearing. But where the younger man's looked like an effort to appear more polished, Raiker's gave him a deceptive sheen of civility that all but the unwary would immediately mistrust. "His brilliance is undeniable. But he was unwavering in his convictions. And I'm told he could be something of a task master."

"He had an admirable work ethic," Dempsey said stiffly, picking a barely visible speck of lint from his lapel. "Of course all of us who clerk for him wanted to support him in any way we could."

"So you worked late last night, too?" Shepherd rolled the pen he held between his thumb and index finger.

The other man bobbed his head. "Of course. Justice Reinbeck was selected to write the dissenting opinion of one of the recent votes. Some of the justices have a clerk write the first draft for them, and then they make changes, put their own stamp on the opinion. But not Reinbeck.

He likes . . . liked"—he seemed to stumble on the self-correction—"to do the writing himself. So even though we knew he had an engagement in the evening, we figured on staying until he finished. In case he needed some research done to be referenced in the opinion. We never lack for something to work on, so it was no hardship."

"No hardship?" Jaid queried. "What if you'd had plans?"

Dempsey shook his head. "You don't apply for a clerkship because you want to check out the DC nightlife. It's for the experience. Part of the job is putting in the same or more hours than the justices do."

"And all of you share that view?"

The man didn't hesitate at Shepherd's question. "If they didn't, they wouldn't be here."

"What about threats? Did you ever hear Justice Reinbeck mention any he'd received since joining the court?"

"That'd be the jurisdiction of the marshals, but no." Sadness flickered across Dempsey's face. "Judge Reinbeck never said anything about that."

"Would he?" Jaid interjected. She waited for the man's attention to shift to her. "Was he the type of person who would have shared that with those who worked most closely with him?"

The clerk hesitated. "He may not have," he finally said with some reluctance. "He was great to work for. Not just because he was brilliant, but also because he genuinely cared about people. He was always asking after our families or giving advice about our futures. He might not have wanted to worry us, although if he thought any of us were in danger, we would have been alerted." He shook his head then. "But I think we would have noticed something different in his demeanor if something like that were bothering him. I don't think he could have hidden it from everyone. And no one has mentioned anything about him seeming off." His jaw quivered a moment before he deliberately set it. "Believe me, I would have heard about it if someone had."

The second interview was almost a duplication of the first, although the clerk this time was female. Krista Temple was a diminutive blonde. Articulate, with a rapid-fire manner of speaking, her intellect was obvious. So was her fascination with Raiker. She appeared unable to tear her gaze away from him, and Jaid suspected her enthrallment was only partially due to the fact that he was leading this interview.

"Flowers?" The woman was shaking her head. "I didn't know anything about that. I'm not surprised to hear that Justice Reinbeck regularly stopped for roses for his wife though. He was pretty thoughtful. But very private. That wasn't something he would have shared with his staff. He was interested in our lives and our opinions, but he didn't reveal much about his own family."

"So no one working with him knew that he occasionally stopped at the same vendor on the way home to pick up flowers?"

Temple's shoulder-length hair swung when she shook her head. "I didn't know. And if one of his own clerks didn't realize it, it's doubtful the knowledge was widespread around here. We're sort of a close-knit group, even though there are nearly forty clerks working for the various justices."

"How close-knit?" Jaid inserted.

The woman flicked a quick glance at her before addressing her answer to Adam. "We tend to socialize together. We share common interests, after all. That's what brought us here. It's not uncommon for a group of us to head downtown after work once or twice a week."

"So." The slight smile Adam graced Temple with had the woman's eyes widening a little. "Close-knit bunch. Frequent get-togethers. I imagine the topic often revolves around work. Like you said, it's what you all have in common."

"I . . . yes . . . I mean . . . mostly of course." The woman seemed to regain her composure by tearing her gaze away from Adam's face and focusing on Shepherd. "But we talked about other things, too. National politics, family, our career plans."

"And office gossip?"

The woman bristled at Jaid's question. "We're professionals in highly sensitive positions. We don't sit around like old ladies in a coffee clatch and discuss the justices' private matters. To suggest anything else is . . ."

"Relax." Adam's ruined voice could never sound soothing, but the woman responded to the note in it, regardless. "We're not suggesting otherwise. But I can't imagine that it's any different than cops on the same task force sitting around with their buddies. Eventually the topic of the current case is going to come up, right?" He waited for the woman's reluctant nod before going on. "So I'm guessing you'd all talk about how your justices might vote on a particular case they were hearing or one that was on the docket."

"Yes. Of course."

"And just from interacting with the other clerks over time, you probably got a pretty good idea of the personalities of the other justices. Even if you didn't work directly for them."

With a sideways look at Jaid, Temple answered, "We knew their politics before taking the job, of course. But sure, you get to know which of the justices are the workhorses. Who's a health nut. Who uses the gym daily. That sort of thing."

"So it's fair to say that the other justices' clerks knew similar things about Reinbeck."

"I'm sure they do. Although it's doubtful any of them would know that he stopped at that place for flowers, since I don't think any of us did."

But they'd know Reinbeck was writing the dissenting opinion yesterday. Jaid recognized where Adam was leading the woman. And it would be common knowledge that his clerks worked late when he did. Given the man's penchant for privacy, would anyone realize his wife was giving a dinner party that evening? And extrapolate from there that his workhorse habits would have him running late for it? It seemed a long shot.

But there had to be some reason the shooter had chosen

that particular evening to take up position on that rooftop. Once an attempt on Reinbeck's life had been made, the assassin wouldn't have gotten another opportunity before the justice had been surrounded by a protective contingent of marshals.

"I understand that Byron was a private man," Shepherd put in. "Who was likely to know the most about his personal life?"

"Mara Sorenson," came the unhesitating reply. "She's his administrative assistant and came here from the circuit with him. I think they've worked together for over ten years."

"When did you hear about Justice Reinbeck's death?"

"On the news." The memory had tears filling Krista's cornflower blue eyes. "I couldn't believe I'd heard correctly. I called Sam . . . Samantha Kingery to ask if she'd heard." Kingery was another of Reinbeck's clerks. "She hadn't. She was out at dinner with a friend. Then I called Larry Dempsey and Cort Phillips, the other clerks. They'd heard the same thing." Her chin wobbled. "We all met at the Black Diamond, a place we hang out a few blocks from here about an hour later." Tears streamed freely down the woman's face. "We just couldn't believe it. Who would want Justice Reinbeck dead? He's worked his whole career to help people."

Which was, Jaid thought, as the woman struggled to compose herself, the million-dollar question. After a few more questions, Temple was dismissed. When the door had closed behind the woman, she asked, "How good did the shooter have to be to make that shot?"

"A lot better than average," Adam mused. "But certainly not sniper quality. He had a clear angle. No wind to compensate for yesterday. With the high-powered scopes they make these days, he didn't have to be an expert."

Not, she thought with a pang, like the one who had almost killed him a few months ago.

"But he had to be very skilled," Shepherd put in. "And maybe we shouldn't read too much into the ease of yesterday's shot. We don't know what conditions the shooter could have been successful in."

"Easier to lie in wait for someone and plan the kill at your leisure, in surroundings that guarantee you a measure of privacy." Adam went silent, as if thinking for a moment. "But the Reinbecks had great security. A walled property with private gates to the drive. Bulletproof glass in all the vehicles they drove and in the windows of their home." And he knew that because he'd discussed the precaution with Byron and Mary Jo years earlier. "Which means the shooter had to do it out in the open, publicly, when Byron was exposed." He stopped then, picked up his pen, and jotted a note on the yellow pad in front of him. *Phone.* Jaid tried, and failed, to make the connection.

"GPS on his car, maybe." Now Shepherd was scribbling something on his pad. "But the location info still wouldn't give the shooter time to set up beforehand."

"It suggests to me that he'd been followed awhile beforehand. His movements studied." Jaid gained the men's attention with her words. "No one can set a shoot up like that on the spur of the moment, even if he had GPS info. But if Reinbeck had been stalked for a period of time, his actions recorded, the shooter might have narrowed the possible kill sites. Prepared for any one of them."

There was an odd glint in Adam's eye that might have been approval. There had been a time, long gone now, when the sight of it would have thrilled her. Their relationship had been that of teacher and student before it had moved into something much more intimate. Much more devastating.

The door opened then, and another woman entered. Her light brown bob was just beginning to show signs of gray, and she had at least two decades on Krista Temple. Everything about her screamed discreet, from her low-heeled shoes to the beige suit she wore with matching sensible bag. Jaid didn't need to glimpse her tear-ravaged face to guess that this was Mara Sorenson.

She sat without speaking for a moment. The ticking of the antique mantel clock filled the silence. "You're Adam

Raiker," she said finally, her voice holding the faintest qua-
ver. "Byron spoke of you. He was beside himself recently
when you were shot. And again several years ago when
you . . ." Her hand fluttered to her neck, which was minus
jewelry. And minus a scar like the one that bisected Adam's.

"He was a good friend." Adam's ruined voice was as
gentle as he could make it. And the two exchanged a look
of shared pain. "He thought highly of you, too."

Mara ducked her head, and her throat worked visibly. "I
was with him for fifteen years." Her voice was choked. "He
was a wonderful man. Intelligent. Passionate about the things
he believed in. And absolutely devoted to his family."

"You've met them?" Jaid inquired. The clerks spoke of
the justice being private about his personal life. But a
fifteen-year relationship would surely mean greater openness.

Sorenson nodded. "Several times over the years. Usually
when they'd come to the offices. Here or before, when he
was on the federal circuit."

"Would he have mentioned it to you if he'd been receiving threats? If something was bothering him?"

"He would have told the marshals, certainly. Byron and
Mary Jo were careful about security. Not hypervigilant by
any means. They wanted their boys' lives to be as normal as
possible. But they were cautious. If there had been a threat,
the USMS would have been informed."

"And he would have confided this to you, as well?"

The woman tilted her head, as if considering her question. And it occurred to Jaid that Sorenson was careful in
her own right. "I'm almost certain that he would," she said
finally. Her hazel eyes filled with tears again, which she
blinked away. "Byron was protective of those he cared
about, and given our long work relationship, that included
me. He insisted on walking me to my car if we worked late.
That sort of thing. If he had reason to believe someone was
going to target him . . ." Her voice broke. It took a moment
for her to steady it. "He would definitely worry about anyone else who could be in danger from their association with

him. His family would be his first concern. And then anyone else who came in contact with him on a daily basis. He
hasn't received a credible threat in years, as far as I know.
The last one was nearly a decade ago, when he was still on
the circuit bench. He arranged for security for me and his
paralegals at that time, until the man responsible was ap-
prehended."

"Who was the last one out of the office last night?"
Adam asked.

"We left together." Sorenson's hands, clasped on the table, clenched more tightly. "As I said, he didn't like me
walking to my car in the dark, even though the lot is fairly
well lit. I think he worked later than he meant to." A smile
trembled at the corner of her mouth. "He was prone to do
that, especially when writing an opinion. I'd already sent the
clerks home, per his request, but I rarely left before he did.
He was in a hurry and I left more hastily than I would have
liked, because he said he was going to be late. He and Mary
Jo had an engagement of some sort, I think."

"Did he mention stopping to buy her flowers?"

She shook her head, fumbled in her purse, and withdrew
a tissue. The tears were streaming again, and her efforts at
stemming the tide was a losing battle. "No, although that
would be like him. Mary Jo loves flowers, and Byron . . ."
Her voice was muffled as she mopped at her face. "Well, he
was a considerate man."

Further probing elicited little additional information.
Sorenson didn't know where the justice bought roses for his
wife, although she recalled it was somewhere on his way
home. Several minutes later when she headed for the door,
Jaid mulled over the words she'd spoken earlier. That Reinbeck had been a considerate man.

And this time that trait had gotten him killed.

———

Jaid exited from the government-issued SUV and rounded
it, waiting for Shepherd to raise the back hatch so they
could retrieve their weapons. It was past eight P.M., which

meant she'd left home that morning fifteen hours earlier. Had eaten once in the intervening time. But as the two men joined her, she looked at her fellow agent. "I'll make the report tonight, if you want. We can take turns."

Shepherd looked surprised, then relieved. "Sounds good. You've got the password?"

She nodded. Hedgelin would stay abreast of the various branches of the investigation through one communal online system. Each team would detail the day's activities, and intelligence analysts would compile them all into one organized cyber file for the assistant director. Although she wasn't looking forward to hours of work ahead, she could only imagine how much time it took Hedgelin to read through all of them. It was, she decided, as she leaned in to reclaim her weapon from the safe Shepherd unlocked, all a matter of perspective.

"Thanks for taking care of that." When they'd all moved away from the SUV, Shepherd activated the button to close the hatch. "My turn tomorrow night. Adam, unless we let you know otherwise, we'll meet back here tomorrow at eight."

He merely nodded at each of them in turn and headed toward his vehicle. Jaid hesitated, watching him, the assistant director's order from this morning ringing in her head. She was tempted to let him go without further conversation. It was highly likely he was heading home, just as she was.

"Been a long day." Shepherd was already heading toward the driver's door. "See you tomorrow."

The other man didn't seem overly concerned about Hedgelin's private instructions to them. Mentally shrugging, she headed toward her car. She wouldn't be, either.

She caught up with Adam halfway across the lot. The evening air held a definite bite, making her grateful for the wool jacket she wore. The breeze that had kicked up was ruffling his hair, but the man looked otherwise impervious to the cold. Seeing his gaze slide her way, she gestured toward her agency-issued dark-colored Impala. "What are you driving these days?"

He used the tip of his cane to point toward the black BMW sedan parked a few yards away from her car. One side of her mouth kicked up. Another thing that hadn't changed, apparently. He'd always favored speed, class, and reliability over flash.

"Where's the GTO?"

"In storage." Thoughts of her lovingly restored '65 muscle car brought a tinge of nostalgia. "I didn't get as much time to drive it as I would have liked last summer." And she always had it tucked safely away for the winter before Halloween rolled around.

One corner of his mouth rose. "You were making the same complaint nine years ago."

"It's still true." Because she very much didn't want the conversation to veer into the personal, she shoved her hands in her coat pockets, searched for another topic. "So. The interviews didn't reveal much today."

"Necessary legwork." His cane made a slight rhythmic sound as they moved across the asphalt. "We learned Reinbeck's clerks admired him, his admin was devoted. There was something there with Dempsey. He and Byron might have had some differences recently."

She sent him a sharp glance. The parking garage that housed their cars was well lit but nearly deserted. "Where'd you get that?"

He lifted a shoulder negligibly. "There was a slight edge of resentment to his tone when he talked about last night. Despite the fact that he espoused a similar sentiment about staying late, he lacked the sincerity of the others. It's probably nothing. Maybe it was as simple as Byron having chosen one of the other clerk's research to reference in his opinion."

Jaid hadn't noted anything untoward in Lawrence Dempsey's interview. If anything, she'd been struck by how close-knit the four clerks seemed to be. And—to a lesser extent—the clerks for all the justices. It had been clear that Krista Temple's words were accurate. The group worked and socialized together, brought closer by proximity and a common purpose. But she knew Raiker well enough not to dismiss any impressions he had of the individuals. The man was as uncanny as a human lie detector.

"The one thing that occurred to me was that if any one of them knew something, it was likely all of them did." Having reached his vehicle, they stopped, turned to face each other. "I'm guessing gossip—at least as far as it concerned the justices and the court—traveled fast among the group."

"Since none of them told us anything of consequence, that doesn't bode well for this line of investigation," Adam said dryly. He reached for his door handle.

"Maybe something brilliant will occur to one of us tonight. Are you heading home?"

It was, Jaid thought, just as nerve-wracking as she recalled to be pinned by that shrewd, blue, assessing gaze. He had always seen too much. Far more than she'd wanted to show. But she was different now. They both were.

"Why?"

She shrugged. "Just wondered if you had any other ideas to follow up on." It took effort to meet his gaze. To not quail beneath the small knowing smile he gave her.

"Hedgelin told you to stick close to me?"

Her distaste for the truth in the words wouldn't be allowed to show. "It's early." Her stomach churned at the need for disassembling. "If you're still working, I can, too."

Unlocking the car door with his key fob, he opened it and got in. "I guess you'll have to tag along and see."

Experience had her hurrying to her vehicle. It didn't escape her notice that he hadn't answered one way or another. That he hadn't mentioned a destination. And she didn't need the sound of his engine starting to realize he wouldn't wait for her.

Chapter 3

"I didn't realize they still heard confession at this time of night." Jaid stared at the darkened church she'd parked in front of and wondered what Adam was up to.

"I'm afraid my tutelage never got that far." He wasn't headed toward the church itself, she realized belatedly as she fell into step beside him, but toward the attached structure adjacent to it.

"Perhaps that's just as well," she said blandly. "Even the Lord can be shocked."

"You give me too much credit." Humor sounded in his voice as they made their way up the two steps to a door. Leaning forward, he rang the doorbell. "There's been precious little worth confessing on my part in the last few months."

She supposed not since he'd spent a couple of them in and out of hospitals, first clinging to life, then recovering from a couple grueling surgeries. Ignoring the clutch in her heart at the memory, she forced herself to say lightly, "Is there a statute of limitations when it comes to the confessional? Because I'm sure your past is rife with unrepented material."

Any rejoinder he would have made to that was lost when the door was pulled open. A figure clad in black stepped out. "Adam."

Jaid watched bemusedly as the white-collared man encased Adam in a bear hug. "Good to see you up and around."

"You just saw me last week." Despite his calm reminder, Adam thumped the man's back companionably.

"And you haven't been maimed or shot in the duration." The priest cast his eyes heavenward. "Proof that God is good."

"There are some who would reach a different conclusion." Adam stepped aside to indicate Jaid. "Special Agent Jaid Marlowe, Monsignor Jerry Benton. Jerry's an old friend."

That last was unnecessary. Even in the dim glow from the security light on the concrete steps, the affection the two men had for each other was clear.

"Come on in." The priest pulled open the door. "It was nice enough earlier today, but the wind's come up."

They followed him inside a vestibule, one wall adorned with an ornately engraved crucifix. Impressions were fleeting as he led them down a dimly lit hallway. The shadowy figures topping tables and stands were, she figured, statues of various saints. She wouldn't hazard a guess at their identities. She knew very little of Catholicism. Would never admit out loud that what she recalled of the deadly sins came from the plot of a movie she'd seen years ago.

"Cardinal Cote's on an energy kick," Jerry informed them as they preceded him into the one well-lit room in the place. "To go along with the rest of his penny-pinching qualities. Less painful to live in the dark than to go over the electric bill with one of his representatives every month."

The room looked comfortable and lived in. Skirting the massive desk facing the window overlooking the street in front, Benton settled himself in a faded navy leather wingback chair. Jaid sank onto the matching sofa that faced it, and Adam lowered himself into a chair next to his friend. There were pictures crowding the wall, all showing Jerry with an assortment of strangers, cutting ribbons, shaking hands, accepting large cardboard facsimiles of checks. Others were framed newspaper articles that featured the man holding signs, shouting. One that had obviously been shot at least fifteen years earlier clearly showed the priest leaning over the hood of a police car, being handcuffed.

Her expression must have shown a little of what she was thinking because Adam said, "Jerry is very passionate about his causes."

She flicked a glance at the older man. "I see that."

Benton scanned the wall of pictures, smiling a little. His still-thick hair had grayed since the handcuff photo had been taken. Well-worn creases softened the lines of his face. But his narrowed brown gaze was bright with intelligence. "I've learned there are other ways to affect change than passive resistance." Surprisingly, there was a flicker of regret in his eyes. "I'd be lying if I claimed I didn't miss it."

"You've been fighting for a cause ever since I've known you," Adam observed.

"In your way, so have you. What does it happen to be this time?"

"I need to brush up on some of my old catechism lessons." Shifting slightly in the chair, Adam stretched one leg out in front of him. "I remember the seven deadly sins. I need a refresher course on the history behind them."

The priest winked at Jaid. "I'm delighted every time he admits to recalling anything from those lessons. He wasn't a particularly apt student, even at nine. Challenged me at every turn."

Fascinated, she shot Adam a glance. "Somehow I'm not surprised."

He raised a sardonic brow. "I was blessed with a questioning nature."

"And a suspicious one." Jerry shrugged. "Since it's kept you alive this long, I've ceased to quibble with that trait." He raised his palms upright, pressed the fingertips together.

Ignoring Adam's question, he asked one of his own. "What exactly do you remember about the list?"

It was Adam's turn to shrug. "I recall the mnemonic SLAGIA. *Superbia, avaritia, luxuria, invidia, gula, ira,* and *acedia.*"

A slight wince crossed the priest's face. "Well, at least your memory is less atrocious than your Latin accent." He looked at Jaid. "Are you Catholic?" He looked unsurprised when she shook her head. "The list he's referring to was first noted by John Cassian, a fifth-century monk, but has developed over time. Pope Gregory I revised the list nearly two hundred years later, and modern Catholic catechism lists the sins as pride, avarice, envy, wrath, lust, gluttony, and acedia or sloth. All leave the soul in a state of mortal sin and left unrepented will damn it to the eternal fires of hell."

"Is there a ranking among them as to which is supposedly the worst?"

Jaid easily followed Adam's line of thought. If the two deaths were linked, hearing that greed and wrath were the gravest would leave hope that the killer was done. If one were inclined to think positively about such things.

"Ah, therein lies the source of centuries of theological discussion." Jerry's face brightened, as if in anticipation of just that. "Most consider pride to be the most grievous. All the other deadlies arise from it."

Which shot their fledgling idea all to hell. It was personal, rather than professional, interest that had her asking, "What makes pride worse than the others? I've seen people and governments do pretty horrible things in the name of the almighty dollar."

"The Almighty has a different connotation in the church, but I follow your meaning."

"That's a joke," Adam inserted, for Jaid's benefit. "Sometimes with Jerry it's hard to tell."

The priest leaned back more comfortably and raised his leg to rest one ankle on the opposite knee. She blinked when she noted that he was wearing Birkenstocks with dark socks. "Adam is rarely a fan of my humor. At any rate, I tend to agree with you that greed is the most grievous as it keeps wealth in the hands of a few while many go without. I spend a great deal of my time, as a matter of fact, doing my part to redistribute some of the riches. But we're in the minority, I'm afraid. Most side with the medieval theologian Thomas Aquinas's argument that pride was the source of every other sin. Lucifer was cast out of heaven for attempting to compete with God, for considering himself God's equal."

"Then there is a ranking?"

"Not necessarily." Jerry answered Adam's question thoughtfully. "Most consider pride to be the worst as I've said, and many would argue that sloth is the least of them all. Oftentimes, it's a sin of omission, the desire for ease, not expending the energy necessary to become closer to God. But even if one accepts that pride and sloth can be ranked, all of them are offensive in His eyes, and the remaining five at least equally so."

Jaid mulled the information over. Crimes of this sort were as much about the offender as the victim. So perhaps wrath and greed were the most egregious of the sins in the eyes of the unknown subject. People rationalized their actions all the time. The only thing unique about this offender was that his rationalization was cloaked in religion. "For the truly devout, they might provide rationale for breaking the law."

Jerry nodded. "I'm hardly a stranger to the concept of bending rules to achieve a greater good. So, yes, of course, one might justify his or her deeds by believing they were righting a wrong or acting on God's behalf. Although the error in that thinking is that in doing so, the perpetrator is guilty of the most grievous of the sins, pride." He gave a small smile. "By placing himself or herself in God's position, he elevates himself to God's status. It's similar to governments meting out capital punishment. Man cannot replace God in the ultimate judgment."

Adam glanced at his watch. "It's much too late to start a discussion on capital punishment."

"It'd be a continuation rather than a beginning on that particular topic, but you're right. I've got seven A.M. mass in the morning, and I still haven't finished my pitch for the metro DC chapter of the American Trial Lawyers next weekend." The look he fixed on Adam was hound-dog hopeful. "I don't suppose you're free?"

"Sorry." Adam sounded anything but. "What's the cause this time?"

"Funding for the Youth Mentorship Program. Sharing a bit of your personal journey could go a long way in shaking loose change from the pockets of those lawyers."

"A tempting prospect, but I'll pass. I've made one appearance for you already this year."

The priest raised both hands as if to ward off argument. "I know. And I'm grateful, believe me."

An unwilling smile tugged at the corner of Adam's mouth. "Bull. You're a pushy do-gooder who's never satisfied."

"And you're a closed-off workaholic who needs someone to open your eyes to what goes on beyond the parameters of your professional world." His voice was as mild as Adam's. Then his look shifted to Jaid. Became appraising. "Perhaps Ms. Marlowe can help with that."

Unease flickered. "Oh. Ah . . . I'm just along for the ride."

Jerry gave her a conspiratorial smile. "My experience has been that rides with Adam tend to be bumpy ones."

Outside the temperature seemed to have dropped several degrees in the short time they had been talking to the priest. "He seems to understand you," Jaid observed as she hunched deeper into her coat. They made their way down the porch steps. In the face of Adam's silence, she continued, "I suppose he should since he's known you since you were a child." And she wouldn't give voice to the questions elicited by *that* fact.

"He thinks he does, anyway." There was a note of wry exasperation in Adam's voice. "Jerry isn't above using our relationship to try to leverage me into participating in his cause of the moment."

They came to the curb where they'd left their cars, and paused. "Sounds like he's been successful a time or two." Which spoke volumes about the men's friendship. She couldn't recall a time when Adam hadn't done exactly as he pleased.

In the dim glow of the streetlight, he looked slightly discomfited. "Well." He moved his shoulders. "He can be incredibly persistent."

She suspected it was more than that. After all, she'd never met anyone more tenacious than Raiker. It would be Adam's regard for the priest that dictated the occasional gracious—or not—acquiescence. And she was intrigued, more than she should have been, about what had forged their relationship.

The strength of that interest drove her to take a step back. And then another. "Well. I'll see you tomorrow." Following him here tonight had elicited nothing of value. Nothing that had anything to do with the case, anyway. And those were the only facts she'd allow herself to care about. Her defenses were a lot stronger these days. She'd had eight years to strengthen them.

Turning, she strode rapidly to her black Impala. Unlocked the door to open it. Slid inside. He made no attempt to stop her. She didn't expect him to. Raiker's good-byes were abrupt.

And final.

Once she'd pulled away from the curb, she checked the clock on the dash, felt a stab of guilt. Fumbling to pull her cell phone from her purse, she hit the speed dial number and waited impatiently for it to be answered.

Traffic was heavy. The Georgetown area that housed Jerry's church was teaming with college kids jostling on the crowded sidewalks. But the view didn't bring back memories of her own long-ago university years. Her mind was on the reason for the call.

"Mother." A flicker of relief met the familiar tone that finally answered. "I suppose Royce is in bed already."

"I'm just fine, Jaidlyn, thank you."

Jaid's teeth ground a bit as she halted for a red light. It was so like Patricia Marlowe to first focus on the social niceties. "I hope you're still well, since I last saw you this morning," she said with barely restrained irony. "I'd like to speak to Royce if he's still up."

The response was preceded by a long-suffering sigh. "Well, of course, he's asleep, dear. You know I'm a stickler about bedtimes, even on weekends."

When the light flashed green, she nosed her car through the intersection. Patricia's last words had been aimed at her. Because last weekend Royce *had* been up past bedtime. Saturdays were their special nights together. Sometimes they'd watch a marathon of those silly comedies young boys thought were so hilarious. Or engage in a brutal Wii marathon. Boxing. Tennis. Football. But for the foreseeable future their time together was going to be curtailed by this case. From experience she knew better than to issue false promises to him to assuage her remorse. Promises that would almost certainly be broken. She wondered how other single parents managed the ensuing guilt that invariably arose from balancing a challenging career with raising a child.

"Of course. How was the birthday party he attended after school?"

"Oh fine." As her mother chattered on about her free hours spent cleaning Jaid's home, cleaning that—in her estimation—had been completely unnecessary, she found her attention wandering. She'd probably be up and gone again before Royce in the morning, but she'd make a point to give him a call sometime during the day tomorrow. The older the boy got, the more she hated to leave him for extended periods of time with her mother. Patricia had come around, softening a bit over the years, but she would never be a warm grandmotherly type. That would have represented a metamorphosis worthy of a Kafka novel.

She considered cutting the call short. Thought better of it. The drone of her mother's voice in her ear was never a pleasant prospect, but it was infinitely preferable to the alternative.

Like spending the long drive home thinking about Adam Raiker.

———

Mose Ferrell watched the cars pull away from the curb before starting his own vehicle. He was in no hurry. If the man was heading home, Mose had an hour's drive ahead of him. And he had to be sure the woman wasn't going to follow the man back to his town house. Mose's orders had been very specific. No witnesses.

At this time of night he wasn't certain he'd find a stretch of interstate that would fit that description, but adrenaline spiked anyway. He had a feeling tonight he'd finally see some excitement.

And so would Adam Raiker.

———

Adam sent a considering look at his silent cell on the console below the dash and the Bluetooth headset beside it. Talking on the phone was a useful evil in his line of work, but never one he'd learned to enjoy. Using the wireless headset or speakerphone lent the act a hellish element. He needed to talk to Paulie Samuels, his right hand at the agency. But the message the man had left had been labeled only "important." Which meant it could wait until he got home, where he could use the video chat each of them preferred. Samuels was no fonder of cell phones than Adam was.

Weaving in and out of traffic as he headed toward Manassas kept his mind occupied for the first leg of the trip. But as the traffic decreased, thoughts of the case intruded. Which would have been fine, had all those thoughts not borne the face of Jaid Marlowe.

It was a memorable one. Her features swam across his mind now, unbidden. Doe-shaped eyes, as dark as her hair, the color of mink. Delicate jaw, angled to a slightly pointed, stubborn chin. He knew from experience just how determined she was. How difficult it could be to shake her from an idea once she got it in her head.

Like when she'd been convinced the two of them had a future.

He scowled, checked the mirrors, and passed the next car. He'd disabused her of that notion finally, while still in CCU after killing John LeCroix eight years ago. It'd been weakness on his part that had led to their intimate relationship to begin with. She'd been young. Green. And achingly unguarded. But their eight-year age difference hadn't been enough to keep him away from her.

His fingers clenched and fisted on the wheel. She was all wrapped up in the biggest mistake of his life. Late at night it was still difficult to decide if the mistake had been starting a relationship with her. Or ending it.

That line of thought was unproductive. Adam checked the rearview mirror again. Much more productive to wonder who was in the light-colored sedan that had been tailing him since he'd left the rectory.

Purposefully, he cut his speed. But the car stayed back. Sometimes four car lengths, other times allowing half-a-dozen vehicles to drift between them. But it was telling that even with the decreased traffic, it didn't speed up enough to close the distance.

Feds most likely. Adam gave a grim smile. Maybe Shepherd had been given the duty after Jaid and he had parted. New vehicle, one he wouldn't recognize . . . Did Hedgelin distrust him that much?

Yes. The answer to the question was automatic. Although to be fair, the idea could have originated much higher in the organization. As if this case didn't come with enough problems without adding in this senseless paranoia about him.

Deliberately, he slowed to take the next exit. And paused long enough at the bottom of the ramp to determine whether he had company. Adrenaline spiked when his tail followed. Damn, but he was going to enjoy this. His recovery from taking three bullets in the chest a few months ago had been slower than he would have liked. He no longer healed like a kid. But the day he couldn't take on some half-witted government drone on a surveillance assignment was the day he'd hang up his weapon for good.

He led the sedan through a series of small towns before coming to the county road he was looking for and turned on it without signaling. Unsurprisingly, his tail did the same. Picked up speed.

The headlights speared through the darkness behind him with the inexorable intent of an oncoming train. There was little traffic on this road, which was the reason Adam had chosen it. No use involving an unwary citizen in what was about to happen.

Because it was appearing less and less likely that whoever was behind him was a fed. An agent would follow orders, and those orders wouldn't have included confronting him. He took a hand off the wheel to unsnap his shoulder holster, leaving his suit coat pushed open to allow better access. The other driver had given up all pretense of hiding his intention. The headlights bounced and swerved as they sped over the poorly lit, ill-maintained road.

Daylight would have distinguished the scenery whipping by the windows as heavily wooded, with trees crowding the roadside, their nude branches entwined in the canopy overhead. But the darkened scenery was the last thing on Adam's mind. There was a series of hairpin curves coming up. He hoped his memory served him well.

He decreased his speed enough to allow the other vehicle to come closer. And closer still. It slammed into the back of the Beemer, hard enough to jolt Adam's teeth together. His lips stretched in a grim smile; he stomped on the accelerator. Timing it to the second, he whipped the wheel at the last moment, tires screeching to make the first of the trio of curves.

The high-pitched screech of metal against an unforgiving century-old tree's trunk filled the air. Lights no longer showed behind him. Slowing the vehicle, Adam stabbed at the button to lower the window. Strained to hear anything else.

But the night was silent.

He brought his car to a gradual halt, navigating the last of the curves from memory, his mind on the vehicle behind him. The Y-turn he executed was tricky on the narrow road. The back wheels left the pavement once, spun, before he was able to right the vehicle. He doused the lights before easing the vehicle back to the scene, one hand on the wheel while drawing his weapon with the other. If he hadn't been cautious by nature, the five attempts on his life last year would have forged that trait.

The seconds dragged as he rounded the middle curve. There was still no sound. He crept around the next. Saw the taillights ahead splitting the shadows from where the car still sat, its grill kissing the trunk of a huge cottonwood.

Every muscle in Adam's body tensed. Stopping thirty meters from the other vehicle, he lowered the window the rest of the way before easing the door open. Stepped out onto the pavement, weapon ready. Using the door between him and the other car like a shield.

"Throw your weapon out the window," he called. "Then get out of the car, hands behind your head." He was guessing the driver was armed. There was little point to this exercise tonight if he weren't.

There was no answer. The vehicle remained still. Was the driver unconscious? Dead?

Adam immediately rejected the latter possibility. But there was notable damage to the front of the car. Its airbag had almost certainly deployed, which could wreak its own injuries.

He was still weighing his options when suddenly the other vehicle roared to life. It shuddered into reverse with a wrenching screech, righted itself, and leapt toward him. Muttering a curse, Adam hurried in an awkward stumble to the area behind his car, taking refuge in the trees hugging the road.

There was a thunderous crash as the other vehicle pushed

the Beemer off the county road. Adam dove out of the way to avoid having his car roll on top of him.

The squeal of the departing vehicle's acceleration rang in his ears like a schoolyard taunt.

———

"Don't bleed on my leather seats."

One of Paulie Samuels's best qualities was that he didn't fuss. "I'm not bleeding anymore." But Adam kept his handkerchief pressed to the wound on his forehead, just in case. The scrapes on his hands were minor. And the head injury had settled to a sullen ooze that he'd already testily refused to have stitched.

"I'm not even going to mention the card hand I threw in to come out here."

Adam laid his head against the rest and closed his eyes. "Thank God for small favors."

"Three ladies. *Three.*" It was too much to hope that Paulie would make good on his word. "Three thousand on the table, and the pot would probably have doubled before it was over."

"Are you telling me you want six thousand dollars for coming out here to pick me up?"

Paulie's response was swift. Vaguely insulted. "It's not about the money."

Amazingly, Adam felt a smile tug his lips. "It's about winning. I get it, believe me."

Nothing about the night left him feeling like a victor. Not when it was his car dangling from the tow truck whose taillights even now winked ahead of them. It still rankled to recall the difficulty he'd had returning to the vehicle. His thigh was seizing and cramping from the punishment it had taken. His chest felt as though it were on fire. Hobbling unaided to the vehicle had been a further indignity. Most of the time Adam managed to forget the physical limitations his three days in LeCroix's captivity had cost him. Intellect trumped physical prowess nearly all the time. But tonight those limitations had been particularly impossible to ignore.

The sheriff's deputy that had responded to the scene had looked a bit dubious at his story of a hit-and-run but had agreed to investigate the car's description and partial plate that Adam had managed to see before taking cover.

"I know there's a lot more to the story than the stingy details you gave the deputy."

Feeling Samuels's gaze on him, Adam straightened and faced him. "You could say that." In a few terse sentences, he filled his friend in and waited for his response. He trusted this man like no one else. Which was odd, since Adam wasn't a person to whom trust came easily. But with one decision eight years ago, he had aligned his fate with Samuels. He'd never had cause to regret it.

"Not feds then." There was a slight frown on the shiny brow beneath Paulie's balding dome. "Send a tail, sure that's their style. But they wouldn't try to kill you."

"If the driver was armed, he never fired. He might have been ordered to just get me out of the picture for a while. Long enough for the case to proceed without me."

There was a long pause. One he read as surely as if the other man had spoken. "You don't agree."

"I might, had it not been for uncovering this earlier to-day." Paulie reached into his wool jacket. Since he'd come from a "friendly" game of cards, he wasn't clad in a suit, so he was sans tie, which was usually adorned with some sort of gambling scene. Instead he wore a hideous sweater in eye-popping green and red argyle. Each diamond in the fabric showed a royal flush.

Unfolding the papers his friend handed him, Adam frowned down at them, immediately irritated. He hated dealing with techy details. That's why he had men like Samuels working for him. But he was able to get the gist of the information on the first page. "You discovered who paid the shooter in Philadelphia?"

"Not exactly. But I was able to do a backward trace of the payments through a front of false overseas accounts to one that rang a bell. It's there on the second sheet."

But Adam had already found it. And the info had the recently healed bullet wounds in his chest throbbing anew. "I'll be damned."

"Most likely, but beside the point. Payment for your shooter came from one of the accounts I tracked the ransom money through last winter for the Mulder kidnapping."

Adam didn't need the reminder. In January he and a couple investigators from his agency had been called to find an eleven-year-old girl snatched from her father's estate in Colorado. They'd found and killed Vincent Dodge, the man who'd abducted her. But whoever had hired Dodge had managed to clear three million of the ten he'd demanded in ransom. Paulie had diverted the rest and devoted a great deal of time and energy to following the three million as it skipped from bank account to bank account across the globe.

"Interesting."

Paulie snorted, sent him a quick look. "Interesting? That's all you've got to say? It's fucking unbelievable. Not only that I was genius enough to find where the accounts intersected— and your awe and gratitude is duly noted—but this means that whoever ordered the girl's kidnapping last January has a hard-on against *you*. Enough to want you dead. Damn near succeeded, too. What were there, four attempts before Jennings turned you into a human sieve in May?"

As usual the man's frank speech relaxed something in Adam. He narrowed his good eye in concentration. "If you count blowing up my town house."

"And why wouldn't that count since you were supposed to be in it?" Without waiting for a response, Paulie continued. "The guy is probably pretty pissed he got less than a third of the ransom he was demanding for the Mulder girl. Decided to go after the man who cost him the remaining seven million."

"Actually, since you were the one with the skills to divert the rest, it's you he should be targeting." Dark humor filled Adam. He looked over at his friend. Noticed the way his hands were clenched on the steering wheel. And was touched by the unspoken concern. "It's actually satisfying to have some evidence that we were right. Neither of us believed the feds' version that Jennings was working alone to avenge his ex-girlfriend's father's death at my hand a decade ago. This makes more sense. Now we'll yank on this connection you've found between the shooter in Philly and the Colorado kidnapping, see if we can finally figure out who was pulling the strings in the Mulder case. But you're grasping at straws if you're suggesting tonight had anything to do with those cases."

"This from the man who doesn't believe in coincidence."

The trees alongside the road were thinning. They were nearing the interstate again. "There's no coincidence. I just have a knack for setting people on edge. Amazing, given my winning personality."

Samuels didn't smile. His tone was dogged. "You can't ignore the possibility that tonight is linked to the other attempts on your life, Adam. The shooter failed in May. Landed you in the hospital and rehab for months, but you're still around. There's no reason to believe the attempts will stop. The bank account discovery ties Jennings to the Colorado kidnapper. Who's still out there and likely still wants you dead. That could be what tonight was all about."

"If tonight was an attempt, it wasn't much of one." Jennings had been nothing if not persistent. Although bullets had been his usual method of choice, he'd turned to incendiary devices twice. The events of a couple hours ago were amateurish in comparison. "It's likelier that tonight was a direct result of the investigation I'm currently working." To distract the man and himself, he filled him in on the case so far. There was disappointingly little to report. They'd barely scratched the surface, and he had no idea what ground the other teams had covered that day.

"Hedgelin's running the investigation?" Paulie's long whistle was fraught with meaning. "How'd that meeting go?"

"About the way you'd expect." Paulie had been in the bureau at the time Hedgelin and Adam were partners. Had worked with Hedgelin himself when the man was still in the cyber crimes unit. "You remember Tom Shepherd? He's on the case."

"Nice to have one friendly face there, I guess." Paulie slanted him a glance in the dim interior of the call. "He's grateful to you. That's why he came down so hard on the field agents in Philly for getting Jennings's whereabouts wrong the night you were shot. He believes you were responsible for getting him out of that shit hole North Dakota field office and reinstalled in DC."

Adam shrugged uncomfortably. He'd never admit to his part in orchestrating just that. The man was a good agent. He hadn't deserved his banishment nearly three years ago. A case of Adam's had intersected with one of Shepherd's back then and returned a missing girl to her parents. The fact that Shepherd and his team had failed to do so must have pissed off someone in the bureau, resulting in the man's demotion.

Petty politics had always frustrated Adam. And he'd give a lot to discover who had been behind Shepherd's reassignment after that case. Hedgelin? Or someone higher up? Maybe one of these days he'd ask. Because it was certain that whoever it was wouldn't have been happy when the senior member on the senate intelligence committee had lobbied the bureau to have Shepherd reinstated to his old post, at Adam's request.

"So are you going to report tonight to Hedgelin?"

Unerringly, Paulie touched on the most troublesome portion of the night.

"The bureau didn't want me anywhere near this case." A thought was forming, fueled only partially by paranoia. "It occurs to me that tonight's little drama could hand them a perfect excuse for my removal."

He didn't have to say more. Samuels followed the line of thought seamlessly. "They'd have to reject their own conclusion that Jennings was working alone and switch gears. Suggest that your would-be assassin is still out there. Still targeting you."

"Or that I'd attracted a copycat. Either of which would be a huge distraction for an investigation that's already knee-deep." The issue settled, he flicked his friend a glance. "I think not."

"Probably a good idea." Paulie eased the car onto the interstate. Headed south. "I'll put some of our people on it. I think Abbie and Ryne are due back from that spree killing case up in Maine, aren't they?"

Adam frowned, didn't answer immediately. He was uncertain whether he wanted to bring more attention to the events of the evening by putting the Robels on it. On the other hand, the husband-and-wife team was free, having just wrapped up their most recent case. And they were very highly skilled.

They had to be, or they wouldn't be working for him.

"I don't think that's necessary. At least not yet." One hand went to his thigh to massage away the cramps that had seized it. They were a leftover from the nerve damage he'd suffered several years ago. He could only hope that an hour in the hot tub later would soothe the worst of them.

Broodingly, he watched the steady stream of lights in the oncoming traffic. It occurred to him that he hadn't mentioned the other agent he was working on the case with. Paulie knew Jaid, too, even better than he did Hedgelin and Shepherd. They'd all been at the bureau together, a lifetime ago. And although the omission hadn't been deliberate, he made no attempt to right it now.

He settled his head against the headrest. The other man would have plenty to say about Jaid's reappearance in his life. At the best of times his comments on the subject would be unwelcome.

Adam was already aware that of all the distractions this case came loaded with, she might well end up being the biggest one of all.

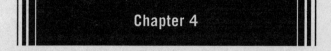

Chapter 4

It was early. Nearly an hour before Adam was due to meet Jaid and Shepherd. But the run-down apartment bearing Danny Shelton's address wasn't all that far away from the Hoover Building in actual miles.

It was a lifetime away in terms of inhabitants.

"Doesn't look like a great place, sir." Reno Tripp's voice dripped doubt. As one of the drivers in Adam's employ, he'd driven in far worse areas. Adam wondered if the man's show of nerves came from recalling the fate of Adam's driver in Philly, who had returned fire with Jennings after Adam had been shot. Had taken a bullet himself. "Relax." His hand went to the door handle. "I won't be inside long." Or maybe not at all if Shelton's family refused to talk to him. "Keep circling until I call."

"Not much choice," the man muttered. And that was true enough. Both sides of the narrow rutted street were lined with vehicles in various stages of disrepair. Given the hour, Adam hadn't expected to see many people about, and other than a few hurrying down steps or along the cracked sidewalks, he was right. The building he was interested in, however, had a steely eyed young man in his twenties sitting on the stoop in a decrepit lawn chair. When Adam exited the car and headed in his direction, the man slowly rose. Positioned himself before the doorway.

Recognizing a sentry when he saw one, Adam climbed a couple steps and halted. "I'd like to talk to Rosa Shelton if she's feeling up to visitors."

"She ain't."

"I'd feel better if you asked her." He reached into the breast pocket of his suit, noted the man's barely perceptible response. He was willing to bet the oversized military-surplus jacket the guy was wearing concealed a weapon.

Cocking a brow, Adam said, "My card?" But the man didn't visibly relax, even when Adam withdrew a business card and handed it to him.

The man didn't look at it. "She ain't talkin' to no press."

"Please." Adam's voice was pained. "Do I look like a member of the press to you?"

"She ain't talkin' to no one strappin', neither." The man gave a meaningful nod to Adam's jacket. "Leastwise no one without a badge."

"Well, I don't have a badge, although I am working with the FBI. So I'll just give this to you to hold, shall I?" This time when Adam reached into his suit jacket, the man's hand disappeared into one large cargo-sized pocket of his coat. Pretending not to notice, Adam withdrew his Glock, hit the magazine release, and racked the slide back to eject the cartridge. Dropping both into his pocket, he handed the empty gun to the younger man. "Maybe you could tell Ms. Shelton she has company."

Indecisive, he stood for a moment, his gaze going from Adam to the weapon. After a moment, he opened up the front door and called, "Tyreque!"

A slighter, much younger man appeared. Still in his teens, Adam estimated. And not nearly as hardened as his companion.

"Stay here." The older man headed into the building leaving the newcomer guarding the entrance.

This guard, however, was chattier than his friend. "You ain't no reporter."

"A fact I give thanks for daily."

The kid cocked his head, giving Adam a thorough once-over. "Don't know exactly what you *do* look like. Maybe Pacino in one of them older flicks. One of them where he gets shot at the end."

Because there was no real answer to that comment— other than to admit how close it came to the truth—Adam asked a question of his own. "Are you related to Danny Shelton?"

"He was my uncle."

"I'm sorry for your loss."

The kid looked away, moving his shoulders jerkily. "Shit happens, right? But it shouldn'ta happen to Danny. He never hurt no one, man. All the time out there sellin' them stupid flowers. And he gets offed doin' that? Life sucks."

Before Adam could agree the older man reappeared and with a jerk of his head motioned Adam inside. "Stay here, Tyreque." The kid settled himself into the vacant lawn chair as Adam stepped by him and through the front door. Upon closer inspection he saw the lock was broken, probably long ago. It wouldn't keep out unwanted visitors.

And in the time since Danny Shelton had been killed in the shooting targeting Byron Reinbeck, there had probably been a lot of unwanted visitors.

At the foot of a rickety staircase, the man shot Adam a glance. "Fourth floor. And the elevator ain't worked since she moved in."

"Lead the way." He wouldn't have trusted an elevator in a place like this in the best of times. But by the time he reached the last flight, Adam was doubly glad for the time he'd spent in the hot tub last night.

Rosa Shelton, mother and legal guardian of Danny Shelton, was standing in the doorway of apartment 431. Nearly filling it, actually. Despite the earliness of the hour, she was fully dressed in a neat navy dress, dark nylons, and low-heeled pumps. Her short hair was styled in soft gray curls around a plump face the color of mocha coffee. She wore her age and weight more easily than her grief. It sat heavy on her shoulders and filled her eyes.

"I'm expectin' the Reverend Andrews anytime now," she said, her gaze not moving off Adam. "So Bobby, you take yourself down those stairs and wait for him."

The man—Bobby—didn't move. "Tyreque's already down there."

"So now you'll both be down there." She glanced away then, and the look she gave Bobby was enough to have him shuffling his feet before slowly turning toward the staircase. Then her look pinned Adam again. "State your business, Mr. Raiker."

"I'm working with the task force formed to look into your son's death, Ms. Shelton. His and Byron Reinbeck's."

Her laugh was short and scoffing. "Weren't no task force formed for Danny's death; we both know that. The task force is for that judge. And those bullets was for the judge." Her large brown eyes filled with tears. "But my Danny's gone, all the same. And no one wants to tell me why. They just want to ask questions 'bout did my Danny do this or know that. Truth is: He knew his flowers and not much more. But he was a good man. Had a kind way 'bout him; I made sure of that. But now the only thing people knows 'bout him was that he got hisself killed because someone wanted the judge dead."

"But he mattered." Adam gave her a slow nod. "His life mattered, too. I'd like to talk to you about that if you have the time."

Rosa studied him for several long moments. "You look like you know a bit about sorrow and sufferin' yourself."

"A bit."

She stepped back then and held the door wide. "Guess you can come in until the reverend gets here. We been plannin' the service. Leastways, as much as we can plan, without knowin' when they'll let us have Danny's body."

He followed her into the dark, cramped apartment. There was a postage–stamp–sized sitting area that opened onto a galley-style kitchen floored with cracked linoleum. The sparse furniture was worn. The shades covering the windows were yellowed and ripped. But the area was neat, and the table holding the lone lamp in the room was polished to a shine. The whole place smelled vaguely of Pine-Sol.

"You must have been very proud of your son." Adam regarded the woman soberly. Agents would have been dispatched to this address immediately upon learning Danny Shelton's identity, but the file Hedgelin had given him yesterday hadn't included copies of the ensuing conversations.

"That school they sent 'im to said he'd never take care of hisself. That he'd have to work at one of them sheltered workshop places. But Mr. Hardt from the church has a flower shop and let Danny sweep up there. Do odd jobs. And Danny learned a lot while he was workin' for him. After a few years he got a hankering to sell his own flowers." Rosa settled herself with surprising grace onto the sagging couch. Adam took the remaining chair. "Mr. Hardt came up with the idea of settin' Danny up as one of them sidewalk vendors. Was always real generous with 'im, too."

"That must have given your son a sense of accomplishment. To be that self-sufficient."

Rosa's chin quivered once before she steadied it. "A man needs to feel he has a purpose. Danny might not've been as smart as others, but he had his pride. Never seen him as happy as he was since he worked with Mr. Hardt. Sorry thing is: Another week or two and Danny wouldn't even have been out on that sidewalk. When it gets too cold, he just works in the shop all day."

"Where's the store?"

Five miles from where Danny set up, Rosa informed him. The man had a cart he pulled with his bike that held his wares, a three-sided shelter, and a chair. In the fall he often took a heater to protect the flowers.

The entire thing sounded like a win-win for the "generous" Mr. Hardt as he was expanding his store walls for what was likely a pittance to his employee. But from the sound of things, the job had made Shelton and his mother happy, so maybe Adam was being too harsh in his assessment.

"By any chance did Danny have a cell phone?"

When Rosa shook her head, Adam felt the fledgling idea he'd gotten at the interviews yesterday die. It gained new life in the next instant, however, when she said, "Well, leastways, not one of his own. He couldn't never have afforded it. But he carried one every day when he was selling out on his own. It belongs to Mr. Hardt, though. That's how he kept tabs on how Danny was doin'. If he was havin' a real good day in the summertime, Mr. Hardt might send someone out to restock him."

"Did you know that Byron Reinbeck was one of Danny's customers?"

Rosa straightened, tension settling into her limbs as her expression grew stern. "Danny didn't go round bragging on himself, if that's what you mean."

Which of course was a yes. Adam eyed her steadily. "You were probably asked that already. Whether your son recognized who and what Byron was. Whether anyone had talked to him about it. Asked for times and dates Byron had been by."

The sigh that emanated from her sounded weary. "They's thinkin' that he tol' someone that man came by sometimes. I tried to explain, but they didn't listen. Danny wouldn't think to tell people 'cuz he didn't understand why's Reinbeck was so important. People was all people to him. Some nicer than others. Danny liked Mr. Reinbeck 'cuz he always treated him real good."

"But you knew who Byron was."

Reluctantly she nodded. "Mr. Hardt tol' me. When the weather was cold, Mr. Reinbeck, he'd stop at the shop sometimes. He'd always call first, and Mr. Hardt would have Danny stay open late to wait for him."

Adam could imagine that the absent Mr. Hardt had also

entertained a visit from the feds. And that they'd had quite a few questions for him. "Did Mr. Reinbeck ever call a day or so in advance?"

"Once in a while, Mr. Hardt said, but usually it was like yesterday. Last minute."

There were voices approaching in the hallway. Adam suspected the reverend had arrived. He rose. "I don't want to keep you any longer, Ms. Shelton. My condolences on the loss of your son."

The nod the woman gave held a surprising dignity. "I thank you for that, Mr. Raiker."

Adam moved to the door, halted with one hand on the knob. After hearing what Rosa had had to say, his mind was already on a couple phone calls he needed to make after leaving here. One to Jo Reinbeck and the other to Paulie. Half turning he asked, "Did Danny have that cell phone with him the day of the shooting?"

The woman shrugged. "I can't say, but I 'spect he did. Like I said, that's how Mr. Hardt kept up with him. He'd tell 'em when it was time to close up. Danny would take any flowers he hadn't sold back to the shop. He had a key. It was his job to put the unsold flowers back in the cooler and then sweep up."

Adam took a notepad from his suit breast pocket. "Do you happen to know that number?" And was unsurprised when Rosa rattled it off without missing a beat.

"I'd check up on Danny, too, sometimes. Or my grandsons would. He's been robbed twice, out on the street like that. Never got hurt, though." This time her effort to stem the tears failed. She snatched a tissue from a box on the table and dabbed at her face. "Leastways, not 'til the other day."

———

"Reinbeck's car was clean," Assistant Director Hedgelin was saying as Adam slipped into the man's office. "And there was no GPS device planted on any of his personal belongings, either."

"What about his chambers?" Jaid crossed one black-clad

leg over the other and tried not to wonder where Adam had been. Or what had caused that knot on his forehead. It hadn't been there when they'd parted last night.

"There was a sweep done on his quarters at the court. On all the areas where he would have spent time. No listening devices were detected. We're looking at the flower vendor, Shelton, and at his boss, who owns the shop that supplied him." He looked at Adam then, but the man said nothing. "We know Justice Reinbeck called Shelton an hour before leaving. We can assume he asked about the availability of the flowers."

"And maybe Shelton tipped someone else off." Shepherd leaned forward, a note of interest in his voice. "He or his boss. Anyone studying Reinbeck's movements would be looking for a routine. If he'd used that vendor in the past, the shooter might have reached out, paid them to tip him off."

"He had," Adam verified. He inclined his head slightly toward Hedgelin. "As I'm sure your agents have already informed you. Mary Jo Reinbeck isn't one for jewelry, but she has a weakness for flowers. Byron regularly surprised her with some, not always from the same place. But he frequently bought from Danny Shelton, either on the street or at Hardt's shop."

The assistant director's gaze sharpened. "We know that. Which is why we're looking into Hardt and Shelton. Their backgrounds. Acquaintances. Anything they might be into."

"Maybe something will show up there," Adam allowed, "although it's doubtful Danny Shelton was into much. He was intellectually limited, his mother said." He waited for Hedgelin's nod before going on. "Which might have meant he could be easily manipulated by others. But surely by now you know if Shelton had a cell on him. And if he did, whether he placed a call after Reinbeck called him."

There was a glint in Cleve's eyes, there and gone almost too quickly to be identified. "You talked to Rosa Shelton?"

"This morning, as a matter of fact." Silence stretched, long enough to be uncomfortable.

Hedgelin removed his glasses and polished them with a handkerchief he removed from his suit breast pocket, a mannerism Jaid always found a bit fussy. "You realize that was outside the scope of your team's assignment."

"Are we going to rehash the parameters of my involvement every day, Cleve?" Adam's voice had lowered. A damaged rumble that sounded like an irritated tiger. "I'm already getting a bit weary of it."

The director made a dismissive gesture with his hand before settling his glasses back on the bridge of his nose. "I suppose it can be delayed for the moment." His tone could only be described as pissy. "As you say, Shelton wasn't batting at the top of the intellectual lineup. He didn't make any calls after Reinbeck's, but he did receive one from his boss minutes later. Hardt claimed he was just checking up on him, telling him to get back there by dark. When he heard that Reinbeck was coming by, he agreed that Shelton should stay put. Of course, he isn't acknowledging that he knew who the customer was. But there's no way of backing up his claim that he didn't."

"And you've been combing through his cell phone and landline LUDs since yesterday." Jaid didn't need his nod to know she was right about a team working on the local usage details. It was their best lead at this point. Certainly more than they'd managed to get from the interviews at the Supreme Court building yesterday.

She also knew that if Adam weren't on the team, pushing the assistant director in a way she and Shepherd would never have dared, none of this information would have been shared with them.

"The warrant for Hardt's phone records came through quickly, given the victim. But there was no call made on the shop's phone or on Hardt's personal cell immediately following his call to Shelton."

"Might have been using a TracFone," Jaid observed. "Or maybe the phone of an employee."

"Both possibilities are being followed up on."

But Adam didn't look convinced. "Mary Jo said this would

have made the second time Byron got her flowers since returning from the last recess. A stalker would have had to follow him, learn his routine. I'm willing to bet there were damn few instances of him returning to the same place in that time period. As Jaid mentioned yesterday, it's likely the shooter scouted out two or three possible kill spots. Waited for his opportunity to present itself."

Jaid turned toward him, frowning. "The problem with my theory is that it requires different informants. The only knowledge Hardt and Shelton would have had would be that of Reinbeck stopping for flowers. It's hard to believe that the shooter would risk making contact with informants for every possible kill site. Neither would he be likely to rely on the flower angle, if Reinbeck used it only once before recently."

She switched her focus to her boss. "What about a bug on Reinbeck's cell phone?" Recalling the note Adam had scribbled on his pad yesterday, she recognized he'd gotten to that idea long before she had. "Or spyware of some sort?" She was a little out of her element here. Unlike Shepherd and Hedgelin, she hadn't come up through the ranks via the e-crimes unit.

A note of impatience entered Hedgelin's tone. "As I've said, we've got the cyber techs going over it. If there's anything there, they haven't found it yet."

"Paulie is unmatched in this area," Adam put in. "He says to look for an incoming text between the time Byron left the building and his death. High-end spyware can be installed via text message or e-mail, but the victim has to download a link first. He's also seen some newer versions that can also be set to self-destruct remotely."

"As I said . . ."

Shepherd leaned forward, interrupting his boss to address Adam. "Either way it would have been discovered. E-mail, even deleted, is likely still on the victim's server. Texts would appear in the SMS log. The agents would have found that."

"Two months ago Paulie consulted on a similar case in

Chicago. The spyware was the best he'd ever seen. Trojan horse installation via a text message containing a link. None of the usual tells. Phone didn't turn on when it wasn't in use, no audible clicks heard during conversations." Adam adjusted the crease in his pants. Stretched his leg out. "The only evidence left behind was likely caused by its self-destruct mechanism. There was a miniscule burned patch on the SIM card. If he hadn't already narrowed it down to spyware, hadn't been looking for it, he would have dismissed it as normal wear."

Interest gleamed in Hedgelin's eyes. "A singed SIM card wouldn't have been evidence enough. How did he prove the spyware existed?"

"He used data recovery to work backward from the text message senders in the in-box list, recovered all the text senders' numbers." His shrug was negligible. "From there it was just focusing in on the right person."

The assistant director scribbled a note on the pad in front of him. "Our lab is second to none. But I'll double-check that. In the meantime, I've got a delicate assignment for the three of you." With deliberation he laid down his pen, clasped his hands on the desk. His pointed gaze swept them in turn. "There were a couple names that popped from the threat assessments. They were deemed very low risk, but that doesn't mean that interviews don't have the potential to turn into a shit storm."

"Who are they with?" Shepherd asked.

"One of them is Congressman Jonas Newell, senator from Virginia." He smiled thinly at their immediate attention. "You see the need for delicacy here. Senator Newell has made no attempt to hide the fact that he was no fan of Byron Reinbeck's. He led the fight to derail Reinbeck's nomination to the court and never misses an opportunity to invoke Reinbeck's name when he rails against activist judges. The feud has been long-running, stemming back to the judge's time in juvenile court."

Jaid wasn't aware of Newell's public animosity toward Reinbeck, but his name was familiar for another reason.

"The way I remember it, he also isn't a fan of our agency." Newell was an outspoken critic of the bureau, often going on news shows to call it antiquated and ineffectual. She didn't know much about the man's politics, but his ravings hadn't placed her in his fan club,.

Hedgelin said, "He has agreed to speak to us and has very generously carved out fifteen minutes from his schedule. You're due in his office," he checked his watch, "at ten thirty. You'll be early. He'll keep you waiting. Regardless, you'll be polite, professional, and thorough, without giving him any reasons to use your visit to further fuel his distaste for our agency."

Jaid and Shepherd nodded, although the barb seemed directed at Adam. She'd been in on interviews with Raiker before. He was masterful with suspects, extracting information without them even being aware of what they were admitting to. But he didn't suffer fools gladly, either. He'd need to summon all his diplomatic skills for the upcoming meeting.

The assistant director was continuing. "I want an immediate report following the interview. And I want it to come from you, not in the form of a phone call from the senator."

"Are there any recent incoming or outgoing phone messages between Reinbeck and Newell, either on Byron's cell or landline?"

Hedgelin shook his head at Shepherd's question. "No. But Newell's questioning of Reinbeck was pretty pointed, and that was all over C-SPAN at the time. After his appointment to the Supreme Court, the senator took aim at him on the media circuit." Hedgelin glanced at his watch again and rose. "I have another appointment in a few minutes. Adam, if I could speak to you for a moment?"

Jaid refrained from casting a look over her shoulder as she preceded Shepherd out of the office. She'd included a brief summary of her and Adam's visit to the priest last night in an e-mail to her boss early this morning. It was ridiculous to feel guilty about that. Not when Adam had guessed her mission last night.

So she mentally shoved aside the niggle of remorse and concentrated on the upcoming face-off with Senator Jonas Newell.

———————

"I understand you had a bit of problem after work yesterday."

Adam deliberately misunderstood. "You mean when your agent insisted on accompanying me to my friend's house? It wasn't a problem really. I've got nothing to hide. I trust she included our conversations in her report to you."

Hedgelin had the grace to look a bit discomfited. But he didn't offer an apology and Adam didn't expect one. "Actually, I was speaking about the accident you reported. The hit-and-run." He waited, but when Adam didn't say anything, he unerringly plucked a page from the sheaf in front of him. "Someone ran you off the road, it says." He raised his brows. "Did you get a look at him?"

"Sounds like you have the report in front of you, so you can see that I didn't." Suddenly weary of the back-and-forth, Adam's tone grew pointed. "I have to admit I thought at first the driver was one of yours."

"You thought I had an agent keeping you under surveillance?" Cleve chuckled and shook his head. "You overestimate your importance. We're stretched thin enough already with this investigation."

Nodding as though it made perfect sense, Adam said, "So you could only spare an agent to follow me until ten but not all the way home? You're right. Thinking otherwise would be a stretch."

When a flush darkened the man's cheekbones, Adam added, "But relax, I didn't think an agent would go so far as to try and run me off the road. Too much paperwork to explain the vehicle damage."

Drumming his fingers on the desktop, the assistant director responded, "Why does it seem that trouble follows you around?"

"Sometimes it's reversed. Sometimes I follow trouble

around. There was a time you followed it with me, remember."

The other man's gaze shifted. "I wasn't talking about Louisiana."

"No." Adam's voice was even. "You never do, at least not with me. But I hear you have plenty to say about it when there's no one around to refute your memories. Such as they are."

Hedgelin's gaze when it returned to him was glacial. "Be very careful, Adam. Remember you're here at my say-so."

Adam rose. "Our memories don't seem to mesh on that point, either. But you have nothing to worry about. Last night was likely the result of some drunk taking a shortcut home after tipping one too many back at the local tavern. Nothing to worry about." He turned and headed to the door.

"I hope you're right. I won't allow any outside diversions in this case. It's too important."

The words summoned a recollection of Adam's and Paulie's conversation about this very thing last night. "Finally," he said as he went through the door. "Something we agree on."

Chapter 5

Senator Newell's quarters were located on the second floor of the Russell Senate Office Building, overlooking C Street. It apparently consisted of a string of offices linked together like beads on a necklace, each with adjoining doors. Jaid made the assumption based on the slow progression they seemed to be making down the line.

Because they arrived fifteen minutes early for the appointment, they were left cooling their heels in the outermost office, guarded by a dragon disguised as a middle-aged woman who was obviously torn between two decades. Although she still dressed like a fifties sitcom mom, someone had obviously taken her in hand at some point and yanked her forward a few decades. And then left her there. Her long wash-and-wear perm with big bangs was straight out of the eighties. She was impervious to Shepherd's charm and looks, and ignored Jaid completely, alternating between her work and casting Adam furtive, suspicious glances.

Her name, amusingly enough, was Imelda Hachette.

A half hour after their arrival, they were herded through

the next office, which seemed crammed full of young fresh-faced twentysomethings, each with a phone to his or her ear or eyes glued to a computer screen. Jaid, Shepherd, and Adam were then deposited, rather unceremoniously, with the young aide there, who had made it quite clear for the last fifteen minutes that he had no idea what to do with them after they all declined his offer of coffee.

Adam was reading a sheaf of papers he'd taken out of his briefcase. If Jaid leaned toward him, just a bit, she could make out enough to recognize that it was a briefing report on the case. She wondered if he had access to the same report she and Shepherd got or if his were more complete. She had a feeling that if it wasn't, Hedgelin would be hearing about it.

Agent Shepherd was bent over an electronic notebook of some sort. She considered her technology skills above average most of the time, until she was surrounded by computers geeks who could eek information out of a piece of equipment faster than she could access the Web with hers.

With a barely audible sigh, she settled back into her chair. Patience wasn't a trait that came naturally to her. It came, she figured, from waiting most of her life for one thing or another. Her first several years were spent as a child anxiously waiting for her father to come home so she could join him in the garage to work on the GTO. It was their quality time, mostly because it excluded her mother.

Then after he'd walked out on them, she'd spent the next seven years waiting for him to come home again.

Rather than delve into the dysfunctional morass of her childhood, she aimed a look at the young man ensconced behind the desk, who'd been introduced as Scott Lambert, junior aide to the senator. After his attempts at small talk had failed, he'd returned to the work on his desk and tried to ignore them.

Jaid considered the man. He wasn't much taller than her at five-ten or so. Slight build. Pale brown hair. Nondescript looks. From her research on the way over she'd discovered that Newell had a staff of nineteen. She couldn't imagine what would keep that many people busy, but from the count she'd done so far, Lambert made number eight. Which left eleven members of staff that likely outranked the junior aide. She hoped that didn't mean they had eleven more offices to make their way through. Most likely it simply meant that Lambert had been designated to babysit them until the senator was ready.

She checked her watch. Eleven oh two. "How long have you been with Senator Newell?"

He perked up at the question. "Four years now. I also worked as a page for him when I was still in college." He beamed a smile at her that looked a bit more relaxed than the barely covered nerves she'd sensed since they came in. Nerves that surfaced every time he glanced at Adam. Obviously, Lambert shared the receptionist's mistrust of the man's appearance.

"What do your duties entail?"

Lambert ran a hand over his short hair. "A number of things, actually. I sort of go where I'm needed. Right now I'm acting as assistant to the communications director," he nodded at a much larger empty desk in the corner of the room. "Our job is to manage the interface between the congressman and the public. I've also filled in as the senator's scheduler, and I actually started as a caseworker, assisting constituents who need help."

"What exactly is the pay grade for managing an interface?"

She could feel both Shepherd and Raiker looking at her. She shrugged. "It's a valid question given Newell's views on downsizing the bureau."

"But perhaps not relevant under the circumstances." Adam's voice was a low rumble, meant for her ears only, with an unusual note of humor threading through it. And the sound of it had memory ambushing her with the devastating impact of a cruise missile.

The two of them, still wrapped around each other in his huge bed, flesh damp, their breathing ragged. "I have to point out . . ." She'd needed to haul in another breath to continue. "If that was meant to bolster your argument about the age difference between us . . . you didn't do much to prove it."

Adam's low, husky chuckle had sent tiny tendrils of heat firing through her veins. Then he'd rolled above her, his face lowering to hers. "Well, damn. I'm guessing this isn't going to prove it, either."

The sneaky snippet from the past slipped in with sly ease, neatly slicing through defenses she'd spent the last eight years building. The familiar pang it left in its wake had her straightening. She reached for another brick to build that inner wall higher. She'd survived Adam Raiker. She'd proved to herself that she didn't need him—didn't need any man to complete her life.

But she'd never managed to exorcise those old ghosts. She could keep them at bay for long stretches at a time. It only took his proximity to unleash them in a battering mental torrent.

Lambert's earnest tones saved her. "Senator Newell is cognizant of the importance of your agency's work. But he believes in a smaller government, and in this economy every government entity has to share the sacrifice."

Everyone, Jaid thought darkly, apparently with the exception of the senator. But she didn't need Adam's polished Italian shoe nudging her foot to have her dropping the line of questioning. Her political views could only be described as eclectic, more issue oriented than partisan. But she had a feeling there were few issues she and Senator Newell would agree on.

Earnestly, Lambert sought to convince them otherwise. "The senator has long fought for tougher sentencing laws for violent crimes. That's admirable from a safety standpoint. He's endorsed by many law-enforcement organizations."

"Well, we can all get on board with that, right?" Shepherd said heartily even as he snuck a look at the clock. As if encouraged by the response, Lambert further regaled them with more than Jaid ever wanted to hear about the senator's accomplishments and agenda.

She tuned him out and turned her thoughts to home. To Royce. His birthday was coming up, and he'd been begging for a new skateboard ramp. Something bigger and meaner than the plywood one she'd built for him a couple years ago. He wanted a six-foot half-pipe these days, which meant he planned to start trying more daring tricks. Stretch his boundaries.

Because that was an urge she understood all too well, she'd probably give in to his pleading, despite her mother's dire warnings. Patricia Marlowe thought all children should be wrapped in cotton batting. The better to not see or hear them. At any rate, Jaid had always found it confining, which meant she better get to ordering the ramp, because it didn't look like she was going to have the time to shop any time in the near future.

Lambert stopped to draw a breath only because the phone on his desk rang. He answered, and then a moment later replaced the receiver in its cradle and shot out of his seat. "The senator can see you now. I'm sorry; he doesn't have much time, so we'll need to hurry."

"Oh, now he's in a hurry," Jaid muttered, but she got up with the two men and followed the aide to the hall door. It was forty-five minutes past their scheduled meeting. She wondered how much of that time the senator had spent conducting business and how much sitting alone in his office, flexing his muscles by making federal agents wait for him.

This time they were led down a hall and past several more doors before arriving at their destination. She could only assume that the other eleven staff members were housed in the space they passed. When Lambert opened another door and she saw that they were in yet another reception area, Jaid had the fleeting thought that they'd been led in a big circle.

But the person behind the desk was male and appeared firmly rooted in this decade. He rose, nodding to Lambert, who murmured a good-bye and exited, not, thought Jaid, without a bit of relief.

"Robert Weaver, the senator's personal assistant." His

voice was as smooth as his stride. He moved toward the adjoining door. "The senator can see you now, but I'm afraid he's only got a few minutes before his next appointment."

The trappings of the opulent office they were shown to didn't reflect the austerity Newell preached. But the man himself did. Spare to the point of gaunt, the senator was seated behind an acre-wide desk of aged polished mahogany. His suit was nondescript, and a cosmetic dentist hadn't enhanced the tight smile he spared them.

He waved them to seats without rising and consulted a sheet in front of him. "Agents Marlowe and Shepherd." Glancing up he demanded, "Which one's which?"

Jaid gritted her teeth, although his attitude was hardly unexpected. "I'm Agent Marlowe. This is Agent Shepherd." She gestured to Shepherd.

But the senator's attention had moved back to his sheet. "And you are . . ." His eyes widened a bit behind his rimless glasses before his attention bounced to Raiker. "Adam Raiker. Well, you I've heard of. Didn't realize you were back with the bureau."

"I run a forensics consulting firm these days. I joined the task force investigating Justice Reinbeck's death at the request of President Jolson."

The senator slapped the desktop lightly, his mouth pursing with displeasure. "Consultant," he scoffed. "Duplication of services, I call it. If we eliminated all the consultants and consulting firms operating in this government, we'd save the taxpayers . . ."

"My services are being offered pro bono." Adam's smile was chilly. "I'll assume that eases your objection."

Making a sound suspiciously close to a sniff, the man leaned back in his desk chair. He was tall, but his width barely filled it. He was a scarecrow of a man. "Remains to be seen what kind of objections I'll have. I'm still trying to figure out why the hell you're all here. I don't have any information for you that will shed light on the shooting that occurred a couple days ago. Horrible atrocity." That last seemed added as an afterthought.

"This is just a routine visit, Senator." Shepherd addressed him with all the deference Hedgelin could hope for. "We have to follow up on everyone who might have had . . . disagreements with the justice in the past."

"Damn right I disagreed with him. He was a left-wing activist judge on the circuit with no respect for the Bible or the constitution, and I did my damnedest to point that out in the Senate Judiciary Committee hearings."

"In fact," Jaid consulted her notes, "during your questioning you called him a liar a half-dozen times, compared him to a Marxist, and suggested his confirmation would result in anarchy breaking out in our country."

The senator bared his teeth. "That's right. Check your notes, missy. Do you also have down there that I use every opinion he writes in my campaign ads to underscore the need to put only strict interpreters of the constitution on the highest court?"

Missy. She smiled with as much sweetness as she could summon. "No, sir. But it does say that you have a poster in your campaign headquarters with a gun sight superimposed over Reinbeck's photo. That you've used the visual to emphasize remarks you've made about removing various menaces to conservative values." The atmosphere in the room went charged.

Newell leaned across his desk, his hands not so much clasped before him as clenched. "Young lady, I can assure you that you've taken my remarks, my meaning, out of context. Reinbeck isn't alone on that poster. Are you accusing me of taking out hits on my Democrat opponents and our esteemed speaker of the house, as well?"

"It's Special Agent Marlowe," she said evenly. "And we are making absolutely no accusations, just informing you of the reason for our visit. Since his confirmation hearing, have you had occasion to speak to Justice Reinbeck in person?"

Apparently getting himself under control, the senator sat back. Straightened his tie. "Not that I recall. We exchange greetings if our paths cross. We would have little to say to each other, at any rate."

Jaid refused to look away from the senator's glare. If she met the man at a social function after some of the things he'd said about the judge, she'd be tempted to spit in his eye. Or at the very least, say something exceeding tactless.

A decade ago she would have done just that. But she'd learned a lot of hard lessons in the last several years. Self-control was only one of them.

"I understand that your oldest grandson, Joseph, volunteers on your reelection campaign."

At Adam's words, the senator's shoulders went tense. "I'm afraid I'm out of time here. I have another appointment."

But Raiker went on. "Is it true that Joseph was arrested at fifteen for setting fire to his algebra teacher's home?"

Rising, Newell said, "If you'll show yourselves out?"

None of them moved. Jaid scarcely dared to breathe. She didn't know where Adam had gotten that information. It certainly wasn't in the notes she'd seen. But he had infinite outside resources, and given Newell's reaction, she didn't doubt the truth of his findings. Could guess where this was headed.

Adam's voice was inexorable. "Joseph didn't get the probation his lawyer was asking for, did he? In fact, he was proclaimed a habitual offender, a delinquent, and spent sixteen months in a juvenile correctional institution."

"Those records were sealed!" The congressman was leaning across his desk as if he'd like nothing more than to leap across it, his weight braced on his fists. "You couldn't have used legal means to access them."

"The legal records are sealed but people's memories can't be, can they?" Adam rose. Silently, the agents did the same. "The fact remains that Byron Reinbeck was the judge who sentenced your grandson. It was early in the judge's career, when he worked the juvenile court. How much of your antipathy for the man arises from his politics and how much from his actions resulting in your grandson being locked up?"

"Reinbeck was a godless ass who ran amuck in every courtroom he oversaw." Newell's voice trembled with fury.

"It was only a matter of time before someone took him out. Are you expecting me to care that he's dead? 'There are many whose mouths must be stopped.' He's trampled the constitution his entire career, and he got exactly what was coming to him. And I will do everything in my power as a member of the Senate Judiciary Committee to be damned sure Jolson doesn't nominate a godless carbon copy of Reinbeck to fill that vacancy." The smile he gave them was chilling. "And that, people, is called a silver lining. Now get the hell out of my office."

This time they left. None of them said a word until they reached their vehicle. Settled themselves inside it. "Nice guy." Shepherd turned the key in the ignition. Looked in the rearview mirror before backing out of the spot. "I'm thinking about campaigning for him."

Jaid turned in her seat so she could see Adam in the back. "Where'd you get that information? And why wasn't it brought out at Reinbeck's confirmation hearings? It should have disqualified Newell from taking part in them, at the very least."

"Those records don't even exist anymore. And you can be sure the people in the system who recalled the case would have been unforthcoming if a U.S. senator brought all his power to bear. Newell's clout didn't affect Reinbeck's ruling on his grandson's case, but he would have used every means at his disposal to get that record sealed and later to have it expunged completely."

Jaid considered this. It was entirely possible that Reinbeck's widow had given the information to Adam. She recalled his friendship with the couple from when she'd worked with him. Reinbeck had still been on the circuit then. Where he'd gotten the details, however, paled in importance to what they meant. "You realize that gives Senator Newell a pretty powerful motive for wanting the judge out of the way."

Shepherd sounded doubtful. "And he waited, what, twenty years or so to enact his revenge? He doesn't seem like the patient sort to me."

"That merely set the stage for his hatred of Byron," Adam said, his head bent over his phone. "No doubt his later rulings cemented it." He stopped for a moment, brought his phone up to better read something on it. "'There are many whose mouths must be stopped.' Old Testament, Titus, chapter ten, verses ten and eleven." His smile was grim. "So we've got a longtime congressman who quotes the Bible and has reason to despise Byron Reinbeck. It'd be interesting to look at the Supreme Court's docket for the year. See what cases are going to be heard that Senator Newell's opinion on could be predicted."

Jaid turned back in her seat, pensive. The senator had taken no pains to disguise his feelings about Reinbeck. Was his confidence born of ego or did he think the power of his position would insulate him?

She needed to take another look at that risk-assessment data. Do a little digging into the other names that appeared there.

"What's Joseph's last name? Newell's grandson?"

"Bailey," Adam answered. "His mother is Newell's oldest daughter."

"Maybe we should have a talk with him, too. If the senator is still carrying a grudge all these years, there's no telling what Bailey feels toward the judge."

Her phone sounded in her hand, signaling an incoming text. She took a moment to read it. Turned to Shepherd. "Hedgelin wants us back in his office immediately."

"You mean Newell already lodged a complaint about us?" Shepherd nosed the car out of the parking garage and onto the street. "That was quick."

"I don't think so." She looked over her shoulder at Adam. "He mentioned Reinbeck's phone."

———

"I had them do another examination of the judge's smart-phone after you left this morning." Hedgelin handed them each a copy of a faxed lab report. "They found a tiny singed area on the SIM card, just like Adam mentioned this morning. It looked like normal wear, which in and of itself wouldn't be evidence of anything, since no sign of spyware exists in the phone's files."

"Did they also examine Patterson's phone?"

The assistant director nodded. "And found the same singed spot. It's unusual enough to raise suspicion."

"That's another link between the murders," Shepherd put in. "The note cards may have been copied, but the phones suggest a connection."

Hedgelin scrubbed a hand over his jaw. For the first time Jaid noted the fatigue that shadowed his face. He'd put in long hours on this case. It was undoubtedly the most high-profile of his career. She'd heard rumors that he had his eye on the bureau director's job when the man's term was up. A successful resolution to a case like this would go a long way toward impressing a future president and the Senate when the next opportunity arose.

Left unsolved, however, the case would be his career coffin.

"So far we've kept the detail about the card found at the site of Reinbeck's shooting out of the press. Done a damn good job of keeping most crime-scene details suppressed, as a matter of fact. I want it to stay that way. The three of you will be assigned to determine if there are any other intersections in the two homicides. Did the victims know each other, have mutual friends, show up at the same social functions?"

"I assume DCPD compiled a client list for Mr. Patterson?" Adam's tone was wry. "Given the bloodbath on Wall Street a couple years ago, it might also act as a list of potential enemies."

The assistant director nodded. "I doubt too many came out on top of that disaster. But the specifics should be in the file Lieutenant Griega sent over." He pulled open a drawer and withdrew three bulging file folders. "Here." He shoved all three across his desktop toward them. "Familiarize yourself with this, and determine your manner of investigation. Clear it with me before you talk to anyone or question anybody." His expression was fierce. "I'm keeping a tight hand on the reins on this case. I don't want any surprises."

The biggest surprise, Jaid thought as she rose to collect the files, was that they were being given the task at all. She wouldn't expect Hedgelin to extend their team any leeway, not with Adam a part of it.

She remembered in the next moment that she and Shepherd were supposed to be keeping Raiker in check for the duration of the case. Maybe that was Hedgelin's ace in the hole. Give Adam enough freedom to come up with something the bureau hadn't—like the evidence of spyware—but keep him contained at the same time. He wasn't above taking advantage of Adam's staggering knowledge and his contacts. He employed some of the most brilliant criminologists in the country, after all. But when the case reached a successful conclusion, it was a certainty that Cleve Hedgelin would make damn sure Adam got none of the credit.

"Find an empty conference room and familiarize yourself with Patterson's case file," the assistant director ordered brusquely. "I'll expect a tentative outline of investigation prior to your taking any action."

Adam and Shepherd stood. Jaid's gaze fell unenthusiastically to the pile of folders she held as she rose. The information would take hours to go through, and that was assuming they each took charge of a folder and summarized it for the others. Stifling a sigh, she turned toward the door.

"Jaid, do you have a makeup mirror?"

Pausing in the midst of rubbing her eyes, she aimed a jaundiced look toward Shepherd. "You trying to tell me something?"

His eyes looked as bleary as hers felt. They'd been poring over the file folders for—she checked the clock on the wall—six hours. Without a break, if one didn't count the run to a nearby deli she'd volunteered for three hours ago. The sandwich and diet soda she'd washed it down with were a distant memory.

Shepherd's handsome face looked puzzled. "What? God, no, I wasn't talking about you. You look incredible, as usual. Don't know how you manage it after the afternoon we've spent."

Adam's head never rose from the pages he was perusing. "Special Agent Marlowe is immune to flattery, Shepherd."

Her ire transferred to the other man. "I don't recall you ever trying any, so how would you know?"

One corner of his mouth pulled up even as he turned to a different sheet in the pile he was going through. Shepherd sent her a woeful look. "Eyedrops." He showed her a small vial he must have taken from his pocket. "I'm too vain to wear reading glasses, so I suffer eye strain under conditions like this."

Without another word, she reached in her purse and took out a compact and handed it to him. Then used the opportunity to watch him just for a moment away from their task. There was something disarming about his admission of vanity. The man wore charm as easily as he did the pin-striped suit. She recalled hearing about his long line of sexual exploits with women from when he was stationed here years ago, but nothing since his return. With his movie-idol jaw and blond good looks, his vanity wasn't surprising, nor was his success with women.

But now, as then, his looks did nothing for her. It took more than charm to catch her eye.

Involuntarily, she looked at Adam. It had been his intellect as much as his ferocious dark looks that had first intrigued her. There was an intensity that radiated from him, a vibrant energy that had held its own allure. Once upon a time she had been well and truly ensnared. Enamored.

In love.

He wasn't a man comfortable with emotion. She forced her eyes back to the folder in front of her. Stared at it blindly. She should have known that. Should have kept hers to herself. Because her declaration had started him back-pedaling out of her life.

His near death at the hands of LeCroix had finished it.

Shepherd handed the compact back to her, and she fumbled with it a little as she dropped it into her purse. "I've cross-referenced the list the DCPD compiled of individuals who made direct threats toward Patterson in the last few years with those on Reinbeck's threat-assessment list," Shepherd said, sitting back down. "I didn't find any intersections."

"What about his clients?" Adam finally looked up. "I'm sure the DCPD took a hard look at anyone who lost huge sums."

"That list goes back five years, and it reads like a who's who of Washington's power brokers. Foreign governments, diplomats, congressmen, religious leaders, as well as one individual the DC police linked to organized crime. If this was about the dive in stocks, there are plenty of people here who would have the means to arrange his death if they chose to."

"If that were the case, the timing is off." Jaid set her pen down and worked her shoulders tiredly. "Why not kill him back when the financial crash first happened? The economy has rebounded recently."

"But few people have regained the former value of their investments."

She'd have to trust Adam on that. The only investment she had was the federal retirement system that took a chunk out of her check every month. Juggling a house payment with raising a growing boy didn't leave her a lot leftover for hedge funds.

"He could have made promises to someone that their portfolio would recover by now, and when it didn't, he was killed." She stopped, looked at Shepherd. "I assume that Justice Reinbeck isn't on that list."

"Neither he nor his wife."

"There might not be any relationship between the two victims at all, other than symbolism." Adam untwisted the cap of the water bottle she'd brought him from the deli. Drank. "The connection then lies in the eyes of the offender. He sets himself up as judge and jury, and determines who is guilty of a specific sin."

"Where's the motivation?" Jaid shifted in her chair to face him.

"If we knew that, we'd have a better idea of where he'll strike next."

Chilled, she could only stare at him for a moment. It would be naïve to assume there wouldn't be another death. There were, after all, seven deadlies, as Benton had called them. The question was, how did a killer hope to turn off that compulsion once the seventh had been acted upon? What did he do with that murderous impulse after he struck seven times?

Adam was going on. "I've got a copy here of Patterson's LUDs for the last two months. Now that we have reason to suspect that spyware was loaded on his phone, too, I'm interested in going through his and Reinbeck's call logs to determine the sender of the infected message."

"Actually, most spyware is downloaded directly onto the victim's phones from software bought off the Internet." Shepherd finished dabbing at his eyes with his handkerchief and then put it away in his suit pocket. "But it can be effectively loaded if a text message to the victim included a link to click on. That link downloads the spyware as a Trojan horse that then takes over the phone."

"Paulie said something about that. He also mentioned that there was no way to discover the content of the messages sent to a phone by going through the providers' records."

"Most people know enough not to click on a link sent to them unless they trust the sender," Jaid pointed out. "And we can guess these two victims were more security-conscious than most." Her eyes felt as though they were filled with sand. But dividing up the folders among the three of them and each giving a verbal summary had saved them hours of time.

"Spoofing?" Shepherd suggested. "It's fairly simple to

make it look like the message is coming from someone else. Again, that capability is found easily on the Internet, too. But the e-wizards should be able to track that, as well, given enough time."

"Shepherd's right. Every contact leaves a trace." Adam's voice was confident. "We need a place to start. I imagine the cyber guys are looking more closely for other similarities in the two phones. Tomorrow we start by getting a copy of Reinbeck's phone logs and comparing it to Patterson's." He stopped as if remembering he wasn't talking to his own operatives. "Unless the two of you have other plans, of course."

Amused, Jaid slanted a glance at him. "Bet that hurt." As the head of Raiker Forensics, Adam had years of experience giving the orders. Truth be told, he'd given plenty in his days at the bureau. His placement on the task force put him in an unfamiliar position of being equals with Shepherd and her. His attempt at diplomacy aside, she doubted he could ever truly be just another member of the investigative team. Some men were born to lead. He was one of them.

Her cell phone buzzed then. When she took it from her pocket and saw that it was her mother, she nearly sighed. Although it was tempting, she didn't dare to ignore it. She'd almost completely broken the woman of calling to see if she'd be home for dinner. That left the off chance that this call was important.

Excusing herself, she got up and walked to the corner of the room for a bit of privacy. "Hello, Mother. I'll probably be . . ." Patricia's strident tones cut off the rest of her sentence. Her words had ice splintering through Jaid's veins. "An accident? How bad is it?"

She wasn't aware of the sudden silence in the room behind her. Wasn't aware of anything but her mother's half-hysterical explanation. Her own bone-chilling fear. After a few more moments, she disconnected the call. Took one deep, shuddering breath before whirling toward the two men who were watching her with concerned expressions.

"I have to go." A strange numbness had washed over her. She strode to her purse. Busied herself putting away the phone. Finding her keys. *There's been an accident . . .*

She couldn't concentrate on that now. Determinedly, she picked up the papers she'd been looking through for the last few hours. Had surprising difficulty fitting them back into the folder.

"Is everything all right?" Shepherd asked concernedly. "Is there anything we can do?"

"I have to go," Jaid repeated. The numbness was sliding away. It was too much to hope that it was going to last. Fear was doing a fast sprint up her spine. She needed to get to the hospital. Dread pooled nastily in her stomach. Patricia was no good in a crisis. She'd barely been coherent. She tended toward melodrama at the best of times. Jaid found herself hoping that was the case today. "I'll call. Later."

"Jaid."

The sound of Adam's quiet voice halted her. "I'll contact my driver. We'll take you wherever you need to go." He was up and rounding the conference table with a swiftness that would have surprised her in any other circumstance.

There's been an accident . . .

"That's not necessary." She looked around for her purse. Found it hanging from the back of her chair, where she'd left it. Hauling in a breath, she grabbed the file folder. Her purse. Turned for the door. Found Adam in her path.

"It is necessary." He nodded to the hand she held her keys in. "You're upset. You shouldn't be driving."

Annoyed, she followed the direction of his gaze and then stopped, surprised. Her hands were shaking like she'd been struck with palsy. She could feel the trembling then. It shook her whole body. "I'll be fine." She moved to skirt him, but he already had his phone out and was texting a command.

"Of course you will." Finished with his cell, he slipped it back into his pocket and moved back to the table to slip his folder into his leather briefcase, with much more finesse than she had managed earlier. "I'll come with you. We'll take care of your car later."

"No!" She hauled in a breath and headed for the door. With a flash of mental clarity, she recognized that the only thing worse than heading into that hospital alone would be to enter it with Adam Raiker at her side. "I can manage this on my own."

Half running down the carpeted hallway, she stabbed impatiently at the button for the elevator. Adam had caught up to her by the time the doors had slid open. He joined her in the empty car. They were silent until it began to move downward.

"You're shaken up. And whatever news you face about your mother when you get to the hospital, you shouldn't have to face alone."

Tears threatened. She beat them back by sheer force of will. "It's not my mother." Ineffectually, she pressed the button for the main floor again, as if that would make the elevator move faster.

The words left her on a whisper. A prayer. "It's my son."

Chapter 6

God, but he hated hospitals.

He was entitled, Adam figured, given the amount of time he'd spent confined to them. Because the mass-produced chairs in the waiting room seemed designed to cause chronic back problems, he leaned against the wall in the corner of the room and did what came least naturally to him.

Waited.

After rushing up to the front desk and speaking to the clerk there, Jaid had been whisked through some double doors and disappeared from sight. That had been nearly three hours ago. More than enough time to recall every torturous moment he'd spent in institutions just like this one over the last several years.

Hell. In the last several months.

His mouth quirked wryly. To be fair, he had it on good authority that the hospitals housing him had been no fonder of the experience than had he. He hadn't achieved model-patient status. Not even close.

People had wandered in and out of the waiting area the

first couple hours, mostly silent. Victims of the same interminable vigil as he. But one by one they'd been called away or collected by a family member. He had no idea if Jaid would even know where the elderly lady in the pink jacket had finally stashed him. She'd been quite insistent that he stay put here after she'd collected him from the ER lounge once Jaid had been shown to her family.

To her son.

Somehow his mind always returned to that word despite the effort he'd been expending to skirt it. Eight years ago she'd finally seen reason and cut off all contact with him as he'd demanded. It wasn't as though he'd expected her life to remain in suspended animation in the time since. He knew she was unmarried. Paulie, damn him, had managed to drop that fact into conversation a few times over the years, although Adam had made it clear enough that the subject of Jaid was off-limits.

But Paulie had never mentioned a son.

Adam narrowed his gaze at the muted tones of the blue wallpaper. He wasn't one to wallow in regrets, but he'd spent more than his share of time in hospital beds over the years. Being bound to a bed gave a man time to think. And more frequently than he wanted to admit, his thoughts had gone to the woman he'd once spent weeks trying to convince that they had no future together.

And he'd spent too much time since berating himself for being successful.

A son meant that she'd found someone in the time since they'd parted. Jaid wasn't a woman who trusted easily. He wondered what had happened to the relationship. If the boy's father were still in the picture. Or if—the thought was like taking a fast right jab to the solar plexus—the man was still in Jaid's life.

He had no right to care. He'd given up that right the last time he'd sent her away. The time she'd finally had the good sense to stay gone.

Knowing that, accepting it, didn't make the thought easier to contemplate.

"I didn't know if you'd still be here."

He looked up then, and she was there, looking drawn but not nearly as worried as she had in the car on the way over. Pushing away from the wall, he approached her. "I wasn't sure you had another ride home. I know your mother must have brought your son in, but . . . is he all right?"

"He's fine." Her expression was half-relieved, half-exasperated. "Other than harboring the delusion that he's Tony Hawk, he's going to be okay. His arm is broken in two places, courtesy of his attempt to do a 5-0 grind on a ledge."

He blinked. "I understood the word ledge. The rest was lost on me."

She gave a small smile. "A skateboard trick and one that is far beyond his skill level at this point. A conversation that will be delayed at least until he's off pain medication." She hesitated then. "I feel bad that you've been waiting out here all this time. But if your offer of a ride home is still good, apparently I'm stranded here. My mother called an ambulance rather than drive Royce to the doctor."

The name struck a memory. "Royce. He's named after your father?"

Her smile vanished. "I'm sorry to bother you like this. I can call a cab."

"Something tells me the ambulance cost is going to be plenty for the day." Her barely perceptible wince told him that his guess was correct. He pulled his cell out of his pocket, sent a quick message to his driver. "Are you done here?"

"Yes." He fell into step beside her, and she headed out of the waiting room and down a white tile hallway. "Mother insisted on a wheelchair, at least as far as the front doors. She can be a bit . . . overbearing in times of stress."

He remembered. He also recalled that Patricia Marlowe and her daughter had been somewhat estranged when he and Jaid had been together. Their relationship was one more bit of evidence that time had clearly marched forward.

"Faster, Grandmother. Like run. I want to see if this thing will do a wheelie."

At the sound of the voice up ahead, Jaid broke into a trot.

"I don't run, dear, and the last thing you need to be trying are more of your tricks. I wouldn't be a bit surprised if your mother takes away that skateboard of yours for good. If she doesn't, I certainly will."

Adam and Jaid rounded the corner to see a tall woman with perfectly coiffed ash brown hair pushing a child-sized wheelchair sedately. The boy in it was leaning forward, as if to add momentum.

"Take it easy, champ. You and your grandmother have had enough excitement for one day." Jaid caught up with them. Laid her hand on the boy's shoulder as she walked beside him.

Adam knew almost nothing about kids. He'd been one— a lifetime ago—in years if not in maturity. So he wasn't much of a judge. But this one appeared to be seven or so, with a mop of dark hair and a freshly plastered right arm in bright blue.

"Can we get McDonald's on the way home, Mom?" The kid sent a wheedling look over his shoulder with eyes the same dark brown as Jaid's. Other than their coloring, the two shared little resemblance. Catching sight of Adam, Royce looked past his mother and went silent for a moment. "Who are you?"

Patricia Marlowe turned her head, frowning, and Adam found himself the focus of the entire family.

"This is Adam Raiker," Jaid put in. "He and I are working together."

"What happened to your eye?"

The elder Marlowe shushed her grandson. "Royce, your manners!"

But when the boy didn't take his gaze off Adam, he pointed at his eye patch. "Knife."

Royce nodded sagely. Pointed to his arm. "Skateboard." Adam could see that he had the vehicle of destruction wedged in the seat next to him. "Hey, you can sign my cast if you want. They gave me a marker. The doctor signed it already. So did Mom. Grandmother didn't want to. She said it would only encourage me."

"Mr. Raiker is going to see us home. My car is still at work."

"How very kind of you, Mr. Raiker." Although it was clear from Patricia Marlowe's expression that she was full of questions, she was much too well-bred to ask them, at least in public. With her light-colored hair and eyes, it was unclear where Jaid had gotten her coloring. "Jaidlyn, how will you get to work if you leave your car in the city tonight?"

Before Jaid could answer, he put in, "My driver will pick her up tomorrow morning."

She slanted him a glance, even as he ushered them through the front door where Reno had pulled up to the curb. "That won't be necessary. I appreciate everything you're doing, but we've put you out enough."

"It's just logical." He broke off to open the front passenger door on the sedan. "Mrs. Marlowe, why don't you sit up front? I think you'll find it most comfortable."

"Oh, but . . ." She looked uncertainly at her daughter.

"Royce can sit in back by the door, so he has the door armrest to prop his cast on. Jaid, you'll want to slide in next to him."

The first two Marlowes did as he suggested. It was the last that shook her head in bemusement, staring at him.

A light mist had begun to fall. Droplets clung to her dark hair. The pavement glistened wetly in the dim glow of a nearby streetlight. "Does the earth spin on its axis when you order it, too?"

"If it's spinning right now, the answer must be yes."

Still she stood on the curb, looking up at him with those doe eyes that had once made him ignore every ounce of sense he'd possessed. "I've been knocked a bit off my stride today. But as a general rule, I don't follow orders as meekly as I did eight years ago."

Meek had never been an adjective he would have applied to her. Tough. Tenacious, but with an underlying vulnerability. He'd spent his fair share of time over the years wondering what would have happened if she hadn't listened to him back then.

Afraid of what she might see in his expression, he gave her a nudge, and she turned and slid into the car. With a feeling of foreboding, he followed her inside and settled himself on the seat next to her.

———

The photos on the computer screen were arrayed in a slideshow. His horror and fear increased with each new view. A dozen shots in all. Anyone else would find them ordinary. Nonthreatening.

But they represented the possible destruction of his entire life. Of everything he'd agonized over.

They'd been careful so long.

He wiped his face, surprised to find tears running down it. The pictures transfixed him. The threat they represented was eviscerating.

Everything they'd worked for could be destroyed upon the whim of one man.

When his cell phone rang a moment later, he started. The number in the call screen was familiar. Dread washed over him. He thought about not answering it. But the pictures on the computer screen warned him otherwise.

Anger rushed in then, and he snatched up the phone. "What are you doing? Leave my family alone!"

Silence for a moment. Then that eerie voice distorted by a voice changer. "You got my slideshow, Junior? How did you like it? I think your mother is quite photogenic for her age."

"Don't call me that." The nickname was from another lifetime ago. How had this man discovered it? His limbs were trembling. He swiped at his wet cheeks. "I know what you did. You killed those two men. You shot Justice Reinbeck."

There was a distant sound in the background of the call.

A moment later Junior recognized it as clapping. "Very good, you can connect the dots. Just remember I couldn't have done it without your help."

"I didn't know what you were planning!"

"But you do now, don't you? And your conscience is being an absolute bitch about it. The photos are just a reminder of how much you have to lose if you decide to tell anyone. After all your mother has sacrificed for you, it'd be sort of unfair for you to abandon her now, wouldn't it? One word from me and her whereabouts will be broadcast to the world. I understand there are still many parties who would be interested in that information. Even more who would like a shot at you. Given who you are."

Sick fear twisted through him. Old demons easily summoned sprang forth, still capable of causing a childlike terror.

"You'll be tempted to use your position to try to find a way out of this. But there is no escape, Junior. I hold your mother's future in my hands. Your future. You'll do anything to protect that, won't you? Think about that every time you're tempted to confess your part in our little scheme."

Junior dropped his head in his hands, crying in earnest now. "But I didn't know!"

"You do now though, don't you?" The voice was inexorable. "Remember what you have to lose. Watch your computer." The call was disconnected.

He raised his gaze, and through his tears he saw the slideshow re-form into a photo array of picture columns before going fuzzy at the edges. Melding. A new picture formed in the center. Of a man long dead. But the visual was enough to turn his bowels to ice.

The images disappeared from the screen. He knew from experience there would be no trace of them on his computer. It was as if his tormentor controlled the machine the same way he did Junior.

Shoving away from the desk, he got up, paced. Shoved the fear back and the past away, and frantically examined his options. Found them limited. He'd moved his mother once, after the first contact. And two days later photos very similar to the ones that had just vanished had appeared in his in-box.

Junior wasn't an accomplice in all this. He wasn't! There was no way he could have known what the man wanted his help for.

But he knew now. His stomach clenched and twisted. For a moment he thought that he would be sick. Coincidence. That's what he'd thought when he heard about Patterson's death. He'd wanted to believe it. But with Reinbeck's he had to face the awful truth. That he'd had a hand in it, however unwittingly. Maybe if he'd gone to the police after Patterson's death, Justice Reinbeck would still be alive.

But he hadn't dared do so then. He didn't dare now, either.

Not even when he knew who the next victim would be.

————

The buzzer sounded in the middle of Adam's third set of reps. He lowered the weights to the stand and sat, grabbing the towel he'd left nearby to swipe at his face and chest. He levered himself up using a bar on the next piece of equipment. Grabbing his cane, he headed toward the door.

The fact that the buzzer sounded three times during the course of his journey said far more about the visitor's impatience than Adam's speed.

He stabbed a finger at the intercom button. "Yes."

"It's me. Buzz me up."

Adam typed in the command on the keypad that would allow Paulie access to his private elevator and stop it at the appropriate floor. Adam swung open the door to the hallway. His friend strolled in from the foyer minutes later.

"Hey, it's looking better in here. You're settling in."

"It's a warehouse. It still looks like a warehouse." Without asking he headed to the wet bar tucked in a corner of the room and splashed some Scotch in a couple glasses. Added ice.

Paulie sighed but accepted the glass and settled onto a stool at the bar. "Loft, Adam. It's a two-story loft. They're considered quite trendy these days."

The correction was lost on Adam. He wasn't in one place long enough to feel at home anywhere. At least so he'd thought until Jennings, his would-be assassin, had blown his penthouse to bits by shooting an incendiary device through a window. Ridiculous to feel loss over a place he rarely spent a week straight in.

He sent a look around the area. It was functional. Exercise room, bathroom, Jacuzzi, wet bar, and a big-screen TV he rarely watched filled the lower area. A large study, two bedrooms, kitchen, and a bathroom big enough to move a bed into dominated the upstairs. The Realtor had certainly agreed with Paulie that it was trendy. More importantly, once it had been outfitted with blast-proof doors and bullet-proof windows, it was a modicum safer.

And he hated the necessity for the added safety features even more than being forced to move to a different place.

"What do you hear about my car?"

"That it's going to be a guest of the body shop for weeks." Paulie took a healthy swallow, his normally effusive mood subdued. His burgundy tie was decorated with dollar bills and poker chips. For him, that was subdued, too.

Studying him over the rim of his glass, Adam guessed, "Bad game?"

"Lost a little more than I wanted at the track this evening, so I called it a night." He raised his glass in a mock salute. "Know when to beat a strategic retreat, right?"

Adam raised the glass. Took a swallow. Tongue firmly in cheek, he offered, "I could probably loan you a fifty if you need it."

Paulie snorted, but his normal good humor made a reappearance. "Thanks, buddy. That'll come in handy next time I want to tip the cabbie. My luck will change. It always does." He gave Adam a pointed look. "Of course, I've never had your kind of luck, at least when it comes to dodging bullets. I figure you've got about one or two of your nine lives left." He dug in his pocket, laid a set of keys and Adam's garage door opener on the marble top of the bar. "Left your new lease in your garage downstairs. Same make and model as yours. Is Reno still around? I'm going to need a ride home."

Adam moved to the end of the bar where he'd left his cell while he worked out. "I'll message Kirby. Just sent Reno home an hour ago."

"An hour ago?" Paulie sipped again. "Where you been?"

Adam gave him a short version of the events of the last several hours. Because he was watching his friend carefully, he noted the lack of surprise on his face. "You knew about Jaid's son."

Paulie gave a slow nod. "I'm not like you. I keep in touch with old friends in the bureau. Heard she had a son. No one knows anything about his father, though." He paused before adding deliberately, "Do you want me to find out?"

"No." Adam was a big believer in privacy. His. Jaid's. She didn't owe him any details. Unless she wanted to tell him, the information had no bearing.

And she hadn't seemed in the mood to share this evening.

"I got a call from the deputy sheriff who took the report the other night." Adam drank, took a moment to savor the flavor of thirty-year-old Scotch. "He never found any trace of the car I had a run-in with." The call had merely been a courtesy. It had been apparent that the man felt that he'd done his duty as far as the investigation went. Adam wasn't surprised. He'd purposefully downplayed the incident. The last thing he needed was for Hedgelin to blow it up as a distraction worthy of having Adam removed from the case. He wouldn't let himself be manipulated that way.

"Backwoods punk. I turned over the partial plate to Kell, and he had a list of possible vehicles from a tristate area within an hour. Also looked for stolen plates." Kellan Burke was one of Adam's operatives. "Culled his findings to a dozen fitting the make, model, and color you described. He followed up with background checks on the owners and interviews with the ones he could find at home. Isn't finished yet, but with our luck he'll discover that the car that ran you off the road is the one on the list whose plates were reported stolen."

"Stolen." Adam drank. "Most likely. Where did they disappear from?"

"From a Safeway parking lot in Arlington two days ago."

"That's when I started with the task force." He leaned his elbows against the bar and gazed into his glass contemplatively.

"If he narrows it down to that car, at least we can let the feds off the hook for this deal."

Adam said nothing. There were plenty in the bureau who hadn't wanted him on this case, but the events of the other night didn't bear their stamp. Hell of it was, they didn't bear the stamp of whoever had been orchestrating the attempts on his life in the last year, either. They hadn't been lethal enough.

"The timing is suspect," he said finally. "I never fully bought that Jennings was acting on his own. Or that his attempts on my life were wrapped up with my having put away his estranged girlfriend's father years earlier."

"You think someone set him on you."

"If I say yes, I'm a paranoid son of a bitch with a suspicious mind."

"It's not paranoid when someone tries to kill you five times in as many months," Paulie pointed out.

Adam smiled wryly. "Which leaves the rest of the description intact. The truth is, I'm not sure what to think. The attempts stopped when Jennings was killed. Even if we're to believe that a new assassin had to be found and hired, the other night wasn't on the same level as the previous attacks. Strictly amateurish. No shots fired. The intent wasn't to kill me."

"Maybe just to put you out of commission for a while." Paulie drummed his pudgy fingers on the marble top counter reflectively. "Which does tie it up in this investigation. Other than the feds, who—let's face it—welcome your presence like they would a case of foot rot, who else would be threatened by your working the investigation?"

"The suspect in the killings." Adam shook his head in frustration. "Who has already proven that he's capable of far more finesse than was displayed the other night. Maybe the whole thing was like I told the deputy. Some boozed up idiot looking for a fight."

"Sure." Paulie drained his glass, cast a hopeful gaze in the direction of the bottle. "An idiot who put stolen plates on his car first."

Adam tipped more liquor into Paulie's glass. Paulie picked it up and saluted Adam with it before taking a drink. "Maybe the killer is more afraid of you than of the FBI."

With black humor, Adam replied, "He should be. I really did like that car."

––––––––

It was the flashing lights that woke him. Adam came from a sound sleep to completely alert in a matter of seconds. The silent alarm was going off. His gaze went immediately to the large computer monitor mounted on the wall next to the bed. Stared hard for several moments until he saw the movement that would have tripped the alarm. Someone was in the garage below.

He sat up. Swung his legs to the side of the bed and pulled himself upright by grasping the bedside table. The gym shorts he'd donned after his shower were on the floor. He pulled them on, then opened the drawer of the table and removed his weapon.

His gaze still on the monitor, he loaded the Glock. The monitor showed one individual moving in the double garage below. Five-ten, eleven maybe. Two hundred and change. Stocky but light on his feet despite his bulk. Right now the intruder's attention wasn't on the gleaming black replacement vehicle Paulie had leased for Adam, nor on the stacks of boxes that he hadn't yet gotten around to unpacking. He seemed to be looking, unsuccessfully, for something else.

Comprehension hit Adam. Cameras. The idiot was looking for the alarm and security cameras. He wouldn't find them. They were too well hidden. But then, it had taken better than decent skills to get into the garage in the first place. Much better.

Maybe Adam had underestimated the intruder.

Because there wasn't a doubt in Adam's mind that the stranger downstairs was the same man who had run into him the other night. The hulking build gave that much away.

As Adam watched, the man gave up his search and turned his attention to the car. Paulie would have made sure it was equipped with their agency's security system before bringing it here. If so much as a finger was laid on the vehicle, an alarm—this one not silent—would begin shrilling.

Adam didn't wait to hear it. He slipped his cell from its spot atop the bedside table and into the pocket of his shorts. Grabbed the cane that was leaning against the table and headed for the door, pausing only to shove his feet into his sneakers.

He and Paulie had kicked around several questions about the possible identity of the man behind the run-in the other night. Maybe he was about to get some answers.

The exit from the garage to the apartment building was a dummy. Even if accessed, a person would find himself in a rabbit warren of a hallway, with none of the passages leading anywhere. There would also be no way to get back inside the garage, as there was no knob on the door from that side.

The real entrance/exit was cleverly hidden in the wall. The high-tech Bond-like silent mechanism that the architect had constructed had a set of shelves along a portion of the wall that slid to the side to allow access to the small foyer with the private elevator. Paulie had been positively giddy at the security measures the man had achieved. Adam found them a royal pain in the ass. But tonight they might come in handy.

The elevator was equipped with a small security monitor, too, like the one upstairs running the live feed from the area that had been breached. The dim overhead light in the area showed the man getting up from the floor, backing away from the car. And Adam recognized for the first time that he might be heading right into a trap.

The car alarm hadn't sounded. The vehicle hadn't been touched. But that wouldn't stop an enterprising prick like the one inside from leaving an explosive beneath it. Maybe set to go off at a certain time. Perhaps one that could be triggered remotely.

Since he conducted a sweep of his car every time he drove it, the device would have been discovered. But perhaps only shortly before he was blown to hell and back.

He pressed the security panel, and the wall moved soundlessly, the dim light from the garage spilling into the opening. The intruder had his back to him, placing something high on the wall opposite the driver's door then stepping back to rappel out some cord. A mini camera, Adam guessed. So the detonator could be triggered remotely as soon as he entered the garage in the morning.

Damn, but this shit was getting tedious.

"Just keep your hands up there," Adam suggested. The man froze for a second before shooting a look over his left shoulder. A stocking mask covered his face, and he wore coveralls, boots, and thin black gloves.

"That's right, turn around. Ah-ah." Adam gestured with the weapon. "The hands stay up." The man turned slowly, fully facing Adam. He held a cell in one gloved palm. "I'm beginning to think you hate foreign cars. But I'm guessing your intent is a bit more personal than that. Drop the cell. And take off the mask."

The man didn't move.

The shot Adam fired kicked up small chips of cement at the guy's feet. He jumped. Slowly reached up his free hand to remove the mask.

He was a stranger. Impatience flared in Adam. Of course he would be. His hair was a grizzled graying brown. Square jaw. Fiftyish. "Who hired you?"

"What do you mean?"

"Don't waste my time." Adam moved closer, looked beyond the man to the narrow opening where the garage door had been forced open. "Are you alone?"

"Yeah."

"I'm sure your word is gold, but I'll reserve judgment." Leaning his cane against his hip, he reached into his shorts pocket and pulled out his phone. Speed dialed a familiar number. "Send police to my place. Now." Leaving the rest to Paulie, he replaced the phone in his pocket. And for the first time noticed the chill in the air. The garage was heated, but dressed like he was, fifty degrees didn't exactly feel like the tropics.

"Jesus, what happened to you?"

Black humor flickered as the man stared at the scars displayed prominently on Adam's body. "Not half the damage you were hoping to inflict, I'm guessing. I'll ask you again—who hired you?"

"No one. I just . . ."

The next shot shaved a bit of leather off the outer edge of the man's boot.

"Christ!" The man jumped a good foot. "Calm down, buddy. I don't got nuthin' to tell you, and that's the truth. I only ever got contacted by phone. And he used one of them voice-changer things. Could have been a woman for all I know."

Could have been, but Adam doubted it. There were far more men than women in this world who'd like to see him dead. Most of his relationships with the opposite sex ended somewhat amicably. With the exception of Jaid. And in the past few days she hadn't seemed especially homicidal in her feelings toward him.

She'd seemed, in fact, to have gotten over any feelings long ago.

"How'd you get paid?"

"He sent me the account number to an overseas bank account he'd set up in my name. Money got deposited there." A whine entered his voice. "Not enough money to get sent back inside, that's for damn sure." The man reached inside his coveralls.

Adam sidestepped to present a moving target. "Really? You're that fast with a gun covering you?"

The guy froze. Seemed torn by indecision.

"If it helps you decide, I shoot to kill, and I rarely miss. Never at close range."

Gradually, the stranger eased his hand back. Raised it again.

"Wise choice. A few years in prison look more attractive than bleeding out on my garage floor. Two fingers. Slowly. Take out the weapon."

The man obeyed. The look he threw Adam was sullen. "I wish I'd blown you to bits, cocksucker."

"I'll bet. Now drop the weapon," he ordered in a steely voice. The gun clattered to the cement. "Kick it over here."

When the gun skittered his way, he kicked it behind him rather than bend down and take his attention off the man.

"Someone wants you dead pretty bad." All of a sudden the man turned conversational. He gave a meaningful nod toward Adam, displaying an odd fascination with the scars crisscrossing his chest. "Not for the first time, from the looks of you."

"No," Adam agreed wryly. "Definitely not for the first time."

Chapter 7

"You look like hell." Jaid's observation was made in an undertone as they waited outside the Hoover Building for Shepherd to bring round their vehicle.

"Nice thing to say to the person who arranged your ride into the city today."

"Thank you," she said dutifully. "You still look like hell." It was a gorgeous morning, promising to be one of those Indian summer days to be recalled wistfully when the temperatures dropped and the wind became frigid.

One corner of his mouth quirked. "Much better. How's Royce?"

She stared at him for a moment then blew out a breath. She should have known better than to expect him to offer an explanation. "Fine. It still hurts a bit, so he was grumpy this morning. I kept him home from school. Frankly, I'm more concerned about the time when the pain goes away and he starts forgetting the need to be careful." She stopped, wondering not for the first time why she felt the need to offer personal information when he so rarely reciprocated. "Thanks for last night," she ended stiffly.

"It was an eventful evening." His words broke off then. When they resumed, his voice had hardened. "Shove off, Bolton."

Surprised, she turned to look behind her. Saw Kale Bolton approaching them down the sidewalk at a fast clip, wearing a sports jacket, flannel slacks, and his usual smug smile. "Bolton," she said without enthusiasm when he stopped beside them. The reporter had a knack for being in the right place at the most inconvenient times. He also had an aversion to taking no for an answer when he was drinking, which was frequently. The slight bump in his nose was a permanent legacy of its contact with Jaid's elbow ten years ago when he'd sought to change her no to a yes in a downtown bar by grabbing her breasts like a high school freshman in the backseat of his daddy's car.

The sight of the slight imperfection still filled her with a sense of satisfaction.

"What can you tell me about the progress on Reinbeck's killing?" He looked from one of them to the other with an expression that managed to be hopeful and sly at once. "Any suspects in the case yet? What leads are you following?"

"All media releases are being handled through the bureau's public relations office, Bolton." And he knew that, damn him. He'd probably come straight from the morning's news conference.

"C'mon, throw me a bone here, Jaid." His smile was wheedling. "You at least owe me that much."

"I gave you what I owed you a decade ago," she said, with a meaningful look at his nose. "We aren't talking about details of the case. Go away."

"Fine." He shifted his gaze to Adam. "Then let's talk about Mr. Raiker here. Why are you attached to this investigation? Whose decision was that? What do you think you can bring to the case that the entire bureau can't?"

"What makes you think I'm working the case?"

"Don't bullshit a bullshitter, Raiker. I've got contacts. You should know that."

Jaid saw Shepherd swing the SUV around the corner. She gave Adam a nudge. "C'mon."

"That's not what I hear." Adam's voice was hard. "I hear the contacts you thought you had aren't giving you the information you want. I heard your publisher is making noises about rescinding the advance they paid you for your next book. What is it, six months past deadline already?"

Mystified, Jaid looked from one man to the other. The two had squared off like pugilists awaiting the starting bell. The other agent forgotten for the moment, she turned her full attention to figuring out what the hell was going on.

"Whoever told you that is full of shit. I got an extension. Happens all the time in the publishing world." The breeze tousled the man's dark brown hair. If she didn't know what a snake he was, she'd consider his dark looks and square jaw attractive. He'd been charming that night they'd talked about his work over a couple drinks. Not so much when he'd gotten more liquor in him, however. From what she'd heard since, he had a taste for the stuff. Maybe that's what was slowing down the production of this book the two were talking about.

"Great. Let me know what happens when you ask for another extension." Adam began to step around him.

"Hell, contacts or not, all I have to do is wait. You provide another chapter for the book every week or so, don't you? Heard about your near escape last night. Have they examined the explosive yet? Was it really powerful enough to take out your whole building?"

Stunned, she stared at Adam, a sick clutch of fear in her chest. "Last night?" A quick scan of his figure assured her there were no injuries other than the one he'd shown up with a couple days ago. The bruise on his forehead was a mottled blue with a cut in the center of it that had almost certainly needed stitches. But she could see no new injuries.

"I'll be sure and call you when all the details are in,"

Adam said with mock politeness. "Anything I can do to help you meet that deadline." He headed away and Jaid started after him. Bolton stepped between them. Grabbed Adam's sleeve.

"Think you're all powerful, don't you?" His face twisted. "Believe me, there are lots who are willing to talk about the mysterious Adam Raiker. I've got plenty of material to go to my publisher with. Plenty. And I will. If you don't want to set the record straight, I'll tell the story without you. Either way this book is getting written."

Adam looked at the man's hand. Then at Bolton. Slowly, the other man loosened his grip. Stepped back. "Is that the deal you made with your publisher? Hard to understand why you missed that first deadline, then." This time when he started walking, the reporter stayed put.

Jaid waited until they were out of earshot of the reporter. "What the hell, Adam?" Her tone was furious. This was so typical of the man. He took closemouthed to new heights. "What happened? Was anyone hurt? Did you catch who did it?"

"I did, yes." The light turned green, and he put a courteous hand at the base of her back as they began to cross, the old-fashioned act curiously intimate.

She shook off his touch. "You're going to have to do better than that."

"It has nothing to do with this investigation . . ."

"So you say." She wasn't sure where the anger was coming from, but it was there, bubbling perilously close the surface. "But it's not your call to make. I'm serious. I want to know what the hell Bolton is referring to. About last night. About the book. You don't get to make the determination of what's relevant and what isn't. You're not running this task force."

His gaze narrowed. Once upon a time the expression on his face would have had her retreating. But that time was long in the past. "I'm serious. If I can't trust you to be open with me, I'm asking to have you placed on another team. Because I damn well won't work with someone I don't trust."

"If you're worried about Hedgelin . . ." he started.

She leaned toward him. "Don't you dare. Don't even try to make this about him."

He studied her for a moment. They'd reached the side of the vehicle. Neither of them made a move to get in it. "My point is that he'll have this information soon enough. Hell, Bolton already had it."

Stonily, she said nothing. Just looked at him.

The window on the SUV buzzed down. "Hey, I'm double-parked here," Shepherd called out.

Adam blew out a breath. "Fine," he muttered bad temperedly. "We'll discuss it after work." When she opened her mouth, he glared at her. "I'd as soon not have this discussion in the vehicle, and we have more important things on our plate today, don't we?"

Because it represented far more of a capitulation than she'd hoped for, she nodded. "After work, then."

Without another word he got in the vehicle. She followed more slowly, getting in the front seat. She was still simmering. Somehow she didn't think sitting next to Adam in back would be especially safe for either of them in their present moods. She embraced the irritation she still felt. Clung to it.

It was far easier to deal with than the cold spear of dread that had pierced her when she'd heard Bolton mention the events of last night.

———

Their tasks for the day included tracing the sources of the text messages to Reinbeck's and Patterson's phones. It quickly became apparent that it would be far easier to follow up on the judge's text messages than on Patterson's.

"Byron wasn't big on technology," Adam informed them as they made their way through the strengthened security at the Supreme Court building for the second time in as many days. "I'm not surprised that the LUDs showed the only sources of texts on his phone for the last six weeks as members of his family or staff. He didn't like to be wired all the time, he said."

"If we strike out here, I'm sure his family will cooperate by letting the techs examine their phones," Jaid put in. She nodded toward the same young Supreme Court policeman who had shown them the way the last time they'd visited. "One of his sons' cells might be the most likely place to look at any rate. Kids are more careless with their personal belongings. Someone could have gotten to one of their phones when it was in their backpack, locker, or car."

The policeman ushered them into the same room where they'd held the interviews last time. After promising to send them the people listed on the sheet they gave him, he closed the door quietly.

"Jaid's right." Tom Shepherd was dressed in a discreet navy wool suit today that made his hair look even lighter above it. "In most instances, kids tend to be advanced compared to adults regarding changes in technology."

"Technology, perhaps, but not murder." Adam set his briefcase on the table in front of him and unlocked it. "And we have to consider that if someone sent the victims a link that downloaded spyware onto their phones, that person is either the murderer or an accessory to the acts."

"I've seen some pretty chilling teenage murderers in my time," Shepherd said. He, too, took his case file from his briefcase and flipped it open. Taking a pen from inside his suit jacket, he looked across the table at Adam. "Ran into a couple in North Dakota a few months before my transfer back. They were burglarizing houses and killed an owner in a panic one time when he came back unexpectedly. Gave them such a thrill that they started hitting houses they knew weren't empty. One of them actually told me it upped the thrill, you believe that?"

Unfortunately, Jaid did. She'd read the agency's statistics on youth gang activity in the country. Access to that sort of information had worn down her resistance to allowing Patricia to play a bigger part in her life again. The truth was she'd needed support. She'd struggled on her own for several months when she'd first brought Royce home as a baby. A single parent with a demanding job had a hard time trying to raise a child alone. As much as she often disagreed with her mother's ideas on child rearing, at least her son had family watching him when he wasn't in school. Too closely, he'd probably say when he got a bit older. Jaid had certainly rebelled at her mother's overbearing ways when she'd been a teen.

The door opened then and a familiar tall figure stood diffidently just inside it. Lawrence Dempsey, one of Byron's clerks.

"The officer said you wanted to talk to me." The slight frown on his face was reflected in his voice. He looked from one of them to the other, making no move to approach the table.

"Yes, thank you for seeing us again, Mr. Dempsey." Jaid sent him a smile and gestured for him to take a seat. "We just have a follow-up question for you regarding the text messages you sent to Justice Reinbeck in the last few weeks."

"The messages?" His tone went puzzled. He still stood inside the door. "What about them?"

"Please sit down." Jaid was a bit chagrined when the man responded to the authority in Adam's tone. "You regularly communicated to the justice by text, is that so?"

"I wouldn't say regularly," he said, his voice, his mannerisms, cautious as he slipped into a chair and sat gingerly on its edge. "Occasionally, if I found case law pertinent to a petition he was reviewing, I'd text it if he were unreachable." He looked from one of them to the other. "What's this about?"

"How about links?" Agent Shepherd asked. "Did you ever send him a link to a website to look at?"

Confusion spread across the man's face. "I don't think so. I don't know why I would have. I mean sometimes we look up articles surrounding legal cases that have been tried, in the course of background and research. No"—he shook his head, slid back a bit in his chair, as he seemed to grow more certain—"I don't recall ever sending him any links."

"Do you mind if we look at your phone?"

Startled, his hand went to his suit jacket pocket. Hesitated. "You mean the out-box? There's nothing in there, I'm afraid. I emptied it a couple days ago." But when Shepherd's hand remained outstretched, Dempsey slowly took the cell out and slid it across the table to the agent. "What's this all about?"

Dodging his question, Jaid asked one of her own. "You don't deny sending texts to the judge on September thirteenth, October thirtieth, and November second?"

"No. I mean, I guess not." He stopped, tried to think, before giving up and shaking his head. "I'd have to check my records to be sure, but I distinctly remember sending him some information he requested at least twice recently. But never a link. I'd recall that."

"Do you ever lend your phone out?" she went on as Shepherd gave him back his cell. "Maybe let someone place a call on it? Leave it where someone can access it? In a gym locker, on the table at a bar when you get up to dance?"

That last had a smile flickering. "I'm not much of a dancer. But no, I keep it with me. That's an expensive model. And sure, I'd let a friend make a call on it if he needed to, but that hasn't happened recently, either."

Krista Temple was next, and the interview was a near duplicate to Dempsey's. Except she recalled both times she'd texted the justice, down to the approximate time of day and the exact reason. The messages she'd sent him were still in her out-box, both citing case law. Neither of them contained a link.

Jaid looked at Adam and Shepherd after the woman left the room. "Those two were the only clerks the justice received text messages from in the last few weeks?"

Adam nodded. "Mara Sorenson is the only other member of his staff listed on his phone records." He looked at Shepherd. "You were in the cyber unit. Can you think of any other ways to attach spyware on a phone other than downloading it?"

The agent shook his head. "I've been out of that line of work for a while, but I like to think I'm still up on the newest technology. I'd agree with your operative's assessment. And the cyber unit's. The spyware has to be downloaded in some manner. There's probably a shitload of ways to hide it in the phone's files once it has been, and that self-destruct element is about the slickest I've heard of. But the infected link has to be opened by the target."

There was a knock on the door then, and the judge's personal assistant stood in the doorway. She was dressed in a simple black suit today, and for a moment Jaid wondered if Reinbeck's funeral arrangements were imminent. But as far as she knew, his body had not yet been released from autopsy. The woman's dress likely was a reflection of her mourning.

"Ms. Sorenson." Adam's ruined voice was as soft as he could make it. "Thank you for your time. We just have a few more questions."

"Yes." Her expression was composed, but her eyes were weary. "About the phones, Krista said?" She approached the table and took the chair Adam pulled out for her. "Did you want to examine the phones in the office?"

"We're not interested in the landlines, just Byron's employees' cell phones." Adam's smile didn't seem to calm the woman's nerves to a significant degree. "You used yours to communicate with the justice at times, didn't you?"

"I used the office phone, usually."

"But you had his cell number."

"Of course." She studied each of them in turn. "But there was no reason to use it when I could just contact him in his chambers. Mostly, I'd call and give him his messages if he were out for some reason that day or left before me." Her smile was fleeting. "That was rare. When he left, he usually demanded that I leave as well."

"His cell phone records indicated that you had called him seven times since court resumed this year."

She gave a little shrug. "Probably. I could check my call log if you want to be sure."

"What we're most interested in, Ms. Sorenson, is the text message you sent to the justice." Jaid consulted the records before her. "On October thirteenth."

Amazingly, the woman laughed a little. "I don't think so. I've never sent a text message in my life. Wouldn't know how to go about it, to tell you the truth."

The room abruptly went charged. Seeming to sense it, Sorenson stiffened a little.

"Can we see your phone, please?" She fumbled with her suit pocket a moment before handing it across the table to Shepherd.

"Do you send e-mails from your phone, Ms. Sorenson?"

Adam's question drew her attention from what the agent was doing with her phone. "Yes, quite often. I take the train home and frequently catch up with my children that way."

"And Byron? Did you ever send him e-mails after work? Possibly about something you forgot to tell him or something that came up after he left . . ."

The woman was already shaking her head. "No, we had a system. There were few things I would have bothered the judge about after hours. If it was important enough to let him know immediately, then I'd call him and leave a message if he wasn't answering."

Shepherd turned to Jaid then and handed the phone to her. Dropping her gaze to the screen, she felt the blood slow in her veins. Despite the woman's words, there was indeed a text message in her out-box. Addressed to Reinbeck's cell phone number. With a link embedded in it.

Jaid leaned across the table to give the phone to Adam. He looked from the screen to the woman beside him. "Ma'am, do you know what an out-box is?"

Sorenson looked flustered. "Yes, of course. An e-mail out-box contains your sent mail."

"Text messaging has in-boxes and out-boxes as well." He showed her the phone with the message on it. Jaid watched puzzlement chase over the woman's pleasant features. "Your phone shows a sent text message to Justice Reinbeck over a month ago. Do you see the blue text in it that's underlined? That's a link. By clicking on it, the judge would be opening a page on the Internet."

"But I never sent that message." Confusion was changing to alarm. Sorenson looked at each of the agents briefly before returning her attention to Adam. "I told you, I have no idea how."

"You didn't send him a message taking him to the donation webpage for the National Center for Missing and Exploited Children?"

"No, of course not."

But something in her voice had Adam pressing on. "Because that's not an organization that you're familiar with? I know Byron has been active in it in the past."

"No. I mean, yes, he has. We both have. I like to think I got him interested in their work years ago." She set the phone on the table with a trembling hand. "I don't understand this. I didn't send that message."

"Have you loaned your phone to anyone in the last month?" Jaid asked. Excitement was flickering. They were on to something here at last. "Could someone have used it at work? Or when you had guests over? Have you ever misplaced it for a time?"

The woman was shaking her head in conjunction with each question, until the last. She froze. "There was once a few weeks ago . . ." She broke off, appeared to search her memory. "October fifth," she said finally. "I was meeting a girlfriend of mine for dinner at the French bistro just around the corner from here. They don't take reservations, and it's always crowded. I put my name in and waited." She shrugged helplessly. "I got jostled and spilled my purse all over the floor. A young man helped me pick things up, but I discovered later that my phone was missing. I called the restaurant, and they had it there. I picked it up the next day."

"So the phone was out of your possession for twenty-four hours?" Jaid asked.

"About that."

Adam picked the phone up again. Clicked through her contact log. "Byron's first name is used to identify his number."

Looking distressed by now, Mara said unsteadily, "I don't understand. Are you telling me someone called Byron on my phone when it was lost? Or, no, sent him a text message, you said, with a link. What does that mean? It couldn't . . . it can't . . ." Words seemed to escape her. When her lips began to tremble, she clamped them together.

"If you didn't send the message to Byron, it might have happened while the phone was lost. In fact, you might have been bumped into on purpose so you would drop your purse." The woman jerked a little at Adam's words. "The act could have been designed for the express purpose of some-one getting access to both yours and the judge's numbers."

Jaid refrained from comment. Given the woman's re-action and her obvious affection for the judge, Jaid was inclined to believe Sorenson wouldn't have sent that link herself. But it was far too soon to cross her off the list of suspects. The story she was telling would be difficult to check out. She could have orchestrated it herself as a cover.

"Do you happen to recall the person who helped you gather up your things? Or was it more than one person?"

At Jaid's question, the other woman said, "It was just the one. A quite nice young man. The crowd sort of shoved us together, and he dropped some of his things, too. I remem-ber specifically because he had a pamphlet for a charity run being done for the NCMEC and I commented on it, said I used to work for them. We spoke briefly about their mission before he saw his friend and went to join him in the bar."

"Did he give his name? Can you recall what he looked like?"

"No name," she told Shepherd. "He was a nice young man. Mid-to-late twenties, perhaps. Light brown hair. Not short but not as tall as Lawrence, for example." She frowned. "He was pleasant looking. I know that's not very helpful, but nothing about him stood out specifically. I think I'd recognize him if I saw him again, though. We did chat for several minutes."

"We need to keep your phone for a while," Jaid told her. And watched as the woman reluctantly handed it to Adam. "The cyber unit is going to want to look at it."

"You're saying my phone is needed for the investigation."

The woman's voice was calm. Almost too steady. "That it was used to contact him, and . . . I don't understand. Please help me understand. Did this message with the link have something to do with his death?"

"We can't be sure of that. But what you've told us is helpful. We'll follow up."

But Adam's noncommittal answer didn't fool her. "I want to know," she insisted. Her pale blue eyes were shadowed now. With fear rather than grief. "I couldn't bear it if something so silly led to . . . I dropped my purse. That's all. It couldn't possibly have anything to do with Byron's death."

"You're likely right." Shepherd's smile was reassuring. "You're going to want to get a loaner phone for a while. I'll see to it that your cell is returned as quickly as possible."

Adam rose and helped her from her chair, although the woman didn't look as though she were ready to leave. "I need to know . . ."

"We'll keep you posted." He led her to the door, opened it for her, the gesture managing to look more gallant than dismissive. "Thank you again for your help." The woman's mouth opened, but whatever she would have said was lost when he closed the door behind her with a gentle *snick*.

The room was silent save for the rhythmic tick of the antique clock on the mantel. Only when Sorenson's footsteps could be heard moving away from the room did Jaid speak. "We need to look at her. Hard. It might have happened just as she described it. Or she might be vulnerable in some way, and the killer exploited that. It'd seem like a harmless enough request. Just send a message with a link in it to the judge."

"I don't know," Shepherd mused. He braced his arms behind his head. Stretched. "She seems pretty by-the-book. And protective of the justice's privacy. She wouldn't have given up his number willingly. But if someone threatened her with something, who knows? Everyone has a vulnerability."

"We'll check her out," Adam affirmed. He was reading something on his phone. As usual, he offered no explanation. Jaid wondered if it had to do with what had happened last night at his town house. Her stomach knotted anew at the memory. "But I think we'll discover she's telling the truth. She'd make an easy target, despite her strong protective instincts for her boss. She'd follow security precautions to a *T*, but she doesn't recognize the technological possibilities."

Jaid cast him a jaundiced look. How much of his feeling was due to those razor-sharp instincts of his and how much due to the woman's air of anguish? Because Jaid was afraid the question stemmed from the personal rather than professional, she refrained from asking. "That's the last from the judge's list, right?"

"The only other incoming texts came from his family," Adam affirmed. "I've been in contact with Byron's widow. She'll make the family computer and phones available to us at our convenience."

"Let's head over there, then, shall we?"

Jaid placed things back in her briefcase and threw a last glance at the antique mantel clock. Since Shepherd seemed to have no problem doing all the driving, the ride over would give her an opportunity to check in on Royce. And then she could start digging into Mara Sorenson's background a bit more.

Something told her that they were going to find nothing in their examination of the Reinbecks' phones and computers. The smoking gun was the text complete with link on Sorenson's phone.

Everyone had a weakness. She got up from the table and followed the two men out the door. Shepherd had called it correctly. Sorenson had children, she'd said. That might be a place to start.

Jaid knew from personal experience the lengths a parent would go to protect her child.

Chapter 8

"How are all of you doing, Jo?"

Jaid and Shepherd were in the study with the family's computers and cell phones. Adam had elected to take the opportunity for a brief word with Mary Jo Reinbeck. It was the first time he'd seen her since the night of Byron's assassination.

With his arm around her waist, she leaned her head against his shoulder for a moment. "Truthfully? Most of the time I feel like I'm sleepwalking. Like I'll wake up, and it will all have been a nightmare." She gave him a wan smile. "But then I recall I haven't been sleeping. At all. So." Drawing in a breath, she released it slowly. Straightened. "We're getting through. My parents are here. Byron's. It helps a little. The boys need all the support they can get. It's been hard for them. The waiting."

"I can check and see how much longer before they release the body," he offered quietly.

"I've done that." She stared into the open doorway of the office. "They don't have an answer for me. I don't want the boys to go back to school until after all the arrangements are over. There's no point in yanking them in and out. But there's not much for them to do here, either. Some of their friends have been visiting them each night. I think that helps."

"And what about you?"

There was a shadow of her old spirit in her blue gaze when she turned it on him again. "What's going to help is you telling me you're unraveling this thing. I heard something disturbing yesterday, and no, I'm not going to tell you from whom." She stemmed the question before it could leave his lips. "Is there any truth to the rumor that Byron's death might be linked to another one?"

Rumor his ass. "Dammit, Jo . . ."

Her gaze was steady. "I've got contacts, too. At all different levels. But I will tell you that someone I trust in the DCPD—someone with brass—told me there may be a connection. I don't need you to confirm or deny it. He wouldn't have told me if there was nothing to it. I just want to know if you've being given the authority to look into a possible link. Because I want you at the highest juncture of this case, and if you haven't been given this information, I can . . ."

"Jo." His voice was as gentle as he could make it. "You have no worries in that department."

She looked as though she'd like to say more, but she finally nodded. "Suffice it to say there will be no leaks from the vault that is Adam Raiker, is that it?"

"I can't afford to give them any reason to remove me. You want Byron's killer." Moodily, his attention shifted to Shepherd's and Jaid's actions in the next room. "So do I."

She touched his arm. "All right. I was just checking. Because that what's I do. Micromanage. You love that about me."

His lips curved in an unwilling smile. "So I have a weakness for pushy women, is that it?"

"Or strong ones." She inclined her head toward the occupants in the next room. "I remember her, you know. At least her name. Byron mentioned her a time or two all those years ago." She waited, but Adam said nothing. Everything within him had gone still. "Don't you want to know what he said?"

He finally found his breath. "I don't think so."

She told him anyway. "He thought you'd finally met your match." Her tone went wistful at the memory. "He was positively gleeful at the prospect. Byron was certain she was the one who would settle you down. But then LeCroix happened and everything changed."

"LeCroix didn't end Jaid and me," he said shortly. He'd started that process himself in the weeks before his capture by the savage child killer. Everything in his life changed after he killed the pedophile and landed in the CCU for the next several months. But not him and Jaid. They'd been over before that.

She'd just taken a bit more convincing.

"Life goes by so fast, Adam. Everything we have is so fleeting." The throb of tears in Jo's voice had his attention swerving to her. "Don't miss an opportunity to grab a chance at happiness. You're as deserving as anyone else, even if you are one of the most maddeningly reticent men I've ever met."

He smiled as he was meant to. And was silently grateful she'd edged the sentiment with humor. Emotions were sticky entanglements that always clouded judgment. He preached that to his operatives. Most of the time he could suppress his own. It was, he was certain, what made him a natural for his job.

But being confronted with others' emotions, especially those he cared about, always made him feel inadequate.

"If you want to help, you can tell me more about your finances."

"You asked about it before. I put a list together of our investments. Byron was good about updating things like that." She left his side to go to a desk in the room Jaid and Shepherd were working in. Jo unlocked a drawer and withdrew a manila envelope. Re-securing the drawer, she made her way back to him.

He took the envelope she handed to him and withdrew the packet of information inside.

"The top sheets are simple listings of who we do business with. The rest gives a bit more information about what that business entails." Her expression was questioning. "I have to say, Adam, of all the possible motives for Byron's death, a financial one seems about the most illogical to me."

His smile was grim as he scanned the top sheet. "You'd be surprised. Money is at the root of the majority of crimes committed in this country." And emotion was at the root of the rest of them.

One name on the page jumped out at him. Interest surging, he pointed it out to Jo.

"Oh, yes. Dennison International. They're a global banking firm. Byron was quite impressed with the broker there. Why? Have you heard of them?"

He had, although he wouldn't be telling Jo where. His attention drifting back to the page, he wondered at the irony that Byron was in business with the same company that employed Joseph Bailey.

Congressman Newell's oldest grandson.

"Well, we were looking for intersections," Jaid murmured, head bent over the paper Adam held. "Here they are in spades."

"But what does it mean?" Shepherd was at a near stop in the congested downtown traffic. Dennison International was located on I Street in the center of DC's bustling financial district. "So Bailey works for the same company Reinbeck has investments with. He's not the broker named on the account is he?"

"No." Jaid leaned over to get a better look at the list Adam had gotten from Mary Jo Reinbeck. "But he's got reason to have nursed a grudge against Reinbeck all this time. And Dennison International is also listed as a client for Patterson Capital." She looked up at Adam, found him much too close. For the first time she realized she was practically in his lap.

Straightening hastily, she continued, "Is his number by any chance listed on Patterson's incoming message logs?"

"Not his personal number, no." Since Adam didn't have to consult his case file before answering, she knew he'd already had the thought and checked it out. "But two cell phones registered to the company are. And Bailey's position there means he might have had access to one of those phones."

"Maybe I should call Assistant Director Hedgelin and advise him of our next interview." This could be potentially more explosive than the one with Newell yesterday. The man had gotten positively ballistic when Adam had introduced the topic of his grandson.

"Wouldn't hurt." Agent Shepherd's gaze met hers in the rearview mirror. "If he's going to get an irate call from the senator, he would appreciate the forewarning."

She took out her phone, very much aware that Adam hadn't rendered an opinion. Amazing how loud his silence could be sometimes. Deliberately, she tapped in the assistant director's number. This would be an opportunity to let him know that they'd struck out with the search of Reinbecks' computers and cell phones. Sorenson remained their best link to the spyware infecting the judge's phone.

And keeping her mind on the investigation remained Jaid's best chance of forgetting the questions that still burned regarding the events at Adam's last night.

————

Heath Carroll steepled his fingers in front of his chin and looked suitably somber. "A terrible tragedy. I'm still trying to wrap my head around the judge's death. Of course, I've left a message for Mary Jo expressing my condolences."

"I'm sure she appreciates that. She told me today how impressed her husband was with you. Where did the two of you meet?"

The broker visibly brightened at Adam's words. "She said that? It means a lot to me, more than you can know. Justice Reinbeck . . . well, he's a hero, isn't he? Or he was.

I've long admired what he stood for. We shared some of the same worldviews, I guess you could say. As for where we met, you might say that you brought us together, Mr. Raiker."

Jaid looked at Adam, shocked. His expression didn't change, but she read his surprise in the slight hesitation before his next word. "Me?"

"Yes, we met at the Boys and Girls Club fund-raiser held a couple months ago. You were one of the speakers." Because she was watching, Jaid noted Adam's barely perceptible wince at the reminder. She recalled what the priest had said when she and Adam had stopped by there. That he occasionally prevailed on Adam to speak at fund-raisers for pet projects of his.

The smile Carroll graced them with was boyish. "You'll be glad to know that I was taken enough with your speech to part with several thousand dollars for Monsignor Benton's cause. When I stopped to introduce myself to Justice Reinbeck, he said the two of you were friends. We had quite a long conversation that evening. Followed it up with a meeting here in my office a few weeks ago when he and Mary Jo started an account with me." He stopped himself, as if just realizing the breach of confidentiality. "By your presence here, I'm assuming you know of the Reinbecks' business with the firm."

Jaid couldn't recall a time when she'd seen Adam look so uncomfortable. Intrigued, she murmured, "That must have been some speech."

Carroll had recovered. Smoothing his thinning blond hair, he said enthusiastically, "It really was. He only spoke for a few minutes, but the crowd was captivated. It's not every day that you get a glimpse into the mysterious Adam Raiker's childhood."

Shock sliced through her, quick and brutal. "No," she agreed around a suddenly full throat. "It certainly isn't." It was particularly hard to imagine the uncommunicative man next to her spilling his secrets to a room full of strangers, so she figured he'd given them only what was necessary to part them from their money for the fund-raiser.

But as little as that may have been, it still represented more than he'd ever shared with her in the fourteen months they'd been lovers.

"Was there anyone else from your company there that night?" Shepherd quizzed the man.

"Several as I recall. The Boys and Girls Club is on our yearly donations list. Many probably support it personally as well." He named a few colleagues he recalled seeing there. "But it was a huge crowd. People coming and going all night. I really can't say for sure."

"How about Joseph Bailey?" With effort Jaid hauled her attention off the now silent man at her side. "Do you recall if he was there?"

"Joe?" Carroll thought for a moment. "I can't say specifically. But he's here today if you'd like to ask him yourself."

"We would." She summoned a small smile. "This is a pretty big outfit. I wasn't sure you'd know him."

The broker leaned back in his chair and hooked an ankle across the opposite knee. "Joe's only been here a few years, but he's interned in several departments. Mine was the last before he got his license. We have a mentoring program for new brokers. I'm one of his."

Connections and more connections, Jaid thought. "I understand your firm also does business with Patterson Capital."

The wince on Carroll's face was barely discernible, but it was there. "We do, yes. Oliver Patterson's death was a terrible shock. And, I don't mind saying, it makes a tenuous financial recovery even more so."

"Your company has a couple cell phone numbers that showed up on Oliver Patterson's business cell records." Shepherd leaned forward and gave Carroll a slip of paper with the two numbers written on them. "Do you recognize either of these?"

"Yes, the first one is for my exclusive use." He gave a firm nod, looked back up at them. "The other is an extra used in my department by interns or assistants doing some routine information updating. I'm surprised that these are the only cells showing up on that list, however. I'm certain the senior partners would have had occasion to contact Mr. Patterson from time to time."

"We're interested only in the text messages that were exchanged."

"Really?" The broker looked intrigued by Shepherd's answer but didn't ask the questions he seemed to have. "Well, I have done so, certainly." He looked abashed. "Ridiculous how quickly we get used to the convenience of technology. I'd use a text rather than e-mail or a phone call when it was quicker."

"Did you have occasion to send him text messages in the last month or so before his death?"

"Let me see." Without being asked he took a cell phone out of his pocket and checked the call log. "Yes, here's one. And another . . ." Swiftly, he counted. "Six all told, in the last five weeks." He gave them a sheepish grin. "I'm terrible about cleaning out my out-box."

"May I see?" Jaid took the phone from him and read each text. All had been accounted for on Patterson's phone log, which they'd consulted on the way over. None of the ones on Carroll's phone contained a link.

She handed it back to him and offered a smile that had him blinking. "I'm afraid I'm terribly dense about your area of expertise. I don't understand why one global investment firm needs to do business with another. Aren't you in competition with each other?"

From the convoluted explanation the man launched into regarding global connectivity, she discerned that the answer was yes. And no.

But most important, she thought, was the expression he was barely able to mask when she first asked the question. When the financial collapse happened a while back, Patterson Capital's downfall had dealt a blow to Dennison International as well.

———

Joseph Bailey bore no resemblance to his grandfather except, Jaid thought, for a faint air of entitlement. His pale brown hair was swept back from a high forehead, and his grandfather's austerity wasn't reflected in the expensive suit Bailey wore or the large diamond winking on his pinky. He was a bit flashier than Carroll's more downplayed look of confident wealth, but maybe the appearance was deliberately cultivated. She supposed no one wanted to invest with someone who looked as though he were a step away from the poorhouse.

What was most surprising, however, was his candor.

"My grandfather called me last night," he told them in his postage–stamp–sized office after refreshments had been offered and declined. "He was . . . agitated about your visit. Mostly because of your mention of me, I think. I brought a great deal of embarrassment to my family when I was a teenager. I think he's afraid that all of it will be dredged up again."

Jaid sent a look at Shepherd. "That wasn't the impression he gave us. He seemed quite upset that you had been treated unfairly by Judge Reinbeck at your sentencing when you were a juvenile."

"Oh, he was." He surveyed them from behind narrow-framed dark glasses. "But back then he was every bit as enraged at me for my actions, I can assure you. Rightfully so," he hastened to add. "I was a punk. Didn't appreciate anything, pissed off in general, and thought I was a whole lot tougher than I was." The wry smile he gave them was tinged with embarrassment. "Quite frankly, I was under the impression that I was untouchable because of my lineage. And Grandfather was equally incensed to discover that wasn't true."

"When Judge Reinbeck sentenced you to juvie."

"The state school for boys." The smile turned to a wince. "Sixteen months of hell, I'll tell you. The lessons I learned there I've carried with me for a lifetime. But if I hadn't ended up there, I'd be in prison now. The road I was on, the rate I was going ... I wouldn't have stopped. Giving me another chance at that point would have been like handing me a length of rope and watching me tie my own noose with it."

"So you're grateful to the judge for ignoring your grandfather's position and sending you away."

"Gratitude?" That surprised a laugh from him. "I'd say that's a reach. Especially given how much time I spent hating the guy for my stay there. I could have learned my lesson in half the time he gave me and still be living on the straight and narrow today. But ..." He lifted a shoulder. "Truth is, that sentence saved me. Allowed me the life I'm living now. I was sincerely sorry to hear about the judge's death. I don't necessarily share my grandfather's worldviews or political beliefs."

"But you still volunteer on his campaign."

"I pitch in when asked." Humor lit his face. "I learned the value of family somewhere along the way. And what it takes to keep the peace. Whatever our differences, Grandfather has always been there for me. We might differ on methods, but family still counts, you know?"

The words resonated. Although in Jaid's experience, family was fraught with the sort of emotional complications that took a lifetime to unsnarl. Her mother's expectations of perfection had slowly driven her husband away. But when the marriage had broken up, he'd left Jaid behind, too.

She looked down to consult her notes. "Have you had occasion to meet Judge Reinbeck since your court appearance as a teenager?"

"Not personally, no."

"You worked in Heath Carroll's department for a time."

Bailey glanced at his watch briefly before responding to Adam's statement. "I interned in a number of departments in the company before getting my license. Heath's was the most recent. He taught me a lot."

"When you were in his department, did you ever have occasion to use the department cell phone?"

"Yes, of course." His smile was wry. "More than half my

work hours are spent on the phone, believe it or not."

His responses to the rest of Jaid's questions was similarly unenlightening. He hadn't been at the fund-raiser where Carroll had met the judge. He'd never had occasion to contact Reinbeck or Patterson. He was aware of the firm's relationship with Patterson Capital but hadn't had reason to know the specifics of it. He was, he explained with charming self-deprecation, still practically a peon at the firm.

He looked at the clock again. "I'm really sorry, but if that's all, I have another commitment in a few minutes."

Because they were done, the three of them got up, headed to the door. "Working late?" Jaid inquired.

"No, we have a basketball league in the wellness center in the basement of the building. It's game night. My team's in the lead for the championship." He gave them a wink. "Only because I'm not opposed to bringing in ringers to round out the positions on the team."

Twenty minutes later, headed back across town to the Hoover Building, Jaid mused, "Bailey got his grandfather's share of humility, I'd say."

"He appears that way on the surface." Shepherd pulled into one of the parking garages for agent use. "But let's face it, despite his claims that he never contacted Patterson, he had access to that phone in Carroll's department. He'd know where to find it, the contacts on it . . . He certainly can't be discounted merely on his say so. And it occurs to me that his physical description matches the one Sorenson gave us of the man who helped her pick up her belongings when she dropped her purse."

That thought had occurred to Jaid, too. "At least we can be fairly certain he won't be complaining to his grandfather about our visit." She glanced at her watch. She wouldn't make it home for dinner, not with the drive she had in front of her, but she'd easily get there before Royce went to bed. "I'll update the task force log tonight, Tom."

He parked and turned to give her a wink. "I'm not going to argue with you. It happens that I have a date tonight."

"What a coincidence." It was the first time Adam had spoken on the way back from Dennison International. "So do I."

Her head swiveled toward him with whiplash speed. It took a moment to discern the flicker of amusement on his face. Another for comprehension to filter in. She'd demanded an explanation from him just this morning about the events of last night. Anticipation hummed. She'd have remembered before allowing him to walk away this evening. Jaid was certain of that. Even if worry for her son had momentarily been her uppermost concern.

"Well, great then," Shepherd was saying in a hearty voice as he gallantly opened the door for Jaid. "Do you good to get out tonight, too, Jaid. I always think I'm sharper after a few hours away from living the case."

"Agent Marlowe has always seemed plenty sharp." Adam's voice was wry as he joined them outside the vehicle. "Too much so sometimes."

But the other agent was already striding away, obviously in a hurry. "See you both tomorrow at the usual time."

She said nothing until Shepherd was well out of earshot. Then she stopped. Looked at Adam pointedly. "About that *date . . .*"

"What, here? I don't think so." He continued toward the elevator of the garage. "You'll want to get home, I imagine, but Mojy's isn't out of the way. This shouldn't take long, at any rate."

She remained rooted in place. Mojy's had been a favorite of theirs once upon a time. A quaint bar tucked in a historically significant hotel, it was just a couple blocks from the Hoover Building. Many an hour had been spent poring over every angle of a case there with Adam.

Even more had been spent in one of the rooms upstairs where he had once kept a suite.

Memories swamped her. They'd confer on the case they were working. And later, when their relationship had turned intimate, the night would end with the two of them in bed.

Communicating physically in a way that they'd never managed to verbally.

He paused. Turned to look at her over his shoulder.
"Coming?"

It took effort to get her feet to move. To shake off the
gossamer web of recollections that had surely been gilded
by the passing years. At any rate his expressionless face
was enough to shoot steel up her spine.

If his memory were following the same path as hers, it
certainly didn't show.

"Fine." On wooden legs she managed to join him in the
elevator. As the doors closed, she looked at him. "I want to
get home before Royce goes to bed. So talk fast. I have a
feeling this is going to be one hell of a story."

"His name is Mose Ferrell." Adam finished the saga of
the last few nights' events as the waitress set down Jaid's
diet soda. Taking the bill he'd laid on the table, the waitress sent him a slow smile and strolled away. He reached
for his glass of water. Drank. "He's a two-bit hood. Has
a rap sheet that includes a recent release after serving a
seven-year stretch for assault with intent in commission of
a burglary. Last night he claimed he didn't know who had
hired him, but today he admits that he was told to call the
man LeCroix."

"LeCroix?" She paled. Clenched the glass a bit more
tightly. "He's dead."

"He is that." And the knowledge never failed to fill Adam
with fierce satisfaction. The man who had cost twenty-
seven boys their innocence and then their lives, the man
who had cost Adam his eye and nearly his leg had been
killed by his hand eight years ago. But not before LeCroix
had left his own mark on Adam. "The name isn't common
enough to be a coincidence. And, of course, with the efforts
he took to disguise his voice, why give his real name?"

"It would only have significance to you." She frowned.

"So whoever is behind these attempts on your life . . . he's wrapped up in your last case for the bureau, is that it?"

"Possibly." He eyed the ice in his glass broodingly. "Or it could just be a name chosen because my enemy imagines himself to be the one to kill me once and for all. As LeCroix came close to once."

"And failed." That information could be gleaned from the numerous articles that had followed Adam's escape. The country had feverishly followed the story of Adam's heroism and tragedy wrapped up in the downfall of John LeCroix, one of the most infamous pedophiles on record.

There'd been a movie loosely based on the facts of the case, she remembered. Jaid had never been able to bring herself to watch it but heard it had been more based on Hollywood glitz then rooted in reality.

Kale Bolton would be looking for the facts to go with the drama.

He had two other books to his credit, both a result of some intensive investigative journalism he'd done. She imagined that meant he needed sources close to Adam to give him information, since Adam obviously wasn't a willing subject.

She raised her gaze to his. "This means the agency was wrong about Jennings. They thought he worked alone when he tried to kill you to avenge his ex-girlfriend's father who you put away."

He picked up the glass. Saluted her with it. "Which I always had a hard time believing actually. Then the attempts stopped, which seemed to lend the claim some credence. But now Paulie has traced payments to Jennings from the same account a ransom drop was made to last winter." She listened, captivated, to his brief encapsulation of the Mulder kidnapping case he'd worked then. "The attempts began about six weeks after we'd returned the girl safely and rerouted seven-tenths of the ransom that was originally wired."

"The timing of the new attempts is suspect." *Suspect.* A dispassionate word for a topic that left her feeling anything but emotionless. He could have been killed. Last night and again a few evenings before. In the last few months, he'd survived in spite of overwhelming odds. A lesser man, one with fewer resources and lacking Adam's innate cunning, wouldn't be sitting in front of her right now.

She toyed with the straw in her drink and tried not to consider how many times one man could conceivably escape certain death. "I wonder if your involvement in a very high-profile case offers your enemy newfound access to you. Or if he regards it as an insult, proof you're going about your life after he's failed to stop you."

"That begs the question of how he'd know I am attached to this case. The information isn't even widely disseminated throughout the bureau. There's a reason we're given individual briefings daily."

She blinked at him. That possibility had escaped her. She'd assumed it was so Hedgelin could keep closer tabs on Adam. "All right. But people *do* know. Look at everyone we've interviewed. And it could have been leaked at a higher level. How else do you explain the sudden recurrence of the attempts?"

"I can't." He shook his head, the gesture frustrated. "This Ferrell . . . he's hardly in the same league as Jennings. Makes it difficult to imagine the same man hiring him." Adam's sudden grin was grim. "But I suppose even assassins can be difficult to line up on short notice."

His humor escaped her. Throat suddenly dry, she bent her head to sip from the soda. "Let's imagine for a moment that it's someone involved with this investigation. Maybe someone we've talked to. Someone who knows your reputation and recalls the media reports about your near-death experience in May. The killer we're looking for could feel threatened by you. Figures any attempts on your life will be blamed on whoever was trying to kill you back then."

"He'd likely be correct." He took his phone out and looked at it as it vibrated. A flicker of impatience crossing his expression, he put it away without answering. "At any rate, if his intent is to get me removed from the case, he very nearly succeeded. He wouldn't have had to kill me necessarily. If I'd shot Ferrell last night, I would have been jammed up in my own investigation, effectively ending my involvement with this case."

"Maybe we're making this too difficult." She tried to push aside emotion and think logically. "Who benefits from your death?"

"That avenue's a dead end. The business would go to Paulie, the estate to Monsignor Benton. I trust both those men with my life."

She considered him for a moment. "Friendship is important to you. I get that. But maybe this time you need to put it aside and think about yourself. This case exposes you. Brings renewed interest to bear. No one would expect you to continue at risk to your own life."

He looked insulted, but she hadn't expected any differently. "If I thought I was putting you or Shepherd at risk, I'd step aside, believe me. But other than the shooting in Philadelphia last May, an attempt has never been made when I'm not alone. I think the two of you are safe enough."

Jaid slapped her hand on the table with enough force to draw the attention of the other patron sitting at the bar. Leaning forward, she demanded, "What about you, Adam? What about your risk? Your safety?"

His stunned expression was as telling as a shout. He didn't have to tell her that it hadn't been a consideration. She straightened in her chair, shaken by the strength of her reaction. He'd told her once that everyone felt fear. That it was a healthy response to danger. But that a good agent used it to fuel logic rather than relying on emotion.

"Fear is a tool—"

"Not an excuse. Yes, I remember the mantra." Because it gave her something to do, she removed the straw and lifted the glass to her lips. "I'd suggest that not acting on it at all is more stupidity than anything else, but it's doubtful you'll listen."

"Do you honestly think I'm standing still on this? I have some of the best people in the country working for me. We're looking into it, Jaid. I've taken precautions, far more than I'm comfortable with. You can't expect much more than that."

"Yes, I learned the danger of expectations with you long ago." The words hung in the air between them, tinged with bitterness. The moment they left her mouth, she wanted to call them back. It was demoralizing to recognize the feelings they elicited. Feelings she'd thought buried years ago.

Adam stilled. The only sign of an answering response was the muscle that jumped in his cheek. For a moment she thought he wouldn't answer. Hoped he didn't. There was no point rehashing old history.

"I don't linger on regrets."

Offering him a tight smile, she gathered up her purse. He'd answered the questions she had. There was no more to be accomplished here. "Good advice."

"But that doesn't mean I don't have them." His voice was low. Intense. "One was losing my weapon at LeCroix's."

There was a light in his eye, a dangerous burn. "You're the other. I handled things badly eight years ago. I know that. But regret doesn't change anything. The strongest are those who put regret behind them and find a way to go on. You did that. Your son is proof of it."

She felt battered by his words and the questions they raised. Was he referring to the way their relationship ended or the fact that he started it in the first place? But now wasn't the time to focus on his meaning. Not when the delicate issue of Royce had been introduced.

No one knew the truth about his parentage. Not even her mother. *Especially* not her mother. "I did, yes. You're right about one thing—regrets are useless. And so is dredging up ancient history." She managed a smile, rose from her seat. "Thanks for the reminder. I need to get home to my son."

The tension eased from his shoulders, and he nodded. "I don't want to place you in the middle of this. I'll be discussing these events with Hedgelin myself."

Comprehension dawned. "That was him on phone just now?"

He nodded. "Not a conversation that I look forward to,

but I made sure a copy of last night's police report was directed to him. He can't say I didn't keep him informed." His smile was humorless. "Although he'll have plenty else to say on the topic, I'm sure."

"I'm not sorry to be missing the conversation. There's an undercurrent between the two of you whenever you're in the same room." Both were powerful men in their own right. Hedgelin by virtue of his position, and Adam because of the reputation he'd built over the years. "I know it has to do with your last case together. When you were partnered to track down LeCroix." She stopped then, a belated sense of caution rearing. She'd never know what had her shoving it aside to add, "There are some who claim he rode that case to his present position. That he put his own spin on the events that led to your capture." She stopped then, certain she'd said too much.

But Adam merely nodded. "We all have our own unique grasp of reality. The final report has my accounting in it. If some chose not to believe it . . ." He shrugged, as if it didn't matter. Maybe it didn't to him. He'd left the bureau for good after his endless surgeries and rehab. Started his own forensics firm a short time later and built an international reputation with it.

Hesitating by the table for a moment, she said, "Try to play nice at your upcoming meeting. He'd make a formidable adversary. And in light of recent events, it doesn't appear that you can afford another one."

Chapter 9

Adam considered the man seated across the table from him as Jaid's parting words echoed in his head. Formidable? Nothing about Cleve Hedgelin's appearance would suggest it. He looked like a banker. An accountant.

But appearances could be deceptive. Hedgelin had been a good agent in his day. But any danger he posed now stemmed solely from his position.

And how he would use it to elbow Adam out of this investigation if he could.

The waitress replaced his water with a Scotch. It was bourbon for Hedgelin. The man reached for the glass and took a healthy swallow before loosening his tie, sending a look around the bar.

"I've never been inside. Nice place." He looked at Adam, brow raised. "What were you doing here?"

"Met an old friend for a chat." It had been a strategic move on his part to suggest this bar for their conversation when he called Hedgelin back. If this meet were going to have more muscle behind it, the man would have insisted on conferencing back at FBI headquarters. His eventual acquiescence on the location had given Adam valuable time and information. Whatever the assistant director wanted to say to him, Hedgelin was still on his own.

Which of course didn't mean he wasn't taking his orders from higher up.

"So." Adam took a sip from his own drink. Approved. Mojy's had always stocked top-shelf liquor. "You got last night's police report."

"Jesus, Adam." Hedgelin's pale brown eyes were magnified behind the rimless glasses. "No offense, but you've got a dark cloud hovering over you."

"Or a lucky one." One finger tapped the side of his glass. "Ferrell didn't succeed in his attempt to turn me into pink mist."

The other man grimaced. "Don't even joke about it. You have to admit there's too much on your plate to continue investigating these murders. Hell, you've got all you can do just dodging would-be assassins and staying alive."

"The attempts usually happen when I'm alone." He parroted the same assurance he'd given to Jaid. Was certain it was met with the same lack of enthusiasm. "Nothing about them has anything to do with my presence on the task force. And despite how hard you try, I don't think you or the director can use this to convince the attorney general otherwise."

When a flush darkened Hedgelin's cheeks, Adam knew he was correct. The man had probably made a flurry of phone calls that day and had obviously been unsuccessful, or he'd have led with that info.

"I'm asking you to do the right thing here. Voluntarily take yourself off the task force. No one would blame you. It's not going to tarnish your carefully cultivated hero status. But you are a distraction on this case."

"That argument would have more merit had you not used it to try to keep me off it to begin with. And there's been no 'carefully cultivated' status. I think that's your MO, not mine."

Hedgelin took off his glasses and carefully cleaned them with a handkerchief taken from his pocket. "I'm not the one with a Pulitzer Prize–winning journalist writing my life story."

Anger flared. Bolton had been a sore spot since he first targeted Adam as a subject for his next release. It took more effort than it should have to keep his voice even. "He hasn't gotten any help from me, and he won't. I wonder if the same can be said for you." Although it had been a shot in the dark, it was obvious his words hit their mark.

Hedgelin settled the glasses back on his nose, brushed at some invisible lint on his lapel. "I don't know what you're talking about."

"Don't you?" Adam murmured. "I'm unconvinced. I know your tells, Cleve. We were partnered for over two years. You get this twitch in your right eye when you're not being entirely truthful. So you talked with Bolton at some point. Why? To get your own version of the LeCroix case in the manuscript?"

"I don't make a habit of . . ."

"You did." Disgusted, Adam sat back in his chair. Few people managed to surprise him. He couldn't say why he was taken aback this time. Maybe if he'd kept better tabs on bureau gossip in the time since he left, he would have suspected as much. It had taken Jaid's warning to plant the idea. Hedgelin's reaction cemented his certainty.

The man gripped his glass tightly, nearly spilling its contents when he leaned over the table to hiss, "I have a position to maintain. I'm not like you; I didn't take the easy way out and quit. I've paid my dues, and then some, and I deserve to be where I'm at based on my own merits. There's nothing to be served by resurrecting that case all over again. And who knows what sort of license a reporter will take with the facts. So damn right, I talked to him, and I set the record straight. You never should have gone after

LeCroix yourself once I was out of contact. What happened to you was a result of your own perceived superpowers, not because I failed you."

"The easy way out?" Adam's laugh was humorless. "You do have an interesting take on things."

The man had the grace to flush, but when he straightened, his hand still clenched the glass in front of him. "I'm not without sympathy for what you suffered."

The word burned through him like a brand. "I don't want your sympathy, Cleve." Sympathy was just another word for pity, and he'd spent his life making damn sure no one had reason to pity him. "By the time I knew you were out of contact, I'd already trailed him to his lair. What was I supposed to do, stand outside with my dick in my hand while he savaged that kid like he did all the others?"

Hedgelin took a long pull from his drink. He looked as though he was in need of the fortitude. "We both made choices. I'm sick of defending mine."

"No one asked you to." Picking up his glass, Adam drained it before returning it to the table. "But maybe you should examine your true reasons for wanting me off this investigation."

"My true reasons are echoed by my superiors. They haven't changed." He hesitated before reluctantly adding, "When do you think you'll have a profile ready?"

The question didn't strike Adam as contradictory. Profiling was a specialty of his, and he was expected to bring something to this investigation that no one else could. "I can finish the preliminary tonight and have it ready for you tomorrow."

The man gave a jerky nod and rose, leaving his drink half-full. "You wanted honesty, so here's some for you. I'm going to continue to do whatever I can to get you removed. Not because of our history, but because your services are unnecessary and the baggage you bring along is a distraction."

Adam inclined his head. He'd expect no less. And as long as he could sidestep the attempts on his life, he'd remain on the case.

He watched Hedgelin exit the bar, tension making his spine ramrod straight. It wasn't Hedgelin's "honesty" that had Adam troubled in any case.

It was wondering how he'd missed the fact that his ex-partner resented him so deeply.

———

Adam Raiker was proving to be a problem.

The man who'd hired Ferrell sat before his bank of computers. But the numbers on the screen showing his overseas bank accounts failed to satisfy as they normally did.

It was unlikely Raiker was going to be removed from the case, despite the carefully orchestrated diversions thrown his way. As much as that knowledge burned, it had to be faced. His involvement was threatening all the careful strategy that had gone into this plan.

He drummed his fingers impatiently on the table. Every problem had a solution, so he'd simply find a way to make this work with Raiker dropped right down in the middle of it. His presence didn't have to change anything. Things might have to be done a bit differently, but the outcome could be the same. The details just needed tweaking.

A germ of an idea occurred. A slow smile crossed his face. Yes, there was a way around Raiker's presence. It could even take the stakes up a notch. How much more satisfying would it be if the great Adam Raiker continued to investigate but was outwitted at every turn?

He examined the idea from all angles. Didn't see a downside. There were far worse fates for Raiker than death. The man was counting on it.

And very soon Adam Raiker would discover that for himself.

———

Somehow, without really planning it, Adam found himself parked outside Jerry's rectory for the second time that week. He hesitated there for a minute, debated going in. He could use a little relaxed conversation with someone outside the investigation. But more importantly, he owed it to the man to give him at least a sanitized version of what had gone down last night. It'd likely be in the papers tomorrow. If Jerry found out that way, there'd be hell to pay.

There were only a few people whose reactions Adam cared anything about, but Jerry was the closest person to a father figure Adam had ever had. And the fact was, he owed the man. Big-time. Adam got out of the car, locked it with the remote, and headed toward the front walk. If nothing else, once the priest had gotten his concern out of the way, Adam might just score some dinner. Lucia, the housekeeper at the rectory, was a helluva cook.

But when he knocked, no one came to the door. Adam backed up, squinted at the building again. One light showing, at least, but that could be for security purposes only, despite the cardinal's attitude about the utility bill. Jerry kept a crammed schedule with his duties for the parish coupled with his myriad do-gooder activities. He was probably out.

Adam knocked once more and half turned, expecting to head back to his car. But then he stopped. Cocked his head. There were voices sounding inside. Loud enough to have drowned out his knock.

Certain of his welcome, he opened the outer door, checked the inner one. With a grimace he noted it was unlocked. Despite his frequent lectures, Jerry was lax about security. Churches and members of the clergy weren't immune from crime.

Adam eased open the door, stepped inside. Immediately realized his mistake. Jerry was obviously there. One of the voices was his, and he was engaged in a high-volume argument with someone who also remained out of sight.

"I'm sick of the constant micromanaging of every single detail of my life. I don't need a keeper. And you of all people are in no position to preach to me about vices. At least I've never tried to hide mine behind the shield of the church. Your hypocrisy is a bit much to swallow."

"You'll keep a civil tongue in your head and remember

whom you're addressing." The response was made in venomous tones. "I am your spiritual leader. Do you know how close you've come to being sanctioned for some of your stunts? Former cardinal White, God rest his soul, should have squelched your disobedience early on, instead of . . ."

It was high time to announce his presence. "Jerry, you here?" Adam called loudly. The voices broke off abruptly to be followed a moment later with the sound of footsteps.

"Adam." His friend's smile looked forced. "I wasn't expecting you."

"I should have called first." Although it was the first time he'd ever had that feeling, it was clearly bad timing on his part. "Call me later. We can talk then."

Another man stepped into the hallway, pulling a long wool coat over his dark clothes. The scarlett zucchetto he wore gave away his identity better than a nametag.

"Cardinal Cote." Although the two men's conversation had halted, the undercurrents were unmistakable. "It's a pleasure to meet you. Adam Raiker." He was wishing more than ever that he'd driven home rather than stopping. After an awkward moment, he extended his hand.

The cardinal returned his handshake. "I've heard of you, Mr. Raiker, and not just from Monsignor Benton." The cardinal was tall and spare, with close-cut gray hair and somber brown eyes. Right now there was a tinge of irritation in his expression that the pleasantries didn't quite mask. "Don't bother leaving. The monsignor and I are done here."

"Quite done," muttered Jerry. Cote sent him one last long look before stepping by Adam to let himself out the door.

Rarely had he felt so uncomfortable. The church had often had that affect on him growing up. "Damn. My timing is usually better."

A bit of tension eased from the priest's shoulders. "Any time I see you still standing is a good time. And actually, we were done here. It was all over but the shouting, literally. Come in." He turned to head back into his office. After a brief hesitation Adam followed him inside.

"Take your coat off. Get comfortable. Need a Scotch? Because I don't mind telling you, I could sure use one myself."

"Not for me but go ahead." Folding his coat over the back of the leather couch, Adam sat, while Jerry seated himself in the matching chair.

"I'll forgo. I have it on good authority that my vices are already numerous enough without adding to them."

Adam eyed Jerry carefully. Although he had never met Cardinal Cote before, he'd heard enough about him. When it came to Jerry's activist causes, the former cardinal of the diocese had been much more . . . understanding would be a stretch. But certainly less judgmental than Cote. Adam understood what it was like to chafe under authority. He and Jerry had something in common there.

"I didn't want you to hear it on the news," Adam said abruptly. The tension that had recently eased from the other man's expression returned. "There was another attempt on my life last night. The suspect is in custody." He'd ensured that the police report made its way to Hedgelin in a timely manner as a matter of self-interest. He couldn't be accused of trying to withhold the information, and there would have been no point once it hit the papers. But his reasons for sharing it with Jerry . . . they were personal. Although it had taken him years to fully accept it, the man worried about him like he would a son.

Jerry rubbed a tired hand over his face. "Details."

After a brief sanitized version of events, the priest was silent, his expression pensive. "You know I wait for the day when I pick up the papers and discover you're dead. I've actually thought about it. It's the only way I'd have of hearing the news, the same way millions of Americans will over their breakfast cereal."

"Paulie has directions to contact you in that event."

Jerry nodded. "Thank you for that. I'm not in the habit of begging for favors, but I'm asking you to lay low for a while, Adam. Can't imagine you sitting on a beach somewhere, but surely there's a place you'd enjoy visiting. Go away somewhere long enough for them to catch whoever is set on killing you."

Adam looked away. Contrary to Jerry's words, the man nagged Adam unmercifully for "favors" when it came to his pet causes. Those requests were casually made, easily refused. But this . . . it came from the heart. And Adam's response had remorse stabbing deep. "I can't."

Silence stretched during which he couldn't meet the other man's gaze. "All right then." The priest's voice sounded old. Tired. "You were always a stubborn one, even at nine. Since I can't interest you in self-preservation, how about some sustenance?"

Grateful for the man's deliberate attempt to lighten the mood, Adam said, "I wouldn't say no to some of Lucia's leftovers."

"Homemade enchiladas with her special sauce."

"Works for me."

"Good." Jerry heaved himself out his chair. "Then you won't mind doing the dishes afterward."

———

The morning sunlight struggling through Hedgelin's blinds was weak and capricious. There one moment. Gone the next. The weather forecast called for snow flurries tonight. The sudden drop in temperatures reminded Adam that the case could grow cold just as quickly.

The assistant director looked up from the profile he'd been reading, a slight frown on his face. "You're saying you don't think the unknown subject is motivated by religion? Despite the notes?"

"Based on what we have right now, not primarily." He lifted a shoulder, aware that Shepherd and Jaid were as intent on his words as was the man on the other side of the desk. "That could change as more information comes to light. Basically the more connections we find between the deaths, the less likely it is that the killer is acting purely out a religious compulsion, and the more probable that we'll discover old-fashioned greed or revenge at the heart of the crimes. I'd expect a religious fanatic to be driven by a need to punish and expose. He wouldn't even necessarily have to personally know the victims. He could draw his opinions from the media, given how high-profile the victims are."

"Then why the note cards?" asked Shepherd from his seat next to Jaid. Each of them had been given copies of the profile as well. "Why bother?"

"Maybe to throw us off, make us waste time looking in another direction." Jaid responded before Adam could. She wore her hair back today in a severe style that delineated her delicate jawline and stubborn chin. "Or maybe he accomplishes two goals at once. Could be he's motivated by revenge and is a Jesus freak to boot. Uses the notes to rationalize his actions."

"The profile is an evolving document." Adam looked at Hedgelin. "There's not enough information at this time to nail down motive, despite the note cards. But the basic descriptor of the type of person we're looking for is solid. A loner or an individual adept at compartmentalizing his life. Highly intelligent and organized. These hits took planning. And he has substantial financial resources, because I don't think whoever is behind them did his own killing."

Stunned silence filled the room. "How can you possibly know that?" demanded the assistant director. There was no sign of the acrimony with which they had parted last night. Adam knew better than to believe it was gone. Only buried for the moment.

"A profile isn't about pretending to know anything." He shifted his cane out of the way to make room to stretch out his leg. "It's part psychology, part logical guesswork. If the killer does turn out to be acting out a sort of religious retribution, we'll discover he committed the murders himself. He'd have to, to get the full satisfaction from the acts, because they would stem from a more personal place. But if he's merely using the deadly sins to cover his tracks rather than to justify them, then we're talking about someone who will be more removed. He won't care how they're carried out, because the final goal is the deaths themselves. His detachment allows him to continue to strike without fear of detection."

"Well." The assistant director deliberately set the document aside. "If we need more facts to solidify the profile, you'd better get to work gathering them."

"I'd like to talk to Saeed Harandi."

The silence in the room following Jaid's words was deafening. Adam watched Hedgelin, but the man was guarding his thoughts closely. "That won't be necessary."

"I think it is, sir." Her voice remained firm. Adam felt a tug of approval. "His was Oliver Patterson's last appointment on the day he was killed."

"He was interviewed shortly after the death." The assistant director's voice was dismissive. "There's nothing more to be gained from going over it again. And since no mention of him was made in the official agency report you have access to, you'll tell me where you came up with his name."

"I was wondering about that, too." Although Hedgelin skewered her with a glare intended to intimidate, Jaid didn't back down. "Why is it missing from our report? Because I found a single mention of him on one of the pages buried in the DCPD report we received. But when I contacted Lieutenant Griega about it last night, he wouldn't say a word about Harandi."

"Perhaps because the lieutenant is better at taking orders than one of my own agents."

"I still believe . . ."

"Agent Marlowe." Hedgelin clasped his hands on his desk, his tone sharp. "The handling of Harandi is sensitive to our country's security and way above your pay grade. I'm satisfied he has nothing more to share on this matter."

Shepherd was looking from one to the other, obviously lost. "Okay, someone catch me up here. I have no idea who this guy is."

"He's an Iranian diplomat," Adam answered. Irritation flared, because, wherever the information about Harandi had been buried in the DCPD report, he'd missed it. The realization rankled. "Been in our country for about a year, I believe."

Shepherd laughed, but no one else joined in. "You're kidding. We haven't had diplomatic relations with Iran for what, nearly thirty years?"

"Before he came here he was the lead economist for President Rashid Akberi, making him the highest-ranking member of Tehran's political elite to relocate here in recent history." He stopped then as Harandi's name sparked another chord of memory, and this time Adam's irritation transferred to Hedgelin. Putting politics before an investigation was always a morass. "Who conducted the interview, Homeland Security? Do you think they can really set aside their agenda—pumping him for insights on Tehran's decision making—to focus on finding information for a murder investigation?"

Hedgelin's glare was furious. "The matter is off-limits. The man was one appointment in a day full of them, and DHS is satisfied with the answers he gave. So am I."

"Would you be as satisfied if you knew that his name was on the guest list to Reinbeck's party the night the justice was killed?"

Adam's question seemed to stop Hedgelin short. He gave a slow nod. "I thought not. You charged this team with following up on the intersections in this case and then made damn sure we wouldn't see an intersection, at least when it came to Harandi. That's not playing political ball, Cleve, it's effectively hamstringing your task force."

The assistant director leaned back in his chair, his expression impassive. But that telltale tick was jumping near his eye. After a long moment he said, "You can probably get some information regarding his invite from Reinbeck's widow."

"And perhaps even more from Harandi himself."

A single slant of watery light arrowed through the shade and dissected Hedgelin's desktop. It wavered there like a fretful butterfly before fading in the next moment. "I have nearly three hundred agents assigned to these murders." Hedgelin's voice sounded tired. "That's not counting the raft of DCPD, DHS, and USMS personnel involved in some capacity. The amount of intelligence coming in daily is staggering."

Adam nodded. He could sympathize with the sheer enormity of the task. But his empathy stopped when it came to being shut out of a vital part of the investigation they'd been charged with.

"Harandi is attached to the Mortara Center for International Studies at Georgetown University as a visiting scholar. Of course, our country is interested in cooperating with him to expand our understanding of President Akberi's administration. This is going to require a certain amount of finesse. If you've been following such things in the news, there's been a series of Iranian elites seeking asylum in foreign countries in protest of their government's regime." Hedgelin's smile looked forced. "Harandi is the highest ranking individual showing an interest in relocating to our country. But I'll arrange an appointment for you with him. I have no idea of his schedule, so you're going to have to head over to the university and wait for my call."

Chairs scraped as everyone got up in unison. Before he walked through the door, Adam threw a last look over his shoulder and saw Hedgelin rubbing his head as if in pain. Adam slipped into the hallway, closing the door quietly behind him. If Jaid was correct, the man had his eye on the top bureau job in the future.

If that was the case, he'd better get used to headaches.

———

The Mortara Center was located close to the Georgetown campus, a two-story cream-colored brick structure with dark green trim. Although there was nothing remarkable about its exterior, the inside was impressive indeed. The huge reception area was wood, gleaming acres of it as floors, paneling, and columns. A graceful matching stairway wound up to the second floor. It didn't much resemble the dusty buildings Jaid remembered attending classes in. But she hadn't spent her university years in such hallowed halls, either.

On the ride over Adam had tried to reach Mrs. Reinbeck, but in the end had to leave a message. Jaid would have preferred to have been armed with more information about the man they were about to meet, but Hedgelin had shown more cooperation than she'd expected in just arranging for them to speak with the professor.

The woman who met them just inside the hushed space was trim and blond, in her midtwenties, with a brisk friendly manner. She reminded Jaid of Kristin Temple a bit in manner, if not in looks. "I'm Carly French, assistant director of the center." She'd obviously been watching for them. Shepherd's and Jaid's shields were scrutinized carefully before French turned her attention to Adam's temporary ID.

Handing them back, the woman said, "Dr. Harandi's class just finished. If we hurry, he can fit you in between his adviser/advisee appointments, but his schedule is quite full." She turned, her heels clicking on the floor as she made her way swiftly across the polished expanse.

They followed her up the open stairway, down another hallway only slightly less lavish than the one downstairs, and around a corner. The door she stopped in front of was standing half-open. French knocked anyway.

"The visitors you've been expecting, Dr. Harandi." Her circumspection was no doubt for the benefit of the students moving through the halls.

"Please come in." The man seated inside the office rose and came out around the desk he was seated behind. While introductions were made and they were getting settled, Jaid measured the man silently. Saeed Harandi was swarthy faced with a stocky build, not much taller than she was. Although his thick mustache was flecked with gray, his hair was still dark. And his expression when he regarded them was pleasantly quizzical.

"I am happy to be of help to you if I can. But if this is about Mr. Patterson's unfortunate death, you should know that I spoke to agents from your Homeland Security once already."

"Yes, we're aware of that." Although, Jaid thought darkly, they'd yet to see a copy of that report. She wondered if they would. "I hope you don't mind the recap. We just have a few follow-up questions." And she hoped she was able to step carefully around the minefield of off-limit topics the assistant director had imparted when he'd called.

"But of course."

She flipped open a folder from the case file, pretended to consult some notes she didn't have. "I understand you were among the last to see Mr. Patterson alive."

"So I am told. But as I said in my earlier interview, our relationship was one of business. He didn't mention to me anything about when he was leaving or who he might be meeting."

"How long had you been in business with Patterson Capital?"

"Since before I came to this country. Two or three years." He smiled a little. "They do business in most of the countries of the world. I found Oliver to be extremely knowledgeable, brilliant with finances. I was happy to meet him in person once I came to this country."

"There are some who blamed him, and companies like his, when the financial crash happened a couple years ago," Jaid observed. "Were you one of the lucky ones who rode it out?"

His slight grimace was her answer. "Luck is in the eye of the beholder, is it not? I prefer to consider myself a survivor. With Oliver's help I hoped that my portfolio would fully recover quite soon. He built a solid company. I will be staying with the business, working with one of his associates, no doubt."

"We understand that you also knew Justice Byron Reinbeck," Shepherd put in. He sent the man a guileless smile. "His death occurred the week after Patterson's."

Harandi's expression grew somber. "I did not know him well, of course, but we had met several times, yes. I was to be a guest in his home the evening of his murder."

"Where had the two of you met?" Jaid sent a sidelong glance at Adam, who had been silent for the conversation. His attention on the man was intense. And from Harandi's occasional glances Adam's way, the Iranian was finding the scrutiny unnerving.

"I don't recall the first time our paths crossed." He gave a gesture with one well-manicured hand. "Perhaps at one of my lectures. I am a frequent guest speaker for many organizations. At any rate, we did meet on several occasions. I enjoyed speaking with him. He was a brilliant man. Your country will be the poorer without his wisdom and insight."

"Do you remember the last time you spoke to him?"

He leaned forward, flipped through the calendar on his desk. "Ah. That would have been nearly three weeks ago. We talked briefly at a function we both attended at the Kennedy Center."

"Did the two of you ever discuss Patterson Capital?"

The other man lifted a shoulder. "I do not think so. Our conversations tended more to international relations and the worldwide economy. Mr. Reinbeck was extremely well-read. It was always a pleasure to argue a viewpoint with him."

"Can you tell us where you were Monday evening around six o'clock?"

His eyes widened slightly. He'd recognize the reason behind the question. No doubt DHS had used more finesse. If they'd leveled the question at all.

"Yes, I was home, readying for the dinner party at the Reinbecks'. I was nearly about to walk out the door, in fact, when I saw the horrible news on the television."

"That must have been a terrible shock for you. Can anyone verify your whereabouts?"

"Does someone need to?" Harandi smoothed his mustache. "I do not spend time thinking of how to commit horrible crimes. But if I did, I can assure you I would plan not to be alone when the act occurred."

After several more minutes of questioning, Jaid rose. Disappointment filtered through her, but she quashed it brutally.

There was little more to discover here, especially given the firm parameters Hedgelin had dictated regarding the interview. "Thank you for your time, Dr. Harandi. I hope it will be all right for us to check back if we have more questions?"

"But of course." He rose and saw them to the door. "You can reach me here weekdays." His smile was brief. "Some evenings as well when I have a night class or a lecture, such as the one scheduled for this evening."

They walked silently back toward the stairway, stepping aside for the occasional small group of students. "He had a relationship with both victims." Shepherd spoke first, but not before flashing a second look at a leggy coed giving him the eye. "But nothing popped in there for me. Killing Patterson after taking a financial bath . . . maybe." They headed down the steps. "But what possible motivation would he have for killing the justice? From all accounts they were friendly. I don't see him appearing on the Reinbeck guest list otherwise."

"Hard to say at this point. But, yeah, it didn't yield anything new." What it had elicited, Jaid thought, was only more loose threads that didn't link to anything else in particular. "I feel better for having talked to him myself, though." They were heading down the wide, ornate downstairs hallway again. Behind a plate glass door she saw the young woman who had shown them upstairs. Carly French.

She swerved in that direction, not waiting to see if the two men would follow. Pushing open the door, she gave the young woman a friendly smile. "Dr. Harandi said I could get a copy of his schedule in here."

"Yes, of course." The blonde turned to her computer and typed rapidly. A moment later, the printer in the corner of the room began to whir. She retrieved the printout and then brought it back to Jaid.

"He mentioned that he has night classes some evenings. That must get to be a long day. For the professors and the students."

"Usually, if the professors are teaching more than one night class a week, they won't have as many day classes, and they can adjust their hours here accordingly. But I think . . ." The girl slipped a strand of hair behind her ear as she leaned over to look at the sheet she'd just handed Jaid. "Yes, he only has one this semester. It meets once a week on Tuesdays. But he also gives lectures occasionally that are open to the public. He has one tonight at seven."

Jaid held up the sheet. "Thanks for this," she said, and rejoined the two men at the front door.

"His schedule." She handed it to Adam, who scanned it before passing it to Shepherd. "Night class on Tuesdays, but that doesn't mean much since neither of the murders happened on those days." They went outside then, and the temperature had her huddling deeper into her coat.

"So he had means and motive for Patterson's death, despite assurances of his consistent faith in the man's financial acumen." Adam ducked his dark head against the bite in the air. The sun had given up its feeble attempts, slinking sullenly off to hide behind the gunmetal clouds. "We need to look harder for a connection to Byron. What would Harandi have to gain with his death?"

"You guys want to wait here? I'll go get the vehicle."

Seeing the way Adam's look sharpened, Jaid made a point of saying carelessly, "We can walk to it together. Saves time." She reached into her pockets to draw on a pair of gloves, shifting her computer bag from one hand to the other. Adam solved the problem by taking the bag from her as they followed Shepherd several blocks toward the parking garage.

"Thanks." But when she would have taken it back from him, he gave her a look that had her subsiding. His manner was sometimes abrupt, but that quality was unexpectedly tempered with an old-fashioned gallantry that had always filled her with warmth. With any other man she'd have made a caustic comment and insisted on carrying her own bag. It was a small thing, perhaps, but the bureau was a macho organization. Female agents were still in the minority, and there was an underlying need to prove herself the equal of any of her peers.

But the man walking silently alongside her could always shred logic and reason with a single look.

She didn't allow herself to wonder just how far he ought to be walking on his leg. The nerve damage he'd suffered on it at LeCroix's hands had been extensive. She'd been in the Louisiana CCU. She'd heard the doctor's dire predictions that they wouldn't be able to save his leg at all. He'd beaten the odds then, too.

A chill skittered down her spine that had nothing to do with the temperature. Odds were a simple matter of probability. And sooner or later, fate always seemed to find a way to even the score.

Chapter 10

"Okay, here are some interesting cases." At the sound of Shepherd's voice, Adam and Jaid looked up from the contents of the case file spread across the table. "Hope my notes makes sense. That girl can really talk fast."

They were back at FBI headquarters, in a frigid conference room without windows. And, apparently, without heat. Jaid hadn't taken off her coat. She was tempted to pull her gloves back on but sufficed by warming her hands in her pockets occasionally. Their first order of business had been to pore over the Supreme Court's scheduled docket for the year. Only to discover that none of them had any idea what the case names meant. It had seemed a whole lot simpler to call one of Reinbeck's clerks for an explanation.

Shepherd rounded the table to stand between Jaid's and Adam's chairs, placing the sheaf of papers on the table in front of them. "Here." He flipped through a couple pages and stabbed his index finger at a host of scribbling. Jaid squinted. "You missed your calling," she said, finally. "Should have been a doctor with that handwriting."

"On January nineteenth the court is scheduled to hear oral arguments for *Kulder vs. Iowa*. The question before the court is the legality of a state law prohibiting people with gun permits from carrying personal firearms in state buildings or meetings."

"Wonder where Senator Newell stands on gun rights," Jaid murmured. "Not hard to guess."

"It's also not hard to check." Adam turned his head to better read the sheet. "What else?"

Shepherd riffled through a couple more pages before stopping. "I marked all the cases that are hot-button items with conservatives. One challenges a Nebraska law that strictly limits abortion. Another scheduled for April fourth will decide if hate-crime laws can be applied to a radical church that disrupts gay people's funerals." He stopped, looked at Adam. "I'm assuming from our talk with Senator Newell that Justice Reinbeck would be seen as potentially coming down on the wrong side of all those issues."

"He was a brilliant jurist, from everyone's accounts. So in my estimation he'd apply the law fairly. But, yes, definitely he and Newell would be at opposite ends of the spectrum in their interpretation of law and the constitution."

"The balance on the court was already split nearly down the middle from the reading I've done on it." A chill shook her, and she took the moment to wonder if the agency had forgotten to pay their utility bill or if it was just their bad luck to find the one room in the place without a working heat duct. "Judge Lexton is a centrist. His vote can't easily be predicted. With Reinbeck gone, I'd expect the president to move quickly for a replacement."

"And confirmation hearings often turn into litmus tests for potential candidates. But you're right." Adam leaned back in his chair and considered. "Someone with a right-wing agenda might consider the removal of Reinbeck as a way to tip the court's balance. But it's a pretty radical way to go about it. And how does that tie into Patterson's death? Is there anything on the docket regarding banking laws or finances?"

"There's something here." Shepherd turned back to the first page. "*Paxton vs. the United States* challenges the right of the government to freeze financial assets of countries indefinitely while protecting the blocked monies from being used to pay out damages awarded to U.S. citizens against those foreign governments."

"Not a clear link to Patterson," Jaid said doubtfully.

"None of them is a smoking gun," Shepherd mused. His suit was charcoal today, with a discreet white pinstripe that matched his snowy white shirt. Unlike her, he seemed impervious to the temperature in the room. "But let's look at the names and backgrounds on the threat list again. I wouldn't be surprised to find more than a few conservative thinkers on it who thought nothing of writing a threatening letter to a judge who embodied everything they think is wrong with the country."

She was about to point out that another team—probably several—had been charged with that very task with nothing to show for it. But Adam nodded and said, "Good idea. It's retracing steps, yes, but that's often necessary when new information comes to light."

Knowing when she was outnumbered, Jaid reached for the case file to find the appropriate pages. "Okay. I'm just hoping they don't find us still hunched over this table tomorrow morning, frozen in place."

His gaze glinting with amusement, Adam said, "That would give a whole new meaning to freezing your assets."

She slapped a hand to her heart, only half feigning shock. "A joke from Adam Raiker? Will wonders never cease?"

"I joke," he said, in affronted tones. When Jaid and Shepherd exchanged a knowing smile, he lifted a shoulder. "Although it's obviously wasted on the two of you. Let's get to work. See if you're better at cross-referencing case intersections than you are at fielding what I can assure you is a well-honed sense of humor."

———

Jaid lifted a hand in response to Shepherd's wave as he pulled out of his spot in the parking garage. Adam was a little behind her, talking on his cell. With a mental shrug she slipped into her car and started it, wondering how long it was going to take for the heater to warm up. And whether she'd thaw by the time she got home this evening.

A moment later Adam was approaching her door. She buzzed the window down.

"That was Mary Jo Reinbeck," he said without preamble. "Byron's funeral is set for a week from Friday."

"So they released the body?"

"Not yet, but they're promising to sometime next week. By setting the service for the end of the week, she's hoping to give them plenty of time to carry through."

She waited, certain there was more. "Did you ask her about Harandi?"

He nodded. "That's where it got interesting. He told us that he hadn't spoken to Byron for about three weeks. But she said a week before his death she was supposed to meet her husband for dinner. Was running late. When she arrived, Byron told her he'd seen Harandi at the restaurant and passed the time talking to him for nearly half an hour."

Jaid stared at him. "Why would he lie?"

"Obviously, because he thought he could get away with it. He didn't see Jo at the restaurant. Maybe he figured Byron wouldn't have mentioned it to her. But he did." There was a measure of excitement showing on his features. A reflection of it revved in her veins. "He also told her how uncomfortable the man made him, insisting on returning to a topic that was too close to a case on the docket for Byron's taste. The legality of freezing financial assets of foreign governments."

"We need to talk to him again," she said with certainty. And parameters be damned this time. While she'd been staying within the confines Hedgelin had dictated, the Iranian was lying through his teeth.

"My thoughts exactly. His lecture starts in"—Adam consulted his watch—"about an hour and a half. We shouldn't have any trouble catching him before it starts."

As it turned out, they did see the man. Without ever leaving their cars.

Across the crowded street from the Mortara Center, Jaid saw a figure hurry out of the building to slip into a cab waiting at the curb. In the nearly constant glow of headlights from the lined-up traffic it was easy to make out Harandi's features.

Well, damn. Jaid smacked the steering wheel in disgust. Where the heck was the man going? He'd said he had a lecture tonight.

She was unsurprised when her cell rang then. Fumbling in her purse for it, she eased around the corner to keep the slow-moving cab in sight. The traffic would keep it tangled up if it stayed in the downtown area.

"I'm going to follow him," she said by way of greeting. "I'd like to know who or what is so important that he canceled his plans for the night."

"He could have gotten sick, I suppose." The ruined rumble of Adam's voice filled her ear. "But I agree. Let's stay with him. If you lose the cab, call me back and I'll redirect you."

"I perfected the art of a tail when I was a rookie," she snapped. But she was talking to herself. He'd already hung up. With a fuming glance at the phone, she disconnected. Noticing the time on the screen, she dialed a familiar number as she nosed the car through the clogged street.

"Hello, Mother." Jaid began to talk fast once Patricia's cultured tones came on the line. "I'm going to be late again."

There was silence, rife with disapproval. "This is beginning to be a habit, Jaidlyn."

"It's my job," she returned, as evenly as she could. "You know what it's like when I'm working a case. If you have plans, let me know, and I'll call Stacy to come over." Stacy Crooks was the teenager next door, a fifteen-year-old with an easygoing manner and a sense of responsibility beyond her years. "Royce loves spending time with her."

There was an audible sniff. "That's just a waste of money when I'm right here. I'll sleep in the spare room. Again."

A knot began to rap at the base of her skull. "I appreciate it. May I talk to Royce?"

The cab turned the corner. She followed Adam as he turned after it. The sidewalks were teaming with people. This close to the Potomac there was an endless supply of restaurants and bars that catered to crowds of all ages. She easily kept both the cab and Adam's vehicle in sight.

"Hi, Mom."

As usual, the sound of Royce's voice could ease other tensions, even those caused by her mother. "Hey, Champ. I just wanted to call and talk to you because I might not make it home before you go to bed tonight."

"Because you got a case?"

"I *have* one," she corrected. "Right."

"Michael at school said you were probably working on a murder. He said someone got shot, and TV showed their guts splattered all over . . ."

"Michael has a vivid imagination." It was always best to quell such conversations before they could start. "Why don't you tell me two good things that happened at school today?"

It was familiar territory. When she was home, they'd end the evening with her sitting on the side of his bed, listening to his favorite parts of the day. Today, it seemed, had been chock-full of all sorts of excitement, most of it surrounding the attention he'd garnered by appearing in class with a cast on his arm. From the sound of her son's rapid-fire litany of events, his classmates had been appropriately awed by his exploits and their results.

"And then that creepy Angelica Herman wrote on my cast with a pink glittery marker. Pink, mom. Do you know how stupid that looked? But Michael and Andrew fixed it later by writing over it with a black one, so it's sorta okay." He wound down for a moment before asking, "Are you with that guy with the eye patch again?"

"Mr. Raiker?" Another car switched lanes, nearly cutting her off. Resisting the impulse to make a juvenile gesture when she passed the driver, she accelerated to keep Adam in her sights. "Sort of. We're going to the same place."

"I told everyone I saw this sorta pirate guy at the hospital, but that he walked with a cane and not a wooden leg and we rode in his really cool car. But no one believed me, not even Michael. They said pirates don't drive cars." His tone was scoffing. "Like they think they still sail ships or something."

She grinned at her son's nonsense. Although she'd mentally used the same description, she was sure Adam's self-proclaimed humor would be absent if he heard it.

"So I was thinking, maybe you could take a picture of him on your phone, and then I could show people at school."

"Sorry, buddy. Mr. Raiker is not a topic for show-and-tell." She cut the imminent wheedling short. "Final answer. Tell you what though, if I have to work late tomorrow night, I'll have Stacy come over for a few hours."

"Cool! She hasn't seen my cast yet."

They were entering the Palisades neighborhood, which paralleled the Potomac. Lights glinted off the water. The street was lined with apartments, town houses, and single-family brick homes. She slowed as the cab ahead stopped. After a minute Harandi exited and hurried up the steps of one of the darkened brick homes. "Okay, Champ, I have to go. Don't give Grandmother any grief about bedtime, okay?"

"Okay. Love you, Mom."

The words always made her heart go tight in a combination of guilt and love. "I love you, too, sweetie."

She cruised past the Iranian man's house and saw Adam shoehorn his BMW into an open parking space on the street. Her phone rang again. "Maybe he was sick." She glanced at the man she was talking to as she drove slowly past his car. "If so, we need to talk to him right away, before he turns in for the night." The evening had turned a little anticlimactic. She'd expected to see Harandi meet with someone. Hopefully, someone with a link to the case. But that would have been too easy. And so far this case had been anything but.

"It's early yet. Why don't you park and join me back here."

That feat was easier said than done. It took Jaid a full fifteen minutes to find a spot. And that much again to make her way back to the darkened vehicle where Adam waited. Just to prove that Mother Nature was a bitch, the sky started spitting tiny frigid needle pricks of ice. When she finally slid into the cushy leather seat of his car, she was thoroughly regretting wearing her hair back that day.

Without asking he leaned forward and turned up the heater. She clasped her gloved hands over her ears. "How is it possible that the temperature has dropped forty degrees in just a few short days?"

"November in DC." His voice was wry. "Give it a few days, though. The weather is likely to change again." She turned in her seat to peer at the house three doors down from where they were parked. A couple lights blazing. A good sign. Facing Adam again she said, "Are you ready?"

He hesitated. "It occurs to me that if he's meeting someone, they may come to his home. Or that he stopped here before heading somewhere else. We can always talk to him tomorrow."

Frowning, she lowered her hands, pulled the gloves off one finger at a time. "Or we can talk to him now and then see what he does."

"We lose nothing by waiting."

"My least favorite word," she muttered.

A note of humor threaded his voice. "Yes, I remember. I don't expect you to stay here all night. Go home. Be with your son."

"All night? You're staking out Harandi's house? Why?"

His shrug was negligible in the darkness. "Call it a

hunch. Most likely he's going to snap those lights off in the next few minutes and go to bed with a bad case of the stomach flu. I'll just hang out here to make sure he stays tucked in for the evening."

Torn, she stared at him. There was little less appealing than spending the long hours of the evening in a dark car with Adam Raiker. The shadows in the vehicle could too quickly begin to feel intimate, eliciting memories of other times. Other nights.

Shaken, she looked out the window. No, she definitely didn't want to go down that road. "I don't think it's necessary."

"I agree. It may well turn out to be a miserable waste of time, and there's no reason for both of us to lose sleep." When she didn't move, his voice hardened. "You're covered, Jaid. You know what I'm doing and why. You can alert Hedgelin and, having done your duty, go home and enjoy what's left of your evening."

Insulted she said, "This isn't about Hedgelin." With a start she realized that since they started out tonight, she hadn't once considered the man or his order to keep him informed of all things regarding Adam. "We can accomplish the same thing by talking to Harandi now."

"Not quite." His tone was getting a little testy. She was reminded that Adam Raiker wasn't used to people questioning his orders. It was unfortunate for him that she had no qualms about doing just that. "If he does have something planned, he may cancel it because of our visit. Patience pays off in the long run."

And that, too, was a familiar line from him. Jaid hadn't liked it any better all those years ago. When she took a moment to consider his logic, it was even more annoying to discover it made sense. "You know one of your most irritating habits is always being right."

His teeth flashed in the darkness. "And one of yours is your tendency to rush in too fast without fully considering the consequences."

She stilled. That so neatly summed up what had happened with them. She'd fallen, hard and fast, spilling her emotions for a man who kept a tight guard on his own. It had been devastating to discover that her judgment had been so flawed. "Yes," she said shakily as she twisted around to take another look at Harandi's house. The lights still glowed. "I learned quickly enough what you thought of that trait."

He was silent for a moment. Then, "Jaid." The gravelly tone lit sparks in her veins that she wished she could will away. "I found it engaging. Like everything about you. Your passion for your work reminded me of the reasons I had for joining the bureau. You were quick and stubborn, and had a thirst for knowledge that made conversations with you exhilarating."

She faced forward in the seat again. Couldn't quite bring herself to turn toward him. "I was green as grass."

He didn't deny it. "Which is why I never should have touched you. The age difference—"

That argument had incensed her then. Made no more sense now. "Was eight years. Hardly enough for you to suspect I had a daddy complex."

"God, I hope not," he said feelingly. "I'm not that old."

"Exactly."

"I was talking world experience rather than years at any rate." A pair of approaching headlights sliced through the night, throwing his face into sharp relief. His expression was brooding. "But it cut deeply, knowing I hurt you. The last thing I wanted was for you to feel . . . rejected again."

Again. She froze. Because, of course, he knew about her father. There was nothing she'd held back from Adam during their time together. Not even the details of her father's abandonment.

He'd left when she was eleven. No warning. No good-byes. Her mother had been dry-eyed and short-tempered in the face of Jaid's confusion. Her heartache. And as the years stretched, she'd almost lost hope of ever seeing him again. Hearing from him.

But nothing in her yearning daydreams had prepared for her for the reality of their eventual meeting.

"Did you ever . . ." Adam's probe was as delicate as a surgeon's cut. Left the same pain in its aftermath.

"He's dead."

There was a moment of shocked silence. She didn't know which of them was more surprised when he reached out a hand. Cupped her jaw. "I'm sorry."

She willed away the tears that threatened, and stared at him, the emotions churning and crashing inside her. "I wish he didn't matter anymore. And I wish *you* didn't matter."

The result of her words was unexpected. Adam's fingers on her jaw tightened reflexively. And then his mouth covered hers with a completeness that rocked her.

His taste was achingly familiar. It summoned a response that she couldn't have withheld if she tried. She didn't want to. But there was something different in the kiss, too. If her response was fueled by years of longing, his matched it. Surpassed it.

She turned more fully toward him, slipped an arm around his neck. He pulled her closer. And the interior of the car went steamy.

He'd always had a way of kissing her that shattered logic. Left her senses reeling.

His lips were demanding and coaxing by turn. Thrilling at one moment. Enticing at the next. She couldn't say which she responded to. But her mouth opened under his. His tongue swept in, and sensation swamped her.

Her hand shifted, so she could thread her fingers through his thick dark hair. She used to tease him that it was silky as a girl's and would laugh at the mock scowl she'd get in response. But humor was far from her mind right now. Bittersweet memories warred with the present, and a hint of desperation flickered. Knowing this wouldn't last, couldn't, just made the hunger sharper.

Her tongue mated with his, their breathing tangled until a dark fist of need clenched in her belly. She tore her mouth away and scored his bottom lip with her teeth. Felt him jerk against her, the arm around her back tightening. And the evidence of his response was heady.

His lips cruised to her jaw. Her throat. Her head lolled, and the blood in her veins went molten.

There was danger in the interlude. A danger that desire so long denied would return with the raging fire she used to feel. A fire that had once driven her to the heights of ecstasy. And when denied, plunged her to the pit of despair.

The memory had caution rearing. With difficulty she arched away from Adam. Opened her eyes. Struggled to focus. When she did, she caught peripheral movement across the street. It took a moment for comprehension to filter in. Excitement quickly followed.

"Adam. Look."

The urgency in her voice had him turning. He stared out the window in silence for a moment. "Well, well. Dr. Harandi appears to be in a hurry."

A taxi had rolled to a stop before the apartment. The professor was hurrying down the walk with two large suitcases in his hands. A pile of more bags waited on the steps, spotlighted by the security light. While they watched, a cab-driver got out, reached for the suitcases, and carried them to the back of the vehicle while Harandi retrieved more luggage. It took several minutes for all of it to be stored in the taxi's trunk and backseat. Adam had already started the car when Harandi got in the front of the cab. Adam let it pull away from the curb and get to the corner. Timing the traffic shrewdly, he made a U-turn and followed.

"He didn't mention an upcoming trip, but I'm guessing the good professor has an international flight in mind," Jaid said. Adrenaline was firing through her veins. She reached for her cell. Dialed a familiar number. "Guilty conscience, you think?"

"It would appear so. I'm still trying to figure out what his motivation for the killings would be." He drove with expertise, keeping a couple cars between them and the cab.

"Hopefully, we're going to get the chance to ask him. Assistant Director Hedgelin," she broke off the conversation when the other man's voice came on the line. "We've got a development regarding Dr. Harandi." She filled him in on the details as they turned off MacArthur Boulevard onto Arizona.

"And you think he's headed toward an airport?" The assistant director's words were sharp with interest.

"With all that baggage it seems a natural assumption."

"All right. Maintain the tail. Is Shepherd with you?"

At the question, she sent a sidelong look at the silent man beside her. "No. Adam is."

The long silence that stretched then had her wondering at the other man's thoughts. Finally, he said, "I need to make some phone calls. I don't have to tell you how delicate a situation this is. Take no action until I get back to you." He disconnected.

"Did he order you to hang back and lay low?"

"Pretty much." Traffic was moving more easily now after making a couple turns along the way. "He said he needed to make some phone calls."

"To DHS most likely. They seem to be calling the shots as far as Harandi is concerned." Conversation lagged for a time then. They followed the car onto George Washington Memorial Parkway. She spent the intervening time using her phone to check flights that might connect through to Iran from Ronald Reagan Washington National Airport and Dulles, although from the route Harandi was taking, National appeared to be his destination. It was another ten minutes before he spoke again. "Who watches your son when you're working?"

"My mother." She was too engrossed in what she was doing to feel the usual flare of caution when her son's name was brought up. "I can't say she's changed over the years, but Royce has mellowed her edges a bit. I still spend a lot of time running interference. Literally. She's always had interesting ideas on child rearing." She fell silent again for several minutes while she read the search results on her phone. "National has the first flight out tonight with a connection to Iran. Eleven fifty-nine P.M. Here's betting the good professor is getting a one-way ticket."

"A safe bet," he murmured.

Traffic to Reagan National was always impossibly congested. They drove until they could see its lights winking in the distance. Jaid looked at her phone, trepidation rearing. She had no idea how long the assistant director would take before getting back to her. If she hadn't heard from him by the time they hit the airport, she was going to keep the professor in her sights. But without a go-ahead from her superior, she didn't dare do more than that.

Adam took the turn to the airport. The heavy rumble of a jet was heard overhead, sounding frighteningly close. She hated using this airport herself. Its approach followed the Potomac, and she always felt like they were going to end up in the river when they landed. But she wasn't an easy flier in any circumstances. Luckily, she wasn't called on to do it often.

"I'm going to let you out several car lengths behind Harandi's taxi." Adam's gravelly voice split the darkness. "You can follow him inside while I look for short-term parking."

"All right. You can call when you get in, and I'll direct you to our location."

"I'll find you. I know the terminal, so it shouldn't prove too difficult."

Her phone rang then. Hedgelin. She identified the number on the screen with relief. After confirming their location, she remained mostly silent while her boss issued terse orders. When he seemed to wind down, she said, "Yes, I understand." The man's sign-off, she reflected as he ended the call, was as abrupt as Adam's.

"He's got agents dispatched. They'll be arriving soon. Airport security has been alerted, but they're instructed to stay back unless assistance is needed. One of them will be inside the terminal doors." Maintaining discretion, she hoped. She didn't want to take the chance of spooking the professor even further.

The cabdriver several cars ahead was unloading Harandi's bags while the man commandeered a luggage cart. Adrenaline pumped through Jaid's veins. When the professor rolled the cart through the double sliding doors, she sent Adam a quick grin. "At the risk of sounding like an almost eight-year-old boy, this is going to be sweet." She didn't see Adam's head swivel at her words. Jaid was already slamming the door and heading down the sidewalk after the elusive Dr. Harandi.

The security guard's name was Olsen. Midfifties and balding, with eyes that looked too kind for a man in his profession. He assured her there were a dozen other officers on the alert; all of whom were stationed nearby. Jaid repeated the instructions Hedgelin had given her, and he nodded. He'd received the same.

There were more passengers than Jaid would have imagined threading through the confined maze to approach the ticket counter. She hung back, stepping behind a large column to shield her from Harandi's view. Once he got to the counter, he took an inordinate amount of time buying his ticket and arguing with the attendant about the fee for shipping his extra luggage. It wasn't until he finished and headed toward the security checkpoint that Jaid made her move.

She didn't attempt to stay out of his line of vision. Saw the second he recognized her. His expression was shocked. He threw a quick glance around, as if checking for possible exits. Then visibly calming himself, he donned a politely quizzical look as she approached. "Agent Marlowe. I did not expect to see you here."

"I'll bet not." She slowed to a stop beside him. Sent him a cheerful smile. "I thought of a few more questions."

"This is a most inconvenient time." He smoothed his mustache, a nervous habit she recalled from that afternoon. "I received a phone call from my home country today. Most upsetting. My mother is ill. Quite ill. I must fly home at once."

"The sick-mother excuse carries a lot more weight when she isn't already dead." The information DHS had shared about the man was scanty, but his family history had been included. "I'm going to need you to come with me."

He lurched around her, the movement sudden. Because she was expecting it, she was able to grab him easily. There was the sound of running footsteps. By the time Jaid looked up to see that the other agents had arrived, she already had the man on the floor, his arms secured behind his back.

"We'll take over from here." The man flashed a DHS badge. Reluctantly Jaid got up, allowed two agents to step forward and flank the man. "Nice job."

But as they walked Harandi away, the only emotion she was feeling was frustration. Seeing Adam in the distance, she began to walk toward him. There was nothing worse than making a case and having another agency step in to take it over. And she had a feeling that getting answers regarding the professor's flight attempt was going to be an exercise in futility.

———————

This would be the easiest job yet. The hooded man waited in the bedroom for his prey. He'd planned on the closet, but there was a large floor-to-ceiling cupboard that held an assortment of vestments. It was a better hiding place. The door could be left open a crack, giving him a good visual of the room.

And as always the anticipation was building to a fever pitch. He flexed the piano wire once, his gloved hands lightly grasping the short dowel on either end. This method always gave him the biggest rush. Up close. Silent. And it didn't get more personal. A death match pitting two adversaries.

But this was a battle the other man couldn't win.

The light in the room turned on as his quarry entered. The hooded man waited several minutes for the evening rituals to be completed. And then, when his prey turned to rummage in the closet for a robe, he struck.

Four quick steps across the room. Quiet, but the other man heard. Started to turn. Too late. The garrote was already around his neck. Stretched tight.

It was almost impossible to kill with a piano-wire garrote without slicing into the neck, causing blood to rush from the jugular. And that, too, was particularly satisfying.

He moved in a death dance with his prey as the other man fought and struggled for survival, fingers clutching uselessly at the wire cutting into his throat. He eased the wire a fraction while he whispered, "See you in hell, padre."

Then he went for the kill.

Chapter 11

The call came directly from Hedgelin while Adam was on the way into the city that morning. Adam slowly tucked the phone away afterward, shock warring with anger. He examined the news from every angle.

But he couldn't imagine how Cardinal Cote tied into the other two deaths.

The assistant director's "request" had been stiffly made. The Evidence Response Team Unit was on the scene. He wanted Adam to take a look, as well.

On the surface the request was surprising. He slowed as traffic started backing up the closer he got to the city. Hedgelin had made no bones about wanting Adam off this case. But he possessed no false modesty. His reputation, and that of the agency he'd built, was internationally acclaimed for a reason. And studying the crime scene first-hand would provide integral details for the profile.

Of course, he thought grimly, as he inched the car forward only to stop again, there was the possibility that Hedgelin wanted to see Adam fail dismally in every aspect of the case he was involved in. At any rate, he hadn't hoped to see the crime scene until well after the fact or, perhaps, only in pictures. This was an opportunity he didn't want to miss.

He glanced over to the next lane and saw a woman shouting into her cell phone as she waited. Rage, he thought, was one of the biggest dangers on the road. And in life.

His mind turned to Jerry then, and something twisted in his belly. Although Adam had been the only witness to the priest and cardinal's yelling match the other night, the animosity that existed between the two men had to be more widely known. Someone would be talking to Jerry, and soon. For the sake of their friendship, Adam wanted to be there for the interview.

Their relationship meant navigating that aspect of the investigation would be a minefield.

The rest of the trip seemed excruciatingly slow. He used the time to consider the case. Figure what this latest murder meant and how it was related. It was a far better use of time than the sleepless hours he'd spent last night.

Running the chronology backward and forward in his head in order to pinpoint the timeline for Jaid's son's birth.

———

The cardinal had lived several blocks away from St. Mark's Cathedral, with which, Adam learned, the man was affiliated. According to his secretary, Denise Quincy, who had found Cote, he had said one of the masses every Sunday. Adam only spoke to her briefly. The agent questioning her was having a difficult time getting answers between the woman's copious sobs.

Security was tight. Adam showed identification at both the outer and inner perimeters before being allowed inside the home. There were, he noted with approval, boxes of gloves, shoe covers, and sterile Tyvek suits just inside the door. Identifying himself yet again to the agent stationed there, Adam was finally allowed to don the protective covering and directed to the cardinal's quarters.

The brownstone that had housed the man was surprisingly lavish. Adam had a pretty good idea what real estate went for in this part of the city. Pretty costly for someone who'd taken a vow of poverty. Although according to recent news stories, the Catholic Church had extensive real estate in this country.

He found the bedroom located on the second floor and waited for yet another agent to once again verify his identity. Then Adam took one step inside the doorway and halted. Just to take it in.

The room was good-sized but looked smaller with all the people working in it. He counted six ERTU techs engaged in their work. None of them looked up when he finally entered.

The cardinal's body hadn't yet been removed. He looked vulnerable in his pajamas, stripped of the dignity and bearing that Adam had noted when he met the man. Death was the great equalizer. The expected note card was lying next to the cardinal. The red letters seemed to scream up from it.

Lust.

Oh, shit. Adam took a deep breath, already calculating the firestorm those four letters would summon. Given the recent scandal the Catholic Church had been hit with regarding pedophile priests, the mere breath of the accusation would be enough to cause some fingers to start pointing. He didn't envy Hedgelin the job of keeping this quiet.

Jerry's angry words to the cardinal blazed across his mind then. *And you of all people are in no position to preach to me about vices. At least I've never tried to hide mine behind the shield of the church.* Trepidation trickled down Adam's spine. This was going to get complicated.

He waited until the tech photographing the body was finished before moving carefully to stand beside it. "May I?"

The tech looked at the agent in the doorway. Shrugged and stepped aside. With a decided lack of grace, Adam knelt on one knee for a better visual. Garroted, he observed immediately. Not with an article of clothing. The wound showed him that. Only one thing would inflict that sort of damage. Piano wire was the tool of choice for assassins using this method.

Rigor and lividity had set in on the body. Adam reached out, tested the man's chest, arm, and then his leg. Large muscle masses were the last to be affected by rigor mortis. It had set into the victim's arms but not completely in his torso and legs.

"Medical examiner hasn't been here yet," the tech standing nearest to him offered. "But from the looks of the body, I'd guess he was killed sometime after midnight."

Adam checked his watch as he rose. "And probably before four A.M." He scanned the area. There were few hiding places to choose from. It was possible the offender had hidden behind the door, but Adam was guessing he chose a place with greater seclusion. That left the closet or the large cupboard in the corner of the room.

Being careful to skirt the areas techs were working in, he made his way over to the cupboard. Pulled it open. No shelves, just the clothing the cardinal would wear in conjunction with his duties. He crossed to the closet, where the door still stood ajar, a velour robe lying on the floor outside it. Looking inside he saw more shoes than he would have supposed a man of the cloth would require. But what he didn't see, though he lowered himself to one knee again to examine the area carefully, was any sign left by a man spending hours in wait.

Adam used the cane to help himself rise again, stifling a wince when his damaged thigh screamed in response. Sending another considering gaze to the cupboard across the room, he had a good indication of where the killer had hidden until he made his move. Crack the door open, wait for the cardinal's back to be turned, four or five steps to reach the man.

A garrote required an attack from behind. Far more difficult and unwieldy to try for a frontal assault, which springing from the closet would have required.

Harandi had the best alibi possible. He'd been in FBI

custody last night. Of course, there was a high probability that this was the work of a professional. If someone had hired the hits, alibis meant nothing.

Adam was mentally updating his profile as his gaze returned to the body. Because hired or not, this looked personal.

Very personal indeed.

————

Denise Quincy didn't look to have calmed much in the duration but Bill Fleur, the agent who'd been questioning her, had gotten some information. Adam waited while the man updated Assistant Director Hedgelin, who was absorbing the news with a grim expression on his face.

That expression didn't ease appreciably when he saw Adam. "You've seen him?"

Adam nodded. "What's the security like?"

Fleur glanced over. "Tight. Decent-model system, touchpad entry. Requires a code, which is changed monthly. And there was no sign of forced entry."

"And who had access to that information?" Hedgelin asked tersely.

Consulting his notes, Fleur said, "Just Ms. Quincy and the housekeeper, a woman by the name of Maria Sanchez. She's been with the cardinal for fifteen years. Ms. Quincy for five. There was a cook, but either Quincy or Sanchez always let her in and locked up after her."

"Where is Sanchez now?" Adam asked the still-teary woman.

"She's only here Mondays, Wednesdays, and Fridays," Quincy said brokenly as she mopped ineffectually at the tears streaming down her freckled face. "The only reason I was going to work today is because I was sick a couple days this week and got behind. Maria probably hasn't even heard yet." The words brought on a renewed bout of weeping.

Correctly interpreting the look Hedgelin leveled at him, Adam nodded. "We'll go over there." He waited for Fleur to write down the address, and armed with that information, he turned to wend his way through the throng to find Jaid and Shepherd.

He found them on the sidewalk out front conducting interviews with some neighbors and waited impatiently for them to finish. Today the sun shone brightly overhead, and the temperatures were edging their way up again. Even so, Jaid wore her hair down, as if in memory of yesterday's chill.

He'd always preferred it that way. Framing that lovely face, following the delicate jawline. Her features had haunted his dreams for much too long. A reminder that no one, not even he, could maintain ironclad control over his emotions.

Recognition of that fact eight years ago had scared the hell out of him in a way that facing down the most vicious criminal couldn't. She'd been his greatest weakness. And he was reluctantly accepting that cutting her out of his life hadn't erased the hold she had on him.

———

Only a handful of miles separated the Columbia Heights neighborhood inhabited by Maria Sanchez from the cardinal's, but they were otherwise light-years apart. The houses wedged between large ramshackle apartment buildings were small, the yards all but nonexistent. Groups of youths huddled on street corners, talking and laughing loudly. Children who looked much too young to be out without adult supervision played in the streets, dodging cars with an ease that spoke of experience.

Sanchez's house was a small white clapboard without a garage. Unlike most of its neighbors, it had a fresh coat of paint and a roof in a good state of repair. The grass that managed to grow in a halfhearted fashion was neatly cut. Someone maintained the place well. Jaid wondered if it was Sanchez herself or another family member.

Shepherd found a place to park behind a decrepit Chevy truck that looked one step away from the salvage yard. They got out of the car and approached the house. "Any background on her family?" Adam's words seemed to echo Jaid's thoughts as they walked up the cracked sidewalk to the small cement stoop.

"The neighbor I spoke to at the cardinal's earlier knows her slightly, because they attend the same church. She only said that Sanchez was a widow."

"Guess we'll find out." Shepherd walked up the two steps and knocked on the door. The porch was too narrow for Jaid and Adam to join him, so they remained below. Moments later the door was opened by a short dark-haired woman. She peered past Shepherd to Jaid and Adam, and her expression became guarded.

"Good morning. Mrs. Maria Sanchez?" At her slow nod Shepherd showed her his ID. "Special Agent Shepherd, FBI. My colleagues, Special Agent Marlowe and Mr. Raiker, special consultant with the bureau. May we come in?"

After a brief hesitation she unlocked the outer door, and they all filed inside.

"I do not understand." Her hands were clasped tightly; her face held a worried expression. "What do you want with me?"

"I'm afraid we have some shocking news, Mrs. Sanchez," Jaid put in. "Cardinal Cote was found dead this morning."

She staggered a bit, like she'd taken a punch. "The cardinal. Madre de Dios, what happened? Just yesterday he was fine. Was it his heart?"

"Did he have a history of a heart condition?" If so, this was the first Jaid had heard about it. But she hadn't had an opportunity to gather much information before heading over here.

"Not recently. But seven or eight years ago. He had those . . . I do not know the name. They widen the plugged arteries to the heart."

"He had stents put in?"

She nodded and ducked her head, reaction setting in. "Why don't you sit down, Mrs. Sanchez," Adam suggested quietly. He handed her a handkerchief, which she accepted gratefully as she sank onto the sagging couch. Each of them found a seat. "I'm afraid it's more serious than that. The cardinal was murdered."

"No!" Her cry was a mix of anguish and shock. She shook her head helplessly as the tears ran freely down her face. "It is not possible. The cardinal was a good man. A holy man. Who would do such a wicked thing?"

They gave her a few minutes to compose herself, which Jaid spent scanning the area. The furniture was old but serviceable. The carpet threadbare. Through the open doorway to the kitchen beyond, she saw yellowed linoleum. A small table with two settings. It looked as though they'd interrupted breakfast.

"We're talking to everyone who had the codes to the security system at the cardinal's house," Jaid finally said, when the woman's quiet sobs had tapered off with a long shudder. "We understand that you're one of them."

"*Sí.*" When Maria looked up, anxiety shone in her dark eyes. "There were only the two of us, Denise and I. And the cardinal, of course. We were very careful. I never left without setting the system again. I would not fail the cardinal in that."

Which, Jaid thought grimly, was exactly the point. "What time did you leave yesterday?"

The woman began wringing her hands. "At five. I work eight to five, three days a week. Sometimes I work a little later if there is more to do. I like to do a good job for Cardinal Cote. But yesterday I left on time."

"Denise Quincy said she left at two yesterday." Adam had heard Fleur relay the information to the assistant director.

"Yes. She works nine to two or two thirty each day, except when the cardinal requests longer."

"Was there anyone else at his home yesterday?" Shepherd put in. "Did he have any meetings planned? Any repairmen scheduled for a visit?"

Her headshake looked woeful. "No, there was no one. It was a quiet day. Cardinal Cote worked all day in his study.

He worked much too hard, I said to him frequently. There was only Denise and I, and Charlotte, the cook. She comes at eleven and prepares lunch for the cardinal and sometimes for guests he has. Then she makes his dinner and leaves it warming in the oven. Always she leaves at four."

"So you let her out?"

She nodded at Shepherd's question. "*Sí.* But I set the alarm after her. And again when I left for the day."

"Did you see the cardinal before you left?" Adam had risen, paced a few steps. Jaid wondered for a moment if his leg were bothering him.

"Always I say good-bye unless he is in a meeting. Yesterday we talked about the cold. He said to bundle up. I walk a few blocks to the bus stop to get home."

"Did he mention his plans for the evening?"

"He said he had to go out for a while later that night. But I do not know where. Denise kept his appointments. It might be on his calendar."

Jaid was sure someone had already checked that. She made a note to ask Hedgelin about it.

"I understand that the security code is changed monthly."

Sanchez looked at Shepherd. "Yes. We are very careful. Always."

With ease, Jaid followed the other agent's line of thought. "That must get confusing." She offered the woman a small smile. "I struggled to remember my new phone number for weeks."

Something flashed in the other woman's face, there and gone too quickly to be identified. "It is necessary."

"And you never shared that information with anyone?" Recalling Sorenson's bout with the dropped purse, she added "Maybe wrote it down somewhere that someone else could find it?"

"I never told anyone, no. Not ever."

"But you might have written it down? At least the first few days of the month until you could remember it."

There was fear lurking in the woman's eyes now. Her fingers clenched and unclenched reflexively. "The cardinal gave Denise and me a slip of paper on the first of the month. We learned the code and threw the papers away."

"How long after getting this month's code did you discard the paper?"

Sanchez hesitated. "I do not remember. Just a few days, surely."

"And where would you have disposed of it?"

Shepherd's question seemed to agitate the woman even further. "Here. I am careful. Always careful. The cardinal is . . . he was a holy man. A great man. I tried to do my best for him."

"I'm certain you did." She threw a grateful look in Adam's direction at his words. "The cardinal must have been very pleased with your work. You've been with him for a long time."

"*Sí.* Fifteen years since my Eduardo died."

"Does someone else live with you, Mrs. Sanchez?" Jaid asked. She nodded toward the kitchen. "It looks like you had a guest for breakfast."

Following the direction of Jaid's gaze, the other woman shook her head. "No, I live alone. But my son, Luis, he comes often. He helps me with the house and the yard."

"Is he still here?" Shepherd sent her a small smile when her attention turned to him. "We'd like to talk to him if he is."

She didn't respond. Jaid looked at her sharply. "Mrs. Sanchez, is your son in the house now?"

Her answer was a slow shake of the head. "He left. Hours ago."

The half-eaten breakfast on the table hadn't been sitting there for hours; Jaid would bet on that. The entire home was spotless. Not a speck of dust was visible on the small coffee table in front of the couch. Maria Sanchez was a woman used to tending house. The dishes would have been cleared and cleaned within minutes after the meal was over.

Most likely their arrival had ended breakfast.

"Do you have Luis's address?" Adam asked. "We'd like to talk to him."

"He . . . he just moved yesterday. He came this morning

to pick up a few more things." Sanchez's attempt at a smile failed. "His new place is bigger, he says, but I have not been there. I do not know the address."

"How about a phone number?" Jaid knew, when the woman shook her head, that Sanchez was lying. At least about her son.

Another fifteen minutes of questioning yielded nothing further, and Maria remained maddeningly reticent about Luis's whereabouts. Finally, they took their leave and headed back to the vehicle.

"I'm guessing Luis Sanchez went through the back door when he saw us out front," Jaid said, as she got in the SUV. "Bet a background check on him is going to yield a lot more of interest than anything his mother offered."

"Already on that." Shepherd pulled out his cell and punched in a number. "What's the DCPD's liaison's name, again? Griega?"

"Lieutenant Frank Griega," she affirmed. And then waited several minutes for Shepherd's call to the man to end.

"We were right." The other agent slipped his cell back in his pocket. "Griega checked their database, and a Luis Sanchez with this address has been in and out of trouble since he was fourteen and took up with a gang. This is not a nice guy. He's been suspected of armed robbery and aggravated assault, among other things. Every time they haul him in he alibis out."

"No doubt because fellow gang members vouch for him." It was an all too common occurrence with bangers. Unless there was positive witness identification, they could be maddeningly elusive until they got caught in the act of committing a crime.

"Perhaps his friends aren't the only ones shielding him," Adam murmured. "Look over there."

Jaid twisted in her seat to see a midtwenties Hispanic man on the Sanchez porch, in the act of leaving. Maria was in the doorway, and they appeared to be having a heated argument. He whirled away, slamming the storm door so hard that the window in it shuddered.

Without a word all three of them got out of the vehicle. Jaid rounded it, caught up with Shepherd. "Luis Sanchez," she called. "FBI. We'd like a word with you."

He threw them one quick glance before dashing down the street. Jaid and Shepherd gave pursuit.

He had the advantage of knowing the neighborhood. They chased him to the corner. Around it. He dodged into a small bodega. They charged in after him, glimpsed him running out the back door and followed. They were led down a long, dark passageway between two apartment buildings. When they came to the end of it, they were in a deserted alley.

Dammit. Wariness surging, Jaid drew her weapon. Saw Shepherd do the same. Scanning the space, she saw that it was boxed in on both sides. Sanchez knew his way around this area. He wouldn't have deliberately chosen this setting if he thought it would effectively cage him.

"Ambush," Shepherd muttered and Jaid nodded. With a gesture she indicated they should separate. She moved left around the corner into the space. The other agent went right. There were three shadowy doorways in this direction. A pull-down fire escape folded against one building. An overflowing Dumpster. Scanning the space, she saw no sign of Sanchez. Adrenaline tap-danced up her spine.

She swung around the first doorway, crouched in a shooting stance. Found it empty. Continued to the next. Her nape prickled. Her breathing slowed.

Casting a look upward, she didn't see a place Sanchez could have scaled. The fire escape was out. She'd never seen one that didn't release without a clatter, and the one in the alley was rusted. It probably hadn't been used in years.

The third doorway was approached. Found empty. She glanced over her shoulder at Shepherd. Looking her way, he shook his head. Both of their gazes were then drawn to the Dumpster.

They found Sanchez's hiding place an instant before he showed himself.

He stepped partly out from behind the hulking garbage

bin. Fired several shots from a semiautomatic. Jaid returned fire, diving for cover. They were exposed here, while the banger had decent concealment. She ducked into a doorway. Heard Shepherd shooting. She waited, barely breathing, until Sanchez popped out again, spraying the area with bullets. He turned his weapon in her direction, edged farther out from the Dumpster to get a better shot. And she saw her chance.

Stepping out from the doorway she fired twice before dodging back inside it again. There was an exclamation of pain. Then silence.

The lack of sound was eerie after the burst of violence. She glanced toward Shepherd. Saw him step out of a doorway farther down the alley and watched his silent motions. Nodded.

Moving in an arc, weapon ready; she crept toward where the man had concealed himself. The other agent approached from the opposite side. Was Sanchez dead? Or was he trying to lure them closer? They'd have no cover once they got near enough to see him.

Unless he showed himself first.

She took the final step that placed her in direct line with the space behind the Dumpster. Saw Sanchez slumped there, still holding his weapon.

"Throw the gun out, Luis," she ordered. He didn't respond. For a moment she thought he was dead, but then he opened his eyes and looked at her.

"Throw out your weapon," Shepherd repeated the order from the opposite side of the opening. "Do you want to die in a garbage heap, Luis? Do it."

The gun skittered over the pavement in Shepherd's direction. "Now crawl out. Slow and easy."

A spate of angry Spanish greeted Jaid's words. "*Puta chingada*, you shot me! I'm dying. Get me an ambulance."

"We're not coming in after you." She kept her weapon trained on the man. He wore jeans. An oversized coat. There was plenty of room for a second weapon inside it.

"*Puta.*" He spat the word. But slowly he inched his way

toward her. When he was in the open, she ordered, "Face-down on the ground."

"I'm wounded," he snarled. One hand was cupped to his shoulder, and blood seeped through his fingers. Her quick duck for cover had marred her shot. She'd aimed for center mass.

"Somehow I'm devoid of sympathy."

He assumed the position as ordered, and Shepherd quickly frisked him. Found no other weapons. Once he'd cuffed the man, she reholstered her weapon. Reaching for her phone, she called for an ambulance. But before the man was taken away, she damn well was going to get some answers.

———

"He claims he was contacted by a white man, late twen-ties or early thirties." Jaid and Shepherd had rejoined Adam in the vehicle. Watched the DCPD officers they'd sum-moned drive off after the ambulance. Once Sanchez was treated, he'd be headed for lockup. "Said it was last week."

"How was he contacted?" Adam squelched the frustra-tion that had been building since Jaid and Shepherd had taken off after the punk. He'd long ago made peace with the physical limitations he was left with. Knowing how close he'd come to losing his leg completely, most days he could even muster up a little gratitude.

But on days like today, it burned like a bitch.

She turned in the seat to face him. "On the street. He says the guy was a stranger."

"So this stranger Sanchez claims approached him knew who his mother was. Knew she had access to the cardinal's security system."

Jaid interrupted Adam's words. "Easy enough to learn that simply by watching the people coming and going from the house. See which ones do the locking up."

He inclined his head. He'd had the same thought. "So what'd he offer Sanchez to get the code for him?"

"According to him, a thousand."

"Little cockroach probably would have done it for a

hundred," Shepherd muttered. "Didn't care why, didn't matter to him how the information was going to be used."

"I assume he claims he has no knowledge of that either."

"He sure wouldn't tell us if he did." Jaid responded to Adam's words wryly. "But there was no need to tell him, so he's probably telling the truth there. Knowing him, the price would have gone up significantly had he been told. In any case we can't be completely certain he isn't just blowing smoke. Surely, he would have met the cardinal before, with his mother working for the man for fifteen years. Maybe he had reason to hate him."

"He's got violent assault on his sheet," Shepherd agreed.

"Garroting someone is a skill that takes practice," Adam pointed out. "You might try Griega again. Have him check the database for unsolved crimes using the same method. If Sanchez was a suspect in any of them, we lean on him hard for this latest murder. But I'm guessing there's no way to tie the actual killing to him. He was likely just a tool."

Jaid's cell rang then. She listened for a time before saying, "Yeah, you're right. We don't work that way. First, he tells us what he's got, and if it pans out, maybe there's a bone we can throw his way at sentencing." She was silent several minutes before Adam saw her expression change. "Would you repeat that? Thanks. He'll have to have his lawyer contact us after we check this out."

She looked at Adam, excitement shining in her eyes. "The ambulance ride must have jarred Sanchez's memory. He's telling the DCPD officer that he once saw the car the stranger drove away in. Dark colored, newer. He wasn't sure of the make. But get this. There was a bumper sticker on it for reelecting Senator Newell."

Chapter 12

Mara Sorenson's tidy brick duplex was on a quiet street with well-manicured lawns and little activity. If Jaid had bothered to picture the woman's residence, her mental image would have closely resembled the reality.

Adam had called ahead to make sure the woman would be home. But he'd given her no reason for their visit over the phone, and Sorenson's expression was worried when she pulled open the door and allowed them inside.

"Agents. Mr. Raiker." She searched their faces carefully. "Is there . . . have you caught the man who killed Byron?"

"Not yet." They stood in a small vestibule papered in muted, soothing colors. Adam reached inside his coat to take out two sheets of paper, tri-folded. "We'd like you to take a look at these copies of photos and see if either of them match the man who bumped into you that night when you spilled your purse."

She studied the sheets he handed her showing Joseph Bailey and Scott Lambert. Her eyes lit with recognition. "Yes, that's him right there." She brought one picture closer to study it more carefully. "He seemed like such a nice young man." There was a slight tremble in her hand when she handed the sheets back to Adam. "Do you think he's the one who killed the judge?"

"No." He folded the sheets again and tucked them back into his coat. "But we're hoping maybe he can tell us who did."

———

They had to do a bit of research to come up with the next address. After a few minutes of discussion, they thought it wisest not to call ahead. And fate was smiling on them. Because when they knocked on the door of the cookie-cutter condo unit, it was only a few moments before Scott Lambert opened it.

He wasn't quite able to mask the flicker of alarm that flashed across his expression at the sight of them. "Agents. Mr. Raiker." He gave a shaky laugh. "This is a surprise. How can I help you?" Unlike Mara Sorenson, he didn't invite them inside.

"You can answer some questions," Jaid said unsmilingly. "We know you're somehow involved in the deaths of Oliver Patterson, Justice Reinbeck, and Cardinal Cote. Tell us the extent of your involvement."

"What?" His eyes bugged. But there was a sheen of fear in them as well. "That's ludicrous. I just heard about Cardinal Cote less than an hour ago on the news. Horribly tragic. How could you think I'd know anything about that?"

"Oh, we more than think it." Adam gave him a long, unswerving stare. "We have a positive ID from a witness. Mara Sorenson, Byron Reinbeck's personal assistant? 'Bumping into her' at that restaurant gave you the opportunity to swipe her phone, get her and the justice's numbers. Which then allowed you to spoof her number and send him a link designed to—"

"She's lying. Or mistaken." Lambert folded his arms over his chest, but not before Jaid noticed his hands were trembling. "I wouldn't recognize the woman if I saw her. In any case it's her word against mine."

"For now," she said. "At least until we show your picture around that restaurant. Maybe check your bank records and see if there's a transaction for that particular place on the night in question. Barring that, we can head over to the DCPD jail and let Luis Sanchez take a look at your photo." Lambert's expression froze. "He saw you twice, Sorenson only once. He also got a look at your car. You drive a 2010 navy Lexus, right?" Which would fit the general description Sanchez had given. "I'm guessing when we take a look at it, we'll find a Newell reelection bumper sticker on it, just like he said."

The man's face seemed to crumple. "It's not like that. You don't understand."

Jaid and Shepherd stepped toward the man in tandem. Taking out her cuffs, she said, "What I understand is that you're under arrest for conspiracy to commit murder."

———

Adam stood shoulder to shoulder with Cleve Hedgelin in the observation room, silently watching the interview through the plate glass window. The room on the other side of the wall was wired with audio. They could hear every question Jaid and Shepherd put to Scott Lambert. The man's replies weren't heard, however. Because he hadn't spoken since being brought in.

"They're losing him." Frustration clutched Adam's gut. The fear and panic on Lambert's face when they'd confronted him at his condo was gone. In its place was an impassive mask that didn't alter, regardless of the questioners' words. "I'm just surprised he hasn't lawyered up yet."

"Give them some more time. Marlowe is solid. And Shepherd will break him down. He's a seasoned agent."

"Hard to imagine then why you banished him to North Dakota a few years back."

The assistant director shot him a look. "I don't answer to you regarding my agents' assignments."

"No." Adam's voice was mild. "Don't have to explain it, either. I already know it was a punishment for me finding

the kidnap victim he'd been searching for over two years."
There was no reason to go into this with the man. But the
petty bureau politics played after Adam had cracked the
child-swap ring still irritated him.

"You're wrong. I needed someone solid in Bismarck; I
chose Shepherd. He's back now, so what's your point?"

The agent was only back because Adam had brought
some pressure to bear in the right places, but there was no
reason for Hedgelin to know that. The man was right about
one thing—Shepherd was a good agent. Even if he and Jaid
were having absolutely no luck with Lambert.

The man's knees were bouncing in increasing agitation.
But he hadn't asked for an attorney. Had barely spoken.
Frequently, his gaze scanned the room, lingering on the
one-way mirror that allowed Adam and Hedgelin to watch
the proceedings.

The assistant director's cell rang. While the man moved
away to answer it, Adam watched the scene through the
glass impotently. It was time to change the method of attack in his estimation. Lambert had shut down. Despite
what Jaid and Shepherd threw at the man, his innate sense
of self-preservation didn't seem to be rising to the surface.

Which meant they needed to change tactics.

He took out his own cell, texted a message to Jaid.
Watched her take out her phone and look at it for a moment.
When annoyance flickered across her face, he grinned. He
hadn't expected her to welcome his interference. She'd
come into her own in the last several years. Developed into
a fine investigator in her own right. And she'd never been
good at accepting orders unquestioningly.

But even so, in the next moment she held up the phone
to Lambert. "So I guess we contact your mother next. See if
she can shed some light on your actions."

The man's response was immediate. Unexpected. He
lunged across the table at her in a sudden movement that
knocked the phone from her hand. Shepherd sprang to his
feet. He stiff-armed the man and forced him to return to his
seat. "You try that again, and the cuffs go back on. Go on,"

he ordered when the younger man failed to sit again.

Lambert's gaze was heated and hadn't left Jaid. "You leave my mother out of this."

Adam's brows rose at his venomous tone. Decidedly different from the mild manner he'd presented both times they'd talked to him in Newell's offices. Hedgelin rejoined him then. "What's going on?"

"Jaid got a reaction when she mentioned paying a visit to his mother."

"What's his mother got to do with this?"

Without taking his gaze off what was happening in the next room, Adam murmured, "According to the background check we ran on him, she's his only living relative. Family exposes vulnerability." Although it remained to be seen how they could use Lambert's mother to shake some answers from him.

"Griega just contacted me. Sanchez couldn't positively ID Lambert's picture but thought it could be the guy who paid him for the code to Cote's security system. And the lieutenant struck out trying to tie Sanchez to any killings similar to the cardinal's. He'll keep working that angle and let us know."

"You must have a team working the ViCAP angle." When Hedgelin didn't answer, Adam cocked a brow at him. "Feed in the garrote, by itself and with the shooting. Both have a professional feel to them." The Violent Crime Apprehension Program was their best chance to find a link to similar crimes.

"Like you say, I've got someone on it," was all the other man would say.

In the interview Jaid was pressing harder. "That's the way it's going to be, Lambert. You don't want to talk to us, fine. We lock you up and start looking for people around you who'll be more forthcoming. Your neighbors. Friends. Coworkers." Her pause was deliberate. "And your mother. We will get answers. It's your choice who we get them from."

The man slumped in his chair. "I'm not going to speak to you." Jaid and Shepherd looked at each other. Rose simultaneously. "Fine. If you need some time in a cage to think things over, we can speak later."

His expression was defiant. "No, I mean I have nothing to say to you two." He turned to stare at the observation mirror. "I'll only talk to Raiker. Get him in here."

Twenty minutes later Adam walked into the interview room. At his entrance Jaid and Shepherd got up and passed silently by him out the door. It closed after them. He approached the table and set a bottle of water in front of Lambert. Remained standing with both hands on the head of his cane, Adam surveyed the younger man.

Lambert took the bottle and twisted off the cap. Took a long swallow. And then another. After setting it back on the table, he picked up the cap. Toyed with it nervously. "I've heard of you, you know," he blurted.

Inclining his head, Adam said nothing. Something was churning inside the man. It would eventually froth out of him without prodding.

Scott set the bottle cap spinning. "Don't you want to know how?"

"Do you want to tell me?"

"You killed that man. It was in all the papers."

Adam waited. There had been more than one man. He'd been at this, after all, for a very long time. Long enough for darkness to settle inside him sometimes. Long enough for black and white to have melded into mottled shades of gray. "Which man is that?"

"John LeCroix."

He stilled. Lambert was watching Adam for a reaction. He made sure that his features would reveal nothing. "Yes. I killed him."

The other man licked his lips, his head hunched lower over his fidgety fingers. His voice had lowered. "I was glad."

"You knew John LeCroix?"

A quick shudder. A jerky nod. "He was my father."

The words hit Adam with the force of a quick right jab. Because, of course, the infamous child killer had had a son. But despite recent rumors to the contrary, he believed the boy had been murdered years earlier, along with his mother. Paulie had been digging since the rumors had surfaced last winter. Had found nothing.

He pulled out a chair. Sat. Stared at the younger man. "I don't believe you."

That had Lambert's head snapping up. "You think I'd make something like that up? That I'm related to the worst child killer in the history of the United States? Why the hell would I?"

"I don't know. You tell me." Because Adam was interested. Very interested in the way that old case kept popping to the surface lately. Mose Ferrell, the man who had attempted to place the explosive under Adam's car, had claimed that his anonymous employer had told him to call him LeCroix. Was he talking about the man seated across the table?

Suddenly, Lambert scraped his chair back. Stood.

"Sit down," Adam ordered in a steely voice. But the man's face was determined. He yanked off his dark suit coat. Twisted off his discreetly patterned tie. Unbuttoned his blue shirt. And pulled the shoulder of the shirt down low enough to bare one bicep. Turned it toward Adam.

"Recognize this?"

The scar was old and white. Spread at the edges as if it had stretched. It was about three inches top to bottom. Two letters. *J. L.*

"That's how he marked his victims, isn't it?" Adam didn't answer. He didn't have to. Lambert shrugged his shoulder back into the shirt. Began buttoning it. "I mean, the papers didn't say, but I'm betting he did it to all of them. I was five, old enough to start fighting. He used a scalpel on me. Said it marked me as his property and he could do anything he wanted with his property. If my mother hadn't found a way to get us away from him, we'd both be dead."

Which was exactly the end that Adam had figured for them. LeCroix had had sizable financial resources with which to mount a search. And there were many in the shadowy world of child lovers who would have joined it to curry favor with the man who was regarded among them as something of a cult figure.

"So." Adam settled back in his chair. "You're the one who hired Ferrell to kill me."

"What?" The man seemed more baffled than outraged. "Why would I? I'm being used here. Me." His eyes filled with tears. "The phone calls started coming about ten weeks ago. Whoever called blocked his number. Distorted his voice. Then the photos started, sent by e-mail. Someone was threatening my mother and me with exposure. He claimed he was going to go public with our true identities. That we'd be considered prizes among the scum my father used to associate with."

"Not to mention what that exposure would do to your career," Adam murmured.

Lambert's face was bitter. "My mother has Alzheimer's. She's confused easily, especially by change. But I had to move her once when the threats started. I got more pictures of her in her new place the next week. There's no getting away from this guy. I had to follow his orders, don't you understand that? If he tells the world who we really are, our lives are over. Maybe literally." He moistened his lips again, his expression pleading. "He said he knew people. Friends of my father's who would come for us. That we'd die in the most hideous way possible. What was I supposed to do?"

"Go to the police?"

"If I did, he'd expose us! He told me so."

"So you have photos he sent you on e-mail?" The IP address could be traced. If there was any truth to Lambert's words, that might provide a link to whoever had hired him. If someone really had.

Unease flickered across the other man's face. "He made them vanish somehow. They'd be on the screen, then they'd just disappear. So would the message. I tried printing them. That always triggered the self-destruct. I tried taking a screen shot. It would vanish later, too. Afterward, it wouldn't show up in my in-box or trash. It'd just be gone. I contacted my service provider. They couldn't help me find it on the server. It was just gone."

Adam regarded him steadily. "How about your phone?"

Visibly brightening, he said, "Yeah, yeah. The calls would appear on my phone statements as anonymous, but that's proof of something, right?"

Unfortunately, it proved little. Lambert could buy himself a TracFone, block his number, and call his own cell. "We'll check it out." Adam's tone was noncommittal. "We know how you got Reinbeck's number. And that you also must have gotten Patterson's."

Shock flickered across the man's expression. His denial was tepid. "No, I swear I never . . ."

"Don't." Adam's terse response effectively halted the lie. "We've linked you to Sorenson. And to Sanchez. It stretches credibility that you weren't involved somehow with obtaining information on Patterson. How'd you do it? I'm guessing through Joseph Bailey." Because he was watching closely, he noted the man's reaction. "You work for Newell; you must have met his grandson."

Clasping his hands before him, Lambert leaned forward. "All right, I play basketball on his team at Dennison, all right? It was just a matter of looking at his company cell in the locker room while he was out warming up. But none of this means anything. I was forced to cooperate by whoever's been murdering these men. I'm a victim here."

"A victim." Adam tasted the word. Found it wanting. "At first, perhaps. But by the second murder you had to have known how your assistance was being used." He waited until he could keep the judgment from his tone. "Which meant you could have saved Cardinal Cote. And you didn't."

The other man broke down at the reminder. "I'm a good man. A Christian. I was forced to choose, don't you understand? If it were just me . . . but it was my mother. You have no idea what she sacrificed for me. No idea."

The words arrowed more deeply than the man could have known. "I think I do."

DEADLY SINS | 189

"I'd do anything to protect her." He wiped his face, his expression determined. "I can help you. Anything you ask. You just have to guarantee my mother protection. You can't let him hurt her."

"Who else?" Adam's voice was deadly. "Where's he going to strike next?"

"I don't know," Lambert insisted. "That's all he had me do. Maybe he's done."

Maybe. And maybe the mysterious man—if he existed—was just getting started.

Jaid and Shepherd had left a yellow legal pad and pen lying on the table. Adam shoved it toward Lambert. "Write down your whereabouts for these dates." One by one he named the evenings that the three victims had been killed. And while the man bent over to write, Adam reflected on the bitter fact that John LeCroix was still causing suffering, even in the grave.

———

"He's lying," Shepherd said flatly in the observation room. He had an opened bottle of water next to him, but he was tapping the keyboard of his electronic notepad, scowling at the screen. "He has to be. Everything I'm finding online matches up with his resume, which he so thoughtfully uploaded on LinkedIn."

Hedgelin only looked at Adam, who shrugged in return. "I worked a case last winter. The Mulder kidnapping. The girl I'd returned safely two years earlier when my case intersected with Tom's was snatched again. Obviously, since she'd been grabbed by a pedophile the first time, we looked hard in that direction. Even reinterviewed the head of the child-swap ring we'd nailed in the case. He later told one of my operatives that LeCroix had a son and suggested the boy might not be dead." What he'd said was that he hoped the boy had become a man consumed with revenge against the person who had killed his father. Considering what Lambert had suffered at LeCroix's hands, if Lambert were telling the truth, it was unlikely he was motivated by that emotion. LeCroix's death had freed him in one respect.

"If you work backward, you're liable to find a place where that online history breaks down." Jaid's suit today was a dark forest green made out of a soft fabric. It highlighted her coloring. Drew attention to those wide dark eyes. "He gave us locations and dates. Places they landed along the way in their escape from his father. It's enough that we'll be able to verify his story, one way or another."

"I have agents checking out his alibis for the dates in question as we speak."

"Maybe he was one of LeCroix's victims at one time," Jaid suggested. "He'd carved his initials in all the bodies you managed to recover, hadn't he?"

"The boys he killed." Adam frowned, remembering the details of the case. "But not the ones he planned to swap later. He wouldn't have wanted to leave any evidence leading back to him." He turned to Hedgelin. "You should also put an officer on Lambert's mother." He intercepted the other man's look and correctly interpreted it. "If he's being honest, she could be in real danger."

"Honest?" The man's mouth twisted. "At worst he's the killer we're hunting. At best an accomplice. He could have saved those victims by coming forward. He's probably only justifying his own actions."

Adam didn't deny it. He wasn't sure himself what to make of the man's claims. "So you err on the side of caution. Because if an elderly woman with Alzheimer's is hurt and the bureau could have prevented it, it'll make for some ugly press. And we're likely to get a higher degree of cooperation from Lambert if he's assured his mother is being kept safe."

The assistant director said nothing. But he pulled out his cell and turned away. A few moments later he barked out, "What's the name and address of the home where Lambert is keeping his mother?" Shepherd read it off to him, and the other man continued his conversation. Shortly, he hung up and fixed Adam with a baleful look. "Satisfied?"

"Lambert may be. And that's the important thing. *If* we

discover he's telling the truth, we aren't a whole lot closer to solving this thing than before. We still don't know the identity of the person who blackmailed him. The one who sent him a thousand dollars cash to give Sanchez in exchange for the code. We need to look harder at Newell." Anticipating the assistant director's objection, Adam reminded him, "Lambert is already his lackey. Think the senator wouldn't have done a thorough background check on him before hiring him? And there's the Bailey connection, too. Some of these strings are tying up too neatly."

"Funny." There was no humor in Hedgelin's response. His gaze was narrowed. "The common thread that keeps cropping up in all these different pieces that concerns me the most is the one that keeps leading back to you."

———

It was late when they left FBI headquarters. They'd started checking on Lambert's story about the journey he and his mother had taken on their escape. The few they'd managed to contact on the list he'd supplied had verified at least parts of what the man had told Adam. A landlord, a clergyman, a counselor . . . even a doctor along the way admitted to helping a woman and her boy years earlier. With the multiple identities they had taken over the years, verifying the story was going to be a laborious process.

"Either Lambert is telling at least part of the truth, or he gave us someone else's background." Shepherd was pulling on his leather gloves as they stepped into the parking garage and headed for their cars.

"I'm inclined to believe he's LeCroix's son." The scar on Lambert's arm had gone a long way toward convincing Adam. "I'm just not so sure about the limitations of his involvement."

Jaid was silent as she walked beside them, her head bent over her phone.

"Hopefully, we'll know more tomorrow." Shepherd stopped at his car. "How long can it take to follow up on his alibis for the nights of the murders, anyway?"

Adam didn't answer. Chances were the agents charged with the task had already reported back to Hedgelin, although Adam hadn't gotten any word yet.

"I'm going to get something to eat. There's a great little Mongolian place a half a mile from here. Anyone hungry?"

"I'm good, thanks." It was the first Jaid had spoken, though she still didn't look up.

"I'm heading home," Adam answered. With a wave Shepherd got into his car and backed it out. With a hand at the base of Jaid's back, Adam steered her out of the way so Shepherd could drive past.

She looked up then. "What?"

"Just getting you out of the way of traffic." Her attention drifted back to her phone where she was typing in a command. "What are you doing there?"

"Trying to get a birthday gift ordered for Royce since it appears that I'm not going to see the inside of a store anytime soon."

He studied her. "And what does a soon-to-be eight-year-old boy want for his birthday?"

Her gaze flew up then. Met his. And he knew she was recalling her words before getting out of the vehicle at the airport last night. Regretting them. Her shoulders braced. "He's not yours."

There was no reason, none at all, for the words to stab deep. "I know." He reached out and pushed a strand of hair back that clung to her jaw in a gesture that was purely involuntary. "You would have told me."

The tension in her stance didn't lessen appreciably. "Yes. I would have."

He'd reached the conclusion last night, but that hadn't stopped his mind from returning to the subject time and again. Because that meant she'd met someone almost immediately after they'd parted. Slept with him. And, since Jaid wasn't a woman to give herself casually, she must have cared for him on some level. There was no denying that the knowledge burned. Even when he'd been the one to end it. Jealousy was an ugly, futile emotion. One he once would have sworn he was incapable of. But this woman seemed to summon his regrets effortlessly. In an effort to lighten the mood, he gestured toward the phone. "The present?"

"Oh." She looked at the screen for a moment. "What Royce wants is a newer, bigger skateboard ramp. After his recent accident, what he's getting is a DS and some games for it."

"Ah."

Obviously seeing the lack of comprehension on his face, she explained, "A DS is a handheld gaming system. And he'll be happy with it. Especially once he accepts the fact that the ramp is not happening in the near future."

"Well. As long as it isn't something he can break bones with, it's probably a wise choice."

"Yeah." She moved toward her car, which was parked next to his. "But this is one of those times it's no fun being the responsible adult."

He watched as she got in the car. Backed out. He whole-heartedly agreed with her last statement: Because doing the right thing was often a bitch.

Adam parked. Looked at the light shining in the window and wished for a reason to avoid the upcoming scene. He took a moment to text Paulie and tell him to meet him at his place in a couple hours. Then he slipped the cell back in his pocket and shoved aside the reluctance he was feeling. Got out of the car and headed up the walk to the rectory.

Jerry opened the door before Adam even knocked. Unlocked the screen for him to enter. Adam stepped inside, examined his friend's face carefully. "How are you doing?"

But he didn't need words for his answer. The priest looked like he had aged a decade since they'd last seen each other. And when he turned without a word and headed back to his office, Adam followed just as silently.

"I counsel grieving family members all the time." Without asking, the priest took another glass out of his desk drawer and poured two fingers of Scotch into it. Handed it to Adam. Picked up his own nearly empty glass and drained it. Refilling it, he continued morosely, "Something that frequently comes up is guilt. 'Father, how can I forgive myself? The last words we exchanged were angry, and then she was dead.' Or variations on the theme." He grimaced. "I wonder if my lecture on forgiving themselves as God forgives sounds as empty to them as it does to me right now."

"Angry words didn't contribute to Cardinal Cote's death."

The priest wagged a finger that didn't look entirely steady. Adam wondered how much of the bottle on the desk had been consumed tonight. "You're getting ahead of me. I tell those grieving parishioners to dwell on the wonderful memories they had with the deceased. That a relationship is about the whole, not the individual parts. But the cardinal and me, well." He drank again. Deeply. "The antipathy between us was the whole. There was little else to the relationship. And because of that, I'm finding the guilt particularly hard to shake."

He stared into the contents of his glass. This was the man who had always had answers for Adam. First as a kid. Then as a surly teenager. Later as an adult. Even when he hadn't liked the answers, they'd been there, delivered with equal measures, he'd always thought, of wisdom and humor.

"Did you see pictures of the scene today?"

Raising his gaze, Adam said soberly, "I was there." Watched his friend wince. "I can't go into detail, but there will be some uncomfortable questions arising from the cardinal's death. Questions about his past, perhaps. Of possible accusations leveled. Of a sexual nature."

Shock flickered over the other man's expression. "Why?"

Ignoring the question, Adam continued deliberately, "Agents will get to you eventually and level those questions. I'll try to be sure the team I'm assigned to will be the ones to visit, but I can't be positive that we'll be the only ones to do so."

Jerry reached for the glass. His hand was trembling. "I figured on that. I'm in trouble, Adam. The kind of trouble that had the cardinal furious with me and rightfully so. It's just a matter of time until it comes out."

His look sharpening, Adam demanded, "What kind of trouble?" But the heaviness in his stomach had already turned leaden.

"You know I sit on the boards of many of my pet causes. I'm at the helm of others. Nonprofits have miniscule budgets. They can't afford to hire people to do what volunteers can." His fingers clenched and unclenched on the glass. "With this economy, giving is down. For churches. For charities. I thought investing the donations for the individual entities, even for the short term, would pay off and make up some of the losses. But the markets . . ."

"Went to hell," Adam finished. The Scotch proved to be handy fortification. He drank. "How much did you lose?"

"Everything I'd invested. I've been juggling funds from one entity to pay the expenses of another and back again to cover costs. Last week one of the organizations discovered what was going on and went straight to the cardinal."

Adam rubbed at the spot between his brows that had begun to throb. "Oh, God."

The other man's response was automatic. "Don't take the Lord's name in . . ."

"How much?" He leaned forward to set his glass on the desk. Then he took his checkbook from his inside suit coat pocket. Flipped it opened and readied a pen.

Hesitating, Jerry said, "I don't expect your help. I got myself into this mess."

Filling out the name on the check, Adam looked up again. "How much? The whole amount, Jerry. What's it going to take to pay back every one of those organizations?"

The figure the man named had the pen jerking in his hand once. Then grimly, he finished writing the check. Ripped it out and handed it to his friend. When the priest wouldn't reach for it, Adam set it on the desk. "You call the people you need to talk to at each organization. Tell them you will have reimbursement payments to them and ready to be picked up the day after tomorrow, for the full amount owed."

Jerry shook his head. "I can't let you do that."

"I just did. Have your housekeeper run the check to the bank in the morning. I want you here all day. Available for the interview."

The priest picked up the check. Stared down at it with an inscrutable expression. "I don't know how to thank you."

"Consider it a down payment on what I owe you for all you've done for me over the years." But his mind was on another question. One he wasn't sure he wanted to hear the answer to. "Mind telling me where you had the money invested?"

Jerry shook his head. Took the check and placed it in his center desk drawer. "Thought it was safe enough. Had it with Patterson Capital. Oliver was a regular contributor to a couple of my causes. He gave me free advice. We talked about getting the highest rate of return in the shortest amount of time." His mouth twisted. "We also talked about risk, but that part sort of skated right by me."

Adam reached for the glass he'd set on the desk. Something told him he was going to need it. "How long ago was this?"

"Last year. At first the investments were responding nicely, then the bottom seemed to drop out. Oliver said it was a hiccup, that the financial world was steadying itself. But it was too late for me."

The headache took on jackhammer status. The news couldn't get much worse. "All right. You don't offer that information. If you're asked directly, answer honestly but with as few details as possible. Maybe there will be no formal complaint from the organizations involved, since they contacted the cardinal directly. If that's the case, the bureau will have no idea about the nature of your latest disagreement with him." And hopefully, by the time it did come to light, the case would be solved, and the information would be of no further interest to the agency. "Where were you last night?"

Looking up, Jerry frowned. "Me? Here. Why . . ." Comprehension dawned in his expression. He picked up the glass. Swirled its contents. "Well. Had I realized I was going to need an alibi, I would have had some dancing girls over." His joke fell flat. Adam could find no humor in the situation.

"All right. You were home alone. If asked, you knew Patterson through some boards you served on together." And Byron, too, Adam realized sickly. He'd been at the fund-raiser where Adam had spoken at Jerry's behest. "Answer the questions honestly and briefly." For his friend's sake, he summoned a smile. "That check should mean the worst of it is behind you." Silence stretched for a minute. "You should have come to me with this, Jerry."

The other man released a sigh. And the look on his face was weary. "I was ashamed. With good cause, don't you think? If I had my way, you would never have found out. But that doesn't mean I'm not grateful."

Adam took a long swallow of Scotch. He didn't know how to tell the man that gratitude probably wasn't going to be enough.

Chapter 13

"Lambert must be lying."

Adam sent Paulie a dry look from his seat on the couch. "Do you really believe LeCroix's son can't be alive, or is it because you just couldn't find him when you checked it out?" Paulie had an uncanny reputation for information mining, one richly deserved. But no one batted a thousand. And it sounded as though the mother and son had gone deep when they'd run.

Adam said as much. The words didn't appear to cheer the man appreciably. "But if what he's saying is true, someone managed to find him, right? Whoever it is he's claiming used him as a tool in the murders. How the hell he managed it when I couldn't is going to give me more than a few sleepless nights."

"Here's something else to add to that mix. Remember Ferrell claimed the man who hired him called himself Le-Croix."

Paulie frowned. "So was it Lambert who hired Ferrell? And possibly Jennings before that?"

Adam's shrug was rife with frustration. "More questions than answers at this point. If he really is John LeCroix's son—and those initials carved into his arm make that seem likely—he certainly wouldn't be motivated by revenge." When his friend's gaze met Adam's, he knew the other man followed his meaning. "But there might be another motivation out there."

"The money." Paulie sank more comfortably into the leather recliner and went silent for several minutes. His tie featured sly-looking dogs engaged in a poker game. One of them was cheating. "That would explain the sudden interest shown to our finances in the last several months."

Adam's look sharpened. "Anything lately?"

Paulie shook his head. "No one will find anything. I've got it buried too well." His expression went pensive. "Do you ever regret the decision you made eight years ago in the CCU when I first came to you about the money?"

"I don't believe in regrets." Adam's tone brooked no further discussion. It didn't matter that every time Jaid entered the equation, those words turned to a lie. In this matter, at least, they were true enough. "But it's getting harder to deny that these three murders are somehow wrapped up with LeCroix's case eight years ago." He shook his head in frustration. "I just can't for the life of me figure out how."

"Maybe not." Paulie stretched his legs out and folded his hands over his slight paunch. "Maybe someone is trying to confuse the issue and make it seem that they're related."

"To what end?"

"To get you removed from this case? We talked about that before. At any rate there are way too many intersections between the Colorado kidnapper and these recent attempts on your life for my liking. The sudden appearance of Le-Croix's kid is just one more." He seemed to have conveniently forgotten that a few minutes earlier he hadn't believed Lambert's claim about his real identity.

"We started tracing his life backward today to verify his story. Seems to check out given the facts he supplied us with. Places he says they were. People he claimed helped them. So far."

"You're wondering if those facts were planted." Paulie's gaze was sharp. "I don't suppose the feds want to go to the expense of digging up John LeCroix's body for a DNA match, so we'll dispatch some people to talk to the so-called witnesses from his past."

Adam nodded. Although he was inclined to believe Lambert's claim to parentage, he'd feel better with personal visits to the places and people who had served to help the boy and his mother hide. "Maybe one of those people will recall someone else asking questions about him. We could find out who it was that discovered his identity first."

"I'm on it."

"There's more." Adam told the man about Jerry's confession this evening. And about the conversation he'd heard between the priest and the cardinal previously. When he'd finished, Paulie's expression was troubled.

"Adam, this doesn't look good."

Broodingly, Adam drummed his fingers on the couch's armrest. "You think I don't know that? Somehow I have to try and make sure the team I'm assigned to is the first to interview him." Not that Adam would take a primary role in that interview. He didn't need Hedgelin screaming about a conflict of interest. But for all the assistant director's posturing about Adam's presence in this case, Jerry's involvement was the first true conflict. And it made Adam more than a little uneasy.

"So how you doing with his news?" His gaze flashed to Paulie, who was eyeing him knowingly. "It's never easy to find out that someone we hold in esteem has feet of clay."

"I don't expect him to be perfect," he said brusquely. "His vulnerability has always been the passion he feels for his causes. It affected his judgment." He looked past Paulie. Stared blindly at the wall. They all had weaknesses. And somehow both of his were tied up in this case.

———

When her cell phone rang, Jaid didn't lift her head from the pillow. Instead, her searching hand slapped the bedside table in a blind search. Discovering the phone, she opened her eyes. Tried to focus. "Marlowe."

"Jaid." The boozy voice was only vaguely familiar, but it was all she needed to realize this call wasn't work related. Sitting up in bed, she snapped on the light over the bed. Checked the alarm. One thirty A.M. Someone should be shot.

"Who is this?"

"It's me. Kale."

Her eyelids slid shut in disgust. "Bolton, how did you get this damn number?"

"I'm an investigative reporter, baby. That's what I do."

"Good-bye." She went to disconnect the call.

"Wait! This is about you and Adam Raiker."

She froze, uncertainty creeping in. "I'm not talking to you about the case."

His laugh was ugly. "It's not 'bout the case. I'm talking about the fact that you and he had a thing. Long time ago. Prob'ly banging him back when you broke my nose. Should have just told me that instead of swinging like a nun protecting her virtue."

"I should have hit you harder."

"Yeah, well, shoulda woulda coulda." He broke off. "What d'ya mean last call? Already? Hell yes, pour me 'nother."

"Sounds like you've had too much already."

"I do my best thinking over a couple drinks. And I've been thinking 'bout you all night."

"I'd feel better if you didn't."

"See I know all 'bout you and Raiker's relationship years ago. Known for a while but big deal. Not relevant to the book. Or so I thought."

Trepidation warred with anger. "You're right. It's not relevant. And neither is this conversation."

Ignoring her he went on. "But then running into you two on the street, I started to think, maybe there's something I can use after all. Information is never wasted. It's knowing when to use it. How to use it."

She moistened her lips. Wanted to hang up. Didn't dare. "You're not making much sense."

"None of it made sense to me, either, until I started digging a bit more. Into you this time instead of Raiker. And . . ." He released a whistle. "Guess what I found? You got a kid. Now that's interesting. So I do a bit more checking, and hey, the age is right, too. So what I wanna know is if you're raising Adam Raiker's bastard."

Ice had formed in her veins, freezing her from the inside out. "The only bastard in this conversation is you."

His laugh was mocking. She could hear the clink of ice in a glass. Probably swilling down another shot before staggering home. "'Cuz, see, that would be of interest in the book. The great Adam Raiker, head of the Mindhunters, he's got a baby mama stashed on the side."

She manufactured a bored tone. A feat, considering the nerves jittering and clashing inside her. "Really? That's what this book is going to be about? Didn't picture you as the type for yellow journalism, Bolton. But I guess the drinking's taking a toll, huh? I mean, how long can those two Pulitzers be expected to carry you before people start calling you washed up? I hear you're only as good as your last book."

"You always were a cocky li'l bitch. Needed a real man to remind you that you're a woman. But I'm guessing you're going to turn into my best source for material on Raiker." His laugh was ugly. "You could say I'm banking on it."

"How do you figure?" But dread was pooling nastily in her gut. She had a feeling she already knew. In the next moment he proved that feeling right.

"'Cuz I'm guessing you have maternal instincts. Even cold, heartless bitches have 'em, right? So you're not going to want the book to come out with all these questions 'bout your kid's father. Don't have the answers to those questions yet, because frankly, I don't give a shit. But I can look into it. You want to keep the kid out of the book? Fine by me. All you have to do is give me the inside information I need to finish Raiker's story."

A vise was squeezing her chest, making it difficult to draw in oxygen. She had the impulse to go sprinting down the hallway, just to make sure Royce was asleep in his own bed. Safe. Secure. The way she'd promised she'd always keep him.

This man wasn't going to change that. "You've made a very big mistake, Bolton." Because there was nothing, absolutely nothing, she wouldn't risk to keep her son safe.

But she wasn't about to throw Adam under a bus to do it.

"You'll come around. After I start sending you pages with your kid front and center. This book is going to make a big splash. How long will it be, y'think, before some kids start saying stuff to your son about it? Maybe you were screwing more than one guy at the time. D'you even know who the father is? Doesn't matter. People will remember the questions raised in the book, not your answers."

It took effort to think logically. To reach for reason. "I think you're full of shit."

"Figured you say that. So I'm just going to write up a sample chapter and send it over to you. Once that convinces you I mean business, I think you'll agree that giving me a little information on the man is a fair trade-off. You sleep on it." The smug satisfaction in his voice had her wanting to reach through the connection and strangle him. "I'm guessing you'll come round. I'll be talking to you."

The call ended. But it was several moments before Jaid could unclench her fingers from the cell. Even more before she set it back on the table. Her mind racing, she sat motionless in bed for a long time.

Bolton was issuing an empty threat. She was almost certain of it. They didn't issue Pulitzers to people for trashing others in tell-all exposés.

But what seemed like exploitative journalism to her may well have passed for investigative reporting to others. And the fact remained that she couldn't be sure his publisher would have a problem with it. At any rate it wasn't the book itself that scared her the most. It was arming Bolton with details that she'd much rather keep hidden.

Driven to move, she threw off the covers. Padded quietly in the dark down the hall to Royce's room. Easing the door open, she saw the familiar outline of her son, lit by the dim glow that spilled from his Baltimore Ravens nightlight. He slept sprawled on his back, his uninjured arm flung out as if sleep had caught him mid motion.

Emotion clogged her throat. She'd spent years keeping him from harm. But in spite of her brave words to Bolton, the thought of the reporter looking into the details of his birth, his parentage, shot ice water into her veins.

Leaning a shoulder against the doorjamb, her gaze fixed on the small form in the bed. And as one hour stretched into another, she mentally grappled for a way to extricate them both from a situation that could easily turn deadly.

Hedgelin looked at them from over the top of steepled fingers. "Due to the sensitive nature of this information, you won't find it in the case file. Only a few are privy to it, but given your assistance with Harandi the other night, I thought you deserved to be apprised of the facts that have come to light in that matter."

Assistance. Adam cocked a brow, looked at Jaid. If not for them, Harandi would be back in his home country right now, so the descriptor seemed tepid. But he supposed this update was the only recognition of that fact they were likely to get from Hedgelin.

The assistant director consulted a sheet on his desk. "The case you found on the Supreme Court docket, *Paxton vs. the United States*, is indeed one that was of interest to Harandi. A couple of years ago another case with similarities made its way to the high court. At its heart was the question of whether an individual who had won damages against the Iranian government could tap the government's frozen assets for payment. That part of the case went unanswered. The Paxton case is similar but will require a more clear-cut conclusion. Agents found volumes of literature on the subject in the professor's home. Even more on his computers, both at home and school. DHS is reevaluating their original assessment of the doctor's reason for being in this country."

It was simple enough to read between the lines. "You mean they now think that Saeed Harandi might be an Iranian spy?"

Hedgelin didn't flinch. "His intentions have come under renewed scrutiny. And that's all I can say on the subject."

Jaid sounded frustrated. "Will we be allowed to question him about this latest homicide? Just because he was in custody didn't mean he couldn't still be pulling the strings. It's likely a professional is carrying out the actual kills anyway."

The assistant director shifted his gaze to Adam. "The probability is high," he conceded. "I've adjusted my original profile somewhat." He reached down to take the revised profile from his briefcase and rose to hand copies to Hedgelin, Jaid, and Shepherd. "There's evidence of a large degree of personal antipathy toward the victims. I doubt that they serve merely as symbols of each sin or that their selection is relatively random."

"How much satisfaction can he get if he's not getting the rush from the acts?"

"It's still possible the one behind the crimes is in fact the killer," Adam allowed in response to Shepherd's question. "Keep in mind that scenario, however, effectively eliminates every person of interest we've spoken to in this case, all of whom have alibis for at least one of the dates." Silence greeted his words. "If, indeed, the homicides are not hired out, you're looking for someone with a personal vendetta against each victim, real or perceived. And our offender would have had to acquire a high degree of skill to kill three different ways."

"Two of the murders were hands-on," Jaid murmured. When she turned to look at him, he had a moment to observe the shadows under her eyes. "Reinbeck's wasn't, but given his position, he'd be difficult to get close to. The rifle might have been a necessity there."

"Or else the offender harbored more anger toward Patterson and Cote than he did Reinbeck," Shepherd added.

"At any rate he'd have to acquire his skill somewhere." Adam addressed Hedgelin. "I imagine someone is already compiling a threat list for the cardinal." He didn't wait for the other man's nod before going on. "I'd suggest you start examining each threat list for someone with former military training." A black-ops soldier might have received the training necessary to carry out these murders. Or a professional who hired out to the highest bidder.

"There hasn't been an intersection on Patterson's and Reinbeck's threat lists," Hedgelin reminded Adam.

He shrugged. "This is a highly intelligent offender. He wouldn't have made threats against every target." Adam thought he'd be too careful to make any at all, but he couldn't ignore the possibility. "All we need is one name on one list. Then we make connections with the two other victims on our own."

"But if you had to make an educated guess," the assistant director pressed him, "is this guy doing his own killings or hiring them out?"

Adam glowered at Hedgelin. Adam hated dealing in conjecture. "What good does guesswork do?" But when the other man didn't look away, he moved his shoulders in frustration. "If Lambert is being honest, the way he was used points to an unknown subject who is quite adept at manipulating people to do his bidding. I think it's a mistake to believe the UNSUB wouldn't be completely satisfied without enacting the killings himself. It's likely gratification comes from multiple levels. And remaining unexposed and able to continue this vendetta would be seen as a necessity as well."

The assistant director pulled the laptop on the desk toward himself and opened it. They waited for several minutes while he typed in commands and scanned information.

Then he looked up again. "Three names from Patterson's and Reinbeck's combined threat lists have military backgrounds. Only one with special-training experience. Donald Vale was dishonorably discharged from the U.S. Marines seven years ago for drug-related offenses. He sent a letter to Judge Reinbeck, before he was elevated to the Supreme Court, ranting about his views on gun control. He was checked out then, and a warning was delivered. But he wasn't considered a serious threat."

Hedgelin broke off to scroll down on the report again. "He was paid a visit the day after Reinbeck's death by a team comprised of USMS, DHS, and FBI personnel. They never got farther than his porch. He was described as combative and uncooperative, but his wife vouched for the fact that they were dining in a local restaurant when they saw the news come on about the justice's death." Hedgelin looked up again, his expression grim. "This was verified by several diners at the establishment as was the fact that Vale cheered loudly at the news report."

"Has anyone followed up on any possible connection he might have to Patterson?" Jaid asked.

"None was found. It's too early to know if he had any link to Cote."

Shepherd looked at Adam. "It wouldn't hurt to find out if he admits to knowing the cardinal. And whether he has an alibi for the night of his death."

Hedgelin wrote down the address. "He lives on a small farm outside Purcellville." Shepherd got up to take the slip of paper from the assistant director. "He wasn't exactly welcoming when the other team stopped out there. Be careful. I understand there is a large collection of weapons in the house. Because he's prohibited from buying them, they were all purchased by the wife."

"Great," Jaid drawled.

But Adam's mind was on something else. He rose when the other two agents did and headed for the door. But halfway there he turned, mentioned as casually as possible, "I know a priest in Cardinal Cote's diocese. Maybe he can shed some light on whether any allegations ever surfaced regarding the cardinal."

Just the reminder of the word scrawled on the note card left at the scene had Hedgelin scowling. "Lieutenant Griega has already looked into it. There is no record of a public complaint about Cote. I don't want that topic even introduced in interviews. We're not going to be responsible for a scandal breaking out after the man's death."

"Actually, Adam's idea has merit," Shepherd put in. He had slipped on a long dark wool overcoat. "The church has a reputation for covering things like that up." He held up a hand in mock surrender. "I'm not saying that's the case here. Just that someone in the church might have been in the position to have heard about an incident that was never reported to the police."

"Fine." Hedgelin bit off the word, his expression fierce. "You're to use the most general of terms and not refer specifically to what was referenced on the note card. Or even mention its existence."

"In other words, fish." Jaid headed out the door. "Got it."

Adam followed her silently. He was pleased enough with the parameters given. More so that they would be the team on record to speak to Jerry. If it became apparent in other interviews that his friend's rocky relationship with the cardinal was widely known, or perhaps more venomous than Adam had been led to believe, there would likely be another visit. This time from a team far less friendly than theirs.

———

"How long have I known Cardinal Cote?" Jerry tipped his head back to consider Jaid's question. "Three decades, I suppose, give or take. Knew him when he was a monsignor, long before he was made cardinal. He was a devout man. An inspiration to all in his diocese."

"That's a long time." Jaid unbuttoned her coat and sent Jerry a smile. "Long enough to know if the man had any enemies."

Jerry huffed out a breath. "Enemies. No, I wouldn't know

about that. We don't worry about enemies in the church, at least not in the way you mean. Our fight is against sin and the presence of evil."

"Which takes a very human shape," Adam noted from his position in the corner of the room.

The priest nodded his agreement. "Of course. And one can't discount the prevalence of mental illness that can make people unpredictable. But I don't know of anyone who has ever posed a physical threat to Cardinal Cote. And I don't have a close enough relationship with him to have been privy to any problems that might have presented themselves."

"What sort of relationship did you have with him?"

Jerry made a show of avoiding Adam's gaze while he answered Shepherd's question. "I would describe it as strained, especially recently."

Adam noted that the words had the agent straightening in his chair, his interest evident. Adam quelled the urge to jump in. Smooth the waters. This was why he'd arranged to come here today. Sometimes getting things on the record early paid off in the long run. The trick here was circumspect candor.

"You and the cardinal had a problem?"

The priest waved a hand at the wall of photos. "I've always believed in taking an active stance where I see social injustice. The cardinal didn't agree with my involvement, although he wasn't my spiritual leader during those years."

"So what was there to object to recently?" Shepherd asked.

"The amount of time I spent engaged in activities not directly related to my parish. I sit on several nonprofit boards. I have an interest in fund-raising for several causes. We had differences in opinion over the issue."

When he left it at that, Adam felt a little of the tension ease from his muscles. Of course, if the details of Jerry's financial transgression came to light, it would be reason for closer scrutiny of his friend. Which would be a waste of time. The man was a liberal bleeding-heart do-gooder. His most dangerous quality might be his ability to talk someone unconscious, but that hardly elevated him to suspect material.

"So you didn't hear of any threats against him." Shepherd lacked his perpetual smile. "But given your long history with him, perhaps you have heard of a reason someone would hold a grudge against the cardinal. An accusation that might have been brought against him and then dismissed, maybe. Or one that wasn't given a hearing at all."

"I have no personal knowledge of any facts relating to something like that."

His careful wording was like gasoline to a fire. Adam watched both agents respond to it. Jaid leaned forward, her voice growing more urgent. "We aren't interested in destroying the man's reputation. But for the purposes of our investigation, if you know of any talk that might have followed the man over the years, we need to check it out. It may well be pertinent to our investigation into his death."

"I'm not going to deal in rumor and innuendo." Adam recognized the implacable tone of his friend's voice. "A man is dead. Nothing will be served by dredging up every vicious word that might have been uttered against him. He devoted his life to the church for more than a generation. I certainly wouldn't want gossip to be my final legacy when I'm gone, would you?"

"Jerry." Adam couldn't remain silent any longer. "Now would be the time to share anything you might know with the agents. Almost none of the details relating to this investigation are being released to the public. You can be assured that anything you tell us would be handled just as discreetly."

The priest avoided Adam's gaze, but his face was mutinous. And being quite familiar with that particular expression, Adam clenched his jaw. "As I said, I have no facts to share, and I won't deal in anything less. The man was savaged brutally in death. I won't follow that up by savaging his good name."

"No offense, Adam, but your friend didn't tell us all that he knows." Shepherd was driving northwest on 267 toward

Purcellville. It was only about fifty miles from DC, but commutes in the area were measured in minutes rather than miles for good reason. The agent had been largely silent since they left the rectory. Adam didn't consider that a good sign.

"He's a priest. Gossip is probably considered a sin of some sort. If he'd had any solid knowledge about any scandal regarding the cardinal, he would have told us." He said the words with more certainty than he was feeling. The man knew about something in the cardinal's past. But Adam wasn't surprised that Jerry refused to share it, even if he'd been tempted to shake the information from the priest earlier.

The guilt Jerry felt over his last meeting with the cardinal was surely the cause of his reticence.

"I can't help but believe we're going to meet the same sort of wall no matter who we talk to in the church about it." Jaid looked up from the phone she'd been bent over. "Our best bet would be to find some longtime churchgoers."

"Parishioners," Shepherd corrected.

"Parishioners, then. Find out what church Cote was at as a priest, monsignor, whatever. Check out the old people. They'll remember, I'll bet."

It wasn't, Adam thought, a half-bad way to get the information. "Priests don't stay at one church forever," he cautioned. "After a few years they're often moved to a different one."

"Why?"

Baffled, he merely looked at her for a moment. "I don't know. I'm not Catholic, remember?"

She lifted a shoulder, her expression amused. "A fact God gives thanks for daily, I'm sure." When he merely looked at her, she added, "Where's that famed Raiker sense of humor?"

"Absent until I hear something funny." He nodded toward her phone. "You still shopping or is that work?"

"Work." She held up the phone so he could see the screen. "Vale's records. Donald Vale is married to one Sarah Matthews Vale, nine years and counting. They own a car and a pickup, both older models, and a five-acre farm. Even outside DC as far as it is, it didn't come cheap, which makes me wonder how Mr. Vale makes his living these days."

Adam should have been wondering the same thing. Instead of observing again that it didn't look as though she'd gotten much sleep the night before. He had enough experience with women, and Jaid in particular, to refrain from pointing out that fact.

Shepherd said, "Jaid's idea about talking to the parishioners is a good one. But I'm betting Hedgelin would frown on any pointed questioning like that, particularly if it pertains to the cardinal's past."

"Most people are only too glad to offer up dirt with very little urging. But you're right, Hedgelin is likely to object." They'd have to strike out trying alternate ways to get the information before the assistant director was likely to consider pursuing that avenue.

Adam's thoughts turned to Lambert. He'd vehemently denied any further involvement. But that didn't necessarily mean the killer planned to stop. Or that he could even if he wanted to.

———

Vale's place was accessed by taking a series of twisting gravel roads that had dust kicking up in the wake of the vehicle. When Shepherd, Jaid, and Adam drove down the drive next to the mailbox emblazoned with Vale's name, Adam studied the ramshackle structures on the property ahead. Whatever else Vale spent his time doing, sprucing up the place obviously wasn't high on his priority list.

A large dog of indeterminate breed chased alongside the vehicle until Shepherd pulled to a stop near the house. Then the animal stood barking a loud alarm for the owners inside the place, announcing the presence of visitors.

But no one came to the door.

"Who wants to distract the canine while I knock at the door?" Jaid asked, not moving to get out of the vehicle. She was watching the animal with a distrustful expression. Adam had the fleeting memory that she'd never been allowed a pet when she was a child. It was one of the few things, outside of work, that they'd discovered they had in common.

"He looks friendly," he said blandly.

"Then you get out first."

With a mental shrug he opened the door. Shepherd followed suit a moment later. The dog didn't stop its incessant racket, but it didn't come nearer, either.

Jaid got out and strode up to the sagging porch, keeping a wary eye on the dog. The screen door shook when she pounded on it. But no one answered.

Shepherd went to peer through one dusty window in the door of the attached garage. "Pickup is here. Car is gone."

Adam stilled. Cocked his head. "Did you hear that?"

"I'm deaf from all that barking. Do dogs come with off switches?" But Jaid stopped. Listened.

It sounded again. A shot. And somewhere in the vicinity.

They looked at each other. "Hunters?" Adam suggested.

"Maybe. Which means when we check it out, keep to cover as much as possible." Shepherd was already striding in the direction the shot had sounded from. Jaid followed.

And Adam fell in behind them. This time he wasn't sitting in the car.

The distance was farther than he'd suspected. At first the land was lightly wooded, but the trees thinned a half mile or so from the house. There was another shot. Louder this time. They were headed in the right direction.

Jaid and Shepherd were slightly ahead of him. Once Adam stepped into the clearing, he caught up with them because they stood there, unmoving.

There was no one in sight. Barbed wire delineated the property line ahead. The trees got heavier where they bordered the edge of the boundary.

Another shot sounded. Still in the distance.

But this time it was followed by the slow fall of a body out of a huge evergreen.

Chapter 14

Jaid and Shepherd raced across the field, weapons drawn. They took cover where they could, but in order to get to the person lying motionless at the base of the fir, they were going to have to cross the clearing in plain sight of the shooter.

"Separate," she muttered, and Shepherd split off silently. They each approached the unmoving person from opposite directions.

The air was still. Quiet. The type of stillness that was only found in the country and always got on her nerves. There were no traffic noises. Nothing but the sounds of the birds that arrowed out of trees when she ran by.

Jaid distrusted the quiet almost as much as she had the dog. In some ways the scene was even creepier than the alley they'd chased Sanchez into.

But as she got closer, she realized she'd been wrong on a couple counts. The person on the ground wasn't a man. And she wasn't dead.

Reaching the woman's side first, Jaid knelt, her gaze skimming over the camouflage coveralls, looking for blood. "Where are you hurt?" Shepherd remained standing above them, scanning the area for the shooter.

"Shit." The woman's face was stark white beneath the hunter's cap. "I think I broke my leg."

"Are you shot?"

"Hell no, I'm not shot. Might be dumb enough to fall out of the damn tree, but not quite dumb enough to shoot myself doing it."

Jaid re-holstered her weapon. "You mean you were hunting?"

The woman propped herself up on her elbows, pain twisting her face. Strands of long red hair had worked free of the cap. "Place is lousy with wild turkeys. Bagged a couple of them and started down the tree to go grab them. Missed my footing and . . . well, I'm guessing you saw the rest."

Gently Jaid ran her hands over the woman's leg, pausing when she winced. Several inches above the ankle, likely a break to the tibia. "Agent Shepherd and I will get you upright. Keep the weight off the leg. We'll help you back to the house."

The woman's gaze narrowed. "Agents?"

Silently Jaid reached into her coat pocket and flipped open her credentials.

"Feds." She all but spat the word. "Don isn't going to like this at all."

"Maybe you'd like us to leave, and you can wait until Don comes back and finds you." Jaid tucked the ID away. "Are you Mrs. Vale?"

"Sarah." Indecision warred on the woman's face before her expression changed. Her eyes widened and fixed on something over Jaid's shoulder. She realized Adam must be approaching.

"Mister, you look like a pack of wild dogs got hold of you and used you as a chew toy."

"A flattering description. And not as far from the truth as you might think."

"Mrs. Vale is trying to decide if she'd like us to leave while she waits for her husband or if she'll accept our help getting to the house with a broken leg." Jaid looked over her shoulder at him.

"Seems like a no-brainer, Sarah. May I call you Sarah?" Still transfixed, the woman nodded. "I'd think the thing to do is have the agents here be of some use to you. Get you to the house. Call your husband and possibly a doctor. And then you can order them off your property."

"I . . . yeah, I guess you're right." Jaid and Shepherd bent to help her to her feet. "But my rifle. Don will skin me if I leave it outside."

"I'll get it." Adam headed in that direction. "But I draw the line at fetching the dead turkeys."

They got Sarah to her feet, and she slipped her arms around their shoulders. The height difference between Jaid and Shepherd made it a bit awkward, but Jaid thought they would have moved along easily enough if the other woman hadn't kept twisting her head to watch Adam.

"I've never met anyone like him before." And despite the earlier description she used, Jaid recognized female fascination when presented with it.

"No." A feeling of resignation filled her. "Nobody has."

In the end Adam beat them to the house. He had the door open and a steaming mug ready to hand Sarah Vale once Jaid and Shepherd deposited her in a sitting position on the couch. She seemed a bit bemused as she took the mug from him. "Green tea," he told her. "I found it in the kitchen and assumed you were the tea drinker."

"Yep." She took the cap off and raked her free hand through her shoulder-length red hair. Then she frowned. "Wasn't the door locked?"

"Was it?"

Jaid managed, barely, to avoid rolling her eyes. The

woman seemed absolutely addled with Adam in the vicinity.

"Maybe I forgot to lock it. Didn't figure I'd be gone long."

"Who would you like to call?"

"Oh." She took a sip of the hot tea. "I probably ought to call Don. He's in town. Maybe he can bring the doc out here with him. I'm really not looking forward to bouncing over these roads on the drive into town. My cell is plugged in on the counter in the kitchen."

Jaid said doubtfully, "I'm pretty sure they'll want X-rays."

The other woman waved off her words. "Why bother. I already know it's broken."

Raising her brows, Jaid looked at Adam. He headed to the kitchen for the phone.

"I understand you already had one group of agents speak to your husband recently."

"They tried. Don ran 'em off with the rifle." She sipped again. "He doesn't have much use for most in the government. He's probably not going to like you being here, either."

Adam pulled a straight-back chair closer to the couch. Sat and handed her the cell.

Since Jaid didn't appear to be needed, she moved to join Shepherd on the opposite side of the room.

"Get a load of this," the man muttered as she joined him.

One wall was lined with glassed-in gun cases. It was easy to see where the Vales spent their money. She studied the weapons closely but didn't observe one that matched the model used to assassinate Justice Reinbeck. But then Vale would hardly be likely to keep that weapon on display if he were behind the shooting.

"Don't start hollering at me." Jaid turned at Sarah's sharply raised voice. She was speaking on her cell. "What'd you want me to do, lay out there until you decided to come home and then maybe a few hours more before you even noticed I wasn't around?"

A long silence during which the woman's pale, freckled face flushed a deep red. "The hell I will. What am I supposed to do if I go into shock or something waiting for you? They aren't hurting anything. Well, if you move your tail, you can tell them that yourself, can't you?" She flipped the phone shut, transferred her glare from it to Jaid. "He's not happy about you all being in the house, I can tell you that much."

That, Jaid thought, was the understatement of the century. She could hear every word the man had spoken on the other end of the line, since he'd been speaking at an ear-deafening decibel. "I'm sure he's mostly worried about you."

Sarah stared at her as if to determine if Jaid were joking. Then she snorted. "Yeah, right. I'm never going to hear the end of this. Of course, falling out of the tree wasn't my brainiest move, but he's pulled some boneheaded stunts, too. Got himself booted out of the marines a few years back for one of them. Didn't say much about that did I? Too late to cry over spilled milk, I said."

"That's a broad-minded way to look at it."

The look she sent Adam was grateful. "I thought so."

"So many of our servicemen are returning to civilian life with problems caused by combat. Did he have trouble adjusting when he came back the States?"

His words seemed to require thought. "I don't know. He's always been a bit of a hothead. But when he came home, his fuse seemed even shorter. And he has terrible nightmares. He was never very political before, but he sure has strong opinions now. He's convinced there's a conspiracy afoot to take guns away from law-abiding citizens."

Which would explain his letter to Reinbeck, Jaid thought. "It's easy to see his interest," she said with a nod toward the wall of guns. "That's quite a collection. Does your husband compete?"

"They're all mine," Sarah said quickly. She was obviously aware of the penalty of buying guns for someone prohibited from owning one. "I got a bunch of trophies in the basement. Every time we add another gun case, I have to clear out more space for it."

"Do you compete with the rifles or handguns?"

"I'm better with handguns. Walt has his military training, so he's . . . he used to be a hotshot with the high-powered rifles. His favorite was the M14."

Since more than half of the weapons in the collection were high-powered rifles, it was clear that Walt's interests remained the same. Jaid would be willing to bet that a good number of those trophies in the basement had Sarah's husband's name on them. From what Jaid recalled, no one checked at those competitions whether the contestants were supposed to have access to guns or not.

But of even more interest was the fact that none of the weapons in the case was the type ballistics had linked to the gun that had killed Reinbeck. "Has he ever handled a Remington 700?"

"Oh, sure." She moved slightly, wincing as she responded to Jaid's question. "He talks about me buying one sometimes. But I said, before I bring one more gun in this house, the place could use a coat of paint. I'm sure you noticed," the aside was intended for Adam. "The whole house could tumble down around our ears before he'd ever worry about the roof."

"I suppose you get the opportunity to fire a number of these weapons when you go to these competitions."

"Not just at competitions." Sarah turned to where Shepherd was still looking at the weapons. "Hey, Slick! Bring me that big black scrapbook on top of the dark brown gun safe there, will you?"

Slick. Suppressing a grin, Jaid slid a gaze at Shepherd. It was an apt enough nickname, one he responded to with little more than a cocked brow. He retrieved the scrapbook and brought it over. Adam vacated the chair he'd been sitting on so the book could be laid on the seat, within reach of Sarah.

"Here's a photo of me after winning a competition where I used a Glock G34, a personal favorite of mine. I've placed before with the Smith & Wesson 625, but I've never won without the Glock."

"It's a reliable weapon." Adam perused the picture closely. "Might as well go with what works."

"That's what I say, but, Walt, he likes to shake things up. He's got more wins than me, but I've placed more overall." She seemed to have forgotten the need to keep quiet about her husband's competing. Sarah reached out to flip the pages to show them. There were a number of pictures with one or the other of them posing, never together, with a trophy or certificate. Jaid tried to position herself close to Adam to get a good view of the photos. She wanted to look for any showing Walt with a Remington 700.

She didn't find one. But she was intrigued to notice that interspersed between the endless pages of competition photos were tucked campaign letters and posters.

"These must be Walt's." Adam reached down for one and unfolded an NRA flier with a list of the organization's political endorsements for the last election. "You said he'd gotten interested in politics."

"Yeah. I hate politics and politicians myself. But Walt thinks we have to support those who are committed to preserving second amendment rights." Adam tucked the sheet back in the book and flipped some more pages. "Like that one. There." He stopped at a page Sarah was indicating. "Like I said, we don't only shoot at club-sponsored competitions. More and more politicians are trying to show how pro-gun they are by hosting informal competitions of their own as campaign events. Went to this one last year." The poster she unfolded was emblazoned with the Reelect Newell banner. Jaid lifted a knowing gaze to Adam. Newell definitely talked the talk. It was hardly surprising that he'd release a photo op of him with a gun.

But seeing Adam's unswerving attention to the poster, she looked at it again. And noted that it wasn't just Newell in the photo, but three younger men, all bearing rifles like the senator. Two of them bore what she thought was an unfortunate family resemblance to Newell. The third was

Joseph Bailey. The caption below the photo identified the others as Newell's sons.

But a moment later she saw what held Adam's focus. Her breath stopped in her throat.

Jonas Newell's face was wreathed in a creaky smile that struck her as more than a little spooky.

And he was holding a Remington 700.

———————

They'd discussed it on the way back from Purcellville. Their chance of getting Hedgelin to seek a warrant for Senator Newell's private residence was zero unless they could present him with a copy of that campaign poster. A copy that was proving exceedingly difficult to produce.

They were back at headquarters, having commandeered another small conference room. Jaid had ensured this one had heat before approving it. They were all on their laptops, trolling the Internet for a copy of the poster that had been tucked inside the Vales' scrapbook. With a singular lack of success.

Adam's phone rang, interrupting his search. Jaid found herself much more interested in his one-sided conversation than in the pages and pages of online Newell stories. Her own cell buzzed, signaling an incoming text.

With a measure of trepidation, she took it out and read it, her mouth tightening.

Considered my offer? Your cooperation is a good deal for all. Especially your son.

Bolton, the son of a bitch, wasn't giving up. She slipped the phone into her pocket again, not even considering responding. Her lack of response wouldn't stop him from trying again, however. Sooner or later she was going to have to confront the man once and for all.

And she would. Just as soon as she could figure out a way to make him back off and still have him lose interest in digging up more details regarding Royce's birth.

Adam ended his call and slipped his phone into his pocket. "That was Sarah Vale. She's on her way home from the hospital. X-rays showed her leg broken in two places, as predicted by the nurse her husband returned to the house with. She'll be in a cast for six to eight weeks."

"We could have taken her there ourselves and saved a lot of time," Jaid pointed out.

"Apparently, that wasn't a possibility until her husband was convinced of the need. It doesn't sound like she makes many decisions without his say-so."

"Think she knows that as a dishonorably discharged former member of the military, he's prohibited from buying or owning a weapon?" Shepherd glanced up from his computer as he spoke.

"Apparently, they don't check on those sorts of things at shooting competitions. And Hedgelin said that the guns are all in Sarah's name."

"But it's still likely a major factor in Vale wanting to keep the last task force team out of his house. In addition to his dislike for the government, that is." Sarah Vale had gotten increasingly agitated the more time that had passed. She'd obviously wanted them gone before her husband arrived. When pressed, she'd told them that she and Walt had spent the night with friends in Middleburg two nights ago. Jaid had already made a call to the couple in question and verified the Vales' whereabouts. Overall, she would have counted the trip to Purcellville a bust. If not for the poster of Newell.

An idea occurred to her. A slow smile crossed her face.

Noting it, Adam said, "I learned a long time ago not to trust that expression."

"We could be at this all night. But it occurs to me that we know one person who could make our lives easier and tell us where to find the photo we're looking for."

There was the glimmer of an answering smile on Adam's face. "Scott Lambert."

Assistant Director Hedgelin gazed at the legal-sized copy they'd made of Senator Newell's campaign poster and looked as though he'd tasted something particularly foul. "And you're absolutely sure about this? Because anyone can Photoshop a few pictures together and make an explosive and completely false new product."

"You can verify it with Transparent Campaigns, which is a nonprofit with the stated mission of looking over campaign speeches and visuals, and cutting through the rhetoric to evaluate the truth of the particular message. They keep records going back two election cycles." Jaid didn't think it was necessary to tell him that Lambert had told them where to look. It was a good guess that Newell wouldn't have been forthcoming if they'd asked him for a copy of it.

"We saw an original at Donald Vale's house," Shepherd put in. "Two years ago it was widely distributed, at least among constituents who would approve of Newell's stand on second amendment rights. The caption on the poster quotes the senator as talking about the type of rifle he's carrying and the number and model of other weapons he owns. He's shown with the exact same type of rifle as the one that killed Justice Reinbeck. He has a long history of animosity toward the judge. We can't afford to ignore that just because of who he is."

"I'm not suggesting we ignore it," Hedgelin snapped. "But getting a warrant for a sitting U.S. senator's home isn't going to be quick or easy. That's assuming, of course, that I can convince the director and a judge that we have cause."

"Of course, we have cause," Jaid started. Her words died abruptly when Adam skewered her with a look. She understood the enormity of the decision about to fall on Hedgelin's shoulders, but she was wearying of the need to tap-dance through the political minefields. It took a moment to swallow the words she wanted to utter and reach for a measure of diplomacy. "We'll wait to hear what you decide."

She held her tongue as they made their way out of Hedgelin's office. Down a couple floors to the conference room they had recently vacated. But once there she could remain silent no longer. "That warrant better come through."

"It'll come through," Adam assured her. He didn't share her level of agitation. But then again she couldn't recall a time when she'd seen him rattled.

With the exception, perhaps, of the other night in front of Harandi's house. Why the memory would pick that particular time to ambush her she couldn't say. She'd successfully dodged it for the last several days.

Even if she'd not always been quite as successful at banishing the taste of his mouth on hers during the long, lonely hours of the nights.

He hadn't made a move since that was less than circumspect. But there was a renewed awareness between them. A current that snapped and sparked to life at the oddest moments. She'd intercepted a couple odd looks from Shepherd lately, as if he, too, had picked up on it.

Or the entire thing could be in her head. Adam had proven once before that he was more than capable of setting aside emotion. Of carving it from his life with the precision of a surgeon. This time Jaid wasn't going to be the one left raw and hurting. She'd developed her own self-preservation instincts over the years. She'd had to.

They sat nearly silently in the conference room, all of them poring over the newest information in the case file today. Shepherd was scribbling notes and making what looked like a chart at the other end of the table. The sheer volume of the material included in the online file made her sympathize with the intelligence analysts whose job it was to compile the information on the reports and fold it into the appropriate places in the case file.

And after a couple hours of studying the latest additions, her sympathies solidified.

"Page four hundred eighty," Adam said in a quiet voice. Her gaze flashed to him then back down at the computer. She scrolled to the appropriate page and scanned it. Then backed up to read it more slowly. "The cyber unit was able to retrieve one of the messages that Lambert says was sent to his computer but then seemed to disappear afterward. It was embedded in the memory. A copy of it is on the page."

Tom Shepherd looked up, interest alight in his blue eyes. "Shows what I know. I thought the guy was making it up, but in any case there are plenty of online programs that allow you to send self-destructing e-mails. Most even have commands you can set, controlling the ability to print or forward the message or setting the time for it to vanish. The programs must have gotten more high-tech if the cyber crimes unit was only able to recover one, though."

He would know, Jaid acknowledged. He'd come from the elite unit himself, years ago. "But the creator of that cell phone spyware was way ahead of what could be bought commercially. It's possible he also came up with a better self-destruct e-mail messaging system."

"It occurs to me that there's a fairly easy way to determine if Lambert authored the message retrieved by the cyber techs. Have a forensic linguist take a look at it, compare it to his written statement, and see if they match."

Jaid looked at Shepherd. "Okay. I imagine the bureau has linguists at Quantico."

Adam's attention had drifted back to his screen. "They do. But I have the top forensic linguist in the country working for me. Macy Reid. Stole her away from California's Bureau of Investigation and Intelligence a few years back. She was instrumental in helping us find the kidnap victim in that case we worked last January."

"Maybe Hedgelin already has someone on that." Jaid took out her phone and called the man. Got no answer. She left him a voice mail, but another thought had occurred. She looked at Adam consideringly. The assistant director was likely neck deep in selling a warrant on Newell's home to his superiors. He wasn't likely to be answering anytime soon.

"I wouldn't mind taking another run at Lambert. See if maybe he has any other written communications that he didn't tell us about."

Shepherd frowned. "What's the point? We've already got what we need to compare the two, right?"

"We could double-check with Sanchez, too. Maybe there

was a note enclosed with the thousand Lambert paid him."

The other agent looked at her quizzically. "Wouldn't he have told us that before?"

"We didn't ask. And he became much more talkative once he got to lockup, remember?"

Adam surveyed her for a moment. Then he rose. "Jaid could be right. It doesn't hurt to check it out. We'll likely wait hours to hear one way or another on the Newell warrant. It may not even come through until tomorrow."

Shepherd looked torn. "I think we should remain here, just in case."

"Why don't you stay? We'll run over to the Alexandria federal holding facility. Lambert and Sanchez are both being housed there for now. You can call us if there's news, and we can meet if needed."

"That works, I guess." The agent looked back down at his notes. "I'm in the middle of something here anyway."

"All right, then. Keep us posted of any developments." The door closed behind them, and Jaid walked silently beside Adam to the elevator. "I'll drive. I think I'm a bit closer than you are in the garage."

The double doors opened noiselessly. They stepped inside. Were joined by a clerk pushing an empty coffee cart. Jaid and Adam moved to opposite corners for the duration of the ride. But when they reached the main level and headed toward the front door, Adam picked up the conversation where it left off. "My car's more comfortable. I'll drive."

She managed, barely, to avoid rolling her eyes. "Whatever."

"You just need to tell me where we're really going before we reach the car."

Jaid couldn't prevent the tiny smile that threatened. Most of the time she hated being so transparent to the man. But there were times when it could be an advantage to have his thoughts so attuned to hers. "It was when you mentioned the forensic linguist," she admitted. "It occurred to me that we can kill two birds with one stone. Why not drop by where your latest would-be assassin is being held, too. What's his name, Ferrell?"

They headed out into the bright sunshine. The temperatures had done a fickle about-face and climbed thirty degrees in the last couple days. In November that was a gift, and one Jaid welcomed.

"I'm not following. What do you hope to accomplish by talking to Ferrell?"

She shot him a sideways glance as they rounded the corner toward the bureau's employee parking garage. "Don't play obtuse. Not with me. Ferrell claims whoever hired him referred to himself as LeCroix. Then lo and behold, Scott Lambert now says he's John LeCroix's son. That didn't seem a wee bit coincidental to you?"

"Let's put it this way. I don't need to provide Hedgelin with any more ammunition to scream conflict of interest and get me removed from this case."

The breeze ruffled his hair. Jaid jammed her free hand deeper into her pocket to squelch a ridiculous urge to smooth it. "Maybe Hedgelin doesn't need to know."

She felt the heat from his intense stare before she met it. "What? I'm not suggesting coloring outside the lines here. We go through the channels and make a formal request for the written communication received by Lambert to be matched with his written statement. Text of both can be found in the case file. You can be up front about it and tell Hedgelin you submitted it to your own forensic linguist. It's not like that damages the evidence in any way."

"Macy has actually conducted classes at Quantico in the past," he murmured, as he walked beside her. "Her name would be familiar to them. She's widely considered one of the national experts in her field."

"Even better. So how can Hedgelin fuss about using her? He can still run it by the linguists in the labs for a second opinion. But this way you can figure out once and for all if your case and the one we're working have any more in common that a long-dead man's name."

At his silence she reached out a hand to tug on his

sleeve. "You need that information. It will help protect you in the future. You can't pass up a chance to get a better idea of who might be targeting you and why."

"I don't want to place you in a bad position with the bureau."

Irritation filled her. She dropped her hand and resumed walking. "Don't be ridiculous. At any rate we don't need to make a decision about how to handle this until and unless we actually know there's something to compare. You know where Ferrell is locked up?"

"The Adult Detention Center in Manassas. He's being held without bond."

She pulled her phone out of her pocket as they entered the parking garage. "I'll call and let them know we're coming. On the way there I can put a call in to Sanchez. But I doubt he has any written communication from whoever bought the cardinal's security code from him. There was no reason to risk it."

There was a small smile playing along Adam's mouth. "So that suggestion in headquarters was just to discourage Shepherd from tagging along?"

She was already bent over her phone. "It would have been difficult to explain a trip to see Ferrell to him, but I'd have thought of some reason to have him wait in the car."

"You've become more devious over the years. A trait that really doesn't get enough credit."

"I'm a woman in a male-dominated career." She found the number she was looking for. Dialed it. "I use the tools required to level the playing field." By the time Adam had unlocked his vehicle and she'd joined him in it, she already had the superintendent at ADC on the line. Before they exited the garage, she'd acquired permission to see Ferrell as soon as they arrived.

"Just so I have this straight, I'm not going to Alexandria at all?"

"I'm putting a call in for Sanchez next. Is it okay if I just have one of the deputies ask the question for us?" She took the lift of his shoulder as agreement. "I don't want to overbook us in case that warrant comes through sooner rather than later." She refused to contemplate the prospect of a judge refusing to issue one. Surely the recent high-profile murders outweighed the possibility of ticking off a high-ranking member of Congress.

They were already on Interstate 66 toward Manassas before Jaid hung up the phone that time. "I spoke to a Deputy Watkins. He promised to get back to me once he speaks with Sanchez." While she spoke, she checked her incoming message box, which had sounded while she was on the phone.

Her mouth tightened when she saw yet another message from Bolton. Same general idea. Cockier now. He thought he had her. He really thought she was going to cave to his threats and intimidation.

Maybe he should have spent more time getting to know her before trying to cop a feel a decade earlier. Because there had to be a way out of the corner he'd boxed her into. She wasn't through looking for it.

"That conversation between you and Bolton a few days ago"—she realized by Adam's immediate stillness that she could have introduced the topic more smoothly—"you said he'd gotten an extension from his publisher."

"I've made it a point to stay abreast of his progress." If he wondered at her sudden renewal of interest in the topic, he didn't reveal it. Just switched lanes to go around a slower-moving passenger bus. "From what I've been able to discover, Bolton sold a proposal for a book on my life with the promise of inside information." His smile was chilly. "He has since learned that the people in position to have those sorts of details aren't willing to share them with him."

Jaid knew she needed to proceed cautiously. The last thing she wanted was for Adam to find out about Bolton's threats. He had a fierce protective instinct. And she didn't want the reporter to get another shot at him on her account.

She also didn't require a man to fight her battles. "How long will the publisher be patient with him?" It'd help to know how much time she had. She just needed to come up with a reason to put him off long enough for her to come up with a way to get rid of him for good.

"Hopefully, if he can't deliver as promised in the next few months, it will cause him some serious issues. I've already had my attorney contact the publisher about our readiness with a lawsuit if he publishes anything not based in fact. Hopefully, that will ensure that they'll be certain he can substantiate anything he puts in the book."

She stared, momentarily distracted from her reason for asking. "That doesn't sound like you."

"I value my privacy," he said shortly. "And I don't intend to become Bolton's stepping stone to his next award."

It was a sentiment she could echo. She had no intention of letting the reporter trample her son in his quest to further his career at Adam's expense, either.

If she were smart, and maybe a bit lucky, she'd come up with a way for both her and Adam to accomplish their goals.

Chapter 15

Mose Ferrell paused just inside the doorway as he was being shown into the interview room, shock apparent in his expression. With a nudge from the green-clad guard at his back, he continued into the room. Neither his hands nor his feet were bound.

"Sit down, Ferrell." Adam slid a chair on the opposite side of the table out with a push from his cane. "I have a couple more questions for you."

The man looked back toward the guard who'd brought him in, only to find the door closed behind him.

"They won't come back for you until we tell them we're finished here. Sit."

The man seemed reluctant to follow Adam's direction. "Who's she?"

"Special Agent Marlowe, FBI." The man's brows rose when Jaid spoke. And he finally approached the table.

"Need to bring backup, this time, Raiker?" The man dropped heavily into the wooden institution-issued chair. Stared at Jaid. "Guess I shouldn't complain. Don't see too many females in this place. And my assistant public defender sure isn't much to look at. She's no damn good at all, tell ya the truth. Couldn't even get bail set."

"Well, give her some slack. You didn't exactly hand her an easy case." Jaid folded her hands on the table. "I hear they're considering adding terrorism to the attempted-murder charge." She'd just made that up, but the idea had merit. From what the superintendent had told her, Ferrell had used enough explosives to take out the entire street Adam's loft sat on. If the prosecutor weren't piling on more charges, he wasn't doing his job.

The man's eyes bugged. "What? That's bullshit! Where'd you hear that? C'mon, Raiker, tell her that's bullshit. I wasn't blowing up the town. Just your place."

"Remind me again how that admission helps you?" Remarkably, there was a note of amusement in Adam's voice. Jaid had the odd thought that his self-proclaimed sense of humor picked the oddest moments to appear.

"This thing," Ferrell wagged his finger between him and Adam, "it was just between the two of us. And nothing personal. Hey, I spilled my guts while you held a gun on me in your garage, right?" The man made an expansive gesture. "I got no secrets. We're looking for a plea deal, but the prosecutors are being dicks about it. Maybe you can do something there for me."

For sheer gall, Jaid figured that suggestion topped the list. But Ferrell uttered it with a straight face. She had to wonder if the man were playing with a full deck. In the next moment she recalled Adam saying this guy was nowhere near the caliber of Jennings, the assassin who had made four attempts before nearly killing him last May. Which made her wonder anew at Ferrell's hiring. Had he been meant to get caught? To fail? If so, she couldn't imagine a reason for that, other than to get Adam off the case.

"Maybe we can work something out." Her attention snapped to Adam. It took a moment to recall that this was exactly why they had come. "Have you ever seen this man before?"

She hadn't realized he'd brought along the likeness of Lambert they'd shown to Sorenson. But there was no flicker of recognition on Ferrell's face. "No, should I know him?"

Raiker just tucked the picture away again and said, "I'd like to hear more about how you were contacted by this mystery employer of yours."

Ferrell's expression went sly. "I been around the block a time or two. I ain't doing anymore talking 'til you put something in writing. Like if I help you out, you drop the charges against me."

Jaid's eyes slid shut in sheer frustration. Where'd this guy been found?

"Only the prosecutor can drop the charges." Adam obviously had far more patience than she did. A discovery that wasn't exactly a news flash. "All I can do is tell them about the level of cooperation you exhibit. It will be up to them to factor that into their consideration when determining the sentence they ask for. I can, however, make a strong suggestion on your behalf."

The man was silent, looking from one to the other of them as if still trying to figure an angle. Jaid pushed her chair back and said to Adam, "We're wasting our time here. He's got nothing."

"Well, maybe I do and maybe I don't." Ferrell appeared to be mulling something over. It didn't seem to be a quick process. "Don't get yourself in a hurry there. To answer your question, I got a package in my mailbox."

Adam fixed him with a dark look. "You said he always contacted you over the phone. Using a voice distorter."

"And he did. Later. But I didn't have a phone at first." Ferrell obviously felt the need to explain this lack to Jaid. "After I got out of the joint, I fell on hard times, y'know? Couldn't get a decent job, and there wasn't money for extras."

"Tough economy," she responded, tongue in cheek.

He nodded vigorously. "You said it. So I'm working odd jobs, just taking what comes my way, right? And about three weeks ago I find this big envelope shoved in my mailbox. In it is one of them phones you can get at the store. With a card of prepaid minutes instead of a plan."

"TracFone," Adam murmured.

"Right. And there's this short typewritten note, saying how if I wanted a job, someone would be contacting me, and I should take the call where no one would hear." He shrugged his massive shoulders. "So I do it, right? Get a call the next night. The guy tells me what he wants me to do and what he'll pay."

"And do you still have this envelope? And the note inside it?"

"That first night, the guy told me to destroy both."

Jaid sat back, a hiss of frustration escaping her. But Ferrell wasn't done. "But I figure, hey, hang on to them until I know the guy is good for the money. In case there was a way to trace either one of them if he stiffed me."

"Where are they?" Her patience had reached the breaking point. "I suppose when they searched your place investigators picked them up."

Ferrell shook his head. "Doubt that. I never kept much in that rat hole I lived in. You could get in the place through the cellar windows with just a screwdriver. I didn't have much to steal, but if I had, it would have been gone the first week. Naw, I stashed it in a box for my sister to keep for me. She lives a couple miles from here. She isn't my biggest fan, but if she still has the box, you can see for yourself that I'm telling the truth."

His gaze bounced from one of them to the other, his eyes anxious. "What I want to know is what's it going to be worth to you?"

"We won't know that until we see what's in that box. If she still has it." Adam rose, went to the door, and gestured for the guard outside. "Let's see if we can get permission for you to make a phone call and let your sister know we're on our way."

———

Martha Montrose didn't share her brother's last name, but she did share an unfortunate resemblance in terms of build and looks. She must have been waiting for them, because when Adam turned into the rutted dirt driveway beside the address they'd been given, the woman opened the door and came out on the porch, holding a cardboard box tied shut with string.

Her hair was a longer version of the grizzled gray-brown of her brother. She wore a black sweater over a flannel shirt and jeans, and a grim expression. Thrusting the box toward Jaid, she said, "You tell that no-good brother of mine that I'm done with him. I don't want to hold any more of his stuff. I don't need feds sniffing round here because of him. He's been nothing but trouble since he first got sent up."

"Has anyone else been by asking about him?" Jaid was unsurprised when the woman shook her head vigorously in response, but it had been worth a shot.

"No, and if they know what's good for 'em they won't be. Don't want the sort he hangs with coming round here any more than I do cops." Her gaze lingered on Adam, as if unsure in what category to place him. But she didn't wonder long. As soon as Jaid took the box from the woman, she stomped back in the house and closed the door with a resounding slam.

"You know, I actually find myself liking her brother better?"

Jaid smiled at Adam's words as they headed back to the car. A couple stray cats darted across their path and disappeared through the broken lattice below the porch. "I'll feel a lot more friendly toward her if that note Ferrell told us about is in here."

When they got in the car, he made no move to start it. Not without some difficulty she removed the string and opened the box. There was little in it. A sheaf of papers outlining the conditions of Ferrell's last parole with a card bearing the parole officer's name and number. A list of businesses, which Jaid thought might have been offered as possible job opportunities. And a folded empty manila envelope.

It was that which she took out, smoothed. There was nothing written on it but Ferrell's name and address, but it carried a local postmark. That alone wouldn't help them trace the sender. Anyone could drive up to the mail drop box and leave a package, as long as plenty of postage was affixed.

She drew out a slip of paper from inside the envelope, smoothed it out. The typed message read:

> I understand you're a man who can be relied upon to get things done. If you're looking for a job, answer the phone when it rings. Take the call where you'll have plenty of privacy.

Excitement kick-started in her system. She looked at Adam. "Is this enough for your linguist to match with Lambert's statement and the message the cyber crimes unit recovered on Lambert's computer?"

"Only one way to find out." He started the car, began to back out of the drive. Jaid noticed that Martha was watching them from between two slats of the blinds covering the front window. "It's almost five. My place isn't far from here. I can scan the information needed and get it sent to Macy from my apartment. Or we can head back into the city, and you can get your vehicle and maybe actually get home in time to see your son tonight."

The silence of her phone took on new meaning. No one had called her about the warrant on Newell's house. Logically, Jaid knew that meant it hadn't come through yet. "How long does it take to run the written communication samples for a match?"

"Macy has to diagram them first." Adam straightened the car and headed across town. "Once she has that done, she feeds them into a database, and from there it's only ten or fifteen minutes."

Jaid hesitated indecisively. She was anxious to get an

answer from the linguist. Unlike other portions of the case, the information wouldn't be a long time coming. And she wasn't unmoved by the prospect of actually tucking her son into bed herself tonight.

"Let me talk to Shepherd," she said finally. "See what's new there. In the meantime let's head over to your apartment and get these communications delivered to your linguist."

"I'll give her a call to let her know to be standing by for them." Adam pulled out his phone as he drove. She did the same, just as her cell rang.

There was a brief flare of panic, followed by a surge of irritation. Deliberately, she checked the screen. It was the deputy who had spoken to Sanchez, not Kale Bolton. Mentally damning her involuntary response, she answered, listened to the brief details the man provided before thanking him and ending the call. Then, since Adam was still occupied on the phone, she dialed Tom Shepherd. He answered on the second ring.

"Hey, did you get anything from Sanchez?"

"No." She was able to answer that much honestly, which helped allay a bit of the guilt she felt for deceiving the man about the nature of their trip. "There was never any sort of written communication delivered. He dealt in person with Lambert each time."

The agent's voice was matter-of-fact. "Well, it was a long shot. I haven't heard from Hedgelin regarding the warrant. Wondering now if there will be any decision tonight. Have you talked to him?"

Disappointment flickered although she'd expected as much from the silence. "No. I imagine I'll hear when you do."

"One way or another." Shepherd sounded unusually gloomy. "I just hope politics don't trump a promising lead."

Silently, she seconded that thought. "I'll submit the report tonight." And when she did, hopefully she'd have some information regarding whether the message from Lambert's computer had been written by him or by someone else.

"Okay, good. There's something else, though." At Shepherd's lowered tone she shot a surreptitious look toward Adam. He was still engaged in his conversation with the linguist. "I've been doing some digging into the witness statements for the cardinal. Made a phone call to Denise Quincy, the cardinal's secretary. According to her, Cardinal Cote had a meeting set up with Monsignor Jerry Benton the night before his death. I thought it was interesting that the pastor didn't think to share that with us."

Trepidation pooled in her stomach. "He mentioned that their relationship was rocky."

"Yeah, but not why. According to Quincy, the good monsignor was the subject of numerous complaints from some of the nonprofit boards he sat on. The complaints were directed to the cardinal, and that's probably the topic of the conversation they had on the night in question."

Just having this conversation made her feel more than a little traitorous. With effort she kept her gaze from traveling to Adam again. "Hard to make the leap from dislike to murder, though, isn't it? Under the circumstances."

"But not impossible." Shepherd sounded stubborn. "At any rate I'm looking harder at Benton. Maybe I'll have more by tomorrow."

Adam had hung up by then. And Jaid didn't want to continue this conversation while he was listening. "All right. We'll catch up then."

"No warrant yet, I take it." She didn't recognize the route he was taking, which consisted of one residential street after another. She was familiar with how to get to Manassas but not the town itself.

"No word from Hedgelin. There has to be a decision one way or another by tomorrow morning, doesn't there?"

"I'm guessing that three homicides of high-profile targets trumps the possibility of pissing off a longtime senator. But that doesn't discount the delicacy needed."

"And delicacy takes time?"

Although he didn't smile, his face lightened. "It does, yes. Although I'll admit that I don't have infinite patience for it, I have, over the years, acquired some expertise in the area. It comes in handy when teaming with the various law enforcement entities that hire us."

Jaid just bet it did. "Lots of egos to massage?"

"People skills are as important as investigative ones these days. A sad fact of life." He was slowing at a large warehouse on a corner near the outskirts of town. But when he turned into the lot in front of it, she frowned. "Where are we . . . oh." Comprehension dawned. She slanted him a look. "Your new penthouse?"

His expression was unenthusiastic. "Paulie says it's trendy. The damn Realtor says it's trendy. But it's a warehouse. That's what you see when you look at it, right?"

She wasn't about to walk into that one. "I haven't seen the inside yet. I'm withholding judgment until then." And Jaid had to admit to a burst of interest at her opportunity to see his new place. She'd never been to the penthouse that had been destroyed months ago when Jennings had shot an incendiary device through the window. Adam had lived in a town house when they'd been together. But it was his suite at Mojy's that she'd always associate with him.

With *them*.

It took effort to sidestep the memories that could so easily swamp her. She raised her brows when he tapped a button on the garage opener attached to his visor and a large metal door rose. As he sent the door descending behind them, she got out of the car and looked around the space. The square footage of the garage they were in would rival the first floor of her house for space. It was mostly empty, save several large boxes stacked along one wall. And a large set of shelves full of power tools and gadgets that she couldn't imagine Adam ever having an interest in using.

To her surprise, he didn't lead her toward the steel door in the far wall. Instead, she followed him to the set of shelves. Restrained an urge to applaud when he reached under one of them and the entire wall slid to the side revealing yet another door.

"Does James Bond know you're living in his house?"

she inquired as she followed him through the opening. With a quick glance over her shoulder, she saw the wall closing silently behind them.

"He can have it back," he said darkly. The vestibule they were in held only an elevator. A private one, obviously, since he had to punch in a code before the doors would open. "It's like living in a fortress. Paulie's in love with the intrigue. I find it all a royal pain in the ass."

She joined him in the elevator. Noted that it required yet another code to move. "If it keeps you safer, I'm with Paulie. It's more than worth it."

Adam looked unconvinced. And maybe she could feel a bit of sympathy for him when there was yet another code to punch in before unlocking the front door to his place. She had enough time to realize there were no other apartments that could be accessed from here. Then he pushed the front door open, and she stepped inside, more than a little curious to see the place he now called home.

The main floor they walked into was little more than a large man cave. Jaid noted the punishing-looking exercise equipment, wet bar, hot tub, and leather furniture grouped around a big-screen TV she couldn't picture him watching. An open staircase was tucked into a far corner, and she wondered what had possessed Paulie to find a place for Adam that required walking a flight of stairs every time he wanted to get from one part of the home to the other.

Realizing his gaze was on her then, she searched for something to say. "It's a loft. With the gentrification going on in downtown DC these days, more and more places like this are cropping up." Not exactly like this one, of course. Certainly not with the level of security she'd seen downstairs. And while she approved wholeheartedly with the measures taken, there was nothing on the inside that told much about the man who lived here.

He'd used a gym when they'd been together. They'd worked out at the same one, in an effort to spend more time together. Without waiting for an invitation, she moved freely into the space, looking her fill. The equipment and hot tub would be more necessary than ever with the extent of his injuries. *Permanent nerve damage.* She could still hear the Louisiana surgeon's voice. *But at least we saved the leg.*

Before the memories could catch and take hold, she moved to the bar. Ran her fingers over the dark marble top. She recognized the brand of Scotch stocking the shelves. It was perhaps the only thing on this floor that reflected what she could recall of the man's tastes.

"My office is upstairs." She followed him to the staircase. Was relieved to see him ascend it with a nimbleness she would have doubted a few moments earlier. Jaid hadn't been around to see how Adam had adapted to the physical limitations he was left with. It was unsurprising that he'd handled them with the same deft equanimity that he'd dealt with the demands of his job.

But it hurt, more than it should have, to recognize that he'd dealt with them relatively alone.

The upstairs held a few more hints of the man's personality than had the lower level. The galley kitchen tucked into one corner of the room looked as though it was rarely touched. A huge office took up most of the area. She imagined the other doorways led to bedrooms.

The office held an array of computers, shelves of books, with a C-shaped desk dominating the center of the space. He went to the desk now and set his briefcase on it. Snapped it open.

She found a seat on a navy armchair made of a rich, buttery leather. Taking out the note they'd gotten from Ferrell's sister, she left her briefcase beside the chair and got up to hand it to Adam. "How much text does the linguist need for a match?"

"I don't know exactly," he admitted. "Lambert's statement will certainly provide her with plenty of content. But the two notes, this one and the one from his computer . . . they'll be more challenging. But she's done it with less. She's brilliant at her job."

While he spoke, he brought up the private case-file site.

Keyed in the code and scrolled until he found the part with Lambert's statement. Printed that section. He repeated the action with the message the cyber unit had retrieved from his computer. The one he claimed had come from the DC killer. Then Adam scanned all of them on the large capable-looking printer next to his desk. Sat down and opened up his e-mail. Sent the whole thing.

"Sort of makes fax machines obsolete, doesn't it?" Jaid nodded toward the printer. The most time-consuming part of the entire process had been looking up the appropriate part of the report to print out.

He swiveled his chair to face her. "And now we've come to your favorite part."

She made a face. "Waiting. How long do you expect it to be?"

"Not more than two hours, I wouldn't think. Probably less. But knowing Macy, she'll verify and re-verify the results before contacting me again."

Jaid checked the clock on her phone. "I suppose I should go back for my car." She hesitated, torn. "I hate to take you away from your computer while you're waiting for results, though."

He shrugged. Rose. "Are you sure you want to go all the way back in to the city? It's closer just to take you home from here. I can send a car for you tomorrow."

"I don't like being without a vehicle at night. If something happens with Royce, I need to be able to get him to a hospital." She correctly interpreted the look he gave her. "Not that I expect anything to . . . it's a mother thing." The cell in her phone rang, and she started a little as she looked down at the screen. "Déjà vu," she muttered.

Turning away from him, she said, "Hey, buddy. I was just talking about you. Sort of."

The tumble of words greeting her ears was practically indecipherable. "Mom, Michael's mom said it was okay, and Andrew's mom said it was okay, and now you just need to say it's okay, and then we can all . . ."

"Whoa. Slow down. I can't understand . . ."

"Here, Stacy, tell my mom so I can go pack!"

"Pack?" Jaid waited impatiently for the babysitter to come on the phone. "Stacy, where does Royce think he's going?"

The girl's easygoing tones filled her ears. "Hey, Ms. M. I told him you had to okay it first. Michael's mom called and asked if Royce could sleep over tonight. I guess another boy is staying, too. She's going to take them to that new animated film they've been talking about. And apparently, there's also pizza involved."

"What?" Jaid frowned. "No. Not on a school night. What is Mrs. Kettleson even thinking to suggest . . ."

"Tomorrow's teacher in-service, remember? You had me lined up to sit all day again?"

At the girl's reminder Jaid's eyelids slid shut in a mental head slap. How she'd managed to forget that already when she'd just hired Stacy for the day last week was beyond her. It was a measure of how the case had taken precedence in her mind.

"I hate to leave you hanging, though. You probably gave up plans."

"No problem. Some of my friends are going to the mall tomorrow. This way I get to hang out with them awhile. And I'll be sure and be back by the time Mrs. Kettleson says she's going to drop Royce off. You won't have to worry about a thing."

Which was easier said than done. There was her son to talk to. And her usual list of warnings and reminders to deliver. Then she had to call Mrs. Kettleson. Pretend that she wasn't the loser mother who had completely lost track of the school calendar. There was small talk to make, thanks to deliver. Laughing warnings shared about her son's appetite. All the while she was mentally wondering when she would have the opportunity to reciprocate. When she was working a case, she didn't even have weekends free.

It was a good twenty minutes later before she turned back to Adam, slipping the phone in her coat pocket.

He appeared engrossed in something on the computer

screen, which rivaled the size of her television at home. "So." He looked up. Turned to face her. "I take it plans for the evening have changed."

"Racking up another nomination for mother of the year. I forgot that there's no school tomorrow. Royce is headed for a friend's house for an overnight, which trumps having his mom home early tonight."

"I imagine in his eyes, allowing him to go with his friend did nudge you up to award territory."

Jaid gave a half smile, wished she could believe it. "Seems like I spend half my time feeling guilty over something I did. Or didn't do. The other half is spent promising myself I'll make it up to him when I'm late. Or have to cancel plans because I have to work through the weekend." She stopped, slightly embarrassed to reveal that much to Adam. Being a parent brought with it a slew of insecurities that once would have been foreign to her.

"I don't know much about the parenting thing, but I imagine the guilt is supposed to go hand in hand with it if you're doing it right."

She blew out a breath. "Then I must be doing something very right, because that's the overwhelming emotion most of the time." She unbuttoned her coat and laid it over the chair where she'd left her briefcase and purse. "Do you have any food at all in this place?"

His hesitation was its own answer. "Ah . . . possibly."

"Sounds promising." She opened cupboards and drawers before checking the refrigerator. The combined contents were meager. "Our choices are soup of a questionable expiration date or"—she took the cheese from the refrigerator, examined it suspiciously—"cheese sandwiches. I'm guessing you'd rather have the sandwich."

"You guess right. But I don't expect you to make me dinner."

"A sandwich isn't dinner, Adam. It barely qualifies as lunch." She slipped out of her tan jacket and hung it on the back of one of the barstools at the counter. The shoulder harness was next. She'd gotten in the habit of locking her weapon in a gun case kept in the trunk of her car to keep it safe from Royce's curiosity. But there were no kids to worry about here. "If you find yourself overcome with gratitude for my culinary talents, you can fetch some wine from that very well-stocked bar of yours downstairs."

After doing so, he shrugged out of his suit coat and loosened his tie while she swiftly cooked the meal. His weapon joined hers on the corner of the counter. They dined elbow to elbow, on the stools that she'd hazard a guess hadn't been used more than a handful of times since he'd moved in. She ate slowly, enjoying the wine he'd chosen as much as the incongruity of sipping it over the basic meal. Adam seemed to have no such problem. He plowed through two sandwiches in between sips of the Scotch he'd poured in lieu of wine.

"Remember when we arrested that wine collector?"

She got up to take their plates to the dishwasher. "I never would have believed that someone would murder over a bottle of merlot." The appliance looked like something out of the future. It took a full minute just to figure how to open the thing.

"He got out of prison early. Turns out the bureau used him to turn state's evidence for a ring of smugglers who were stealing wine in Europe from the top vineyards, putting on a new label, and then shipping them over here. And they were unbelievably vicious. Last I heard they'd uncovered no fewer than half-a-dozen homicides enacted as they—" He broke off, cocking his head. "I'll grab that for you."

A bit disconcerted by the non sequitur, she straightened from putting the dishes in the washer, closed the door of the machine, and looked over to where he was striding across the room. To her coat.

"Text message, sounds like." He reached into her coat pocket and withdrew the phone, turning to take it to her. "Hopefully it's not your son asking another . . ."

After the last phone conversation Royce was uppermost on her mind, too. But she realized her mistake in the next instant. The moment Adam's hand faltered in the act of handing the cell to her. When he looked at it more closely, his expression went flat and impassive.

He set it on the counter between them, slid it toward her. "Better answer that. I know from personal experience just how impatient Kale Bolton can get."

For a moment she stood frozen. Then she snatched the phone up to read the latest text.

Tired of waiting. Call me.

Shock was replaced with a futile fury. And irrationally, it was directed as much toward Adam as to the man who'd sent the text. "I'm trying to decide right now which of you two is the biggest ass."

His head jerked up. "Me?"

Deliberately misunderstanding him, she nodded. "Yeah, I think so, too." Rounding the corner of the counter she dropped the cell in the pocket of her jacket. Then she stood facing him, arms folded across her chest. "Tell me that you didn't immediately assume the worst just then."

"Don't be ridiculous." He reached out for his glass. Brought it to his lips for a drink. "I don't deal in assumptions."

"I'm not helping him with the book." Anxiety was riding her. She had to figure out a way to handle the reporter. And time was running out. "I haven't quite figured out a way to dissuade him of that notion yet, but I wouldn't give him information about you. And it pisses me off that you'd think otherwise."

His face went still. "The book?"

Immediately, she realized her mistake. He hadn't even considered that the reporter would tap her as a potential source of material. Try as she might, she couldn't figure out another reason for his reaction. "He's not above a little blackmail if he thinks it will get him the inside details he's looking for. I'm handling it."

"Blackmail?" The word was uttered deliberately. Dangerously.

She mentally backpedaled, searching for the right explanation to offer. Enough to pacify him. Not enough to raise more questions. "He knows about our past. Thinks he can use it to leverage information about you." She shrugged carelessly. Hoped he was satisfied.

Judging from his shrewd look, he wasn't. "How does he hope to use that against you? Hedgelin isn't my biggest fan but our relationship eight years ago isn't likely to derail your career."

Jaid hesitated. Knew he noted the pause and would probe more deeply because of it. "There are circumstances surrounding Royce's birth that I have gone to great pains to keep secret. For my son's safety, I need to keep them that way."

It was one of the first times she'd ever seen Adam look stunned. The expression was gone in the next moment, to be replaced by a lethal determination. "I'm sorry you've been dragged into this. I'll take care of it."

"No!" Her palm slapped against the counter. "This is exactly why I didn't tell you in the first place. I can handle this." She was convinced of that. She just needed a plan. "Every time you talk to Bolton, you give him more material for that damn book. You stay away from him."

His fingers were clenched tightly around the glass. "He's dragging you into something because of me. I'll convince him to back off." His smile was grim. "Actually, I'll enjoy it."

"You'll make it worse," she said bluntly. "He's like a dog with a bone. Make him think something is there, and he'll just dig more. I'll do this my way." His silence was its own answer. "I mean it, Adam. If I need your help, I'll ask for it."

"You may not realize you need my help until it's too late."

"And you might piss him off so much by rushing to the rescue that he'll go after the information about Royce regardless." Their gazes battled. Sparks all but jumped between them. Steel meeting flint. "Leave it alone. Or so help me, I'll tell him about you being afraid of mimes."

"Freaks of nature," he muttered. "But I'm not afraid of them."

"By the time he tells the story, you will be. You're not interfering in this, agreed?"

His silence was telling. Then, reluctantly, he nodded. "If he doesn't give it up in the next couple days, though, I'll approach this my way." The words were uttered fiercely. "He doesn't get to threaten you or your son in my name, Jaid. I won't allow it."

Two days. Knowing it was the best offer she was likely to get, she nodded. Somehow she'd think of a way to dissuade Bolton.

"He's lucky to have you. Your son." Her gaze flew to Adam's. Held. There was a softness to his expression that was rarely seen there. "You always had such passion. It was apparent in everything you did. But when you talk about protecting Royce . . . it turns formidable. Bolton isn't going to know what hit him."

Her throat went thick. "I think that's the nicest thing you've ever said to me."

His bright blue gaze grew intense. And somehow he seemed closer than before. "If that's the nicest thing I ever said to you, Jaid . . ." His hand went to the base of her throat, fingers covering the pulse that beat madly there. "Then I failed you miserably."

Chapter 16

Adam never should have touched her. He'd learned just a few short nights ago that once he did, stopping wasn't an option.

And tonight they didn't have a Harandi getaway to distract them.

He brushed his thumb across her soft skin, relished the evidence of her response. Replaced his thumb with his lips a moment later and felt his own pulse rev in reaction.

She could always do that to him. His free hand went to her waist. Fingered the filmy turquoise material of her blouse. Felt the warm promise of flesh beneath. She made him want until the hunger was raging in his blood, fueling the addiction in his system. Therein had lain her danger. For a man used to keeping a tight leash on his control, losing it with her, relishing its loss, was as frightening as it was intoxicating. Resisting her as long as he had years ago should have qualified him for sainthood. He nipped at her throat lightly with his teeth, and she softened against him.

He'd never pretended to be a damn saint.

Settling his mouth over hers, he let her familiar flavor jolt through him. He was a man who prized honesty. Insisted on it from others. But he'd spent the last eight years lying to himself. That he didn't miss this. Need this. Need *her*.

There was a moment when he almost thought he could back away. But her mouth was twisting beneath his in an answering demand. Without a glimmer of shyness. Not a hint of reserve. She gave as she did everything else. Openly. Freely. It had always made him fear for her. Everyone needed defenses. A guard to protect vulnerabilities.

And the regret that he'd been the one to teach her that lesson seared through him like a bitter flame.

He pulled her closer as their lips parted, tongues met. It was enough for a moment just to taste. To steep his senses in her, senses that felt raw and deprived. No matter how many times he'd had her, the hunger would start anew. She'd been an appetite he'd never been able to sate. The knowledge had been challenging. Maddening. And he knew, even as her tongue glided and battled with his, that this time would be no different. But he was compelled to try.

The buttons on her blouse were small. Difficult to release. Or perhaps he used to be capable of far more finesse. He heard one of them bounce and skitter on the floor tiles. But he was distracted from the small noise by the sweet feel of bare flesh beneath his palms. His fingers clenched reflexively. Loosened to stroke. Her waist was still narrow. The satiny stomach taut, the muscles quivering beneath his touch.

He had a sudden vivid mental image of long hours engaged on a voyage of discovery. Of soft skin stretched over toned muscle. And of all the places that made her moan and sigh when he'd linger over them. Memory could be a sharply wielded weapon, nicking away internally with every snippet of recollection.

Knowing that, accepting it, Adam transferred his attention to her jaw, strewing kisses along it before cruising down her throat. He undid the remaining button on her blouse and lifted his head, anticipation snapping in his veins. Her bra was white and sheer; the flesh it encased was just a shade darker. Her nipples were plainly visible behind the lace and were already taut. Lowering his head, he took one between his teeth. Lashed it with his tongue, dampening the fabric. And her sharply indrawn breath only whetted his desire.

Jaid unknotted his tie impatiently, and he reluctantly leaned back to pull it off. Toss it over the chair. But when he would have reached for her again, she took one of his hands in hers. "Which room is yours?"

A slow smile crossed his lips. With one quick tug he had her in his arms again, his kiss hard and urgent. She returned it with an answering fervor that made his blood flash and strobe. And without lifting his mouth from hers, he moved them both in the direction of his bedroom.

The large bed was unmade and showed effects of a sleepless night. He wondered if she could look at it and guess that she'd been the cause. He hadn't had a night's sleep free from dreams of her since this case started.

Jaid braced her hands on his chest. Exerted slight pressure. Reluctantly, he dropped his arms. Let her back away. And then felt his skin grow tight and hot when her fingers went to her waistband. The button was released with agonizing care. The zipper descended in slow motion. And surely, her pants weren't tight enough to require that she peel them, at an excruciating pace, over her hips. Down those long, slender legs. When they pooled at her ankles, she toed off her shoes and stepped out of them.

The glow from the security monitors and equipment lit the otherwise dark room. He'd gotten used to sleeping that way. But now the filtered light they afforded highlighted the sexy striptease. His throat went dry when she bent to roll first one dark stocking over her slim calf. Then the other.

His forehead was damp. His heart lurching and bucking in his chest like a racehorse. Patience was a trait that had been hard learned. But every moment spent with her tantalizingly out of reach had his patience fraying thread by thread.

He closed the distance between them, his limp more pronounced without the cane. And when he brought her close again, his palm shaping one of her breasts as his mouth ate at hers, all thought of finesse evaporated. There was only need too long denied. And a thirst for her that had never been completely quenched.

Her bra was released, and the shirt pushed from her shoulders. Both fell forgotten to the floor while he feasted on her in a desperate quest for flesh. In a dim and distant part of his brain, he knew he needed to slow down. To harness his restraint before it snapped and left him in uncharted territory.

He moved his attention lower, kneading the sweet flesh in his palm while he feasted on its twin. The sound of her breath shuddering out in breathy pants merely honed the need to a fever pitch. In primitive hunger he drew her nipple more deeply into his mouth, suckling strongly. Her hips did a quick grind against his, and he knew he'd been fooling himself earlier.

His control had always been in question when it came to Jaid.

His palms moved to cup her butt, encased in the same sheer fabric her breasts had been, while her hands wedged between them to unbutton his shirt. And it helped calm his raging pulse, just a bit, to notice the tremble in them as they worked.

It was torturous to feel the warm skin separated from him by only a filmy layer of fabric. He increased the torment by tracing the thin elastic beneath her cheeks, to where it disappeared between her legs. The first touch of her fingers against his bare chest had him jerking against her. The next had a dash of cold water rushing through his veins.

His hand came up to catch hers. To halt it. And the look they shared in the semidarkness was full of unspoken understanding.

"Adam." It was the softness in her voice that undid him. Coupled by a lack of the pity that would have wounded far worse than LeCroix's sharpest blade. He tugged off the shirt, let it fall. Steeled himself for her reaction. But she only swayed forward, pressing against him. Close. Curves flattened against angles. And the sheer pleasure of that first contact had his senses howling.

Her palms raced over him, trailing heat in their wake. He reached to sweep the panties over her hips, down her thighs and returned to stroke the flesh he'd bared. Deliberately, he traced the seam of her legs, the softness of her folds, and felt the slight sting of her nails against his biceps as she jerked helplessly against him.

And the dark magic they always created enveloped them. Cocooned them from the world. From a reality that could too often be cruel.

He found the taut bundle of nerves between her legs and brushed it rhythmically with his thumb as he kissed her deeply. When she jerked against him, he used her reaction to bring her closer. And let himself drown in the sensations she summoned.

Her fingers were at his zipper, and he hauled in a deep, shuddering breath. Too much. Too soon. And his much-vaunted restraint had never been further out of reach. He stepped out of his trousers when they hit the floor. But when she reached out to trace his hardness through the boxer briefs, his vision abruptly grayed at the edges. Catching her hand to still those questing fingers, he drew in a breath. Then another. It took a moment before he was able to move them, with less grace than he would have liked, to the bed.

He dropped down beside her, rolled to cover her. Razor-edged lust was clawing through him, a relentless drive for release. He looked at her, willed the fog of passion to lift. But what he saw in her expression nearly sent him over the edge.

Her eyes were heavy with desire. But her touch was sure, knowing, as she rid him of the last barrier between them. When she took him in her hands to stroke and tease, every clever clutch and slide of her fingers seemed destined to shatter his resolve.

He withstood it as long as he could. Until the need for completion was a primitive urge surging through his system. He could focus on nothing but her. Nothing but the primitive desire to mate with her once more. And to make it be enough this time.

Levering himself away, he reached for the bedside table, his fingers going in a blind search for a condom. Was almost undone when she took it and spent an inordinate amount of time sheathing him. When she'd finished, every muscle in his body was clenching and quivering in a futile clutch for restraint.

Surely, the years apart had been a waste. Her hold on him was as certain as it had ever been. And the dark and desperate longing for her was still a fever in his blood, a hammering in his chest. If it had been only physical, she wouldn't have represented such a threat. But she'd been more. She was still more.

She straddled his hips, and he watched her, his eye slitted. Her long dark hair teased her bare shoulders, moving with every motion. Her face was filled with emotion, a sight that once would have concerned him. But it was part of her response, and he was suddenly greedy. He wanted it all. Everything she had to give. Even if once it had been more than he'd dared accept.

Demand pounded through him, fueled by a desperation that was new. She seemed to feel it. Reciprocate it. Because she lifted herself then and guided him inside her.

And with a sense of homecoming, he surged up into her, the force of his thrust stealing his breath; the sensation of being steeped in her, surrounded by her, fired through his system. His hunger leapt and raged like a beast unleashed. His hands went to her hips. Her fingers clutched at his shoulders. The pace quickened. Became harder. Faster. His urgency was fed by a brutal need that he was helpless to control. And when he heard her crest, felt her orgasm, he followed her over the edge, his mind wiped clean of everything but her.

————

They'd collapsed in a spent sweaty heap, and he'd yet to let go of her. He'd held plenty of women before Jaid. More after her. But none gave him this sense of peace he found just by having her close.

That alone made her dangerous. The realization had tempered his response at one time. Resulted in decisions that he couldn't undo.

"Seeing you with Royce, it reminds me of my mother." He felt her still at his words. Knew the reason. He'd rarely offered the least bit of personal information. Not, as she might believe, to keep her at a distance. But because his past held no appeal for him. There was only the present. The future.

But he found himself offering her a slice of his past now. Because it was the only way she would understand. "You wouldn't care for the comparison. Glenna was a simple woman. Uneducated. And prone to bad decisions. But she did her best by me. It was little enough, but I knew what she did, she did out of love. That matters. Even now that matters."

He felt her fingers tracing the shallow indentations around his heart. A legacy from the three bullets he'd taken last May. He'd been fortunate then. But knew that most people wouldn't share his view of luck. "What'd she do?"

His hand swept down her back, then up again to trace each individual vertebra there. Such a delicate spine to be capable of such inner strength. "She cleaned houses. Apartments. That paid the rent but little else. So sometimes on the weekends she would, ah, supplement her income. She'd take me to a church first. It was her way of keeping me safe, not exposing me to whatever, whomever, she brought home. We weren't Catholic, but churches were always unlocked back then. And where safer to leave a young boy? I proved adept at finding spots to hide myself away. Sleeping or playing with whatever toys she'd packed in my bag. And on Sundays after the noon mass, she was always there. Always came to take me home again."

"How long did this go on?"

"A couple years." He continued because there was nothing in her voice but interest. No judgment for the woman who had done her best for the child she was ill-equipped to care for. He'd come across far worse parents in his career. Enough to make him remember Glenna with fondness. To recognize her best quality in spite of her flaws.

Jaid lifted her head a little to look at him in the darkness. "That's how you met Jerry."

"It is, yes." The memory had a smile curling his lips. "I imagine he knew I was there long before he tried to coax me out. In the end it was the comic books that got me. He'd leave them at the end of a pew. Farther into the church each time. Until finally, if I wanted to get my hands on the newest adventures of the Green Hornet, I had to take it directly from him."

"He had to earn your trust."

"Much like one would coax a wild animal, I expect. At any rate he kept my secret. Never told anyone that I know of. But after a while I'd find a pillow and a blanket in the choir loft. Knew they were mine for the weekend."

He felt her smile against his chest. "He's a good man."

"The best. He helped when the inevitable happened. Because one Sunday Glenna didn't come back. The next day I finally gave him my address. And when he came back from checking things out, I didn't want to believe what he told me." He halted then. No, he'd had to see it for himself. Had to return home only to see the rickety apartment door covered with police tape. And when he'd let himself inside, he'd known what the chalk outline and the bloodstains on the floor meant.

"Did you live with him then?"

"That wouldn't have been allowed. There were foster homes." The passing of time had helped frame them for what they'd been. None better or worse than necessary. "But he made time for me every week. He's my family, as much as I have one. I realized later that my mother tried to prepare me for the worst. She had to have known the risks of the lifestyle she was dabbling in. Every Friday when she dropped me off, she'd tell me, 'If anything happens to me, it's going to seem really bad. But know that it will be the worst thing that can ever happen to you. And nothing in your life can ever get that bad again.' For a long time I believed that." Hell, he'd lived his life according to that mantra. "But turned out she was wrong. LeCroix was bad. So was losing you."

Something clutched in his chest when he felt the dampness there. Her tears were all the more gut-wrenching for being silent. But her voice when it came was steady. "You didn't lose me, Adam. You pushed me away. There's a difference between the tragedies that befall us and the ones we bring on ourselves."

As usual she didn't give an inch. He settled his head more comfortably on the pillow. Brushed his fingers over the curve of her shoulder. That quality of hers had been appealing when they were together. She'd been a rookie, yes, but she'd gone toe-to-toe with him to argue a point when she disagreed.

And she'd disagreed, vehemently, when he'd ended things between them.

All the reasons he'd given her then were still valid. He stared blindly at the ceiling. And it was hard to convince himself that a willingness to ignore them now was any more than selfishness on his part.

And maybe ego. His fingers stilled. Because despite the fact that she was in his arms, in his bed, he had no reason to believe that Jaid was open to renewing their relationship. Eight years was a long time. Emotions faded. Circumstances changed. She had a son to consider now.

He frowned. One that Bolton was somehow threatening in Adam's name.

That news had been worse, far worse, than the unfamiliar pang he'd experienced when he'd recognized the number on the phone's screen. Since he wasn't a man to feel jealousy, it had to have stemmed from something else.

He rolled to face her. "I think we need to make a plan about what to do about the reporter. He can't be allowed to . . ." Adam broke off when a tiny noise sounded. Not without regret, he disengaged himself from Jaid and sat up, levering himself to the edge of the bed.

"Is that your phone?"

He used the bedside table to push himself to his feet. Grabbed his trousers and pulled them on quickly. "No. It's an e-mail."

By the time she'd dressed and joined him at the computer in the room, he was at the bottom of the message documenting Macy's thorough, well-researched findings. Stunned, he didn't object when Jaid pushed his fingers aside and scrolled back to the top. Read it for herself.

He waited for her reaction. It wasn't long coming.

Halfway down the page she stopped. "Oh my God." Her voice was threaded with excitement. "It's not a match. Lambert's statement and the message the cyber agents found embedded on his computer are by different authors. He was telling the truth about being threatened by someone."

"Probably."

His terse response seemed to warn her. She sent him a sidelong glance before scanning the rest of the message. "Ninety percent accuracy, it says. That's pretty good odds. I'd be interested in knowing how she does . . ." Her words tapered off abruptly.

"She is good." His voice was bleak as he looked at the screen and read the results of the second test again. "So I'm going to have to accept the fact once and for all that the man who hired Lambert—ostensibly the one behind the homicides of Patterson, Reinbeck, and Cote—is the same man who hired Mose Ferrell to kill me."

———

"You look good, kid." Paulie Samuels finally set Jaid down and released her from the bone-crushing hug. "You should have run away with me years ago when you had the chance."

It was impossible to dislike the man. The three of them went way back, to when he and Adam were still in the bureau, although Paulie had bounced between the forensic accountant and cyber units at the time. It had been he who had notified her when Adam had been in the CCU, clinging to life. Both times. He'd earned a permanent place in her heart for that alone. "So you're saying there's a statute of limitations on the offer? I'm crushed." She smoothed a hand down his vest decorated with greenbacks. "I've never found a more dapper dresser. You've ruined me for other men." She smiled at his bark of laughter.

"You remember Kellan Burke from Philadelphia, right?" Paulie jerked a thumb at the younger man who had followed him silently into the apartment. She nodded at Burke, whom she'd seen from a distance, along with several of Adam's other operatives, when she'd made a brief visit to Adam's bedside in May. That had been their only meeting, but she recalled his name from when she and Adam had been together. There was a relationship between the two that had never been fully explained. Which wasn't unusual, given Adam's reticence.

Which made his earlier openness all the more out of character. She and Adam had been together for fourteen months. She'd never been introduced to Kellan. Or to Jerry. She couldn't recall a time that he had mentioned his mother. Foster homes. He'd told her once he refused to live in the past. But she recognized now that he'd effectively compartmentalized his life by shutting segments of it away from her. Which had been, she assumed, one more way to keep her from getting too close.

That made tonight's reversal all the more intriguing.

"Macy's findings sure kicked up a firestorm, didn't they?" Kellan's light green eyes were shrewd behind the fashionable glasses. "Discovering a connection between Ferrell and whoever's pulling the strings in the DC murders puts Adam right in the center of this."

"I was worried about that from the beginning," Paulie muttered as he made a beeline for the bar. "Told you we needed to consider that idea carefully. Oh, no, you said. Ferrell's attempts weren't of the same caliber as the other homicides, you said."

"No one appreciates an I-told-you-so, Paulie." Adam's voice was relatively mild as he headed to the bar to play host. "What I said then is still true. And I believe more than ever that Ferrell was a red herring. Meant to get me removed from the case, one way or another."

"The question is, why?" Kell moseyed over and wedged a place for himself between the other two men. Jaid had thought to bring her wineglass and laptop down with her. She had some familiarity with war meetings, as Paulie liked to call these nights. They often ran late into the night. Might as well get comfortable. She carried her things over to the sage leather couch and curled up on one end.

"When Jennings's place was searched after he was killed trying to assassinate Adam last May," Jaid managed the words in a fairly steady voice, "did the bureau happen to find any written communication from whoever hired him?"

"Good idea." Paulie pointed at her while he swallowed from the drink Adam had poured him. "Try to tie whoever hired Jennings to the DC mastermind." He looked at Burke. "What was in the final report?"

He shook his head. "Nothing like that. The only link I know of is when you traced the money in his account from part of the ransom paid last January in the Mulder kidnapping."

Disappointment reared. "And what about the ransom notes received in that case? Can Macy use those to test and see if their authorship matches with these latest communications she tested?"

Kellan shook his head. "Macy and I were the operatives on that case. Whoever was calling the shots was damn careful to have someone else assume all the risk. The victim's father is Stephen Mulder of Mulder Department Stores. Very deep pockets. But it was his longtime friend and attorney who was blackmailed, he claims, into sending the ransom notes and stealing the security specs for the estate."

Jaid looked at Adam meaningfully. "That sounds familiar. People are disposable tools to the offender we're looking for. Sorenson. Lambert. Sanchez. And you've already said in your latest profile that the hits are professional."

"Hired a professional to snatch the Mulder girl, too." Kell stopped, took a sip, and grimaced. To Adam he demanded, "Seriously. You have to have more behind that bar than Scotch."

In response Paulie reached out and grabbed the other man's glass to dump the liquor into his. "It's wasted on him, Adam. Give him the cheap stuff."

Burke continued, "Vincent Dodge was the kidnapper's name. But his background was far more colorful than that. He'd been directed to kill the girl as soon as the ransom cleared. We arrived before he could carry out his orders. And we'd barely gotten clear of the cabin he was keeping her in when the place blew." He accepted the replacement drink Adam slid toward him. "Which tells us that the mastermind of the whole thing does not like loose strings."

She wasn't ready to drop the idea. "What about this Dodge? Maybe he had some sort of written . . ."

Kell was already shaking his head. The overhead lights shot his dark hair with reddish highlights. "He's not around to ask. Macy killed him when he tried one final time to get at the girl." He grinned fondly. "It's always a mistake to underestimate my fiancée."

"Fiancée?" She looked at Adam. He grimaced. Set the whiskey bottle back under the bar.

"I have no idea what it is with these people. I send them out on assignment, and they come back wanting to get married." He looked honestly baffled. "Damnedest thing I ever saw."

"Yeah." Kell's voice was good-natured. "We're all waiting for the time when you meet your match and we can all . . ." He was interrupted then by Paulie's fit of coughing. "Geez, Paulie, don't lose a lung." Burke gave the man a companionable thump on the back.

Jaid had an idea what had brought on the man's coughing spasm. Deliberately, she skirted Adam's gaze. "So if we find the professional carrying out the DC murders, maybe he'll have some sort of written . . ." Her head snapped up. "We don't need him. I mean we do, but why don't we get written statements from everyone we've looked at so far? Bailey, Newell, Harandi . . . Macy can run matches and see if any of them wrote the messages to Lambert. And Ferrell." There was a measure of disappointment when she saw the expression on Adam's face. "You'd already thought of that."

"It's a good idea," he allowed. "But we can't get ahead of ourselves. This task hasn't been OK'd by Hedgelin, and we have no idea how he's going to react to us having used a linguist outside the agency. At the least he'll want to have the tests duplicated by one of his own people."

"Macy can run circles around any of those guys," Kell scoffed. "She's the best in the country. I'd say the world, but there's this funny little guy in Belgium she's always talking about. Seems he's revolutionizing forensic linguistics over there, and . . ."

"Burke."

It took just the single word from Adam to silence the man. Jaid arched a brow. It was a neat trick. It was a wonder he could manage at all in a world where everyone didn't treat him with such deference. "I don't think the assistant director will completely discount this lead. He can't afford to. And going forward with trying to match suspect statements to the matches Macy has already run gives us an idea where to focus our energies."

Adam regarded her over the top of his glass. Drank. Then set the glass down again. "I think you're overlooking one thing. Once Hedgelin sees the link tying Ferrell to the DC killer, he's finally proven his contention of conflict of interest. This time when he asks for my removal, he's likely to get it."

The words rocked her. The possibility hadn't even occurred to her, although it should have. And he was right.

The assistant director had never made any bones about his reluctance to accept Adam's help. No doubt this latest development would have the man positively gleeful.

Her gaze dropped to her laptop. "I promised Shepherd I'd file the report tonight. I'd planned to update the assistant director that way about our findings this evening." She looked up then. Caught all three men staring at her. "But I'll probably forget to add the part about the match in authorship between Ferrell's note and the e-mail recovered from Lambert's computer. I can file that first thing in the morning. That should give Adam a minimum of twenty-four more hours on the case." It'd take that long for the intelligence analysts to fold the details into the case file.

"Twenty-four hours to stop the offender before he kills again." His eye glinted as he lifted his glass again. "That seems fair enough."

————

It was all coming together too easily. The man being hunted by nearly three hundred federal agents sat with his feet up, watching a Redskins game he'd DVR'd. And really, the game he'd started bore much similarity to the football being played on the screen. Like the coach, he was the brains. But they both had to rely a bit more than they'd like on the players on the field.

The team members he'd selected so far had ranged from functional to near brilliant. But all that mattered in the end was that they'd carried out the plays he'd called. So far it had gone off without a hitch. And the satisfaction felt at a well-executed kill couldn't be overstated.

But the next one would definitely kick the exercise up to a whole new level.

He looked down at the white card with its red lettering, already safely encased in its Ziploc.

The Redskins were in for the game of their lives. And very soon, so was Adam Raiker.

Chapter 17

"The warrant came through. How far out are you?"

Jaid sat up in bed, momentarily disconcerted. The alarm on the bedside table said four A.M. The driver had just dropped her off from Adam's three hours earlier. "I'm in Centerville. Adam's in Manassas."

The suppressed excitement in Shepherd's voice had an answering emotion firing through her veins. "Okay. Newell's estate is in Great Falls. Can you be on the road in a half hour? Hedgelin is shooting for seven A.M. to serve the warrant."

She was already swinging her legs over the side of the bed. "Better give me the address. It'd be easier to meet you there." She fumbled in the drawer of the bedside table for a paper and pencil, writing as the agent recited it to her. "I'll call you when I get closer."

"Sounds good. Talk to you then." After the agent disconnected, she dialed Adam's cell. Was unsurprised to hear him answer immediately, sounding alert.

"We got the warrant. We're to serve it at seven in Great Falls."

"See, wouldn't this have been easier if you'd stayed here last night like I suggested?"

"This way I'll have fresh clothes," she reminded him. She got up, padded toward the shower. "You picking me up?"

"What are the chances you'd stand for being left behind?"

She grinned into the phone, adrenaline doing a quick sprint up her spine. "Nonexistent."

———

The senator lived on an estate set on acres of rolling green lawns in one of the most exclusive suburbs of DC. Driving in Great Falls was usually one of Jaid's favorite ways to spend a scenic afternoon. The roads were narrow and resembled a roller coaster with the dips and peaks, twists and turns. In the summer the trees formed a canopy overhead, meshing into a solid green overhang with only occasional patches of the sky peeking through.

Some of that charm was lost in the late fall, with the naked branches resembling entwined, skeletal fingers. Still, watching the horses shake their manes and gallop lazily around the paddocks at the estates they passed by, she imagined she could get used to it year round.

"There's Shepherd. Parked in that drive up ahead." She leaned forward in her seat. She'd been in contact with the agent along the way and knew where the meeting place was. But when they pulled alongside him and Shepherd buzzed down the window, she could tell immediately from his expression that something was wrong.

"Someone leaked the warrant to Newell. They had to have." He jerked his head toward the drive down the road. A long black luxury sedan was pulling into it. "I've been here twenty minutes, and six cars have arrived so far."

Her stomach plummeting, Jaid stared up at the next house. "Did you recognize any of them?"

"Too far away. I called Hedgelin, and he said there's nothing to do but go ahead with the process. But damn, I'd like to get hold of whoever leaked the warrant."

"Given the circumstances, they probably outrank us." The news was a bit deflating. But after last night, she had hopes of coming away with more than the high-powered rifle they'd seen in Newell's campaign photo. "Let's get it over with."

Jaid was unsurprised when Joseph Bailey answered the door, dressed for the day in a Savile Row suit that rivaled anything she'd seen Adam wear, and Raiker was a known clothes horse. "Mr. Bailey." She sent him a bright smile. "What a surprise to see you here this morning. We'd like to speak to your grandfather. Is he in?"

"I'm afraid he's indisposed this morning." Gone was the affable, candid young man they'd first spoken to at Dennison International. His manner was aloof. Cold.

"We won't disturb him then." Jaid took a copy of the warrant from the outside pocket of her briefcase and handed it to him. "We have a warrant to search the premises."

He did no more than glance at it, which solidified Shepherd's earlier assumption that Bailey had known it was coming. "This is absurd. Surely you can't believe a sitting U.S. senator had something to do with those killings in DC." When none of them said anything, his gaze narrowed. "Is this because of Lambert? Did he tell you something that incriminated my grandfather? Because if he did, he's lying."

"Lambert said he was able to access Patterson's phone number from the business cell you carried with you in the locker room for basketball practice."

His expression was arrested. "So? What does that have to do with this warrant?"

"Actually, nothing. The warrant has everything to do with this." She handed him a folded-up copy of the campaign poster from a couple years ago. "Good likeness, by the way. Wouldn't have figured you for an outdoorsman."

Bailey looked at it, his expression growing more and more confused. "I'm not. It was just one of those photo-op things." Another man approached, this one taller. Older. With a bearing meant to cow lowly public servants. Had to be the high-powered attorney.

"Joseph, I'll take over from here." He took the warrant and the sheet from Bailey but didn't look at them right away. "Darren Smythe, of Smythe, Spencer, and Davies. I'll need to see some identification."

Jaid didn't point out that Bailey clearly knew who they were. She'd expected to be put through a song and dance, although in truth she'd thought Newell himself would be calling the shots.

The IDs were presented, and either Smythe was an extraordinarily slow reader or he was trying to put them off. She suspected the latter. Finally, he handed them back and said, "Wait here while I go over the scope of the warrant."

"You wait here." The three of them stepped around him and continued into the house. "We're conducting the search."

"Now just a minute . . ."

But they'd already moved down the huge hallway, their footsteps sounding abnormally loud against the gleaming marble floors. Jaid sneaked a look up. The hallway was open to the second story, where a double-tiered chandelier was suspended, each crystal shooting prisms of color. She caught a glimpse of a stern-faced older woman watching them from behind a railing upstairs. Newell's wife. From her demeanor the two appeared perfectly matched.

The first door on the left was a formal living room, with an accent on the formal. Jaid gave an inner shudder just thinking of the damage Royce could do in that room in under ten minutes. There were dark framed pictures of horses along with busts and statuettes, all hanging or sitting in a place that a carelessly thrown ball would find in an instant. There were no guns here. If Jaid didn't miss her bet, this room was the jurisdiction of the senator's wife.

Across the hall was a smaller study, and it was filled with the people Shepherd had noted coming this morning. Bailey had retreated there, as had Smythe, who was at a long conference table poring over the warrant with two colleagues. A couple of the men Jaid recognized. They'd also been armed in the campaign photo and captioned. Newell's sons.

But it was the senator himself who addressed them. "Agents. Mr. Raiker." His smile was chilly. "Enjoy your last day on the job. I will bury you for this."

"I'm sure you're willing to do your part to bring the DC killer to justice, Senator." It was Adam who spoke. Newell might be the one who wielded the power, but it was Adam who seemed the more formidable. "Since you do run on a law-and-order platform."

"I have a phone call into the bureau director. This search of yours will be over before it starts."

"In that case we better get busy." Jaid withdrew from the room and headed to the next. Shepherd hurried to catch up with her.

"Okay, I don't think we need to go out of our way to irritate him," he said in a low voice.

Throwing him an amused glance, she said, "You don't think the warrant itself accomplished that? We can pretend we're the lowly servants just following orders from higher up, but we're the ones who brought the poster to Hedgelin's notice. I'd like to see the sparks when Newell decides to take on Judge Carter for signing it."

An elegant dining room with an acre-long table was situated next to the living room. They crossed the hall again and opened the door to the room next to the study, and Jaid's breath caught. "Bingo." If the living room was Mrs. Newell's domain, this room was Newell's. There was a large leather sectional situated around the requisite big-screen TV. Heads of dead animals stared balefully down at them from their mountings high on the wall. Stuffed birds appeared ready to take flight. But it was the gun cases that drew her eyes.

Although the wall of weapons couldn't rival Sarah and Walter Vale's in number, she'd be willing to bet the guns were all top quality. She followed the two men across the room, scanning the cases.

"There's the Remington 700."

Jaid stopped beside Adam and looked at the case he was gesturing to. The weapon looked like a match to the one Newell was holding in the campaign picture. The same sort of weapon that ballistics said was used to kill Justice Reinbeck. Shepherd slipped on a pair of plastic gloves, went to open the case. Found it locked.

"Before you take anything out of this house, you'll be signing a receipt." Jaid recognized Bailey's voice behind them.

"Of course." She gestured toward the case. "Unlock it."

His mouth tight, he stepped forward with a key. Shepherd moved forward as the door swung open, but the other man was already reaching inside. With one hand gripping the stock and the other the barrel, he handed it to Shepherd, his gaze meeting Jaid's.

"There's a soft cover for it that I'll get for you. My grandfather isn't going to stand for it being damaged while it's in the FBI's possession."

While he went to some cupboards on the next wall and began to rummage through them, Jaid exchanged a glance with Shepherd. Bailey had gone to great pains to make sure they saw a reason for his prints to be on the gun, which was intriguing. They weren't yet at the stage where they'd be asking for elimination prints, however. First ballistics would have to determine if this was, indeed, the weapon that had killed the judge.

Bailey came up with the case in question and handed it to Shepherd. "If you'd come with me, Mr. Bailey, we'll rejoin the others in the library. I'll write out a receipt for your grandfather," Jaid said.

Although it was clear from the backward glances he threw over his shoulder that he was reluctant to leave the two men in the room, she walked him out the door and down the hall to the study.

The lawyer saw her first. Rising, he straightened his suit jacket, which was already precisely aligned. "Agent Marlowe. I trust you've finished this intrusion now?"

"I just wanted to write out a receipt for the senator," she responded, neatly sidestepping the question. "And ask if perhaps the senator and his family would like to write a short description explaining the photo campaign in which they were holding the weapons."

Although she was looking at Newell, it was Smythe who answered. "Absolutely not. No one is putting anything in writing."

Shrugging, she set her briefcase on the corner of the conference table and opened it to take out a pad of blank receipts. "They certainly aren't obligated to, of course. I merely suggested it as a courtesy. Things can look differently to those outside the political arena. I thought the senator might like to get his explanation for the poster into the formal report." She stopped long enough to make out the receipt, before ripping it off the pad and handing it to the attorney.

"Father, that might not be a bad idea." She made sure she showed no reaction when she heard the low murmur behind her. "It gives us the opportunity to offset any negative spin put on this."

"Spin." She turned slightly to see Newell glaring at her venomously. "I'm not afraid of spin. Miss Marlowe should be concerned, though. When I get through with the agency, she's going to be looking for a job as a parking attendant."

Her smile was beatific. "It's Special Agent Marlowe. And some days that would seem like a step up, Senator. If no one is interested in the written explanation, I'll join the others."

"Clive's right." It was the second Newell son. It was difficult to tell the two of them apart. This one looked older. They both appeared like younger renditions of their father. "Darren, what's the downside of this?"

Watching the lawyer hem and haw, then consult with his cohorts, Jaid knew the man had no real objection. He was doing what all good attorneys do—offering only what was legally called for.

After some wrangling back and forth, it was finally de-

cided that the four who had posed for the poster, the senator, his two sons, and Bailey, would write a short paragraph
about the intent of that particular photo campaign. Jaid
agreed to the content of the writing with alacrity. The explanation would serve no purpose to the bureau, a fact she
was certain Smythe suspected. But their communication
samples could prove of great assistance when they were
turned over to Macy Reid.

"What have you done with my assistant, Scott Lambert?" The senator gave his statement to the son who was
collecting them, and stared at her.

"He's being held without bond in federal lockup for
conspiracy to commit murder."

His narrow face didn't show a flicker of emotion. She
was willing to bet he'd known that much already. With his
connections it wouldn't have been difficult to discover.

"You've linked him to these DC killings, then? And because of his involvement you're turning your interest to me
because of my animosity toward Reinbeck." He didn't wait
for an answer. He leaned forward in the cushy recliner he
was seated in. "If there are any links found to my office,
they'd all be suspect. For all I know Lambert was operating
some of sort of clandestine scheme out of my space."

Because he'd opened the avenue of questioning, Jaid
was more than happy to follow it. "How well did you know
him?"

"Not well at all." He silenced the words that his grandson would have spoken with merely a look. "He was just
another employee. I can't even tell you for sure who hired
him. I think he was with me for about three years. I barely
spoke to him in all that time. He certainly wasn't in my
inner circle of advisers or assistants."

Jaid felt a tiny flicker of sympathy for Lambert. The
senator would have made a powerful ally, but the man was
cutting Lambert loose like he would a tangled fishing line.
She was willing to bet, based on what Lambert had said and
given the man's friendship with Bailey, that there was a
closer relationship between Newell and LeCroix's son than

the older man was willing to let on. But she wasn't going to get confirmation of that here.

She put their statements into her briefcase. Locked it. Then looked up at the occupants of the room and said brightly, "Thank you all for your cooperation. We'll be out of your way shortly."

"Shortly?" Smythe rose, propping his fists on the table in front of him. "With all due respect, Agent, you're done here. Joseph said he helped you pack up what you came for. I expect all of you off the premises in minutes."

"Soon." She nodded to the warrant unfolded on the table in front of the man. "After we make sure there aren't any other weapons of that make and model on the property."

As she walked toward the door, Smythe sputtering behind her, she heard Newell utter a word that his conservative base would surely disapprove of. She figured he was entitled. It had to be frustrating when his power and position didn't insulate him from little things like the law.

———

It was another three hours before they finished searching the house and outbuildings, and headed back toward their vehicles. Jaid's cell had been emitting pings all morning, signaling incoming texts. Since all of them were from Bolton, and read only, *URGENT! CALL ME IMMEDIATELY!* she figured they could be ignored. She hadn't come up with a fail-safe plan to shake the man loose yet, so she was toying with simply going with violence. It was a ballsy move to try and threaten an FBI agent in any case. Maybe she should just tell him she was turning him into the bureau for extortion. If nothing else, the threat would buy her time.

Shepherd was carrying the rifle case tucked under one arm. He caught her sleeve with his free hand and drew her aside as Adam continued toward the car. "I was working all night," he said in undertones. "There are things about Adam's priest friend, that Benton, that bear a closer look."

"I've got some things to catch you up on, too . . ."

"I don't want you mentioning anything to Adam about this." A note in the man's tone had her looking at him more carefully. "I owe the guy, more than you know. If not for him, I'd still be freezing my ass off in Bismarck. But these things I'm discovering about the priest . . . they have to be looked into. And I don't want Raiker maybe saying something to the man that will warn him off."

She gave a half laugh, but there was no answering amusement in the other man's expression. "Seriously? You think a priest shot Justice Reinbeck, stabbed Patterson in the heart, oh, and garroted Cardinal Cote? I'm pretty sure all those would rank pretty high on the mortal-sin list."

"He had a relationship with Patterson. I don't know all of it yet, but there's a connection." The agent sent a quick glance in Adam's direction. "And Reinbeck was at a fund-raiser Benton and Raiker attended not long ago. Then there's the animosity he admitted to regarding the cardinal. Hell, maybe he didn't do it himself. Adam thinks there's a professional actually doing the work, right? Or maybe he thought he could copycat the other killings as a cover to get rid of Cote. I don't know. But I do know there's more there than he's admitting to."

She stared at the man, disbelieving. "Shepherd, he's a *priest*."

The agent looked grim. "Yeah, well, some pretty horrible things have been done over the centuries in the name of religion. And guess what he does every month? Visiting chaplain at the Alexandria Detention Center, just in case you were wondering where he might meet someone to do the wet work for him."

Her phone sounded again. She clenched her teeth. She wasn't sure she could deal with Bolton and this ridiculous line from Shepherd at the same time. "All right. I've met the man twice, and I think you're way off base, but you and I will find some time this afternoon to sit down alone and go over everything you've got, okay?"

He took a step back, looking a bit relieved. "That's all I'm asking."

Her phone was ringing now. Taking it out of her pocket, she recognized Bolton's number. "I have to get this. We'll talk later."

Shepherd nodded and headed toward his vehicle. Jaid remained in place. She waited until the agent was out of hearing distance before answering, her voice hard. "I have to warn you, Bolton, I'm seriously considering just shooting you and putting an end to this harassment."

"Jaid. My God, what does it take to get you to answer a fucking message?" Lost were the smug tones that usually had her wanting to smack him within a few minutes. The man's voice was as agitated as she'd ever heard it. "This is big. This is the fucking story of the century."

"You know what's going to be a big story, Bolton? The one where a hotshot prize-winning journalist ends up in prison bunking with a toothless hillbilly named Sweetums. Extortion. Attempted blackmail of a federal agent. Tough sentencing, Bolton. You'll be inside long enough for you and Sweetums to get real friendly."

"What are you talking about? Never mind, just listen. I was contacted today by the DC killer."

Her heart stopped for an instant. When it renewed beating, its hammering filled her ears. "What are you talking about? Why would he contact you?"

"Give me a little credit, Jaid. I'm sort of a big deal in the news world. He wants me to tell his story. He sent along a clue to who his next victim will be. He wants me to get it to the bureau."

She shook her head. Nothing about this story was making sense. "I swear, Bolton, if this is some sort of elaborate ruse to get me to meet with you, I'll break more than your nose."

A bit of his usual smarm entered his voice. "Violence again. I'm beginning to get turned on."

"It still doesn't make sense. Why you? And why me?"

"We've already covered my part. As far as you, I was told to get it to the bureau. You're an agent." A shrug sounded in his voice. "If you want me to contact someone else, I know lots of agents."

"No, I'll come." The words left her mouth before she could consider them. But she saw no other choice. If this was a trick by the reporter, she'd make him regret it. "What sort of proof did he send you?"

"No more information until the actual meet. How soon can you get here?"

A measure of cynicism returned. She wasn't convinced that this wasn't some huge hoax perpetuated by Bolton just to get her roped into a meet. But he'd be the one surprised when she slapped a pair of cuffs on him if he tried the blackmail number again.

"Depends on where we're meeting." She saw Adam get out of the vehicle again, leaning a hand on the driver's door, a questioning look on his face. Belatedly, she started walking in his direction again, noting that Shepherd had already pulled out of the drive.

"I can't get away long. How about right outside the *Gazette*, at noon?"

It seemed an innocuous enough place. The building for the newspaper giant ate up an entire city block in downtown DC, but it wasn't all that far away from the Hoover Building. "Better make it one. I'm a ways out of the city."

"One, then." The quiver of excitement was back in his voice. "You won't be sorry." The call disconnected.

"I'm already sorry," she muttered, slipping the cell back in her pocket and hurrying toward the vehicle. She opened the door and got in, sinking a little into the plush leather seats. She had a feeling it would be all too easy to get used to little luxuries like this.

"Everything all right at home?" Adam started the ignition.

"That was Bolton." She filled him in on the short conversation as he backed out of the drive, ending with, "He's probably blowing smoke, right? Has to be. But I figure I'll check it out. If nothing else, it will give me the chance to put the fear of God in him, so he'll back off on his threats to drag Royce into this." Another thought occurred. The reporter had mentioned writing up a sample chapter of innuendoes about her son. Maybe he was going to present her with it.

Her spine stiffened. If that were the case, she'd use the writing as proof of his harassment. But whatever the man was up to, it ended today. "The *Gazette* isn't all that far from headquarters. You can drop me off, and I'll pick up some sandwiches on my way back. It's only a few blocks on foot."

"That's one option."

She shot him a narrowed look. "And that's Adamspeak for no way in hell. I know your lingo, buddy."

"Obviously, you do." He didn't take his attention off the road. "But if you knew me as well as you thought, you would never have considered seeing him alone."

"We went over this last night."

"Yes, I recall. I promise not to ride in on my white horse. But if the outcome of your meeting is not to your liking, we do things my way."

She considered his words. Figured she wasn't going to get a better deal. But one way or the other, within the hour she was going to get a few more answers.

Cody Tweed pulled the black panel van into the parking garage and waited for his ticket. The garage would be fairly full, despite its size. Parking in DC was always at a premium. Any slots left would likely be on top, several stories up, out in the elements. But that wouldn't be the special spot he'd be looking for.

He cruised around, saw several areas that would work on the second level. Away from the prying eyes of parking attendants. Of course all of the spaces were filled. He'd expected no less.

It took two trips around for him to settle on the perfect spot. An older model Nissan Pathfinder was parked there. Pathfinders were easy marks. They may as well come with a neon arrow. *Pick me. Here I am.* Cody wasn't one to ignore signs.

Checking for cars behind him, he waited for one white Cadillac to move by before getting out of the van with his tools and approaching the driver's door of the Pathfinder. Ten seconds to slide the small wedge of plastic into the seam where the door met the body of the vehicle. Pry it open slightly, slip in the larger plastic wedge to act as a doorstop. He sent one quick look over his shoulder. Another car was passing slowly by, but he'd appear to be just another guy fumbling for his keys. Cody waited until the vehicle went past before sliding the long, thick wire wrapped with a rubber band at the top into the opening provided by the wedge. Two tries. Three before he reached the unlock button and slid it back. Less than a minute and the door was open. Another ten seconds to find and memorize the ignition key-code number, and he headed back to the van. It took a little over five minutes to make a duplicate key with the portable key maker, during which time he received a couple more irritated looks as people drove by.

He grinned. They didn't know irritated.

The key ready, he backed his van up a ways and got in the Pathfinder, reversed out of the space, and pulled ahead several yards before getting out again to back the van into the prime spot he'd chosen. He locked up and then got back in the Nissan, started trolling for a new spot somewhere near the top of the garage. He didn't give a shit where. The clock on the dash said he had an hour to set up his shot. Plenty of time, because he had it timed to the minute.

That's what professionals did.

———

"The offer's still open."

Adam had double-parked at the end of the street. Noted that Bolton was already pacing nervously outside the *Gazette* building, a manila envelope in his hand. Jaid paused, one hand on the door handle. "I'll let you know if I need reinforcements."

He nodded. She had the odd sense that she had disappointed him. Or maybe he was just let down that he was missing the upcoming scene. "Maybe I'll drive around the block a few times until you're done."

"Don't bother." Although the sun was shining brightly today, the temps had settled into the forties. That might seem balmy in Minnesota, but it was about twenty degrees cooler than her personal comfort zone. "One way or another, this isn't going to take long. If a traffic cop comes along, flash him your ID."

"I look forward to it."

Smiling at his unenthusiastic tone, she got out of the car and rounded the hood, waiting for a break in traffic before she darted across the street.

The reporter noticed her when she hit the sidewalk. But he let her come to him. "Marlowe. You're looking as delicious as ever. Ready for me to rock your world?"

She managed, barely, to avoid rolling her eyes. "I have a feeling I'm just one in a long line of women who will wait in vain for that to happen, Bolton."

He sent a suspicious look across the street, where Adam waited in the car. "Is that Shepherd? I told you to come alone."

"As a matter of fact, you didn't, but here I am. Alone. What do you have?"

The excitement was back in his tone. And its appearance made her wonder if she'd misjudged the man's intentions about the purpose of this meeting. "Okay, last night about three A.M. someone was pounding on my door. But no one's there. Just this"—he held up the envelope—"in the mailbox. I didn't bring it in right away. I mean, I'm thinking bomb, anthrax, right? Gotta be careful these days. But after about fifteen minutes the package starts to *ring*. So yeah, there's a phone in there. I finally figure what the hell and go out and answer it."

"And?"

His eyes widened. "And . . . there's some guy on the other end using a voice distorter, claiming to be the DC killer. Says you guys don't have dick on him—I'm paraphrasing here—and that his messages aren't getting out to the public. He wants his side told, says I'm the one to do it, and sends something along he claims you can use as a clue to the next victim. Says to call you . . ."

Everything inside her froze. "Wait. He said to call *me*?"

"That's right. Think I don't have contacts higher up in the agency to take this to? But he was asking about you, so I told him what I know. He told me to set up a meet, and I got back to him with the specifics after I talked to you . . . just left a message is all."

Time seemed to slow down then. "Bolton." Her voice was urgent. "Did he tell you where to meet me?"

"Yeah." He reached into the envelope and pulled out a Ziploc bag. With a white note card inside it. "Said to show you this."

A car horn blared on the street across from them at the same time her cell went off. Something had her looking in the direction of the horn. Adam had driven up the street and stopped across from them, and his driver's window was down. He was shouting something. Waving frantically. Pointing at the parking garage directly behind him.

Suspicion turned to comprehension. She tackled Bolton even as she was drawing her weapon.

But the sound of the rifle shot was heard before either of them hit the ground.

Chapter 18

Adam heard the shot. Saw them both fall. And his lungs stopped drawing in air. People on the sidewalk were screaming, pushing each other frantically in an effort to escape. A bus rumbled by then, blocking his view.

And the thought of Jaid lying crumpled and bleeding on the sidewalk a few yards away made him want to give a primal howl of anguish.

He raced around the edge of the bus and was halfway across the street before he saw Jaid rise, and bile rose in his throat. She was covered in blood. In gray matter. And Bolton wasn't moving.

"Are you hit?" The words were torn from somewhere deep inside him.

She shook her head vehemently. She had her weapon in one hand, her cell in the other. "Secure the garage!" she shouted.

Cars blared their horns as they passed him on each side. He was in the middle of the street and wanted, needed to go to her. To assure himself she was unhurt.

He didn't ever recall having to wrestle between duty and emotion. But this time, it wasn't even a battle. Adam headed toward her.

"Go! I'm fine!"

If nothing else, the urgency in her voice convinced him. Grimly, he backtracked, halting for vehicles that showed no signs of stopping, dodging between others to get back to his car. It took an endless minute to get to the entrance of the parking garage. He left his vehicle in one of the lanes and got out, dialing 911 as he strode up to the attendant's booth.

"Hey!" The attendant ignored the car on the other side waiting to pay. "You can't leave your car there."

"There's been a shooting in front of the *Gazette* building." He rattled off the address. "One person down. An FBI agent securing the scene. Shooter is likely still inside the parking garage directly across the street. Send cars to secure both entrances." The attendant's eyes had grown huge as Adam spoke.

Ignoring the dispatcher's questions, he dropped the phone back in his pocket. Fished in his pocket to flash his ID at the attendant. "Get security to the area. Have them posted at every exit. Shut down the elevators. Is there another way for cars to get out of here?"

One of the vehicles waiting to pay honked impatiently. To his credit, the attendant, a twentysomething with a bad case of acne, was already on his radio. "Yes, sir, the east entrance."

"Radio that attendant. Have any cars currently in the lanes vacated and left in place." They would act as a sort of barricade. "Have security lock down the elevators. Take anybody on foot to a secured area. Vehicle in question is likely a panel van."

Adam didn't wait to see if the man obeyed. He was already moving to the cars in the lanes next to him. "Out of the vehicle. FBI." His temporary ID was pressed against the driver's window. The man, a midthirties suit, started to argue until he saw the gun in Adam's other hand.

"Leave the keys," Adam barked. He heard the sound of

running footsteps. Turned his head to see a security officer approaching. "Go with him." The man was slow to obey so Adam gave him a slight push. "It's important that you cooperate, sir."

"But what about my car?"

He was moving on to the next vehicle. The driver, an elderly woman with a mop of improbably gold curls, was staring at him with her mouth an O. He repeated the direction and got her out of the car. He vacated several more waiting in line, and the guard hurried the drivers away. Then Adam waited, hoping he'd chosen the right entrance.

The garage's back entrance would provide the shooter with the most privacy. It opened onto Klur, a street much less well traveled than the one out front. But Klur was one way, with no stoplight at the next corner. Cars could sit for an hour trying to find a break in traffic to get across it.

If it were him, he'd try this entrance.

"Do you have the other exit blocked?"

The attendant looked frightened. "I think so. I told him what you said to do."

Adam nodded. Then looked at the vehicle doing a slow roll around the second level. "You need to find a safe place. Follow that guard to wherever he took the others."

The young man needed no further urging. He hurried away. Adam didn't watch to see which direction he went. He was too busy looking at the black panel van rounding the corner and rolling toward him.

His weapon aimed at the vehicle, he approached it, keeping close to the parked cars along the wall. If he was wrong, he'd scare the hell out some driver who would never use public parking again. If he was correct . . .

He noted the exact moment the van driver realized the cars in the lanes ahead were empty. Adam stepped out from his cover, weapon aimed. "Get out of the vehicle. Hands in the air."

There was a second when the man driving turned to him. Smiled. Adam had an instant to observe that he was younger than he would have thought. Then the driver threw the van in reverse, before switching gears to accelerate forward.

He hit the first car blocking the lane at the same time that Adam's shot shattered the driver's window. The impact had slammed the first empty vehicle into the next one. But the lanes were still solidly blocked.

Adam moved parallel to the vehicle. It remained unmoving. Then it's passenger door opened. The driver got out. Raised the barrel of his rifle.

Bullets tore into metal. Adam's face was on the pavement, his cane lost in his dive to safety. He used the fender of the nearest car to haul himself upright, saw the man running toward the exit.

"Drop your weapon." He fired a warning shot.

The shooter turned then. Brought up his rifle again.

Three shots sounded in quick succession. Adam watched the man wheel back, drop his weapon. Fall to the garage floor.

"Put down your gun! Hands behind your head."

The police had arrived. Adam set the weapon on the trunk of the nearest car and clasped his fingers behind his head. He watched two uniformed officers approach the man as another came toward him, weapon aimed. Arriving late on the scene, they'd have no way of knowing how it'd gone down.

"FBI. My ID is in my left inside-coat pocket."

"Take it out," the officer told him, his weapon still pointed. "Carefully."

Adam obeyed, holding it out so the man could take it. Examine it more closely. After he did he lowered his weapon but didn't holster it. "We're clear here," he called to his colleagues.

"Is he alive?" Adam called out to the other two officers who were rising. But he was afraid he already knew the answer.

"Not a chance. Three shots, center mass, all within an inch of each other. That's some pretty good shooting."

But Adam wasn't feeling celebratory. They'd just lost a chance to tie the assassin to the mastermind behind the DC killings.

———

"I already went over this a half-a-dozen times," Jaid said tiredly. "I'm sure Adam has, too." At least she hadn't had to go through a shooting review like he would have been put through.

"Not with me, you haven't." Recognizing the tone in Hedgelin's voice, she ran through it once more. Then listened, with growing horror, as Adam gave a brief recitation of what had occurred in the parking garage.

"A security guard has backed up your story." Hedgelin inclined his head toward Adam. "Although it's unfortunate you killed the shooter, effectively shutting down that avenue of questioning, we at least have an identification. Cody Tweed. Did a stretch at Leavenworth, disappeared five years ago, and his parole officer never heard from him again. This is the first time he's surfaced."

"What was he sentenced for?"

"Murder one. He ended up getting his time commuted in return for his testimony that brought down a drug cartel in Miami. The same cartel he'd provided muscle for. Either he started a solo business and started hiring out, or he developed a strong dislike for the four DC victims."

The number had her wincing slightly. Four. Bolton had been executed right in front of her. In mid-sentence. Mid-life. If she let it, today's events would drag her into a dark place it would take time to recover from. "Who was the target? Me or Bolton?"

Hedgelin looked at her sharply. "We're assuming the reporter." He reached for a file folder on his desk, flipped it open, and turned it around so they could see the digital picture of a white card. Red lettering. Encased in a Ziploc. "I'm told he had an alcohol problem."

"Gluttony." Adam's gaze met hers. "That's what he was showing you when I caught your attention."

She nodded tiredly. "I'd already gotten spooked because it sounded like he'd been told not only to arrange the meet with me but where. There was only one reason for that to be predetermined—if the killer was planning to be there, too." Jaid wanted nothing more than for this day to end. She was wearing ill-fitting sneakers and scrubs that someone had brought her. She didn't know where her clothes were. Didn't care. There was no way she wanted them back.

Every time she had an instant to think, anxiety filled her. She'd had a chance to send a quick text to Stacy, telling her to keep Royce away from the television, but there was no way of knowing if the girl had been successful.

But he was asking about you, so I told him what I know.

Whenever she recalled the reporter's words, ice water washed through her veins. What had the man told him? And how much of it was about Royce?

"I read your linguist's report denying a match of authorship from the communications found on Lambert's computer and his written statement." The assistant director directed the words at Adam. "Intriguing. Naturally, I'll want to duplicate the tests with our own experts."

Adam inclined his head. "Naturally."

"We thought we could also run authorship match tests on that e-mail found on Lambert's computer and writing samples of the people of interest in this case," Jaid put in. "I got some statements from Senator Newell, his two sons, and Joseph Bailey today. If you can get us a sample from Dr. Harandi, we can at least start narrowing our search."

"I'll see what I can do." Hedgelin shifted his attention to Adam. "How does this latest death affect the profile?"

The demand implicit in the question was ridiculous. A profile was a researched, tediously developed document, not something offered off the cuff. So she was surprised when Adam answered the assistant director. "I think it supports the last profile I gave you. Tweed's background makes it likely that it was a work for hire, allowing the mastermind of these killings to remain in the background, safely pulling the strings." He smiled grimly. "Chess pieces. That's how he's likely to think of all the people affected. He's personally motivated and gratified by each death. And he's not done."

"What makes you think that?"

"He orchestrated that last death in front of an FBI agent." She read the apology in the gaze he sent her. It fortified something inside her. "He's taking things up a notch. Thumbing his nose at the attempts to stop him. He's saying, 'See this? You could be next.'"

"You think he's escalating?"

"I think he's had every act planned from the start," Adam said flatly. "Executed to a tee. And he's working up to his grand denouement."

———

It was after eight as Jaid walked down the hallway. She had her briefcase and purse; her phone was in hand as she strode through the building. "Stacy?" she said in relief when the girl answered. "How's Royce? Were you able to keep him away from the news?"

The girl sounded worried. "He's fine, Ms. M. And I made sure he didn't watch any TV. But Mrs. Kettleson called your place and asked me about it. And there have been some calls from some newspapers and television networks. I didn't answer, and I turned off the machine so Royce wouldn't hear any of the messages they left. I hope that's okay."

Relief flickered through her. Had she been that responsible at fifteen? Somehow she doubted it. "That's great. Thanks so much. I'm on my way home now."

"That's okay, your mom came over a few hours ago."

Relief turned to trepidation. "Oh."

"She sent me home. Said Royce needed to be with family. I'm sure she wouldn't say anything to him about what happened, though. She's, like, real protective, right?"

"Yes. She is. Thank you again, Stacy. You did great today."

She felt something on her shoulders and turned to find Adam cloaking her with his overcoat.

"Those scrubs aren't going to be much protection against the cold."

She stared at him, her phone still clutched in her hand. "All I thought about today was shielding Royce from the news. But Mother . . . she had to have seen it. She's a world-class worrier. I never thought to call."

"Well." Settling the coat around her shoulders, he placed a palm at the small of her back and guided her through the glass doors to the outside. "The clip I saw did mention your name," he ignored her slight wince, "but it went on to say that you were uninjured. If she watched it, she knows you're all right."

Somehow that did little to lift the mantle of concern. They rounded the corner in front of headquarters. Headed for the parking garage. "Bolton said something today about the killer asking about me. Said he told him 'all he knows.' How do I find out exactly what that entailed? What if he relayed his questions about my son's birth?"

"Jaid." Adam's ruined voice sounded like rumpled velvet. "Do you trust me?"

She stopped. Looked at him. And halted the immediate agreement on her lips. Did she? Not with her heart. Certainly not with that. But in all other matters . . . "Yes," she whispered.

"Then I think it's time you tell me just what you're protecting that boy from."

She ducked her head. Began walking again. Refusal was on her tongue. She'd spent years guarding Royce's secret. It had long been second nature.

But protecting it from a careless journalist and keeping it from the madman targeting victims all over the city were two different things. "He's adopted," she said finally, eyes straight ahead. There were few people on the street and none near them. Even so, she kept her voice pitched low. "He was a few months old when I took him. His mother was dead. His father dying. And I'd been warned that the people responsible for his mother's death were hunting for his father. For him. I promised I'd raise him as my own and keep his birth a secret. Adopt him, so his last name would be different. Take him to a new suburb. In essence, help the boy vanish, so he wouldn't become victim to a revenge killing."

She had said nothing to hint at it. But Adam's hand on her elbow stopped her. The expression on his face told her he realized the truth.

"He's your father's son, isn't he?"

The words sounded foreign. She'd spoken them to no one. Not to the judge at the adoption hearing. Not to the social workers that had come for visits before the adoption was final. Certainly not to her mother after they'd repaired their rocky relationship when Royce was two. She'd never risked even breathing them aloud.

Until now. "Yes." She was barely conscious that they'd started walking again. "He was waiting for me outside headquarters one afternoon. It was a couple weeks after . . . after the last time I'd seen you in the Louisiana CCU." The time when he'd been weak but awake. Strong enough to order her to go back to the city. Strong enough to convince her that their relationship was over for good.

"You'd always hoped he'd reach out again."

Her mouth twisted. "Yeah, well, I guess delivering the GTO to my front door with the keys in it on my sixteenth birthday was all he was capable of. He left when I was eleven and stayed gone. But suddenly, he was there again. I met him several times after that. Wary, you know? But . . . hopeful. I thought maybe there was something there to salvage."

"He was dying, you said."

"Liver cancer. And I don't know what he and Royce's mother were into, or whether they just saw something they shouldn't have. But she was gunned down in a drive-by shooting weeks after Royce's birth. And my father . . . they were after him, too. One way or another, he didn't have a lot of time left. But I didn't know about Royce until our fifth meeting. He brought him along, and when I saw him, I knew. I realized my father hadn't returned for me. He'd returned because he needed something and I was all he had."

"He knew he could rely on you to do the right thing. Even though he never had where you were concerned."

"He couldn't have known that." The shadowy confines of the parking garage were fitting companions for the dark turn of her thoughts. She didn't want to admit aloud the odd moments of resentment she'd had, toward an infant of all things. Royce had disrupted her life. Dropped her down in the middle of a world she knew nothing about. "He went to great lengths to protect his son."

"While he'd left his daughter behind."

She forgot sometimes that he was a forensic psychologist by training. It was what made him brilliant at his job. But it could be uncomfortable to have that insight turned on her. "I don't know what my father's relationship was with Royce's mother. Just that the baby bore her last name. And I'm not proud of how I handled things with Royce for those first few months. But somewhere along the way, I stopped caring for him merely as a favor to my father. It was about our relationship, my son's and mine. Because he'd become that by then. I might not have been such a great place for him to land at first, but I'll give my life to protect him now. And after today . . ." A quick shudder worked down her spine as she stopped at her car. She looked at Adam. Saw understanding on his face. "I can't risk him. I can't risk what Bolton might have told the killer or what he plans to do with that information."

"So we keep him safe."

As if it were that easy. That simple. Adam took the key fob from her hand because she hadn't yet used it and unlocked the car door for her. "Would your mother accompany him if we sent him away for a while?"

Her stomach did a quick, vicious lurch at the thought. She hadn't been separated from her son for more than a weekend since she'd brought him home. "I think I can convince her of the need. But I don't know where they can go."

He handed her back the fob. Reached for his cell. "Disney World should be nice this time of year." When she stared, he looked uncertain. "That's the name, right? Orlando? Mickey Mouse?"

"Yes." She did a mental shake. "But I thought maybe a place to stash them, where there'd be no money trail."

"Dear Jaid. Have some faith. I know a bit about this sort of thing." He opened her car door as he began speaking on the phone. "Paulie, what do we have Ramsey on right now?" He frowned. "He is? Are they joined at the hip these days? Yes, I know they're married." Adam covered the phone for a moment. "I'll follow you home. It'll be arranged by the time we get there."

"Arranged? Adam, I need some input into this. I'm not going to just send my son off with strangers who I've never . . ." With a gentle pressure on her shoulder, she was guided into the car. Tossed the keys.

"We'll talk later."

Then he was striding for his vehicle, his voice trailing behind him. "I need cash. A bank card accessing one of our unassociated accounts. And I want Ramsey to drive them down there. Their names can't show up on a passenger manifest anywhere. Yeah, send Stryker along, too. He might come in handy charming the grandmother."

It was a bit like being picked up and spun around by a tornado. Finally, Jaid put the key in the ignition. Started the car. Dealing with Adam could be like that. Overpowering. Devastating. It took strength to stand up to him.

She backed out of the parking spot. Straightened the car and headed toward the entrance.

But when it came to keeping her son safe, she was willing to do whatever it took. Even if that meant letting Adam take over.

———

The taillights winked for the last time before the departing car turned at the corner down the street. Was lost from sight. Adam slanted a look at the woman by his side. He saw her swallow hard. Her bottom lip trembled once before she deliberately firmed it. Then she turned back toward the small home where she lived. Headed inside.

He thought he could guess what it cost her to send the boy away. Figured it took a particular type of courage to put her son's fate in the hands of strangers, even if those strangers happened to work for Adam.

Following her into the house, he locked the door behind him. Went to sit next to her on the couch. He wasn't accustomed to giving comfort. But it seemed all too natural to draw her into his arms. To have her head rest, just for a moment, against his shoulder.

"They'll be safe. I promise you. I'm told there are countless parks and shows to keep them occupied for several days. When this is over, Ramsey and Dev will go back and bring them home again. No one will ever be the wiser. Here." He dug in his suit-coat pocket. Handed her a nondescript cell phone. "This number is programmed into the cell we gave to your mother and vice versa. You'll be able to communicate as needed."

She leaned back a little to take it. Something inside him mourned the loss of contact. "You've thought of everything."

"Everything that can be planned for has been." He stared at her, his gut clenching. "It's the things you don't plan for, can't imagine, that grab you by the throat. Today, on the street, when I saw you go down . . ." A vise squeezed in his chest. That moment when the bus had obstructed his view had been a torturous eternity.

Her gaze was caught by something in his expression. He didn't worry about what might show there. Couldn't. Instead he cupped her face in his hands and took her mouth in a hard, desperate kiss. Let the warmth, the pressure, heal something inside him that had threatened to split when the rifle sounded.

"Well." Her hands came up to caress the backs of his. She whispered against his lips, "Now, you have an inkling of what I went through when you were in the CCU. Both times."

He didn't want to consider it. Not the worry that she'd experienced while she'd sat at his bedside, nor how near he'd come to being placed in that same situation with her today. Or worse.

The phone vibrated in his pocket. He leaned in for another quick kiss. "Don't go anywhere." He pushed himself to a standing position with one hand on the arm of the couch. Took his cell out with one hand. Loosened his tie with the other. "Because I don't intend to. Not tonight."

Her slow smile had heat flaring in his belly. And proved entirely too distracting when he answered the phone. "Raiker."

Paulie's tone filled his ear. Talking fast. Urgently.

"That's impossible," he interrupted tersely. Paulie's voice grew more urgent. And disbelief was elbowed aside by anger. And frustration at his own blindness.

"Call a code eight. Shut it all down. Yes, now." He stopped, listened a few more moments. "No, I'm at Jaid's. Centerville." His gaze went to her again, and wished he wasn't responsible for putting that expression on her face. "Not here. Call on the safe phone when you get closer. I'll meet you."

"What's wrong?"

She didn't need another hit today after everything she'd been through. But there was no way to keep it from her. For all he knew she'd be getting her own phone call from the bureau shortly.

"Paulie got a tip. There's a warrant out for my arrest."

Jaid bounced off the couch, her face a mask of shock. "What? Why?"

Strangely, her reaction, so similar to his a moment earlier, calmed something inside him. "I'm wanted for questioning regarding the DC murders. That card Bolton had today . . . apparently, they lifted my thumbprint from it."

Chapter 19

"That's impossible." Nothing about the news made sense. Jaid shook her head, as if that would clear it. "You never got near the card. I didn't take it out of the bag."

His expression was grim. "I expect that's their point."

She stared at him, her mind working furiously. "It was a setup. The whole thing today . . . a big, splashy, in-your-face, are-you-watching-this-world setup?" Driven to move, she started to pace. "Hedgelin has to see it. You've practically been tied up in a bow and delivered to him on a platter. He can't possibly buy this."

"I'm thinking he might be only too happy to buy it." He went for his coat, where it was folded over an armchair. "You may have noticed, he's not my biggest fan. Tomorrow he's going to see the report that Macy Reid tied the man who blackmailed Lambert to Ferrell, who tried to kill me. He's going to consider that proof that I'm all wrapped up in this thing." He slipped into his overcoat. "I'm not going to wait around to hear what spin he puts on it."

She folded her arms across her chest, suddenly cold, although she'd changed out of the scrubs immediately upon arriving home. "What will you do? What was that you said to Paulie? What's a code eight?"

"I'm shutting down Raiker Forensics headquarters. When they don't find me at home, they'll go there." He looked around for his briefcase. Discovered it just inside the door. "We have a plan in place for just such an eventuality. A secondary secret location where we'll prepare."

"Prepare? To do what?"

"To figure out who the hell is behind this and why they're so intent on pinning it on me." His tone was fierce. "Somehow, I don't think I can count on the bureau to clear my name."

Sick fear twisted through her. "I should have seen this today. Should have put it all together. It was too weird, what Bolton said about the caller asking about me. Where's that interest coming from?"

"Where indeed? At the risk of sounding egomaniacal, Bolton ties to me. Reinbeck. Cote, a more nebulous link there, only through Jerry. Nothing that I can think of with Patterson. Then there's Ferrell, who's connected to Lambert through the written communications from the killer. And Lambert's link to LeCroix, which leads right back to me."

He stopped then, and she read his thoughts as easily as if he'd spoken them out loud. "There's no reason to believe I'm the next target."

"The possibility can't be discounted. Why draw you into the scene with Bolton? As the reporter told you, he has lots of contacts in the bureau. But you're tied to me, too. And right now anyone with a connection could be in danger."

"How would the DC killer know about us?" She shook her head. Adam was an enigmatic man at the best of times, but she knew how his mind worked. "I'm not leaving. I'm not joining Royce in Disney World or whatever plan you're hatching in that mind of yours."

The look of affront he wore told her better than words that she'd followed his line of thought seamlessly. "It would be safer all around . . ."

"Here's what I am going to do," she told him calmly. The best way to handle Adam Raiker was with logic and unyielding determination. "I'll continue working the investigation from the inside. Focusing on the ties to you without getting caught up in the ridiculous assumption that you're the DC killer. I can do more here, especially now that I don't have to worry about Royce."

She returned his glare with equanimity. "I want to hear from Hedgelin himself what he's thinking. Maybe I can make him see reason." She knew Adam recognized the futility of the thought. But there were suspects in this case who hadn't been fully investigated yet, angles that had yet to be explored. She wasn't going to allow the assistant director to focus on Adam while ignoring the countless other possibilities.

"I don't have time to debate this with you."

The irritation in his voice almost made her smile in spite of the seriousness of the situation. He wasn't used to people arguing with him. Which was all the more reason she couldn't give the man an inch. "You're right; you don't. Go meet Paulie. Give me the number of that safe cell you mentioned."

Grudgingly, he told her. She mentally repeated the digits until she was certain she had them memorized. "Wait. You'll need the statements I had the Newell family write today for Macy to run tests on." She carried her briefcase into her bedroom, took them out, and made copies.

Reentering the living room, she found him standing in the same place she'd left him. She handed him the pages, watched him fold them and tuck them in the pocket of his overcoat. Then she looked at the clock. "You need to go." The words brought a pang, one that had to be firmly set aside. There was no telling how long ago the warrant had been issued. "They'll be looking for your car."

"And they'll find it at Ray's Auto Body in Manassas. This is a rental, so it might take them longer, but you're right. It won't be long." He was at the door. Easy enough to turn. Go through it. He was known for his abrupt departures.

But he made no movement toward it. And something in his gaze had her heart doing a slow flip in her chest. It was she who crossed the room in the end. Walked into his arms and hugged his hard waist. "Don't be a hero."

His laugh sounded choked. "Haven't you heard? My press has taken a definite downturn." With one crooked finger beneath her chin, he tilted her face up. The brush of his lips across her forehead was whisper light. "Love and sex just muddy the issue."

Immediately recognizing his oft repeated phrase, she supplied the rest of the quote. "'People always see much clearer without either clouding their instincts.'" He'd preached that time and again in classes. On the job. "I heard a brilliant investigator say that once."

"Too bad he can't take his own advice."

When her head jerked up so she could look at him, he took the opportunity to take her mouth in a bruising kiss. Released her. "Lock the door after me."

She folded her arms around her middle. Nodded. Then watched the man walk out her door without a backward glance.

And at that moment, the threat posed by the DC killer didn't seem like the biggest danger she was facing.

Diving headlong into love with Adam Raiker again was.

Shepherd was already in Hedgelin's office when Jaid arrived. She slipped into a seat, surreptitiously watching the assistant director's expression for signs of his thoughts. But nothing showed in his expression but the familiar vague impatience. "Special Agent Marlowe. I trust you've recovered from the incident you were involved in yesterday?"

No weaknesses were ever allowed to show on the job. In this environment personal vulnerabilities could be used to bury an agent. Her voice was clear when she responded. "I'm fine, sir."

"Because you know we have counselors available for that sort of thing."

Jaid wasn't entirely sure she was able to keep her reaction to those words from showing on her face. "That won't be necessary."

Hedgelin took off his glasses. Withdrew a handkerchief from his pocket and began to polish them. "I was just updating Special Agent Shepherd. We have a warrant out for the arrest of Adam Raiker. Hence his absence this morning."

Her voice hardening slightly, she said, "Yes, I heard."

"You heard." Examining the results of his efforts, he finally resettled the glasses back on his nose. "So maybe you have an idea how his fingerprint got on the note card Bolton was showing you when he was shot."

"The evidence was never out of my possession." She glanced at Shepherd. His face looked drawn. Worried. Shifting her focus back to her superior, she said, "Adam was in shooting review, and I was reporting in my own sessions. He didn't have access to it."

"Which makes it even more suspect to find his thumbprint on the note card, doesn't it?"

"Suspect?" She didn't attempt to mask her sarcasm. "What's *suspect* is believing that the most brilliant criminologist in the country"—she noted his immediate reaction—"excuse me, *one* of them was so careless that he accidentally made an amateurish mistake on the fourth card left at a murder scene. We need to be thinking about how else his print could have gotten there."

"When we hear hoofbeats on a ranch, Agent Marlowe, we don't go looking for zebras. But you make a valid point. I'd very much like an opportunity to discuss the matter with him. Coupled with the report you filed connecting the man who tried to blow up Raiker's place with whoever was manipulating Lambert . . . surely you see how he's tied into this investigation." He took a moment to survey them both. "If either of you has any knowledge of his whereabouts, now would be the time to tell me."

Relief flared. It took effort to keep it from her expression. Her voice. "He hasn't been located?"

"Not yet. But that's just a matter of time. Agent Shepherd." Hedgelin's change of topic was swift. "Have you located that priest, Jerry Benton, yet?"

Jaw dropping, she demanded, "You're arresting Benton, too?" Adam would be devastated if he learned his friend was caught up in this mess because of their association.

"No," Shepherd put in hastily, seeing her expression. "There are just more questions I want to ask him. But no, sir, I haven't been able to find him. There's a retired priest covering his duties at the church, and all I've been told is that Benton had an emergency to tend to."

"Convenient. Keep digging in that area."

"Have the linguists at Quantico duplicated the authorship tests run by Adam's forensic linguist yet?"

"The impetus of the investigation has shifted." Hedgelin flicked a glance at the other agent after answering Jaid's question. "You're excused, Shepherd."

After a brief hesitation, the other agent rose. Left the room silently. Dread pooled in Jaid's stomach. She steeled herself for what might be coming next. Hoped she was wrong.

"Special Agent Marlowe, it occurs to me that despite your vows otherwise, you may need some time away from the demands of this investigation."

The words ambushed her. "I am more than capable of continuing my work, sir." Anxiety had her muscles tensing. Of all the scenarios she'd envisioned, somehow being removed from the case hadn't even occurred.

"The personal nature of Bolton's request, the way he sought you out to meet with him is troublesome."

Her breath came out in a rush. She hadn't been aware that she was holding it. "I'm willing to assume that risk, sir."

"Well, I'm not." He avoided meeting her gaze by straightening the file folders on his desk. "Not to make light of your contributions to this case, but I have nearly three hundred investigators involved here. I can afford to lose one, especially if your removal ensures your safety."

"Sir . . ."

He did look at her then, and his voice turned cutting. "Don't make the mistake of believing you have a choice in this matter, Agent. You've been reassigned. Talk to your immediate supervisor for your new duties."

Tamping down her disappointment and anger, she said, "I was going to ask, sir, to take some personal leave now instead." His sharp look was full of suspicion. "My son broke his arm a few days ago. I haven't been able to spend much time with him."

It took effort not to squirm under his penetrating stare. After a long moment he gave a jerky nod. "See human resources."

She got up. Reached for her briefcase and purse. She got as far as the door before his voice stopped her. "Please turn in your copy of the case file. If I hear you are involving yourself in this investigation in any way in the future, Agent, there will be disciplinary action involved."

Jaid sent him a look over her shoulder. "Not to worry, Assistant Director. I'm going for a little R and R."

———————

It had taken over an hour to fill out the necessary leave paperwork.

So when Jaid saw Agent Shepherd lingering near the elevator when she finished with human resources, she immediately knew he'd been waiting for her. "Tom." She stabbed the Down button with her index finger.

"I wanted to talk to you one-on-one about Adam's friend. That priest."

The doors opened silently. When Jaid entered the compartment, the agent followed her. "I've been removed from the case."

Shepherd looked dumfounded. "Removed? Why?"

Rolling her shoulders, she said, "Party line or the real reason? Hedgelin claims it's for my safety. Somehow, I think his motives are somewhat less altruistic, but who knows."

He lowered his voice as if someone would hear him. "This whole thing smells bad. This perpetrator is one of the most careful, organized ones I've ever seen. But all of a sudden he makes a rookie mistake like leaving a print? Bullshit."

Because it was an apt description, she nodded. But she was also careful to say little. She had no idea if this conversation would be repeated to the assistant director. Suspicion had started to haze every aspect of this case. She couldn't afford for it to be otherwise. The stakes were too high.

They were heading for the front doors. "I know you don't want to hear this. That Adam wouldn't believe it, but Jaid"—the agent's hand on her arm stopped her—"if Raiker isn't behind these murders, then someone planted his print on that card. Where'd they get it? How? Only someone close to him would have that kind of access."

His words made sense. And echoed similar thoughts she'd wrestled with in the wakeful hours of the night. "You think that someone might be Benton. To what purpose?"

Frustration stamped the man's handsome face. "I haven't gotten that far. But I'm not going to drop it. There are a lot of people in this agency who still hold Raiker in high regard. A lot who aren't going to take this latest twist at face value. If someone is trying to frame him, it's someone he trusts."

And that, she thought sickly, was a harsh sentence for a man to whom the emotion came so reluctantly. "I agree. I hope your efforts turn something up on that end."

He seemed to be choosing his words carefully. "If you would happen to speak to him . . ."

Delicately, she freed herself from his grasp. "I won't. But I hope you find something that proves your hunch." Because if he didn't, she thought as she turned and went through the front doors, the manhunt surrounding Adam would intensify. And even with his resources, he couldn't stay underground forever.

———

The West Virginia site was tucked into a rural mountain-ous region where the black bears outnumbered county residents. Its seclusion had been one of the factors that had led to its selection for a backup facility when Adam had started his agency.

But having a process in place to vacate his primary location had simply seemed a security precaution at the time. He'd never imagined a time when he would have to utilize the code eight operation. Shutting down the Manassas facility and moving a smaller, more select group of operatives to this site.

He scanned the area with a careful eye but could find nothing that required his immediate attention. From the exterior the area looked like a camping property. Small cabins were scattered in a perimeter around a large structure that looked like a huge warehouse. Inside a mobile lab was housed in one corner. Alfred Jones, the one scientist who had made the trip, was currently inside it, fussily arranging his domain. There were large conference rooms set up with movable walls and flooring. And there was a small cyber center with operatives busy handling the download of backup files from the main server.

If things went according to plan, by the time law enforcement seized what remained of the computers at the Manassas headquarters, the motherboard of each would be fried and useless.

Paulie came up beside Adam and silently joined his perusal of the activity. "Should be ready to go in another couple hours."

"Have they hit the main facility yet?"

"Served a warrant there a couple hours ago." Paulie seemed to understand Adam's black thoughts. "We knew, when they couldn't find you at home, that the facility would be next. We had plenty of time to shut things down there. They aren't going to access any information about our back cases. Or anything else. Gavin and I made sure of that."

Gavin Pounds was their resident cyber wizard, currently

in the e-center bringing their computers up to speed. Paulie matched him in brilliance with all things electronic. "I know."

"But it's the idea of law enforcement swarming in there and putting their grubby paws all over what we've built." He laid a pudgy hand over his chest, which was clad in a light blue shirt decorated with tiny poker chips. "Believe me, I feel violated, too, and not in the way I usually prefer. But whoever is behind this will pay, Adam. Maybe the government will, too, when we hit them with a suit for unlawful arrest."

"Since I have no intention of allowing them to arrest me, that may be a moot point," he responded dryly. His cell rang, and he tensed. The news in the last few hours had only brought complications.

But recognizing the number of the safe phone he'd left with Jaid, something inside him eased. He turned away to answer it. "Jaid."

"I've been removed from the case. You can either have me join you, or I'll continue the investigation here alone. But make no mistake, Adam, I will continue with or without you."

He wasn't totally surprised at the first part of the news. But the last statement had ice-cold fear spearing through him. "I think it'd be best if you joined your son."

"Two options, Adam, and that wasn't among them."

Cursing mentally, he shot a look at his friend, who was pretending to be interested in the activity in the corner. And wondered why he'd ever found independence in a woman to be so damned attractive.

"All right," he bit the words out. "Follow directions precisely. And if you give my operatives any trouble, I'm giving them permission to drop you off, mid flight, without a parachute."

The empty lot south of Manassas had a high security fence surrounding its perimeter. The fence was topped with barbed wire that carried an electrical current. At least that's what the warning sign posted at the double gates said. Jaid could see no reason for the security. The huge open space that it encompassed was empty.

But she punched in the series of codes Adam had given her, and the light on the security modem flashed green. The gates slowly swung open, and she got back in her car and drove through. Parked a quarter mile inside near the center of the area.

The gates closed automatically behind her. Probably locked. She sat for about fifteen minutes. Long enough to peer anxiously in all directions several times to see if she had been followed. If she'd acquired a tail, it wasn't visible. And there'd be no way to follow her from this point, at any rate.

She heard the 'copter long before she saw it. And she recognized that the area, the ownership of which couldn't be traced back to Adam, had one purpose only. And that was to serve as a private landing strip.

She waited until the helicopter bounced lightly a few times, settled, and a door opened before she got out of her car. Taking her purse, briefcase, and a duffel bag out of the backseat, she locked the vehicle and ran in a crouch toward her ride.

All three occupants inside were unfamiliar. But Adam had told her whom to expect. The raven-haired woman with the brilliant green eyes would be Caitlin Fleming. The muscular dark-haired man next to Hank, the pilot, would be her husband, Zach Sharper.

"That all you brought?" Cait helped her stow her gear in the tiny interior space. "Good thing. We're sardines in here."

The door closed automatically as they buckled themselves into the two backseats. "Just so you know," Jaid pitched her voice loudly enough to be heard over the sound of the copter's blades, "if you have any thought at all of taking me somewhere other than where Adam is, I am armed." She gave the woman next to her a cheerful smile. "I'll shoot to maim."

The helicopter lifted as Cait gave her a long, assessing

look. Her sudden smile elevated her features to cover-girl status. "I like her," she shouted, leaning forward to thump her husband's bicep.

He looked over his shoulder at them, his expression indulgent. "I'm not surprised."

———

Jerry Benton kissed the rosary he held, made the sign of the cross. Once again he was the only one in the small chapel. Alone with his regrets. His prayers. His despair.

He began the Our Father, hoping another decade of the rosary would bring him what confession hadn't. A feeling of peace and forgiveness.

But he knew somehow that forgiveness was a long way off. He couldn't deny Pastor Gleason's words of absolution. He'd functioned for far too long believing, in some respects, that the ends justified the means.

It was the unintended consequences to plans set in motion long ago that brought the most grief now. The strength of his convictions had hurt those he worked with. Involved Adam in a way Jerry had never intended.

His head bowed, he prayed for a way to make it up to him.

———

"Has Macy run authorship matches on the written statements I got at Senator Newell's yesterday?"

Jaid's question was directed at Adam, but a small dark-haired woman with quiet gray eyes answered from the end of the conference table. "That'd be me. And yes, I ran the tests. None of them matched the author of the e-mail found on Lambert's computer or the note Ferrell had."

Slightly deflated, Jaid reached into a pocket of her briefcase. "I never was able to get a copy of Dr. Harandi's statement. But I did find a couple papers he's published that were accessible on the Web." She took the sheets out and got up to walk them to the linguist. "Will that work?"

"It might. Although I would expect a research document

such as this to be written in a more formal manner than, say, a paragraph or written statement, it's my understanding that Dr. Harandi is not a native English speaker. In that case, his syntax may well tend to be more formal anyway. At any rate, it'll just take an hour or so to diagram the samples and run the tests."

There were nine of them around the table. Jaid didn't know any of them, really, other than Adam and Paulie. But she'd met Kell a couple days earlier. Cait and Zach on the ride over. And the still absent Ramsey and Devlin Stryker had been the operatives tasked with driving Royce and her mother to Orlando. She assumed they'd be joining them later. There was something strikingly familiar about Risa Chandler, the long-legged woman with the dark blond hair on Adam's other side. A dark-haired man flanked her. In the next moment Jaid recalled that both of them, along with Devlin Stryker, had been at the Philadelphia hospital when she'd gone to visit Adam after he'd been shot.

The sheer number of people who were involved in what should be a covert investigation made her nervous. There were a few others bent over the computers in the next room. An oddball of a scientist in the mobile lab with a black Mohawk and enough piercings to set off metal detectors. And Adam had mentioned another couple of investigators on the road checking out Lambert's story about his childhood.

More people meant more possibilities for leaks. But Adam didn't look worried. If anything, he appeared in his element. In command.

"We need to concentrate on how the crimes relate to me, since someone is making damn sure that I'm at the center of this," he said.

Certain of the unpopularity of her next comments, Jaid nonetheless said, "Agreed. And whoever is attempting to frame you is someone who knows you well. Someone is familiar with your history and is using it against you. Agent Shepherd told me again this morning that he is pursuing an avenue regarding your friend. Father Benton."

Adam's glare was lethal. Everyone else in the room seemed to be holding their collective breath. "Jerry's biggest fault is caring too deeply about causes others don't even think about. I hope you're not suggesting that a man of God would put aside all vows and enact not one but four murders?"

Her voice was even. "I'm just telling you one line of investigation going on. They are looking for Benton for another round of questioning. He's nowhere to be found." Taking in the stillness of his expression, she felt a stab of remorse for adding that worry atop his other more urgent ones.

"Risa, see if you and Nate can track his whereabouts."

The slender woman with eyes nearly as gold as her hair nodded. "It'll give me a chance to break the newbie in."

"Eight years in Philadelphia homicide," Nate murmured. Jaid figured that Risa's sudden start meant she'd been the recipient of surreptitious pinch. "I think I'm up to it."

"Paulie and I are questioning whether the assistant director is involved." Adam's next words commanded everyone's immediate attention. And the statement gave voice to a terrible suspicion she'd never dared contemplate. But one that made a horrible sort of sense.

"He . . . resents you," she said slowly. She'd told Adam as much before. "It's connected to the LeCroix case you worked together." The outcome of that case might have elevated Adam to cult hero status, but Hedgelin has ridden it to his current position in the agency. "I know he was unhappy about Bolton's proposed book on you."

Adam nodded. "He admitted to me that he had spoken to the man; I assume to get his side of the LeCroix case on record."

Jaid's gaze traveled around the table. "So yesterday's murder eliminated one of the assistant director's concerns."

"I believe he was upset a few years back when a case of mine intersected with one of the bureau's. Shepherd was working it at the time." Several at the table were scribbling notes as Adam spoke. "I solved their kidnapping case when

I broke up a child-swap ring. Shepherd was banished to North Dakota; probably for embarrassing the agency."

"Or Hedgelin," Jaid murmured.

Risa spoke then, her gaze steely. "It was an FBI screw-up that led to Jennings shooting Adam. According to their agents, they had the shooter contained in a residence, surrounded. It turned out they'd been duped by a lookalike."

"And the icing on the cake?" There was an uncharacteristic hardness in Paulie's usually ebullient expression. "It was also the bureau who handed us a nice and neat little motivation for Jennings, which I never bought. That he was revenging an ex-girlfriend's father's arrest?" He made a scoffing sound. "There's not much I'd do for ex-girlfriends, and murder doesn't even make the list."

"So we focus on Hedgelin. Look for links, however remote, to Jennings, Ferrell, Lambert, Tweed. He had to have come into contact with them somewhere."

"It's possible he heard the same rumors we did last January." This from an unsmiling Macy. "That the LeCroix boy was alive. And now he's appeared as Scott Lambert. Is there any chance he was more deeply involved in this than he says?"

Adam shook his head. "I don't think so. Abbie and Ryne Robel are checking out his story about his childhood, though. Maybe they can discover someone else who was digging around in the Lamberts' pasts. The profile I developed of the DC killer suggests he's selecting targets for personal reasons. I still think this holds true if Hedgelin turns out to be the offender. I don't have a connection to Patterson, and I barely knew Cote. Look for links from Hedgelin to each of the victims. Their selection will be about him, not me."

He stopped then as his phone rang. "It's the Robels," he said in an aside to Paulie, and the two men got up and left the room.

Jaid rose, closed the door after them, and surveyed the remaining occupants. "I think we need to look hard at Hedgelin, and I'm willing to admit he fits. But it would be a mistake not to look at the obvious, and that is the offender could be anyone close to Adam." She watched the quick glances they shot each other and smiled grimly. "Yes, by all means, count me in that group. And I say that because I want to remind you that no one is above suspicion. Not me. Not Pastor Benton."

"And not Paulie Samuels."

"Mace, what the hell?" It was Kell who responded to his fiancée's words, but from the shocked expressions on everyone else's faces, they were similarly taken aback.

The petite woman ran a nervous hand through her dark hair, but her voice was mutinous. "I just learned recently that my stepfather, the man who raised me, the man I would have trusted with my life, was responsible for my kidnapping when I was eight."

Jaid blinked in shock at the news, but it was apparent from the sympathy in the others' expressions that they knew about it already. Macy looked at them all grimly. "Betrayal is hardest to see from those closest to you. That's all I'm saying. Jaid is right. We can't afford to overlook anyone. Not with Adam's life at stake."

"I saw Paulie with Adam in Philly," Risa said slowly. "But not on the night he was shot."

"He ran the wireless ransom pickup in Colorado last winter when we worked that Mulder kidnapping." Kell shook his head. "I hate this."

"He's been with Adam since the beginning, right?" Cait's green eyes were troubled. "They were in the agency together even at the time of the LeCroix case."

Jaid felt a little queasy about where her warning had led. She'd known Samuels for over a decade. Would never have doubted his devotion to Adam. Hated hearing it questioned now.

But she hated even more the thought of him vulnerable to someone he trusted and would never suspect. "Paulie inherits the business in the event of Adam's death," she told them. "And the money goes to Father Benton."

"Sort of a big-fucking motive on both counts." Kell's

gaze was hard. "Risa and Nate pursue the Benton line. Jaid, you know more about Hedgelin than anyone but Paulie and Adam, so you help Cait on that end." She nodded. "Macy has the Harandi sample to run, then she'll help me see if Paulie ties in to this in anyway."

"He was with the agency, too," Cait put in. "Maybe he has links to Jennings and the others."

"He was in the cyber unit," Jaid reminded her. "But, yes, that's definitely something to be checked into."

Zach Sharper looked at the group. "I don't work for this outfit, but you might as well put me to work. I've tackled a few things along the way since getting tied up with this one." He jerked a thumb at Cait, who gave him a feline smile.

"Always a sweet talker. Stick with me. I'll find something to keep you busy."

Chairs scraped as they all rose. Jaid noted that no one had mentioned checking on her. But she didn't fool herself into thinking that her relationship with Adam would be overlooked. The thought didn't bother her. She wanted thorough. Adam deserved no less. And if his own operatives couldn't be relied on to keep the man safe, she didn't know who could.

No one would anticipate a strike again so soon. Events had spiraled a bit quicker than he'd planned, but adaptability was always key.

He hadn't expected Cody Tweed to be taken out yesterday, but maybe Raiker had done him a favor there. The assassin was quickly becoming a loose end. And he could take it from here.

A slow smile formed at the thought. As a matter of fact, his plan called for a more personal touch.

Put on the vinyl gloves. That was important, wasn't it? Reach across the table for the white note card and a red marker. Prepare for the next victim.

Next to Raiker, this one was the most deserving of all.

Chapter 20

The e-lab looked like something out of Hollywood. Or at the very least an upgrade to what she'd seen at Quantico.

Jaid's eyes widened when she saw what was, she had to remind herself, merely a secondary site for Adam. Each of the operatives had uploaded the data they'd compiled. Paulie had explained, in a lengthy, detailed discussion that had been lost on her, how he and Gavin ensured their backup server was secure. She'd have to take his word on it. But it had occurred to her, with a quick glance at Kell, that if the man wanted to advertise their location electronically, he was in position to do just that and none of them would be the wiser.

There were half-a-dozen desktop computers in the lab, with screens the size of the one at Adam's loft. But it was the touch screen on the wall that held her attention. It was enormous. Easily eight feet by six feet. And portions of their reports were projected up on it, with Adam moving the data around with the brush of a finger.

"Here's what everyone has come up with on Hedgelin so

far." He pulled a data report over, enlarged it with a flick of his fingers. "He was the special agent in charge who was responsible for putting away Jennings fifteen years ago."

"The man who did his damnedest to kill you last winter and spring," Risa murmured.

Inclining his head, Adam continued, using his index finger to pull another data report across the screen so the two sat side by side. "He had five years in the cyber unit for the bureau before switching to field agent. So he's got the skills to be the one sniffing around the agency's financials for the last several months."

Jaid intercepted the surprised looks from his operatives. Apparently, this was news to them as well as to her.

"Someone needed a great deal of electronics know-how to set up that wireless ransom payment for the Mulder girl's kidnapping last winter," he went on. "Paulie managed to circumvent seven million of it, but he still got three. There's also evidence that some of that ransom money ended up in a wireless account for the assassin sent after me in May."

"And it takes a cyber background to come up with the spyware on the first two victims' cell phones," Jaid put in, fascinated as Adam manipulated each piece of data into a linear sequence. "Not to mention the self-destructing e-mails sent to Lambert's computer."

"Any sign of that money in Hedgelin's financials?"

Paulie shook his head woefully at Kell's question. "I've spent months trying to trace the money from the ransom last winter, and there are three overseas accounts I've got flagged. But whoever is the owner has done a good job keeping his identity secret. Of course, it helps that he chose countries that don't follow international banking regulations."

A chill worked down Jaid's skin. The cyber wizardry described could just as easily be attributed to Paulie himself.

"If the DC killer is the same one who's behind the Mulder kidnapping, at least we know how he financed the assassins. Jennings. Ferrell. Yes," Macy nodded to Adam when he would have interrupted, "we have to include him.

Tweed. And Vincent Dodge, the man who actually snatched the girl in Colorado. That's a lot of money. Sure, he had the three million from the ransom, but he's expended some serious cash in this effort. How does he hope to recoup it?"

"That's a question we'll have to ask him."

Jaid propped her hips against one of the desks behind her and stared at Adam. Wondered what he wasn't telling them. It was slightly frightening to realize how well she knew the man. But he'd shut her out enough in the past to make her certain that there was something he wasn't disclosing right now.

"If I can go on." His voice was silky. A sign of his flagging patience. "Connections to the victims. I know we never saw his name on Patterson's client list, but as we discovered by talking to the other investment manager at Dennison International, Heath Carroll, all these companies are interrelated to some extent. Hedgelin does have an investment account with another large corporation, Stanley International."

"How could you possibly have learned that?"

The room went silent at Jaid's question. "Seriously, this is private information. It wouldn't be accessible . . ." Comprehension struck her.

"Every database we access at headquarters at Raiker Forensics is strictly legit," Paulie assured her.

"And here?"

"Not."

Adam, damn him, looked amused. "Hacking is a serious crime, Special Agent Marlowe. Feel free to make an arrest."

"Don't tempt me," she muttered.

"As I was saying," he went on with an exaggerated inflection, "it's nebulous. Requires speculation. But that's a tenuous tie to Patterson, if Hedgelin blamed that firm's actions when his investments went south."

"And he lost money?" she asked, already knowing the answer. Because if they had found Hedgelin's investment firm, she knew for a fact they'd delved into his portfolio.

"Faster than Paulie at the racetrack." Everyone in the

room laughed at Adam's response except for the man in question.

"Luck's going to turn around. Then you're all going to be singing a different tune."

"What about Reinbeck?" Jaid asked doubtfully. She couldn't recall anything on the upcoming court calendar that would have interested Hedgelin. "There was that case on this year's docket about outlawing weapons in government buildings, but I don't know a law enforcement officer who isn't in support of regulating that."

"We might have been focusing on the wrong docket." Adam turned to the touch screen and pulled up a couple more bits of information. "Unless Cleve has changed his opinions since I worked with him at the bureau, he was anti–gun control. Last year Byron wrote a scathing minority dissent on a ruling dealing with the open-carry legislation in Virginia. The majority ruling was seen as a victory for gun rights, but Byron cited a flaw in the way the law was written that the anti-gun lobby has been using to fire up their supporters."

He looked at Cait, who nodded. "That organization is working on getting a challenge to the law based on the technicality that Reinbeck cited, hoping to get it to the high court again and this time have the law overturned."

"Wrath." Adam's ruined voice sounded soft. "No one was more passionate about the law, or his interpretations of it, than Byron." Turning back to the screen, he cleared his throat. "Notice we came up empty on a relationship between Hedgelin and Cardinal Cote."

"We came up empty linking the cardinal to any of our persons of interest in this case," Jaid put in wryly.

"Something we still need to work on. But Bolton." With a brush of his index finger, he pulled over another report. Spread it to make it bigger. "Easy link there. Cleve wasn't at all happy about the book the reporter had in progress. He gets rid of him, and the book goes away."

"And hanging the entire series of murders on you wraps it all in a neat little bundle." She thought for a moment. To

Macy she said, "Did you get a match with the Harandi document?" When the other woman shook her head, she looked at Adam. "Do we have something written we can use from Hedgelin? That would be the quickest way to tie him to this."

"We've only gotten a couple reports signed by him available on the Web. There was nothing written by him in my copy of the case files."

"I tried matching that report with his signature for authorship," Macy said, "and struck out. But frankly, the document isn't a good sample. We have no way of knowing if he dictated it or used a secretary to write the gist of it from notes he provided. Either way would give us a false negative. We really need something that we can be certain he wrote himself."

"There's still the little matter of how he got your finger-print on the note card left with Bolton," Kell put in. His frown was reflective. "Could have transferred it from some-thing you touched recently, I suppose. And it wouldn't take them long to match it, since your prints were still on file from your days as an agent. They would have identified them when they ran the elimination prints of the task force members in the vicinity of the evidence."

"Everything we have that points at Hedgelin is circum-stantial," Jaid pointed out. "We need something solid."

"I'll get that. When I meet with him."

Splinters of fear pricked her. Jaid shoved away from the desk as a chorus of voices met Adam's words. "No."

He flicked a glance at her, even as he addressed the group as a whole. "We're not going to find the evidence we need, short of a search of his home. But I think I can draw him out in a face-to-face." His smile was grim. "That will be the next order of business. We collectively come up with the best plan for doing just that."

Brooking no argument, he picked up a remote and with a click emptied the touch screen. "Who followed up on Jerry's whereabouts?"

"That'd be Nate and me," Risa put in. She shoved her

dark blond hair behind one ear as she spoke. "I finally got in touch with the monsignor's cook. Nobody else who worked for him would talk to me, but she said the emergency that took him away was 'a crisis of faith.'"

Nate took over from here. "He used his bank card at the ATM at the Swenson's Grocery Store near the rectory. That was the night before last, and there's been no activity on it since. His credit cards have also been inactive. I couldn't do a GPS trace on his cell phone." He raised a brow at Adam.

He shook his head, a half smile on his face. "Jerry's cell is the oldest one he can still use with his network. It wouldn't have any of the bells and whistles on it."

"Triangulation also didn't work. I suspect he may have the phone shut off or the battery is dead."

"I called St. Ambrose and talked to the priest there." Risa took up the story again. "I asked him to explain to me what a crisis of faith meant to a member of the priesthood, and he was pretty thorough. He said it referred to an incident in which a priest comes to doubt a religious conviction, a belief, or even his own worthiness in his chosen vocation."

Because she was watching, Jaid saw the effect the words had on Adam. And even though Shepherd's concerns about the priest rang in her ears, she couldn't help but sympathize with the way Adam hurt for his friend right now. After what he'd told her about his childhood, she knew what the priest meant to him.

"The St. Ambrose priest even listed a half-dozen places a member of the clergy might go to pray for guidance. Nate called a retired cop he knows down here and didn't give him any information but the addresses of these places and Benton's plates. He found Benton's car at the third place. A Franciscan monastery closed to the public and on the outskirts of the city." Risa looked at Adam. "Do you want me to have him check further?"

"No." He checked his watch. "It's after one. I trust each of you is already situated in one of the cabins. If not, claim one and be ready for a brainstorming session at seven A.M. sharp."

Jaid had no idea where her bag had ended up, but Adam was engrossed in conversation with a balding man sitting before one of the large monitors. She noticed his operatives heading out the door in a group and followed them into the same conference room they'd been in earlier.

The door was barely shut behind her before Kell was speaking. "All jokes aside, Paulie has had a run of bad luck lately, and his accounts are leaking red ink. I'm not sure that would motivate the man to betray Adam, but it's a fact we have to consider."

"You looked in Paulie's accounts?" This from Cait. She looked at the others. "He's going to know that, right? I mean he probably has his personal information cyber booby-trapped."

Kell threw her an impatient look. "No, Gavin told me. He and Paulie work closely on all the cyber work for the agency. He loaned Samuels some money last month. Hasn't gotten paid back yet. I struck out trying to link him to any of the hired killers but did discover that he and Mose Ferrell came from the same hometown. Middleburg." He lifted a shoulder. "Okay, it's not much. But first thing to-morrow morning Macy and I are going to figure a way to get a writing sample from him. And then we can put an end to the speculation, right?"

"Kell is going to figure a way," Macy put in, her eyes anxious. "I'm not good at making things up on the spot like that."

"While I'm an incurable liar." Kell gave a wry grin, reaching over to tug a strand of her hair. "Anyway, in the meantime I think we all need to be careful about any plan Paulie might suggest tomorrow about the upcoming meet between Adam and Hedgelin. Whatever he comes up with, we all outvote him, right?"

There was a murmur of agreement, then the door opened behind them. Adam stood inside it, frowning at them. "I thought I told you people to call it a night."

Everyone rose hastily. Headed for the exit. In just a few moments Jaid and Adam were alone in the room. "Neat trick." She got up. Turned to face him. "Their strings are practically invisible, and you're masterful with the controls."

One dark brow arched over the eye patch. "You think I'm a puppet master? You obviously believe my employees are better trained than they really are. What were you all doing in here?"

"Planning mutiny. There's grumbling about running out of pizza, and we're already worried about breakfast."

"Uh-huh." She was getting good at withstanding the intensity of that laser blue stare. It helped when she didn't look directly at it, turning instead toward her briefcase and purse. "I'm guessing I can pry the information out of you since we're sharing a cabin."

That had her attention bouncing to his. "What exactly are you suggesting?" She reached out to flip the light switch behind her. The lighting in the rest of the structure was dim. It looked like everyone had followed his order to turn in.

"I'm suggesting that I have the leftover cookies in my pocket." There was a smile working around the edges of his mouth. "And knowing your weakness in that area, you'll be spilling your secrets inside the hour."

In the end he yielded the cookies without much of a fight, and they shared them while sitting on the bed. The cabin was too small to have any other furniture. "Did you get time to contact your son?"

She nodded, her mouth full. After swallowing, Jaid added, "They went to the Magic Kingdom today, and he was full of news about how many times he rode the roller coaster. Tomorrow they're planning on Epcot. I think that might be more to Mother's liking than Royce's, but there's enough to do on the property to keep them busy for as long as we need to keep them out of the way."

"Hopefully, this will be over soon." He reached over and brushed a crumb from the corner of her mouth. "Maybe you'll even get a chance to join them before your leave is up."

"I'm not thinking that far ahead," she responded deliberately. "We still have to get through tomorrow."

318 | KYLIE BRANT

"I have no doubt that together we can all come up with a plan that even you will find agreeable."

Agreeable. She restrained a wild laugh. Despite their best efforts Adam would be the one taking the risk. What were the chances that Hedgelin would want to meet alone? They didn't have enough incriminating evidence to take to law enforcement, and the assistant director would have to know that. "He's too smart to admit to anything, so what can possibly be gained with a face-to-face?"

She saw his answer in the way his gaze skidded from hers. "You." It took effort to force the word out. "He'll come because he wants you."

"I'm counting on it. That it won't be enough to merely ruin my reputation, possibly hang multiple murders on me. Why stop there when he can have all that and kill me, too? He's certainly expended plenty of time and energy to that end up to this point. No." He flicked a stray crumb from his pants leg. "If we're right about Hedgelin being the DC killer, he won't be able to resist a meet. He has to tell me how smart he's been, or it won't be nearly as gratifying. I'm counting on his ego to do his thinking."

"And if he comes out with guns blazing?" she asked tartly. It was easier, far easier, to draw on temper than to dwell on the sick fear circling in her stomach. "You don't have nine lives, Adam. At some point your luck is going to run out."

"I can't consider the worst outcome when I go into something like this. Have to visualize the best because otherwise I help him beat me. But it would be easier . . . far easier to contemplate squaring off with Hedgelin if I didn't have in the back of my mind what I stand to lose." Her breath caught at the light in his eye. It left his meaning impossible to misinterpret. "It's selfish, I know. But I don't want to spend the night going over what-ifs. There will be time for that tomorrow morning. I just want . . ." His words tapered to a whisper against her lips. Their kiss was bittersweet. But before it ended Jaid decided that he was right.

She didn't want to spend the next few hours talking, either.

Her lips parted in welcome. The stakes he was facing made desperation flicker to life, igniting greed. She couldn't let herself think about the worst outcome tomorrow, but the worry was there, tucked away in a corner of her mind. Tomorrow, it would incite panic and fear, but right now it summoned a reckless desire that she was unwilling to turn away from.

His taste reminded her of dark nights spent tangled together, their mutual needs equalizing them in a way nothing else ever could. Her head lolled back as he pressed a line of hard, stinging kisses down her throat. He nipped at the sensitive cord there, and she shivered. When he immediately laved it with his tongue, her blood began a primal beat.

Pushing away from him, she stood and faced him, stripping at a pace that wasn't meant to entice. Last time had been about tempting, teasing, and rediscovering, but an urgency was building that had as much to do with the mounting danger as passion. Tiny flickers of flame lit beneath her skin, heating her from the inside out.

He pushed off the bed, shedding his clothes at a pace that rivaled hers. The sight of all that naked flesh was as exciting as the haste in his actions, the hunger in his expression. There could be nothing quite as arousing as being wanted by a man who showed only a dispassionate face to the world. Being the recipient of all the pent-up emotion that was so rarely in his gaze.

She pressed against him, her eyes sliding shut at that first delicious feel of flesh against flesh. Then, releasing a shuddering breath, she pressed one hand lightly to his chest and pushed. He dropped to the bed but took her with him.

His mouth found hers again, devoured it wildly. The primitive response called to something inside her, something untamed, a reaction only he could elicit. Her hands raced over his arms, his shoulders, his back. And feeling the patterns of ridged raised flesh under her palms, another need rose. Refused to be banished.

She rolled over him, stretched out until every inch of them touched. Curves to angles. Sinew to softness. With her lips she mapped every inch of puckered skin, each jagged scar. And nearly wept at the thought of the pain he'd endured.

She traced the web of scars on the back of his hands, on those long sculptor fingers, capable of trailing heat in their wake. Followed the erratic pattern of nicks and creases, white with age, up his arm, where they met the long crooked seam across his throat. Jaid didn't think of them, any of them, as disfiguring. They were badges of what he'd endured. Marks of survival.

The tip of her tongue dipped in the indentations around his heart. Journeyed over the design of scars left from a madman's knife. Her heart was full. Overflowing with a need to have a part in healing wounds that had wrought such devastation on the outside. Had left the man unmarked within.

He withstood her ministrations for long minutes, his muscles jumping and quivering beneath her lips. But then, in a show of flagging control, he rolled her to her back and cupped her breasts in his hands. Lowered his head and feasted.

Colors pinwheeled behind her eyelids. Pleasure shimmied from nerve ending to nerve ending. With each greedy tug of his mouth, there was a corresponding pull deep in her womb. Her nails bit at his shoulders, an edgy blade of hunger twisting inside her, building to a fever pitch. It was too much. Too fast. Too soon.

And then his hand moved between her legs and rocketed her from wanting to demanding in the space of a few moments.

"Open your eyes. I want to watch you go over." His ruined voice sounded a harsh mutter in her ear. "It's greedy. You make me feel that way." His quick and clever fingers had her twisting against him in just a few wicked strokes. "You make me want in a way that's dangerous. I want to have you. All of you." His thumb pressed against her clitoris in rhythm with his words, wringing a sudden orgasm from her that hazed her vision. Tore a cry from deep in her throat.

"And more." He was over her and inside her in one smooth stroke, possessing her with a single powerful lunge that drove the breath from them both. Then he began to move, his thrusts hard. A bit frantic. And the passion so recently sated began to build anew.

His desperation fed her own. Her legs climbed his to clasp around his back. She met each thrust with equal demand. The night rushed in, draping them in intimacy. Desire was firing through her veins, fogging her vision.

But she kept her eyes open, fixed on his as their hips pounded together. She could see nothing but him. He filled her senses. There was only the dampness of their flesh. The beat of her blood, roaring in her ears. And when he surged against her one final time, his climax shuddering through him, it was the sound of her name on his lips that took her over the edge with him.

———

He was silent a long time. But one of his arms held her curved against him. His hand stroked her hair. And although there were no words, she could sense the war that was waging inside him. She said nothing, knowing it was a battle he had to fight alone. But when he finally spoke, the subject couldn't have surprised her more.

"You know LeCroix was a pediatrician. That's how we narrowed in on him eventually. He had treated three of the missing boys sometime in their lives. He was a doctor. Sworn to heal. And he used his skills for torture."

He must have felt the shiver that shook her then, because he pulled her closer. "I was an adult. Could withstand more trauma and pain than his young captives. And it became a game with him, I think. To see how far the human body could be pushed. Lots of the scars . . . they were shallow cuts. A slit of the scalpel, but before the blood loss was too great, he'd stitch it up. Start again somewhere else."

Bile filled her throat, and her eyes slid shut. She steeled herself against the rest. Knowing he had to get it out for his own reasons. "He was ecstatic over my capture, but he made me suffer, too, for costing him the escape of his newest captive. He was punishing me as much for that as anything. And he was distracted. Once he'd tire of his games, he'd go outside for hours, leaving me cuffed to a metal gurney. I could hear him hammering and the sound of power tools, but I didn't know what he was up to. Not then.

"I thought Cleve was right in back of me. The woods along the bayou were dark. We'd called for backup before we headed in after LeCroix. By the time I'd spotted where he'd taken the boy, I wasn't able to get an answer when I called Hedgelin. I discovered later that he'd dropped his phone. Reached down for it and caught his finger in a trap meant for beaver, I suppose. Maybe raccoon. I don't know how long it took him to get free. Long enough to lose me."

"For three days," she whispered. Thirty-six hours of agony, of facing certain death.

"I thought I'd die there in that swamp." His voice was chillingly matter-of-fact. "I'd gotten the drop on him when I surprised him in the act of savaging that boy. Knocked him out. But the place he had there, it was a rabbit warren of blind corridors that crisscrossed and led nowhere. Had them booby-trapped, too. I finally lowered the kid out a window, one too small for me to follow him through. Was trying to find my way out when I triggered a trapdoor that landed me in a cage. Lost my weapon. And I quickly learned what happened when LeCroix had someone at his mercy."

She brought her hand up to hug his arm tight while she pressed more closely against him. Knew there was nothing she could do to ease the razor-edged memories that could never be erased.

"He'd been building a guillotine. I was to be its first victim. But he had a bit of a problem on his hands." There was grim humor in Adam's voice. "He had to get me out there, and the gurney wouldn't fit through the door. So he cuffed my hands in front of me and kept a scalpel handy to move me in the right direction. I suppose he thought I'd be weak from blood loss. Shock. God knows I should have been. But I managed to catch him off guard. Got my cuffed wrists around his neck and choked him with the short chain.

"I got this in the struggle." She felt him finger the scar across his throat. "But I killed him. And somehow stumbled far enough out of the woods to run into the agents who had been looking for me for three days."

Nerves clashed and twisted in her stomach. She knew there was far more to the story than what he'd told. But it was also more than she'd ever expected to hear. Of more interest was the reason he'd told it. Now. Like this. And it was that knowledge that had her holding her breath.

"Paulie was at my bedside throughout."

Her heart lurched then. She'd been, too, until he'd ordered her away, his voice weak but implacable. He'd been injured beyond comprehension, had months of recovery ahead of him. But he'd managed to convince her, once and for all, that there was nothing to be salvaged between them.

"When I was well enough, Paulie told me what he'd done. He'd been working the case, too, tracking LeCroix's finances. The man had overseas accounts under several different names. Some of the boys he kidnapped he killed. Others he sold. I imagine those boys were the source of the money. We never figured out any other avenue for it."

Tears welled at the thought of those faceless children whose parents would never have closure. Who might be out there, still suffering. Or dying alone. The thought nearly had her stomach heaving. When she could manage to speak, she asked, "What had Paulie done?"

"Erased traces of the accounts. Transferred the money to other banks under other names. And gradually surrounded the finances with an impenetrable firewall." There was a long pregnant pause. "And he put all of it in my name."

Shocked, she twisted in his arms to look at him.

"I could do good with that kind of money, he said. He knew it wasn't safe in his hands, but together we could build something that would help bring men like LeCroix to justice. Law enforcement is constrained by finances. Case loads. Politics. But we'd be free agents. And when we took a case, we could follow up on it until it was solved." Soberly, he returned her stare. "I knew the bureau would confiscate it. And it wouldn't go to waste. God knows there are always unmet needs. But black-and-white had gone gray for me during those days with LeCroix. And I realized Paulie was right. We had an opportunity to help even out justice a bit in the world. So I agreed. Every dime of it was poured into our agency."

"And that's how Raiker Forensics began," she said slowly.

Even in the darkness, she could feel the intensity of his gaze. "I only tell you this because you have a right to know the truth. You have a right to know who I've become."

Adam's candor was a rare gift. He'd spent his life dealing in secrets, while shielding his own. Jaid wasn't sure what to make of the information he'd just shared with her. But she knew what it had cost him to do so. "You haven't *become* anything," she whispered. "You're the same man I fell in love with nearly ten years ago."

She stopped before leading with her heart, remembering what the words had cost her the last time she'd uttered them.

But the truth reverberated inside her. Because in reality, nothing had changed in the years apart.

She was still in love with Adam Raiker.

———

The church was dimly lit. It was early; there was another half hour before mass would start. But his quarry was in a pew near the back, prayer book in his hand. Utterly predictable in his daily routine. And utterly accessible.

Slipping into a pew in back of his prey, he lowered the kneeler. Waited a few moments as if he were sending up a prayer. The man in front of him finally made the sign of the cross. Sat. The silenced weapon rested against a fat hymnal, pressed to his nape.

"Shh."

His prey froze in place.

Whisper now. Other early churchgoers would join them

soon, and this was just between the two of them. "You know if you were really as devout as you pretended, it might not have come to this."

"Who are . . ."

"Shut up. You're a damn hypocrite. Don't care who you hurt as long as you get all the glory, do you? Turn around now. I want you to see my face."

The next victim turned enough to see. For his eyes to widen. "Why would you be . . ."

"I think you know." The hymnal and silencer helped muffle the blast, but even so, the noise had the hunched over blue-haired lady coming inside looking around, confused.

Unhurried, the man rose, keeping his back to her as reached in his coat for the note card in the Ziploc bag. Dropped it over the back of the pew on the body folded forward.

Envy.

Then unhurriedly, he retrieved his cane and headed for the exit.

———

"Apparently, you thought of everything when stocking this place." Jaid handed Adam a cup of coffee while he picked up the remote and turned on the TV in the conference room.

"We'll see what you say when you tire of instant oatmeal and coffee for your morning meal," he murmured, flipping through the channels for a news program. Most of his employees were moving around the structure, here on time but still rounding up breakfast. He settled on a program that had his photo splashed across the screen. It was the one Hedgelin had insisted he have taken for his temporary ID.

"And the manhunt continues for Adam Raiker, ex–FBI agent and head of Raiker Forensics, better known as the Mindhunters," a vapid-looking blonde was telling the camera. "A spokesman for the bureau has verified that Raiker is a person of interest in the DC killings, a case, ironically enough, he was assigned to as an independent consultant." A phone number scrolled across the bottom of the screen. "Residents are warned not to approach Raiker if they see him, as he is considered armed and dangerous. Instead call the number on the bottom of this screen, or 911. And be sure to check in for regular updates on this chilling ongoing investigation." With a brilliant smile she turned to her co-host. "Back to you, Chet."

As the male anchor began the national news, Jaid set her mug carefully on the table, her hand shaking slightly. Setting up the meet with Hedgelin wasn't their only problem, she realized, fear threading through her. They also had to move undetected through the city, when every officer in the area was looking for Adam.

"Hey, boss, just caught you on the news." A sleepy-looking Kell pushed open the door, held it for Macy, who looked as fresh and crisp as her fiancé looked rumpled. "Terrible picture of you. Where'd they get it?"

"That's sort of the least of his worries, don't you think?" A lanky woman with green-gold eyes and sun-streaked short hair followed them in, blowing on a cup of coffee. Ramsey Stryker. She and her husband Dev had driven Royce and Jaid's mother to Orlando.

Jaid gave her a faint smile. "I hope my family didn't give you too much trouble on the trip."

"Your kid is pretty funny. Him I like. Your mother should be locked in my mom's trailer for twenty-four hours while we take bets on which of them comes out alive."

"Don't mind her." Dev trailed behind his wife, giving her a reproving nudge on the shoulder. "Your mother is charming."

Ramsey rolled her eyes, but her expression was amused. "Women seem to get that way around him. I'm still getting used to it."

"I can see why." Jaid smiled warmly at the man. He'd been a balm to her fractured nerves at the hospital in Philly, she recalled. She hadn't forgotten his kindness.

"Macy and I kicked around a couple ideas for arranging the meet with Hedgelin," Kell started. The others filed in and took chairs around the conference table. Jaid caught Macy's eye surreptitiously. The other woman made a show of fiddling with a folded paper in her hand. Then shook her head. The communication sample she'd promised to get from Paulie, Jaid realized. Apparently, she'd run it, and it hadn't been a match. Jaid couldn't help but feel relieved. She hadn't wanted to discover Paulie was implicated in this. Adam didn't deserve to live in a world where his closest friend betrayed him.

"All right." Adam was seated at the head of the table, Paulie at his side. "Since you're so anxious to be first, you can—" His voice abruptly broke off as he grabbed the remote. Turned up the volume on the TV.

"Breaking news. This just in." The blond news anchor looked appropriately somber. "One of our affiliates has informed us that the DC killer may have struck again." A photo of a church appeared in the right corner of the screen before the camera panned to its parking lot and then to the street. "An eyewitness gave a description of a man hurrying out of the church, leaving another male fatally shot in the pew ahead of him. The victim's name is being withheld at this time, and officers on the scene will not confirm or deny the association of this latest homicide with the DC killings. The witness is described as having dark hair, wearing a long black coat and an eye patch, and using a cane."

The outbursts of the people in the room effectively drowned out what the woman said next. Jaid felt frozen in place. Her gaze was still on the screen, full of horror. She recognized a car in the parking lot shown. It was almost as familiar as the description of the assailant.

Risa's voice was heard over all the others. "Adam, what the hell's going on?"

He looked at the group, his expression a grim mask. "You heard the news. It appears that this morning before breakfast I shot and killed FBI assistant director Hedgelin."

Chapter 21

"Shit, with Hedgelin out of this, we're right back to where we started. No suspects." Nate's face was equal parts shock and frustration. "First you're framed with a thumb-print on the card, now someone pretends to be you while claiming another victim."

"We're not back at the beginning," Jaid said. "We can't be." She refused to believe it. It would be too heartbreaking to have come this far and to be left with nothing. "There has to be someone with motive as solid as Hedgelin's. Who else would know about the connection to LeCroix? And conceivably be tied in with the Mulder kidnapping case last winter? We know some of that ransom money found its way into accounts for at least two would-be assassins sent for Adam." Her smile was tight. "Maybe we need to focus on that avenue. Who'd have access to multiple hit men for hire? They're not exactly in the Yellow Pages."

"It leaves one very good suspect."

Adam felt Paulie's eyes on him as the man spoke the words. In one part of his mind he marveled at the uncanny way the man's thinking so closely paralleled his own. "Paulie's right. I should have thought of it before, but Hedgelin fit so neatly."

He held his hand up to quell the clamor of voices. Meeting Jaid's eye for a moment, he saw by the stunned realization there that she knew exactly who they should have looking at all along. "Abbie and Ryne Robel called last night from the road. They've been checking with people in the towns where Lambert claims he and his mother stayed when they escaped from LeCroix. I told them to specifically ask if others had been asking about the two. One woman told them yesterday that last summer someone from the FBI was asking her similar questions about them. I assumed she was referring to Hedgelin. Everything else fit. But we've been looking in the wrong direction all along."

Ramsey looked around the table. "Will someone please fill me in?"

"Shepherd?" Shocked realization was on Jaid's face. "I can barely believe that. He told me more than once how much he—"

"Owed me?" Adam smiled grimly. "Apparently, he wasn't talking about my getting him transferred from the Bismarck office. He must fault me for his landing there to begin with. His failure to rescue the Mulder girl the first time she was kidnapped was bad enough. Having me solve the case and return her safely to her parents was a personal affront."

"And rather than taking responsibility for the failure, he blamed you. And her father," Kell guessed.

Adam nodded. The pieces were falling into place with a dizzying rapidity. "His career might have been deep-sixed, but he could strike back at one of the men responsible for his landing in North Dakota and get rich at the same time. He arranged for Ellie Mulder to be snatched again last winter, but this time he had no intention of the child being found safely. She was to die as soon as the ransom got paid."

"Except we showed up on the scene and rescued her." Kell's pale green eyes glinted at the memory. "And thanks to Paulie, Shepherd didn't rake in nearly as much as he'd hoped."

"Imagine how it must have fried him to be bested by you again," Paulie murmured to Adam in an aside. His tie today was sprinkled with mini slot machines. "And then the attempts on your life started shortly after that kidnapping case was solved."

"When he failed to get you killed, he regrouped." Nate's midnight-dark eyes were narrowed in concentration. "You weren't the only target."

"No." There was a fire burning in his belly. Shepherd, if he was behind this, had much to answer for. "If he can't kill me, what's the next best thing? Laying all these murders at my doorstep." He scanned the group. "I want to confront him tonight. We find out everything we can about Shepherd in the next few hours." His gaze landed on Kell. "Burke, your misspent youth is about to come in handy. You join Jaid, Paulie, and me. The rest of you, I need every tiny bit of information you can get on the man.

"This ends today."

———

Tom Shepherd let himself into the double-unit condo and reset the security alarm. It was nearly eight. Agents had been expected to want to work through the night, to avenge their beloved boss.

The entire day had been a rush. First killing that bastard who had railroaded his career. And then spending hours immersed with the so-called best the country had to offer and inwardly laughing his ass off. Raiker wouldn't be able to so much as breathe without God's own wrath coming down on him. He couldn't stay hidden away forever. Shepherd just hoped some rookie law enforcement officer with an itchy trigger finger didn't shoot Raiker and ruin all his plans for the bastard. The realization might have come too late, but there were far worse things than death. Raiker was going to find that out when he was sentenced for the five DC killings.

Shepherd hung up his coat in the hall closet and toed off his shoes. Took off his suit jacket and hung it on the door-knob. Loosening his tie, he padded to the kitchen for a beer. Maybe two. He'd take them into the study and get caught up on the twenty-four-hour news channels. After all the planning over the course of the last year and a half, it was difficult to get used to the fact that his work was done. All he had to do now was sit back and watch the final act play out.

Taking a couple bottles from the twelve-pack in the re-frigerator, he ambled to his recliner and settled himself comfortably, setting one bottle on the end table next to him and opening the other. He took off his shoulder harness and laid it with his weapon next to the spare beer before picking up the remote. As he channel surfed, he took a long swal-low from the bottle in his hand and considered his next move.

There was a trick in knowing when to leave well enough alone. But the information he'd gotten from the reporter regarding Jaid Marlowe's son intrigued him. He was tempted to do a little investigating there himself. Once Adam was sent away for these crimes, wouldn't that be one more stake in his heart knowing Marlowe was suffering, too? There had to be something between the two of them. The woman had traveled to Philly to visit the son of a bitch when he'd managed to survive three bullets to the chest. It was a con-sideration for the future. Shepherd took another pull of the beer, while settling in to see what CNN had to offer.

A cell rang, the sound muffled. Instinctively, his hand went to his shirt pocket, but his phone there was silent. It rang again, insistently, and he straightened in his chair. There was no one left alive who knew the other cell num-ber. It had been the one he used to communicate with Tweed, and Raiker had taken care of the man for him.

So it was a wrong number. Had to be. But he still had to make sure.

He used his laptop in the study when he worked from home, but his real workspace required a bit more seclusion. The large walk-in closet in the spare bedroom had been doubled in size, and that's where his most sensitive work was done. By the time he keyed in the touchpad code, the phone had fallen silent. But curiosity, and a zing of something else, compelled him to check it out.

The number displayed in the missed call log was unfamiliar. Just as he'd expected. He set it down again on the counter holding the electronics equipment and turned to leave.

The phone rang again before he could resecure the door. He picked it up, saying nothing until he plugged in the voice distorter attached to it.

"I believe I'm talking to the DC killer. Do you know who I am?"

A flood of anticipation rushed through him. "Adam Raiker." Ballsy. But then, he hadn't expected the man to be hiding under a rock cowering somewhere. "How did you get this number?"

"You're not as careful as you think. Left a few loose ends. Not many, mind you. But they're there if a person knows where to look."

"Is that what you've been doing since you ran away?" Shepherd tipped the bottle that he'd carried with him from the study to his lips, enjoying himself hugely.

"I have had some time to think," came the mild response. "I've decided that you aren't going to be fully satisfied with letting the FBI be the ones to bring me in. That'd be sort of a letdown, wouldn't it? I'm sure you have a sin already in mind for me."

"Pride." Shepherd's hand clenched on the bottle. "That's supposed to be the worst, although my religious education never got that far. It came to an abrupt halt when Cote started taking me aside for some private tutelage. My old man might have been an abusive old drunk, but he tried to do right by me. Problem was, no one wanted to hear that sort of thing back then."

"Revenge was a long time coming."

He chuckled. "I have to admit, it would have given me a great deal of pleasure to do that one myself."

"Like you did Hedgelin this morning?"

Shepherd took another drink. "That was you, remember? It was on all the news."

"Let me guess. He was guilty of envy."

"See. It *was* you."

"Ah, yes. I assume Bolton was for my benefit. But you've admitted to personal reasons for Cote. So I'm guessing you had a similar excuse for wanting Patterson and Reinbeck dead."

"Patterson." Just the mention of the man's name was enough to have anger flaring. "He and I had a sweet little thing going. I was signed up as a dummy client, and he'd throw information my way about corporate takeovers in the making. I'd buy stock in the company relatively cheap and sell it for double or triple the price. Split the profits with him. But the greedy bastard sold us all down the river when the index funds driven by the commodities bubble he and his ilk created burst. He got off easy."

He emptied his beer. "As far as Reinbeck . . . have you read his decisions? Judges like that put dirtbags back on the street faster than we can get them in a cage, and call it justice. The country should have given me a medal for that one."

"Why don't you meet me? I can deliver the medal myself."

The temptation was great. The fates had been smiling on Raiker for too long. It'd be sweet to take him out with his own hand. Mulling the possibilities, Shepherd wondered if it could be managed. Or maybe there was a way to set the man up, draw him out while having agents secreted nearby. He'd be the hero then. His career would skyrocket from the hole Hedgelin had buried it in. Hell, he might even end up with the assistant directorship. There *was* a vacancy.

"Maybe that can be arranged. What do you have in mind?"

When there was no answer, he thought for a moment that the man had disconnected. "Raiker. Are you there?"

"No. I'm here."

Shepherd froze. The voice hadn't come over the phone. It was right behind him. Whirling, he dove for the counter.

Adam was ready for the move. Unconcerned. The weapon the man kept there had already been emptied. But Shepherd wasn't after the drawer where he kept his gun. What he was after became clear a moment later.

The lights went out.

Moving backward, Adam slapped a hand on the wall, flipped on the light switch. Nothing. The power had been cut. And the closet where Shepherd had been standing was completely enclosed. While the window in the room allowed enough filtered moonlight for Adam to be highlighted.

He was moving before the first shot fired. Tiny flakes of plaster stung his cheek before he ducked around the doorway. Now he had the same advantage that Shepherd had.

Darkness.

Silence stretched. Shepherd must have drawn a clutch piece. Adam crept several feet to the doorway opposite the room the agent was in. He reached inside his coat pocket. Found the object he was seeking and tossed it in the doorway across the hall to land with a soft thud. Instantly, multiple shots were fired, kicking up splinters of wood flooring. But smoke was filling the small room from the smoke bomb he'd thrown. Shepherd had two ways out. The window or the door.

Adam braced himself. He was betting on the door.

The other man rolled through the opening, firing as he moved. A bullet tore through the Sheetrock. There was a flame of pain in Adam's arm. He lunged to the other side of the doorjamb, shooting at the rolling target. Shepherd gave a grunt. One of the shots had found its mark. But then the figure was melding with the shadows, crawling along the floor. And the agent had the clear advantage. He knew the house. Adam was the stranger here.

He left the cover of the room and headed into the hallway after the man. Knew immediately it had been a trap. Then Shepherd turned and fired. Adam dove to the ground. Landed on his bad leg. Damaged nerve endings sent up a chorus of agony. He rolled to his stomach, stretched his arms out in front of him, and emptied his gun.

And this time the huddled mass on the floor didn't move again.

Dizziness crowded his vision. An answering hum was in his ears. With difficulty Adam crawled to the wall and struggled to a sitting position, his weapon still trained on Shepherd. With his free hand he pulled out his cell phone. Paulie and Kell burst in the back door an instant after he sent them the predetermined signal.

"Check Shepherd."

Paulie kicked the weapon out of the man's loosened grip and knelt down next to him. "Breathing," he announced. "Barely. I'll get an ambulance. Some first aid here, Burke."

A small penlight snapped on as Kell bent over the agent's body. A moment later he was shrugging out of his coat, making a compress to press against the wound. After a few minutes Kell looked up and turned the light on Adam. "You're bleeding, boss."

The words seemed to come from a distance. "Yeah. Jaid isn't going to be very happy about that."

———

"You owe us. All of you." The truculence in Ryne Robel's tone was offset by his wry smile. "You get in on a code eight while we're doing legwork on Lambert in Ohio. You know how long I'm going to have to wait for another code eight?"

"Hopefully forever," Adam said dryly.

Silently, Jaid agreed. They were having a celebration of sorts, having just gotten the main site for Raiker Forensics operational again. But there was a sense of déjà vu in the scene. The table Adam's operatives were gathered around might be littered with sandwich wrappers, but it reminded her a bit of the time spent hunched over a similar table at the temporary site.

Trying to come up with a way to keep Adam alive.

The look she sent his way was meant to be surreptitious. Although the bullet had passed through his arm without hitting anything major, it'd bled profusely. The Kevlar she'd insisted he wear had left his head and limbs unprotected. But she was hoping this would be the last time that she'd have to worry about someone shooting at him.

Abbie Robel caught her eye, a slight smile on her lips. Jaid had just met her and her husband, but she didn't think there was much that got by the very pregnant forensic psychologist. Not Jaid's worry about Adam.

And certainly not the cause of it.

Her attention was caught by the rise in voices among the operatives, each of them striving to outdo the other as they filled the Robels in on what they'd missed.

"Yeah, okay, Paulie and Gavin hacking in to TKM Security System's mainframe helped," Kell allowed, his arm stretched along the back of Macy's chair, his fingers playing lightly with his fiancée's hair. "But I still disabled the system. In thirty seconds flat on the first try when we did the scouting mission. I made Paulie time me."

"Honestly." Macy gave Paulie a commiserating glance. "He does that. He's like a twelve-year-old."

"Doesn't matter." Samuels waved dismissively. "I'm the one who swept Shepherd's place for listening devices and cameras. And disabled them, I might add. And added our own. Your part was little more than a locksmith, Burke."

"Uh, and who discovered the information about what security system Shepherd was using?" Risa chimed in. "Nate and I did the intelligence gathering while you glory hogs take all the credit."

"I found the TracFone for Adam to call," Kell pointed out.

"Hey, Zach and I drove the truck and got the DC Water uniforms for you two to wear for your cover," Dev drawled. "Pretty good for a couple rank amateurs."

Abbie put in, "But what's the word from the feds? Were they satisfied with the recording of that phone conversation between Shepherd and Adam?"

"Coupled with what they found on his computers and in his office, yeah," Ramsey put in. She reached over and snuck a couple of her husband's fries. "They've got bank books to overseas accounts. Evidence that his was the computer sending the e-mails to Lambert. And with Paulie's help they'll soon be tracking the path Shepherd's finances took, with money ending up in overseas accounts set up for Dodge, Ferrell, and Tweed. There's enough evidence to convict him twice over. He probably would have rather died from his injuries than end up imprisoned for the rest of his life."

Feeling Adam's gaze on her, Jaid looked up. And catching the barely perceptible tilt of his head, she waited a few minutes after he'd let himself out of the room before following him, unaware of the knowing glances passed around the room she exited.

She found him outside the building, his head tipped back as if trying to catch a wintry ray of sunlight. It was chilly enough to have her buttoning her coat as she went to join him where he leaned against the building.

"I finally heard from Jerry," he said abruptly. "He's having a tough time dealing with the cardinal's death, but I think he'll be okay. Maybe not unchanged." His expression was brooding. "But none of us skate through things like this unscathed."

"What about Mary Jo Reinbeck?" Jaid knew the woman had called him earlier. He'd been on the phone with her for a long time.

"The funeral's tomorrow. She wants to talk to Lambert. Despite his culpability in this whole thing, she's got some sympathy for how Shepherd used him. When it comes time for sentencing, I think he's got a valuable ally."

Jaid didn't know the woman but thought she must be empathetic indeed to forgive the part the young man had ended up playing in her husband's death, even if it had been unwillingly.

"And I've been giving a lot of thought to Royce."

She blinked. They weren't the words she'd expected to hear from him. "It concerns me that Bolton spoke to Shepherd about him. I don't trust the man not to try something from prison. If he thinks he can make one of us suffer, that would be plenty of motivation for him."

Anxiety surged. She looked in the distance. Her son would be home in another two days. And she still couldn't be sure that he was safe.

But she should have realized Adam wasn't done. "Sometimes the best way to protect a secret is to remove the reason for it." His expression was somber. "This afternoon I'll put everyone on your father's past. Figure out what he and Royce's mother were involved in and, more importantly, who might still harbor a grudge over it. When we know that, we can neutralize the threat."

His voice was assured, as if he didn't even contemplate failure. And it eased something inside her. "Mother still can't know. She'd never be able to handle the fact that she's helping raise her ex-husband's child." Jaid's smile flickered. Disappeared. "She isn't the forgiving sort."

His gaze was bright blue. Unswervingly intense. "Did she pass that trait on to her daughter?" Jaid's breath caught. Held. Her eyes searched his. "It's a bit humbling to discover that I've been fooling myself all these years. Thinking that carving you from my life could also mean extricating the feelings I had for you. In all I've experienced, the most frightening was the hold you had on me. The hold you still have, whether you're in my life or not."

Emotion thudded in her chest, flooded her heart. But still she said nothing. Whatever their relationship had been in the past, if they were to go on, it'd be a new kind of partnership. One of equals. There was no equality where one felt more than the other.

"You have to wonder about a man who takes as long as I have to recognize what was right in front of me." The uncertainty in his expression, when it was usually so sure, made something inside her go soft. "I thought what I felt for you made me weak. But it was weakness that had me driving you away the first time. What I need to know is if it was for good."

She looked at him. Saw what was in his heart but so rarely in his expression. "I can be pretty hard to shake."

Something eased in his face then. His arm reached out to snag her around the waist. Bring her close. "I won't be finding that out on my own. I intend to keep the woman I love pretty close to my side."

Her lips curved, even as her pulse jittered. And when his mouth lowered to hers, she whispered against his lips, "Just try to get rid of me."